GO ON PRETENDING

ALINA ADAMS

ISBNs: 978-1-963452-07-5 (pb);
978-1-963452-08-2 (hc);
978-1-963452-09-9 (eBook)

Book Cover Design: The Book Cover Whisperer, OpenBookDesign.biz
Interior Book Design: Inanna Arthen, inannaarthen.com

Library of Congress Control Number: 2024938049
First Printing: 2025
Printed in the United States of America

Names: Adams, Alina, author.
Title: Go on pretending / Alina Adams.
Description: [Roseville, Minnesota] : History Through Fiction, [2025]
Identifiers: ISBN: 978-1-963452-07-5 (paperback) | 978-1-963452-08-2 (hardcover) | 978-1-963452-09-9 (ebook) | LCCN: 2024938049
Subjects: LCSH: Women--Social conditions--Fiction. | Mothers and daughters--Fiction. | Interracial dating--Fiction. | Television soap operas--Fiction. | Liberty--Fiction. | Family secrets--Fiction. | United States--History--20th century--Fiction. | Soviet Union--History--1985-1991--Fiction. | Syria--History--Civil War, 2011---Fiction. | LCGFT: Historical fiction. | BISAC: FICTION / Historical / General. | FICTION / Political. | FICTION / Historical / 20th Century / General.
Classification: LCC: PS3601.D367 G66 2025 | DDC: 813/.6--dc23

You and I
We've seen it all
Chasing our hearts desire
But we go on pretending
Stories like ours
Have happy endings.

"You and I" by Tim Rice

FOR MY SON, ADAM,
WHO TAUGHT ME ABOUT BEING BIRACIAL IN MOSCOW

FOR MY SON, GREGORY,
WHO TAUGHT ME ABOUT BEING AN ANARCHIST IN ROJAVA

FOR MY DAUGHTER, ARIES,
WHO TAUGHT ME ABOUT BEING HAPPY ANYWHERE

Prologue: Spain

1939

Rose Janowitz wasn't sure exactly where she was. Riding an open-top jeep somewhere along the northern Spanish coast was the best her jostled, overstimulated, sleep-deprived brain could ascertain at the moment.

Rose was a bit more sure of why she was there. To do battle with the Nationalist Army of General Francisco Franco alongside the Republicans of the Popular Front government as part of the volunteer international Abraham Lincoln Brigade.

Where Rose sat stymied was what she was supposed to be doing. She'd come to fight. Back home in New York, Rose had listened to stirring tales about the heroic acts performed by the *Milicianas*, the over 1000 women who'd risen up to defend Madrid in the early days of this Spanish Civil War. They came from trade unions and militant libertarian organizations. Their speedy assembly was reported to be one of the reasons why the Nationalist coup d'état didn't start and end in July of 1936, turning, instead, into a going-on-three-year campaign.

The *Milicianas* served in single-sex and mixed gender battalions, raiding prisons to rescue captured comrades, erecting barricades to protect regained territory, and charging onto battlefields, fully armed, with a specialty in manning machine guns.

That was the duty Rose had volunteered for, albeit as part of an international, rather than native Spanish force.

Reality proved somewhat different.

She'd come prepared to face the fog of war at the front. She'd expected chaos among the carnage, the deafening din of gunfire, the blinding haze of smoke, the bleeding wounds, the screaming fallen, the painfully silent dead. She wouldn't say she'd been looking forward to it, exactly. That would be macabre. But she had been eagerly anticipating the opportunity to do her part, to prove herself an equal of the brave women who'd come before her.

What she hadn't expected was the bureaucratic confusion. Especially in the columns of self-proclaimed anarchists, communists, and socialists, where a chain of command would seem to go against everything they said they stood for. As they fought for their lives against Franco's Fascist, Nazi-aligned forces, nobody could agree on what role women should play in their struggle. While some insisted that Largo Caballero's October 1936 decree expelled women from the self-organized militias, others countered that it was, in fact, the opposite. That Caballero's decree folded the otherwise independent militias into the Republican Army and thus specifically called for an obligatory militarization of women to serve.

In the meantime, rumors regarding how women were treated by both warring sides ran rampant, designed to scare off volunteers and to smear the other as particularly depraved. Republicans touted the bravery of Lina Odena, who committed suicide rather than be captured by Nationalist forces. They insisted that she had every right to fear a fate worse than death and pointed to the Fascists' threats of rape by Moorish soldiers, as well as their history of violating women and young children in every village they conquered, after which they would parade with the victim's bloody underwear on their rifles. The Nationalists countered that there was never a threat of rape, and accused Odena of committing suicide not because she feared their wrath, but in order to avoid facing the punishment she was due for her part in the slaughter of priests and nuns behind Republican lines. This was dismissed on the left as a lie spread by Franco's minions. As was the preposterous claim that female Stalinists were purging Trotskyite comrades in Barcelona. The women of the left were united for their cause. There was no dissent between them. They were an emancipated, liberated fighting force. It was women volunteers on the right who were forbidden from wearing pants, forced into long skirts and sleeves for modesty, and shuffled to supporting tasks like office work, and the care of widows, orphans, and refugees.

Thankfully, even if there was some lingering confusion about the precise role of women in the merged Republican forces, Caballero's edict wielded no power over foreign volunteers. The decision regarding how best to utilize women in this struggle for freedom and equality would be up to their individual Abraham Lincoln Brigade unit leaders.

Rose had faith in her commander. He was only a few years older than her, barely out of college. He had red hair and blue eyes and, as a result, skin that had burned and blistered so many times in the Spanish sun that it would crack and bleed if he turned his head too quickly. He didn't believe in an autocratic chain of command, and so told everyone to call him Ludwick, noting that it meant "famous fighter" in Polish. He'd never led a battalion before, but he was a dedicated progressive, a loyal member of the Chicago Communist Party, where he'd been one of the ringleaders in exposing the city's self-proclaimed liberals as socialist-fascist betrayers of the worker's cause. Ludwick spent most of their jeep ride to the front telling Rose about how, unlike New York City, their organization had Mexicans and Coloreds. The Party supported them during the 1894 Pullman Boycott, so damn tootin' those South Side boys owed them fealty.

Rose had come prepared to fight. She'd been practicing with a pistol, a rifle, and, when given the opportunity, a machine gun. Even if, up to this point, she'd been primarily assigned secretarial duties. She understood that keeping track of supply lines, communication positions, and troop movements was vital work, and that Rose was in Spain to do what was needed, not necessarily what she preferred. But that was back at the training camp. Now that they would finally be seeing action, she expected to be issued a weapon as soon as they arrived on site. They were to be a back-up force for those who'd already broken through the Nationalist lines and occupied several tactically critical positions.

Yet, when Ludwick gestured two dozen men to follow him onto the battlefield, he held up his palm to indicate that Rose and the handful of other women who'd come with them should stay behind. The drone of grenades and anti-tank guns going off what felt like barely a few yards away from them, yet, in reality, was a half mile, made it impossible for Rose to ask why, even if she shouted.

The men charged off. The women stayed behind. When Rose first signed up to come to Spain, she and the other volunteers had shaken their heads at the Second Republic's slogan, *Men to the Front, Women to the Home Front.* Good thing there was no such division in the Abraham Lincoln Brigade, they told themselves.

Now, they looked for something to do to make themselves useful. The best they could think of was to make sure their spare Kropatschek, Tigre Modelo, Berthier, and Ross rifles were loaded and ready to go as soldiers came running back to grab fresh supplies.

Periodically, one of those left behind would pick up a pair of binoculars to see if they could make out what was happening. They saw grass, rocks, and shrubs blown into the air as if from a subterranean exhale, a volcano of earth that swept up anybody standing adjacent to it. The explosions covered up any screams. Or maybe it was all one, incessant scream. They were too far away to view the precise damage, still they imagined they could smell it, the wind wafting traces of sulfurous gun powder, a bitter acid of fear sweat, the copper of fresh blood. The thrashing limbs reduced to marionettes through their field glasses had, only a few hours ago, been young men they'd driven up with. The ones who'd bummed cigarettes and told dirty jokes and flung their arms around only some of their fellow comrades' shoulders, expressing astonishment that their hands should fall on an utterly unexpected breast. *What a surprise!*

And now they were... what? Martyrs? Heroes? Cannon fodder? Were they corpses? Were they fragments? Would there be enough left to bury? Would there be enough left to keep living? Would there be enough left that they'd want to keep living? Rose and the other women should be out there among them. They should be helping in any way they could.

When Ludwick briefly returned, Rose inhaled as deeply as possible and screamed into his ear, "Let us deliver fresh weapons straight onto the field!"

Ludwick shook his head, blood from the cracks of his skin melding with the tears spilling from his eyes due to the all-encompassing smoke.

"No," he croaked, throat ripped from attempting to be heard over the clangor. "Orders. No exposing women on the battlefield."

It wasn't until Ludwick stumbled back a second time hours later, grabbing the door of a jeep to keep from sinking to his knees, that he commanded Rose and the other women, "Go. Get the wounded. Bring them back. Set up a medical tent."

Rose knew she should listen to her superior officer. Even though Ludwick had made a point of saying no one was superior in a true people's army. But she had to make it clear in case he hadn't been briefed. "I'm not a nurse. I don't have any medical training. I was taught to do artillery."

"Go get the wounded," Ludwick repeated. "Hurry. Before the Nationalists come back. We might only have a few minutes."

"The Nationalists are still out there?" Rose clarified, even as the women around her; the better soldiers, clearly, hopped to attention and began loading their jeeps with stretchers, gauze, and splints.

Ludwick nodded, closing his eyes, gasping for fresh air. Rose understood that he had his own concerns at the moment, and that now was neither the time nor the place for her to ask: *So, you can't expose women on the battlefield with a weapon as combatants, but you can expose them on the battlefield without a weapon as nurses?*

She mentally shushed herself. Leave it to Rose to rebel in the midst of a rebellion. She reminded herself that an army consisting exclusively of Roses would never get anything done. They would be anarchists who'd devolved into anarchy. That was no way to win a war.

Rose forcibly swallowed her question. It tasted like the grime, gunpowder, and blood reeking off Ludwick's uniform. They hadn't been imagining it. It was the smell of the battle. She joined the other women in doing what he'd ordered.

This was bigger than her. This was bigger than this company, this engagement, this strip of land, this territory, this war. This was about the future of humanity. Men, women, Americans, Europeans, Africans, Orientals.

This was the most important thing that Rose Janowitz would ever do.

SHE WAS WRONG.

Of course, she was wrong.

What seventeen-year-old in the history of seventeen-year-olds was ever right when it came to understanding what was actually important, and how little they truly mattered in the great, cosmic scheme of things?

She hardly ever talked about Spain. She certainly never talked about what had really happened to her in Spain. Even the stories she told her granddaughter, Libby, were heavily censored and, according to Rose's daughter, Emma, embellished. Rose let Emma think so. It was preferable to confessing the truth. She hadn't even told Emma's father the truth.

Rose knew now that her charging off to bring about a brand new, better world hadn't been important at all. It had affected absolutely nothing. It had affected absolutely no one. Even if it had completely destroyed her.

That is until a staggering seventy-three years after Rose's ill-advised misadventure, when Emma came storming into Rose's apartment, shoving her cellphone in Rose's face, an email from Libby front and center: *I'm going, Mom. Please understand.*

"She's doing this because of you," Emma accused Rose. "So, you're the one who has to bring her back home."

Part One: New York City

Chapter One

1949

"If you don't tell them, no one ever needs to know."

Rose's mother followed her to their Lower East Side apartment door, flipping up the collar of Rose's beige, virgin wool sheen gabardine coat, the one *Vogue Magazine* swore was brilliantly manipulated to give tall girls the impression of a slim waist, then smoothing it down again. As if an article of clothing Rose would remove before being shown in for her interview, even if it were the most expensive thing Rose or her mother ever owned—or touched—would make the difference between Rose getting hired, or her resume being shunted into the trash.

"They'll have questions," Rose predicted. The gap between her dropping out of Seward Park High School and starting at Hunter College couldn't be papered over with a coat costing more than the weekly salary of the job Rose was applying for.

"You traveled. Every civilized young lady takes a tour of the continent. It's in Henry James. And Ernest Hemingway."

Mama was no fool. Unlike Rose, she'd actually graduated from high school. She knew that the women in Henry James and Ernest

Hemingway were named Daisy Miller and Brett Ashley. Not Rose Janowitz.

"If they don't ask, there's no need for you to bring it up." Mama paused to give Rose a final once over. Thanks to an investment they couldn't afford to repeat, Rose was the epitome of Christian Dior's chic New Look silhouette; a full, triangular skirt in black with a cinched waist, softened by the rounded shoulders of her cream blouse. Definitely more Daisy Miller and Brett Ashley than Rose Janowitz. Not that the rest of her would have fooled anyone. She'd brushed out her ebony curls and pulled the result into a bun, yet stray tufts still insisted on springing forth no matter how often Mama spit on her finger and attempted to smooth them into place. Rose's elongated neck jutted beneath a pointed chin that might have been her most prominent feature, if not for a nose that superseded it. Her eyes loomed as dark as her hair, the only benefit being equally raven lashes so thick she needn't bother with mascara, though it also resulted in brows perpetually requiring plucking. Mama smiled, projecting a confidence neither felt. She pinched Rose's cheek for luck—and a final burst of color. *"Zei gezunt," be healthy*—a traditional way of saying good-bye in Yiddish. She added the less commonly evoked, *"Un shtark." And strong.*

THE PROCTER & GAMBLE COMPANY may have operated a plant on the northwestern corner of Staten Island so massive that locals dubbed it Port Ivory—after the institution's best-known product—but their corporate offices, including their advertising division, Compton, were located in midtown Manhattan. Rose could hardly believe that, after she took the elevator to the 11th floor and given her name, the girl sitting at the front, simultaneously answering two telephones, typing, and vetting guests, didn't so much as blink when Rose said she was there to meet with Irna Phillips.

The Irna Phillips.

The woman who had single-handedly invented radio soap operas (their nickname coming from the same product which inspired Port Ivory) and was currently the head writer of *The Road of Life, Young Dr. Malone, The Brighter Day, Today's Children, Joyce Jordan, MD, The*

Right to Happiness, Masquerade, The Guiding Light, and, on television, *These Are My Children.* Irna traditionally wrote and produced her shows out of Chicago. Three years earlier, after a lawsuit that began as copyright infringement then turned into non-payment of taxes, Irna moved *The Guiding Light* to CBS Radio and relocated its production to Los Angeles. But Irna was unhappy with the acting on the West Coast. She didn't think the Hollywood types sounded authentic enough for her wholesome, midwestern characters. So, *The Guiding Light* was moving again, this time to CBS Studios on East 58th Street. Irna being Irna, had managed to requisition Liederkrantz Hall, the larger of the second-floor studios. Now she needed someone to supervise production while she returned to her other shows in Chicago.

Rose intended to be that someone. She'd spent money she didn't have on an outfit that wasn't her in order to make sure Irna saw through the artifice and recognized how perfect the authentic Rose was for the job.

Except Rose didn't feel sure of anything at the moment. The girl who'd checked her name off a list and beckoned her to take a seat, kept typing and answering phones. Rose kept waiting. The more she waited, the worse of an idea this adventure seemed. Who was Rose to think she was worthy of stepping in for Irna Phillips? What had Rose done with her life up to this point? The solitary chance she'd taken, the one time she'd thought for herself and not done the expected nice, Jewish girl thing, had been such a disaster Mama still needed to remind Rose to keep quiet about it, over a decade after the fact.

And yet, Irna—or someone who worked for Irna—had seen Rose's resume. They'd deemed it good enough to call Rose for an interview. Maybe they knew something she didn't? Odds are, they knew lots of things Rose didn't. Like how to move ahead in the world by staying out of trouble. She could learn a lot working here. If she got the chance.

A voice over the phone prompted the girl at the desk to stand up, grab a stack of papers and run from the room. Rose was alone. Still waiting.

After a few minutes, she wondered if the solitude was getting to her. Because she quite clearly heard a woman's voice call out, "Rose!"

It was coming from behind the closed office door. Rose climbed to her feet and inched towards it. "Rose! Now!"

This time, she definitely heard it. Rose rested her hand on the knob, twisting it slightly. She swore it opened on its own. The office behind it was occupied by two women. The smaller sat behind a desk so mammoth she might have fit into one of its drawers. Irna Phillips. After obsessively studying the paragon in preparation for this interview, Rose would've recognized that wavy, swept off the forehead bob anywhere. Irna wore a gray and black striped blazer, no softening of the shoulders here, with a golden brooch in the shape of a leaf at the collar. The other woman was taller, her hair longer and rolled about her head in a style held over from the war. Yet it was obvious who the dominant figure was. Irna talked and talked and talked. The other woman merely nodded.

"Take this money and use it to build Cedars Hospital in Selby Flats. Oh, Dr. Matthews, we couldn't! You're too generous! It's not generosity, I believe in Dr. Parker, Dr. Boling, and Dr. Leland. A woman can be as good of a doctor as any man. We'll never forget you, Dr. Matthews. You take care of yourself, Bill. That new bride of yours is a special woman. Bert will be touched you said so. And your sister, Meta. You knew her as Jan Carter. Do you think she'll be able to get her son, Chuckie, back from Ray and Charlotte? She aims to try, but we don't know if that would be best for the boy. She's his mother! She's a stranger! So much heartache ahead!"

Rose's head spun. Especially when this bizarre stream of consciousness was once again punctuated with the cry of, "Rose!"

"Yes?" she piped up instinctively.

Both women turned to stare at her.

"Who are you?" Irna barked, her tone completely different from the soothing, hypnotic drone of earlier.

"I'm… Rose. You called me?"

"I'm Rose," the taller woman corrected. "Rose Cooperman. Miss Phillips' assistant."

Well, that explained that. Rose—Janowitz—felt like a complete idiot. She wanted to bow her head and slink out of the office, back to the Lower East Side, where she could pull off these foreign clothes and tell herself it was for the best. Rose didn't deserve a job as potentially life-changing as this one. Rose deserved only the life she'd made for herself. Or, as Mama called it, the hole she'd dug for herself.

Irna was looking at Rose now the way Mama had when Rose first returned home ten years ago, humiliated and humbled. A combination of disappointment, self-satisfaction and, she couldn't help thinking, disappointment that Rose had failed, even if that was exactly what Mama had expected. Rose couldn't stand up to Mama. She'd seen what happened that one time she'd tried. But Rose could stand up to Irna. She'd already made a fool of herself. Foolishness, Rose had great experience with.

Instead of lowering her head, Rose raised her formidable chin—and the nose that came with it. Instead of slumping her shoulders, she squared them. Instead of meekly avoiding Irna's gaze, she met it. "I'm Rose Janowitz. We had an appointment for..." she consulted her watch. "Twenty minutes ago."

"Twenty-two," Irna corrected. Rose wasn't sure if she was being put in her place—or complimented.

Irna and her Rose exchanged a silent look across the desk. It conveyed whatever Irna deemed necessary. The assistant stood, tucked her steno pad under one arm, and headed for the door, discreetly closing it behind her.

Irna barely waited for the other woman to depart before demanding, "Your writing sample?"

"I sent it in. As requested."

Irna was still sitting. She'd made no gesture for Rose to do the same. Would it be presumptuous of Rose to take the initiative? Presumptuousness, Rose also had a great deal of experience with. She claimed the spot Irna's preferred Rose had occupied earlier. When Irna didn't snap for her to keep standing at attention, Rose chose to interpret it as a sign of approval.

The grand dame dug around in the stack of papers to her left and wrenched out a script Rose recognized as her own. The paper was onion-skin translucent, but it was all Rose could afford.

Irna blinked as if to clear blurry vision. "It's not in English."

"It's Yiddish. I thought you might..."

"I'm Unitarian," Irna informed Rose, making it clear that whatever faith Irna might have been born into, Rose would be scoring no co-religionist points with her.

"There's a translation attached. I thought you might want to read it in the original. To get the true flavor of what I can do."

Irna skimmed Rose's cover letter. "You wrote for *Mayn Muter Un Ikh?*"

Rose noted the conversion to Unitarianism hadn't rendered Irna incapable of reading the title of the world's first and, as far as Rose knew, only Yiddish language radio soap-opera.

"For WEVD? The Communist station?"

"Socialist," Rose corrected. "The call letters stand for Eugene V. Debs. And it was owned by the *Jewish Daily Forward* by the time I got there."

"My shows are all-American, nothing subversive." Irna's tone made it clear that was one area on which there would be no discussion.

"I know." Rose nodded fervently, eager to show off what she'd studied. "*Guiding Light*, Reverend Rutledge, his lamp in the window: *There is a destiny that makes us brothers/ None goes his way alone./ All that we send out into the lives of others/ Come back into our own.*"

"This isn't a writing position," Irna said. "You do realize that? I write my scripts."

The loose pieces clicked into place. "That's what you were doing. Dictating your scripts." That still didn't explain… "But you never indicated who was saying what. You just recited all the dialogue straight through."

"Rose understands. She'll type it up, make it clear."

"That's incredible."

"Why serials?" Irna asked her questions the same way she wrote her scripts, a stream of consciousness that she expected the listener to make sense of on their own time. "Why not *Baby Snooks* or *Ozzie and Harriet* or *Life of Riley*? Why not films?"

The obvious answer was that they weren't hiring. Irna was. But Rose suspected she knew what answer the doyenne of daytime was looking for. Luckily, it was even true. "Films end. Situation comedies are once a week. If you make a bad decision in a film and don't rectify it by the conclusion, that's how it stays forever. If you make a mistake in a primetime comedy, you have to wait seven days to fix it. Serials offer chance after chance to get life right daily. You can keep trying, over and over. Bad people can become good, seek forgiveness."

"Seek redemption?"

"Isn't that why Reverend Rutledge keeps that lamp burning in his window?"

"I expect a great deal from my employees." Rose wondered if this was another of Irna's wild swerves or whether she saw it as a natural transition. Redemption through hard work—and suffering—was a favorite theme of hers, after all. "Are you married?"

That was definitely a swerve. The change of topic caught Rose off guard. "No." At twenty-seven, she knew she should be mortified and ashamed of that fact.

"Neither am I." Irna didn't appear either mortified or ashamed. "Why would I want to be? If I need to fight, I can call up one of my P&G buffoons!"

Rose didn't know how to react. Was Irna bringing Rose into her confidence, or testing her? And if she was testing her, was it to see if Rose would agree with her, disagree with her, or go running to the P&G executives to tattle? A job interview with Irna Phillips was proving as full of twists and turns as one of her shows!

Rose's reaction, however, turned out to be unnecessary. Irna went on, "I expect absolute loyalty. Husbands tend to not understand that. Wives are bad enough. Phoning me to complain about their men's long hours, them working on the weekends. The show must come first."

"You said this wasn't a writing position." Rose opted to focus on the concrete details, the better to make Irna feel like she'd already given Rose the job. "Why did you ask to see a sample of my writing then?"

"The position is Supervising Producer. Your responsibility will be to ensure my scripts get recorded the way I intended. You'll be involved in scheduling, casting, budgets—and, once in a while, if there's a last-minute problem, a script needs some slight adjustment and I'm not available by phone, you may need to step in and alter a word or two. But no more."

She'd said *your responsibility*. Either Rose already did have the job, or Irna offered it to every candidate—and Rose was the only one foolish enough to think of accepting.

"It sounds wonderful," Rose told her honestly.

"It is," Irna sighed, softening for the first time since Rose had come in. "It is absolutely wonderful. I can think of no better way to spend my life."

"When do I start?" She rose from her chair, one arm already outstretched, looking to shake hands and formally seal the deal, when Rose caught sight of Irna hesitating. She was looking down at Rose's resume.

Rose anticipated the question seconds before Irna articulated it. "You didn't graduate from high school? The year between it and college…" Irna let the question hang in the air. Like on one of her shows.

Rose had done her research. In addition to knowing that Irna had been born Jewish, Rose also knew that, when she was eighteen years old, Irna had become pregnant by an older, married doctor. He'd refused to acknowledge paternity or pay child support, so Irna took him to court—and actually won. Tragically, the baby was stillborn. Nevertheless, on *The Guiding Light*, Irna wrote a similar story for the character of Rose Kransky—coincidentally, the only Jewish girl on her otherwise "all-American" program—and allowed that fictional baby to live and be raised not only by his single mother but, eventually, by the weak-willed father who returned, admitted the error of his ways, and begged for another chance.

Rose looked Irna in the eye. "I thought you, Miss Phillips, would understand."

Irna opened her mouth as if to follow up. But all she said was, "You start tomorrow."

Chapter Two

There were llama droppings on the marble stairs.

Rose couldn't have been happier.

"Props!" she shouted, leading to a chorus of chuckles and groans. The studio where they staged *The Guiding Light* for fifteen minutes live every weekday, year-round, also broadcast periodic, experimental television programs. Said programs featured a disproportionate number of animal acts. As the building had no elevator, the cast, sets, and assorted creatures arrived via marble staircase. This not only made a clatter—while they broadcast, Rose stationed boys at the top and bottom to stop anyone from interrupting; an aspect of Rose's job Irna had neglected to mention—but also proved a magnet for fecal droppings of many sizes and textures. There was an ongoing building argument about which department's responsibility clean-up fell under. Most recently, it had been dumped on—pardon the expression—props. Hence, Rose's call.

While such matters, technically, did not fall under her job description, Rose didn't mind. She was happy to do whatever it took to keep the wheels of production churning. Because, as she'd promised Irna, the show came first. Everybody from Network Head to actors with a single line, not to mention the sound effects crew, the director, and the engineers put their personal needs on the back burner and rallied to ensure their product was the best it could be from the moment the organ announced its histrionic beginning, until the music adroitly faded "until next time." Rose would have expected to experience the height of worker solidarity at proudly socialist WEVD. It turned out, though, that there was nothing like money to be made to get everybody enthusiastically rowing in the same direction.

Money, of course, was also the source of some of their greatest conflicts. Not among the staff, but among those who created the shows and those who controlled them. Sponsors loved getting into the act, demanding characters use their products, talk about using their products, and marvel at the convenience and thrift of using their products. Irna was a wizard at scripting heart-clenching drama to take place amidst a variety of cleaning supplies. If a villain wasn't being threatened to have his mouth washed out with soap (only one brand would do!), then the heroine was hurrying to get her laundry done before her husband arrived home and learned she'd been out all day, engaging in who knows what mischief. How lucky she was that this brand of detergent took half the time for twice the results!

Their bigger problems stemmed from all that they weren't allowed to do by Standards and Practices. According to "daytime morality," good men and women could not smoke. This infuriated Irna, who saw thousands of dollars in potential sponsorship monies wafting away like, well, smoke. It was Rose who came up with having the bad characters be the smokers, while having the good ones constantly remark on it. "Go and take your [brand of] cigarettes with you!" and "I knew you'd been there. I could smell your [brand of] cigarette the second I arrived!" That way, they wouldn't be going against the censors, but the product would still be associated with the voices of heroes and heroines.

They faced the same obstacles with alcohol. Even beer and sherry were off limits. Tea or coffee were the mandated beverages of choice, no matter what the crises. (They could always select from hot or iced, in case anyone complained of feeling creatively shackled.) Inspired by prohibition, Rose suggested to Irna that she write any drinking as either religious or medicinal. When Rose submitted that having Jewish characters would make a sip on Friday a directive from God Himself—what pious censor could deny that?—she actually pried a smile out of her redoubtable boss.

Their biggest problem, however, was sex. They couldn't show it. This was radio, not the movies. They couldn't speak of it. This was radio, not… the Bible. (Irna had chortled at that one, too, which was the biggest compliment Rose could hope for.) On *The Romance of Helen Trent*, one of the few radio soaps not created by Irna, where the titular heroine had been proving that "romance can begin at thirty-five" for seventeen years; while managing to remain thirty-five— they spoke of the "emotional understanding" that could only come with marriage. And not a second before. They meant sex. Everyone knew they meant sex. But no one was allowed to say it. Irna gave notice she wasn't going to adopt that awkward turn of phrase for her own shows.

So, on *The Guiding Light*, characters begged each other to "hold me and never let me go." They embraced. Quite a bit. They stared into each other's eyes. Sometimes from one day to the next. And then they somehow ended up pregnant. Viewers filled in the gaps on their own.

Rose wished she could do the same. She'd told Irna the truth when she answered she wasn't married. But she'd never confirmed the implicit promise that she never would be. She'd like to be. No matter how many times Mama told Rose she'd ruined whatever chance she'd had—what man would want her after what she'd done, what woman would want a man who would; it was quite the recursive question— Rose never quite managed to give up hope. She was a year short of thirty now. If Helen Trent could "find romance" at an even more decrepit age, why not Rose Janowitz?

She spent her days surrounded by men. For a woman's genre, daytime drama—save Irna—was suspiciously dominated by men. Men at Procter & Gamble, men at the network, men at the advertising agency, men in the production booth, men on the studio floor. There were men in tailored suits and men in shirtsleeves. Men in fedoras and men in caps. Men wearing the latest *No. 89 by Floris* cologne, and men who smelled of the Ivory P&G gifted each employee at Christmastime. There were men wherever Rose looked. So why was she still alone?

Naturally, a majority of those men were married. Rose wasn't ready to go the mistress route yet—though she knew Irna had a stable of such philanderers in her life. Irna preferred doctors and lawyers, just like on her shows. If Rose were twenty, the pickings might have been broader. But men her age were interested in younger women. And older men were either divorced—which came with children and alimony… and bitterness—or… well, Mama said Rose was picky. As tall as she was, she had to accept that some men would be shorter. As opinionated as she was, she had to accept that silence could be golden. And certainly, she must never talk about how much money she was making. No man would stand to be emasculated in such a manner. Yet, after all that, remember, he had to be Jewish. Anything less would be unthinkable.

The worst part was, Mama was right. Rose was too picky. She could put up with short. She could put up with poor. She could put up with old. The one thing she could not put up with was: boring. Compared to the hustle, bustle, constant crises and close calls of production, the conversation proffered by the majority of men Rose met for dinner dates left much to be desired. Mama said it was because Rose challenged them. Rose should be sitting quietly and listening. Yes, even when the men were wrong. Especially when they were wrong. A good man, Mama lectured, didn't expect the woman across from him to know more about a given subject than he did. And he certainly didn't appreciate her demonstrating it. When a man waxed poetic about a film he'd seen, he didn't need Rose breaking down the dialogue and scene structure. When he talked facts and figures about his job, he didn't need to know that Rose also oversaw a budget—and it was greater than his. And he definitely had no interest in anything she had to say about politics! Rose found the men she stepped out with boring. She could only imagine what they thought about her.

Luckily, she had very little time to dwell on it. Irna lived up to her promise. She kept Rose so preoccupied, the only love lives Rose agonized over were Bill and Bertha "Bert" Bauer as they battled that floozy, Gloria, and whether widowed reporter Joe should choose Nurse Peggy, whom his children preferred, or ex-jailbird Meta, who made Joe's heart flutter. Irna was thinking bigger than radio. She'd already produced one television soap-opera, *These Are My Children,* which sputtered out after less than a month of episodes on NBC. Yet Irna remained convinced the fledgling medium was her serials' future. To that end, she was battling to convince Procter & Gamble to resettle *The Guiding Light* on the small screen. To assuage their doubts about its viability, Irna used her own money to produce a pilot. When it failed to convince her sponsors, she set to work on a second one.

This meant Irna had less time for the radio version. Outside of writing, which Irna still guarded ferociously, the bulk of responsibilities were now Rose's. Rose raced from advertiser meeting to rehearsal to casting session. When the latter was plunked in her lap, Rose switched all auditions to the telephone. It allowed her to sift through paperwork without the actor noticing her distraction and getting—rightfully—offended. It also kept Rose from basing her decisions on appearance. It was difficult to picture a dashing, romantic leading man when the applicant was balding and barely came up to Rose's chest, or an ingenue when the lady reading for the part looked more appropriate for grand opera. Since all that mattered was how they sounded, Rose holding auditions over the phone was more likely to yield unprejudiced results. Which was best for the show. Because the show always came first.

On the schedule for today were tryouts for a new role, that of ne-er-do-well Edmund Bard, who'd be coming to town to set every young and not so young lady's heart aflame, toy with them mercilessly, then be revealed as the illegitimate son of a pillar of the community. It was a fun, juicy role, and Rose was looking forward to hearing her candidates' takes on it.

The first six proved a disappointment. They were playing it too evil right from the start. There was no tension, no surprise, nothing to reveal or learn. Rose couldn't imagine listeners at home not seeing right through the literal bastard and wondering why the women of *The Guiding Light* couldn't do so, as well.

For the seventh applicant, Rose didn't even glance at his name until after he'd been speaking for almost a minute. She didn't even listen to the words—she'd heard them so many times—until she realized that—what was his name, now? Cain… Jonas Cain—was offering a completely different interpretation from the men who'd preceded him. Where they'd snarled, he purred. Where they'd bellowed, he murmured. Where they'd insisted on seduction, he made the listener want to be seduced. No, he made the listener ache to be.

"Mr… Cain," Rose needed to clear her throat, lest her voice crack.

"Yes, Miss Janowitz?" His speaking voice was the same as his auditioning voice. Which meant he was either always on, or always himself.

"That was… that was quite… good."

"I thank you for saying so." Yes, he was definitely always… something. Impossible to believe he didn't realize precisely what effect his speaking voice had on the listener. And that he wielded it for all it could do for him. Rose didn't blame him. She'd do the same in his position.

"May I ask what inspired your take on this character? It's so different from how every other actor saw him."

"Is it now?"

A drawl? A bass clarinet? A full-throated pipe organ? Just what was it about this man's voice that made Rose vibrate from hipbone to hipbone as surely as if he'd plucked a string, like Rose might melt through her desk-chair, dissolving towards the carpet.

"Yes." This time, she swallowed instead of coughing. Hardly less obvious.

"Well, it's obviously Shakespeare, isn't it?"

"I'm sorry, what?"

"Edmund Bard?" His laugh rolled in like a fog diffusing throughout her senses. "You gave the whole game away right there. He's Edmund the Bastard from *King Lear*." Jonas quoted, "*To both these sisters have I sworn my love; each jealous of the other, as the stung are of the adder, which of them shall I take?*" When Rose didn't reply quickly enough; primarily because she'd run out of coughs and gulps and felt pressed to come up with an alternative; speaking was out of the question, his confidence wavered. "Did I get it wrong, then? How terribly embarrassing."

"No." Rose found her voice, because his had briefly tottered. "You're one hundred percent correct. When Irna—Miss Phillips—when she told me about the character, I suggested the name. As sort of a little joke between the two of us."

"Ah! So, you're the Shakespearean scholar."

"Hardly!" Her snort was instinctive. If utterly unladylike.

"It was precisely the guidance I required to understand this man. He commits villainous acts, seducing married women, attempting to murder his father and brother, but he does not see himself as the villain. After being cast aside for an accident of birth, he feels righteously justified to, as they say: *top the legitimate. I grow; I prosper: Now, gods, stand up for bastards!* Surely, a sentiment we've all experienced. Whether or not we'd admit it."

Was that the moment Rose fell in love with him? When Jonas Cain—with a pinch of help from William Shakespeare—put words, put poetry, to the feelings Rose had been pressing down her entire life? Because the one time she'd let them roam free, she'd ruined everything.

She'd read those words. If she hadn't read *King Lear* she wouldn't have known of Edmund, and if she hadn't known of Edmund, she never would have suggested that name to Irna. And if she'd never suggested that name to Irna, what would Rose and Mr. Cain be speaking about now?

She'd read those words. But she'd never heard them outside a well-meaning college professor who made as apt an Edmund as she did a Juliet. Rose had read the words; she'd heard the words recited. She'd never realized they were about her until they came undulating over the phone line at her office on the East Side of Manhattan.

Rose might have fallen in love with Jonas then and there. But the only thing she said was, "You've got the job."

ROSE SENT THE STANDARD CONTRACT to Mr. Cain's agent, perplexed when it was returned promptly, without a change. She wondered if her new employee had inexpert representation—it was an unknown to her agency—or whether they were desperate to see the document counter-signed before… what?

What could they be hiding? She'd heard the voice. The voice was all that mattered. The worst Rose could conceive of was Jonas Cain might be a pseudonym, and he was employed on another show which forbade him from performing on competing programs. But Rose listened to a lot of radio. She felt certain that, if she'd heard his voice before, she'd have proven incapable of forgetting it.

On the morning Jonas Cain was scheduled to come in for his first broadcast, Rose made a point of not dressing any differently. It was just another day. No longer did a chic autumn coat cost more than her weekly salary. Thanks to Irna, Rose could afford a closet full of crepe and taffeta tunic dresses with their touted slenderizing waists and straight three-gore skirts. She'd paid extra to have the lapels and pockets dotted in rhinestones, as per the current fashion. The sole reason Rose chose the lightweight green over the navy fine-ribbed was because the day was shaping up warm. She didn't want to over-heat. It wasn't because the white jabot of the latter made Rose appear older—she saved those for meetings with the sponsors—while the overbodice of the former brought out the hazel in her otherwise dull brown eyes. A pair of black Capezios with sharply pointed toe-tips completed the ensemble. Rose opted for flatties. No reason to appear any taller than she needed to.

Because one thing that Rose had already braced herself for was the possibility of Jonas Cain being short. She had no idea why a disproportionate number of deep-voiced men seemed to be challenged in the height—and follicle—department. Maybe a compressed entity was vital to generate such a profound resonance? Rose told herself she didn't wish to intimidate Mr. Cain by towering over him. Not on his first day.

"Jonas Cain is…" the voice of the unspeakably competent assistant Rose met the day of her interview and now knew to be named Hazel, that she was twenty-four years old, working to pay her husband, Ike's, way through medical school, counting the days until she could quit and just be a normal wife and, hopefully soon, mother to a brood of baby Ikes, echoed through the intercom on Rose's desk, "...he's... uhm, he's... here."

"Send him in," Rose chirped, oblivious to the message Hazel was trying to transmit with her uncharacteristic stammer. Rose was too eager to finally set eyes on Mr. Cain to notice.

"How do you do, Miss Janowitz? Jonas Cain, at your service."

Rose had been in the process of rising to greet him. She'd just pressed her palms into the desktop, which came in handy when she nearly lurched forward, only stopping herself from plunging face first by the fact that her arms were already locked at the elbows.

She'd braced herself for Jonas Cain being short. She'd braced herself for him being ancient, him being a child half her age. She'd braced herself for his having a face Mama called "perfect for radio," and a host of other deficiencies, as well.

She hadn't braced herself for him being a Negro.

Chapter Three

He wasn't ancient, and he wasn't a child. He looked to be about Rose's age. He wasn't short. He looked to be about Rose's height. He wore a gray suit, broad at the shoulders, straight cut to mid-thigh, single-breasted with long, wide lapels and three buttons along the front. The hat he held in his hand, having removed it upon entering the building like a proper gentleman, was a matching Stetson Whippet, the band a slightly darker shade of gray encircling the crown.

And he was a Negro.

A strikingly handsome one. Eyes as dark as their irises, surrounded by a thick fringe of lashes any woman, save possibly Rose, would envy. Nose cut as sharp as his cheekbones; a smile as dulcet as his voice. It unfurled languidly, an unstoppable, volcanic drift that caressed everything in its path, enveloping, pulling you closer. Not a forced seduction, but a desired one.

"Am I not whom you envisioned for your Edmund Bard?" The smile made it into his query. They both knew exactly what he was asking.

Rose's impulse was to deny, to be polite, to place herself in the best possible light under the pretense of sparing his feelings. She understood that would be self-serving. And insulting. It would be patronizing to treat him like a child. This was obviously a man. A man who knew the score and deserved the respect of her acknowledging it.

"No."

"Should I see myself out?" He made a gesture to return the hat back atop his head.

He was giving her the opportunity to protect herself. To terminate the awkwardness with the least amount of embarrassment. He was a gentleman, offering Rose the option to return to business as usual as if their encounter had never happened.

Now, gods, stand up for bastards!

Rose was no god. And Jonas was no bastard. Yet, this was her chance to top the legitimate, as she'd once so passionately burned to do. This was Rose's chance to do the right thing, to ameliorate some of the wrong she'd already done. Plus, there were those eyes, that smile, and that voice… oh, that voice!

"No." Rose straightened up, no longer needing the desk to support her, prepared to stand on her own two feet, no matter what. She walked past Jonas, towards the door, and beckoned him forward, "I will see you to the studio."

THEY MADE THE TRIP in near silence, interrupted only when Jonas, invoking the stairs, softly recited, "*Not marble, not the gilded monuments/Of princes, shall outlive this powerful rhyme/But you shall shine more bright in these contents/Than unswept stone.*" And then he smiled again. The man certainly had her number. That voice, that face, and poetry, too.

"We only briefly covered the sonnets in school," Rose admitted.

"You don't know what you're missing."

The way he said it made Rose desperate to find out.

She led him into the soundproofed studio, a plate of glass separating the actors from the production staff. A dual keyboard organ stood at the far-left corner, Rosa Rio, who played it daily for each intro, outro, and dramatic pause in between, setting up her sheet-music. The sound effects bench was on the left, featuring every tool necessary to make doorbells ring, coffee-pots pour, cards shuffle, trains chug, brooks babble, and fists fly. To the right of the organ hung three microphones, a CBS logo engraved along the bottom, from three separate poles dropped from the ceiling. Each set-up could accommodate up to five actors. Leads with the most dialogue would gather in groups of two or three around the first two mics, while those covering smaller parts rotated around the remaining. They stood on mats to muffle the sound of shoes on studio floor concrete. They held scripts in their hands, dropping pages to the ground once done to avoid the rustle of turning. Though they wouldn't be seen, everyone reported formally dressed. Men in suits, women in dresses, skirts, blouses, hair styled, wearing full make-up. They were professionals. No different from theater or movie performers. Though they didn't engender a fraction of their respect—or their salaries. They were just selling soap. To housewives, no less.

"Good morning." Rose addressed her cast, the various members of *The Guiding Light's* Bauer family, from the patriarch known as Papa to the actors playing his children, their assorted love interests, friends, and nemeses. Faces swiveled in her direction, including the director and audio technicians. When Irna was in Chicago, Rose was the established authority. "This is Mr. Jonas Cain. He will be assuming the role of Edmund Bard."

If the expressions Rose was seeing came close to what must have splashed across her features when she spied Jonas, any hope she harbored of coming off as unflustered skipped out the window. Recalling his resume, which she surely hadn't been reading obsessively since the audition, Rose enlightened, "Mr. Cain is a graduate of Columbia University. English major. And a veteran." Even six years after the war's end, a former soldier still garnered some respect. "Where did you serve, Mr. Cain?"

"In the European theater," he answered cautiously, not nearly as pleased with Rose's line of questioning as she was. "The Battle of the Bulge."

A snort from the back of the room, an actor Rose wasn't familiar with—she didn't bother with casting the smaller, under-five lines roles—raised his chin to drawl, "I was at the Bulge. There were no colored soldiers at the Bulge. You're a liar, boy."

"With all due respect, sir," Jonas emphasized the final word, setting an example of how one should address a fellow man, "my 761st Tank Battalion broke through the German lines in Tillet so the rest of you could come strolling in after. One of our tankers, Private Ernest Jenkins, received the Silver Star from General George Patton himself for our efforts. Kraut bastards got a pounding they won't soon forget from The Harlem Hellfighters."

Rose was about to step in to shield Theo Goetz, who played Papa Bauer. He was a Jew, born in Vienna, Austria. A proud naturalized American, but Jonas' Kraut slur could still prove offensive to him, when the unnamed actor countered, "Eleanor's niggers is more like it."

Mrs. Roosevelt's outspoken efforts to end Jim Crow laws and integrate the military, all of which came to a head when she was photographed personally handing out refreshments inside Washington DC's first mixed canteen amongst Negro servicemen and white hostesses, earned all colored soldiers the demeaning sobriquet.

Rose was about to chastise the use of the epithet Kraut. But now she stood frozen in the face of an even worse slander. There was no question it was up to her. When Irna was in Chicago, Rose was the established authority.

Except she had no idea what to say.

They had a half-hour until today's episode went live on the air. They had time for only one rehearsal. In theory, Rose could replace any performer at any time. She could fire the under-five actor and shift his lines to someone else. She could rewrite the script so that another character said them. She could cut them altogether. She could also hand off the role of Edmund to another actor, either just for today and then begin the casting process all over again, or for the long-term. It was Edmund's first appearance. Nobody would know that he didn't sound the way Rose had fantasized him sounding. Yet, Edmund was scheduled to be a major player for months. He was critical to the long story. The judicious thing to do was get rid of the less salient actor and make it clear that such behavior would not be tolerated on *The Guiding Light* set.

Now they only had twenty-seven minutes until today's episode went live on the air.

Rose didn't want to waste the time it would take to exorcize one actor, then rearrange the whole episode to gloss over his absence.

At least, that's what she would say if asked.

She knew nobody would ask.

Just like she knew the real reason Rose didn't want to fire the actor who'd challenged Jonas was because she didn't know how many of his colleagues felt the same way. And Rose couldn't risk a mutiny. Not twenty-five minutes now before airtime.

The cast was looking to her. Jonas' gaze was the only one that felt like a weight pressing down on her breastbone, making it difficult for Rose to breathe.

His face reposed absolutely neutral. Why then, did Rose feel like he was tracking every thought which flitted through her head the moment she considered it? Why did she feel like he was judging her? And why did she feel like he not only anticipated her verdict, he approved it?

Perhaps because she was already rationalizing her decision? To herself most of all.

"I'll leave you to your rehearsal." Rose handed off her authority to the director, slinking out of the studio a great deal less confident than she'd originally come in.

SHE LISTENED TO THE LIVE SHOW in her office. Jonas sounded exactly as she'd dreamed. He was letter perfect, even better than in the audition. Before the fifteen-minute episode was over, Rose was getting reports from Hazel that the CBS switchboard was lighting up with fans calling to demand more Edmund Bard.

If it were any other actor, she would have gone down to the floor to share the news with him, the cast and crew. Good news for any one character was good news for the show, which was good news for them all. As Irna always said, "The show must come first."

But Rose didn't do that today. Instead, she stood at her window, looking down onto the East 58th Street sidewalk and the building's exit. She stayed there until she'd witnessed Jonas depart the building, identifying him by the cut of his hat and the breadth of his shoulders.

Only then did she dare leave her office and continue with her day.

At the production meeting later that afternoon, she informed the director, "I'm cutting the under-fives from tomorrow's show. We're a bit over-budget and I can rewrite the dialogue, so we'll make do without them."

"Yes, Miss Janowitz." He drew a line through that spot in the script. And declined to meet Rose's eyes.

THE CALL FROM IRNA CAME at 9 p.m. that evening, eight in Chicago. Word had gotten to Miss Phillips about the… unpleasantness which transpired that afternoon. Rose had a strong suspicion she knew who'd felt compelled to enlighten her. The American Federation of Radio Artists union was always most unhappy when a performer was cut. Rose stayed at the office to await Irna's call. She didn't relish puttering at home, on edge, cooking dinner, reading, laying out her clothes for the next day… jumping at every new sound, a bird outside her window or a water pipe banging, as she anticipated the phone ringing, Irna on the other end, already mid-tirade.

Rose lifted the receiver gingerly, using two fingers, as if loathe to ruin a wet manicure.

She had an explanation—a defense, really—prepared. But all her boss said was, "Give 'em hell."

ROSE UNDERSTOOD that Irna had more important matters on her mind than one newly hired actor—and a handful of unhappy under-five players. Irna had just launched a revolutionary new story on *The Guiding Light*. Meta Bauer was another of Irna's strong single mother characters. Meta bravely fought for custody of her baby boy, Chuckie, from his adoptive parents, then felt pressured by her family to marry Chuckie's biological father, Ted, who'd initially wanted nothing to do with either of them. But Ted proved a horrible parent, bullying the shy, sensitive boy and insisting Chuckie take boxing lessons so he wouldn't grow up a sissy. The five-year-old fell out of the boxing ring, struck his head and, after lingering in a coma for weeks, tragically died. Blaming Ted for the loss of the child she'd fought so hard for, Meta shot and killed her no-good husband. She was sent to prison and put on trial, where every mistake she ever made was dredged up by the prosecution. So far, so typical. Where Irna broke new ground was in letting the audience play jury. She asked her listeners to call, write and send telegrams declaring Meta either innocent or guilty. CBS received over 75,000 votes, with those advocating for Meta's freedom outnumbering those who wanted to see her punished nearly one hundred to one. The show's ratings spiked higher than they ever had before. And the success of the Meta Bauer trial finally convinced CBS to launch *The Guiding Light* on television.

The show was scheduled to debut on June 30, 1952. But to hedge their bets, the network demanded two concessions: They wanted the radio version to continue. Actors would arrive at the radio studio at 2 p.m. They'd rehearse the latest episode and record it for airing the following day. The next morning, they'd arrive at the television studio and block out the show they'd recorded previously for airing on television live from 12:45 to 1 p.m. They would then travel back to the radio studio in order to start the cycle over again.

CBS' second demand was that, in case the television version failed to catch on, Irna create a spin-off from *The Guiding Light*, exclusively for radio, so they could hold onto the fans they'd picked up with Meta's sensational trial.

Irna told Rose she didn't have the time to produce *The Guiding Light* for radio, television, and a spin-off. She informed Rose she was being promoted. Rose would handle the secondary show. And, as such, she could decide which current *Guiding Light* character to build it around.

Rose didn't hesitate. "Edmund Bard."

Irna hesitated. For a moment, Rose feared she might say no. There were many reasons for Irna to say no. Rose bet she'd thought of even more of them than her boss could.

There wasn't a single better reason to say yes.

"Yes," Irna finally said.

HAZEL POINTED OUT the obvious problem. While Edmund had been a supporting *Guiding Light* player, it posed no difficulty to keep his countenance from the press. Though radio was an audio medium, fan magazines like *Photoplay* and local newspapers often asked *Guiding Light* for images they could run alongside stories about the actors and plots. In honor of Bert Bauer giving birth, Rose and Hazel staged a photo shoot of actress Charita Bauer laying in a hospital bed, her nightgown pristine, her dark, cascading hair tied up in a bow, clutching a stiff, tightly wrapped doll that was supposed to represent newborn baby Michael… while on the television screen next to her beamed the image of Gloria LaRue, the trashy singer Bert's husband, Bill, was stepping out on poor, postpartum Bert with. It was a scene that never transpired on the radio show, but it summarized the engrossing goings on nicely.

If Rose made Edmund the centerpiece of *Guiding Light's* spin-off, there'd be no hiding him from the press. That meant there'd be no hiding Jonas Cain. So far, they'd been able to keep details about their new sensation under wraps. Without categorically putting out a general command to do so. Plenty saw Jonas on a daily basis. Yet, except for the initial complaint to the union, everyone had zipped their lips. Once his co-stars realized Jonas wouldn't be immediately fired, they comprehended that what was good for the show was good for them, and anything which brought negative publicity would ultimately hurt them too. No one wanted a boycott. Rose expected the production crew and actors to remain mum. But what to do about photographs…

Hazel came up with a solution. "Edmund is a mystery man, right? So, we photograph him to enhance the mystery. In the shadows, from the back, from the side. They'll see just enough to be intrigued, but not enough…"

"To get us canceled?"

Now all Rose needed was to figure out how to tell Jonas that they'd be building a show around him, they'd be promoting him, they'd be making money off him… without revealing who he really was.

ROSE NEEDED TO SPEAK to Jonas alone. She knew what time he arrived at the studio and what time he left. Not because she stood at her office window, glancing casually down at the street and inadvertently catching a glimpse of him. Rose waited until she knew he was on the way out to call the studio and ask them to send Mr. Cain up to see her. She could have done it as soon as Jonas came in, but she didn't want to keep him from rehearsal or distract him before the air show. Not because she was stalling for time, hoping a magic—and tactful—explanation would pop into her brain to make their state of affairs less offensive. Or, at the very least, less blatantly insulting.

Hazel ushered Jonas into Rose's office. His presence filled the room. Rose's months of only catching a glimpse of the top of his head, the width of his shoulders, the power of his stride, had failed to inoculate her from the force of encountering Jonas head on. His smile seemed broader and brighter than she recalled from their first and only meeting. His eyes deeper and sharper and more alive. Of course, once he opened his mouth to speak—"You wanted me, Miss Janowitz?"—Rose was completely overcome.

She hoped she didn't show it. She gestured for Jonas to take a seat. Weeks of listening to him on the radio—Rose listened to every show, as did Irna, it was quality control, it was part of the job—failed to acclimatize her to how much more orotund his voice tolled up close. Rose pressed and rotated her palms in front of her on the desk. She didn't feel worthy of speech in comparison. Yet, she'd have to speak. She'd called the meeting.

Jonas settled, as directed, and waited patiently, hat literally in hand between a pair of neatly tapered fingers. He tapped it against his knee as he crossed his legs, still waiting.

As briefly as possible, lest her voice give out without warning, Rose outlined Irna's plans for a *Guiding Light* radio spin-off while the main program transitioned to television. If she'd told any other of her actors they were about to become the centerpiece of a show all but guaranteed to be a runaway success thanks to its pedigree, Rose might have expected shock, block-long grins, tears of joy, demands to renegotiate their contract. Jonas' facial expression didn't change. He listened politely. He waited for the other shoe to drop. Because this wasn't a mere shoe. This was a steel heeled boot. And Jonas harbored his suspicions regarding whose neck it was about to come crashing down upon.

Rose reassured Jonas he wasn't being replaced. She and Irna would like him to keep on voicing Edmund. They'd reach out to his agent with details about his upgraded contract. They'd scheduled a photo session for artwork to send out with a news release about the spin-off. Rose outlined Hazel's plan for the pictures. She didn't attribute the idea to Hazel. Rose accepted full responsibility. If Jonas grew incensed, she preferred it be with her.

It was difficult to tell how he felt about the proposal. Jonas' face remained maddeningly placid. He kept listening. So, Rose kept talking. Babbling, really. "Think about The Shadow. From *The Shadow* series. The Shadow knows!" Rose tried to sound as mysterious as the announcer who opened with that weekly did. Mystery and babbling made strange bedfellows. "Not having a face to go with the voice only increases interest. We want to do the same for Edmund. Build up suspense, anticipation. We want America eagerly tuning in every day to learn more about you—him. It's a publicity stunt, really." *Not an attempt to hide you from a reactionary and judgmental listening public.* "Will you do it?" Rose pleaded, as eager to hear his answer as she'd promised America would be to see his face.

She could tell he was thinking. The placid expression shifted ever so slightly, eyebrows creeping towards the bridge of his nose. He scratched beneath his ear. He looked down at the hat in his lap. He looked up at the window. Rose wondered if he could tell what a stellar view she had of her employees' comings and goings?

His chin began to bob up and down, and then that smile, the one that had nearly robbed Rose of the ability to speak only a few moments earlier. When Jonas finally spoke, it was in the same timbre which had gotten him the job, the one that made you ache to be seduced, even if you knew disillusionment must soon follow. "Only for you, Miss Janowitz."

Chapter Four

The picture session ended up occupying most of the afternoon and into the evening. The photographer they'd hired, one who'd shot dozens of stills for them previously, seemed unable—or unwilling—to give Rose what she asked for. He claimed the lighting was wrong, he claimed the costuming was wrong. The only thing he didn't claim—out loud—was that the subject was wrong. Since it had been Hazel's idea, Hazel tried repeatedly to demonstrate what they had in mind. The photographer dismissed her set-ups as unworkable. After three hours of back and forth, during which Jonas might as well have been a mannequin for all the consideration the photographer showed him, Rose dismissed the man and turned to Hazel, "Would you like to do this shoot, instead?"

Rose realized she perhaps should have made her inquiry prior to firing the photographer, but there was a reason Rose worked in live radio and not film. She preferred tackling problems as they came up, making decisions on the spot and adjusting to the consequences as she went along rather than painstakingly plotting each move, anticipating every eventuality. Where was the surprise in that? Where was the fun? Mama would say Rose lived her personal, not just her professional, life in the same manner. Mama was right. And no fun.

The way Hazel's chin bounced up at the suggestion, the way her eyes widened, and she pressed both hands to her chest, mouth forming a delighted circle suggested Hazel would very much like to do this shoot. But then her gaze shifted to the clock on the wall. A wrinkle split her forehead and her front teeth snagged her lower lip.

"I'm sorry, Hazel. I didn't realize the time." Hazel was an extraordinary assistant. Efficient because she made sure to get every lick of work done before 5 p.m., stepping out on the dot and catching the subway to Washington Heights, greeting her husband with freshly prepared dinner after his grueling day of medical school. If there was work still to be done, Hazel did it from home, after Ike had gone to bed, because, as she earnestly explained to Rose, the poor, exhausted darling needed his rest. She'd even set up her phone line so she could connect Irna and Rose, and join in any last-minute conferences, which Hazel confessed she did from their hallway closet, muffling her voice so as not to disturb Ike.

Hazel's eyes drifted from the clock to her watch. Rose wondered if her assistant was hoping the latter would reveal a markedly different verdict.

"You go on ahead," Rose urged, "we'll make do."

"Thank you for your assistance today," Jonas added. "It was much appreciated."

Hazel's square-heeled white Emma Jetticks shoes were pointed towards the door. But her eyes couldn't quite detach from the Rolleiflex camera, the kind Margaret Bourke-White had reportedly rescued and used after her ship was sunk in the middle of the night while covering the North African campaign of World War II. It was the camera of heroines.

Hazel reached for it, whispering, more to herself than to Rose or Jonas, "Ike's constantly calling to say he's being held up. It should be fine for me to do it just once…"

ROSE SENT THE PHOTOGRAPHS to be developed, gave Hazel money for a taxi home so she might arrive faster, and somehow found herself walking out of the studio alongside Jonas, who tipped his hat to the security guard as they exited.

The sun had set. Rose was accustomed to clocking out this late, but Jonas had stayed long past his call time.

"Is there somewhere you need to be?" Rose inquired, to indicate she recognized he'd gone above and beyond. "Is someone waiting for you?" She struggled not to sound as curious as she felt. It was none of her business.

Jonas shook his head.

"You've missed dinner," Rose said. Because stating the obvious was safer than stating what she desperately hoped wasn't equally as obvious.

"Shall we?" Jonas offered her his arm.

Was he asking her out? Was he offering to escort her… somewhere?

Rose didn't know. Rose didn't care. Rose linked her elbow through his and told Jonas what she'd been dying to tell him from the first moment. "Let's."

NEW YORK CITY, Manhattan in particular, delighted in their sophisticated, enlightened ethos. They clutched their pearls when talking about those backward people down South and their horrid Jim Crow laws. They sent generous donations to the Leadership Conference on Civil Rights to strike down cloture practices. They agreed that Marian Anderson should absolutely be allowed to sing at the Metropolitan Opera. Soon as Maestro Rudolf Bing found an appropriate role for her. There were so few. A shame, truly, as she was so talented.

When Jonas walked into the French restaurant around the corner from *The Guiding Light's* East Side studio, the maître d' took in the cut of his suit, the make of his hat, the brand of his shoes, and approvingly reached for a menu. When he spied Rose, he asked whether the gentleman would object to their seating the lady, first? It was the gallant thing to do.

"We're together," Jonas said.

That was the end of their chit-chat. Rose and Jonas were walked to a table furthest from the bay windows, left to pull out their own chairs and unfurl their own napkins. Jonas performed the former task for Rose, allowing her to sit with her back to the wall, leaving himself the seat with its back to the rest of the dining room. Rose started fidgeting in discomfort for him, knowing how strange it felt to be watched, unable to look back. Images were constantly darting through one's peripheral vision, triggering a fight or flight response that sped up Rose's heartbeat. And she wasn't even experiencing the worst of it. Yet Jonas' features remained as placid as ever.

They waited for someone jauntily dressed to take their order. When no one volunteered, Jonas raised his arm, a single finger extended. Because of where they'd been placed, right next to the kitchen, his gesture was impossible to miss. It forced every single figure passing directly by them to deliberately avert their eyes and scurry onward. Every time a fellow patron looked towards the doors, they caught sight of the preposterous scene, which drew more attention to a situation the management clearly wanted to avoid.

Realizing it was in their best interests to serve and get Jonas and Rose out as soon as possible rather than prolong their presence, a sacrificial waiter was pressed in to asking what they wanted. He tried to take their drink, appetizer, salad, main course, and dessert order all in one go. Jonas wondered what Rose would like to drink. She requested a martini. Jonas said he would have the same. He told the waiter to come back for the rest after they'd been served. The waiter looked helplessly at the maitre'd, who gave a brusk shake of the head and gestured for him to march to the bar and make it snappy. He glowered Jonas' way.

It made Rose want to giggle.

It was all so ridiculous. Jonas was making the staff look like fools simply by acting like a regular customer. He had them flustered, all but taking orders from him, when, in the beginning, they'd been the ones attempting to make Jonas feel like an interloper.

The realization sobered Rose. Here she was, laughing at their ignominy, when the reason for it was Jonas' unwanted presence. Jonas' race. Jonas himself. Jonas and her. She snuck a peek his way, dreading the censure she expected to see. But there was nothing. No change. No hint of irritation. No hint that he'd even noticed anything was awry.

"How do you do it?" Rose asked in awe. "That under-five on your first day of work? The photographer earlier? Now this? How do you stay so—so unbothered? When I get disrespected—when the waiter asks my date what I want to order, when they hand the man I'm with the bill though I'm the one paying, when the show executives talk to the stage manager instead of to Irna or me—I get livid. I can barely control myself!"

"A beautiful woman who can barely control herself is exhilarating," Jonas said. "A colored man who raises his voice—who raises so much as an eyebrow—is a threat."

Rose understood she should be focusing on what Jonas was trying to tell her. It was very interesting and insightful and instructional. As a writer, Rose should open herself to all peoples' life experiences so that it could inform her work. But had he called her beautiful?

Now wasn't the time for a follow up question. Not about that. Instead, Rose asked, "How do you manage to stay composed?"

"It's how I was brought up." Jonas accepted the drink he was handed, finally putting in his order for the main course—after indicating Rose should go first. "My parents live their lives by Booker T. Washington's maxim: *The thing to do when one feels sure that he has said or done the right thing and is condemned, is to stand still and keep quiet. If he is right, time will show it.*"

"Oh," Rose admitted. "I'm afraid I lack the patience for such civility."

"*It is a hard matter to convert an individual by abusing him. It is more often accomplished by giving credit for all the praiseworthy actions performed than by calling attention alone to all the evil done.* Also, a quote from our Mr. Washington. Growing up, I swore the man had a pithy lesson for any and all occasions. Especially where I was concerned. It's alright," Jonas prompted her. "You may laugh again. I'm being terribly amusing. If you don't, I may feel compelled to stop."

So, she did. Though still not without an aftertaste of guilt. Was she laughing at him? At all he'd been forced to suffer simply due to the color of his skin—and those who took issue with it?

Jonas went on, "My father is in the publishing business. We're said to be living in the golden age of The New Negro, or so one publication dubbed it. Alain Locke, W.E.B DuBois, Countee Cullen, Langston Hughes, they're publishing essays, poetry, fiction. My father does not wish to be a member of the Harlem Niggarati. Every day, he goes to an office in midtown. He toils for a white publisher. They only let him edit the colored writers for now. But, one day— one day he thinks he'll be allowed to do more. And, until that day comes, he will *stand still and keep quiet.* Because he knows he is right. And he expects time will show it."

"That sounds awful." Rose didn't think about what she'd said until after she'd said it. A common occurrence she really should work on.

"*Negroes,*" Jonas recited. "*Sweet and docile. Meek, humble, and kind: Beware the day—They change their mind.* That," he told Rose, "is not Booker T. Washington."

Rose wanted to interrupt. She desperately wanted to tell Jonas that she wasn't what she seemed like. She knew what she seemed like. But if she interrupted him now, then she'd be acting exactly like what she needed him to understand she wasn't. Even if she could barely untangle her own sentence gymnastics to prove her point. So, she'd waited through dinner, as Jonas neatly cut his steak while regaling Rose with tales of his days traversing the country as part of an assortment of theater companies, often shuffled off to cities so miniscule they couldn't even be found on a map.

"When I grew weary of the touring life, I took a stab at cinema. There were a few roles as Pullman porters. *Yes, sir; No, sir; Thank you, sir; Your luggage, sir,* were the extent of my dialogue. Quite the challenge to memorize, as you may well imagine. But I did notch one remarkable opportunity, a role in Oscar Micheaux's final film."

"Oscar Micheaux?" While Rose wasn't a habitual moviegoer—she was, frankly, too busy with work and her own imaginary worlds— she did make an effort to keep up with that side of the entertainment industry. But this failed to ring a bell. "Who's he?"

Any other man Rose had ever sat across a restaurant table from would have leapt on the opportunity to patronizingly fill in Rose's tragic gaps of general knowledge and demonstrate that, no matter how much more money she made than him—it didn't matter that Jonas was about to headline his own radio show, Rose still made more money than him—he, nonetheless, knew far more than she could ever hope to.

But that wasn't the case here. Jonas' visible delight in spinning his story flowed not from the glee of putting Rose in her place, but out of his obvious passion for the topic. She could tell the difference. "Mr. Micheaux was America's first colored filmmaker. He has quite the biography. Son of a freed slave, he was a homesteader, a mill worker, a Pullman porter, naturally—we do it in real life, not merely in the movies—a shoe-shiner, and a novelist. Had seven books published. And that was all before he turned to film production. His company, Lincoln Motion Pictures—note who is credited in the title—was the first owned by a colored man."

Lincoln, Rose thought. Yes, she was familiar with entities named after Abraham Lincoln. She hoped Oscar Micheaux's adventure had a happier ending than hers.

"Mr. Micheaux wrote, he directed, he produced. Forty-four finished films, silents and talkies. He was quite the success, even sold stock in his corporation—primarily to wealthy white folks he charmed during his days with the railroad. I only met him briefly on *The Betrayal*. It was the first race story to open at a white theater, right here in New York City at the Mansfield, in 1948. A generous critic called it the greatest Negro photoplay of all time. *The New York Times*, of course, hated it. Especially the suggestion that Negroes and whites might find many points of commonality, not merely in professional and community endeavors, but possibly in marriage."

"Oh," Rose said. It was already more than she'd intended to say.

"Box office receipts were abysmal, and that was the end of Lincoln Motion Pictures. He died a few years later."

So, no, then. No happier ending for this Lincoln namesake, either.

"I'd love to see it," Rose said. "The movie, I mean. I'd love to see you in it."

"Impossible, I'm afraid. All prints were destroyed, it's considered a lost film. By the way, I don't want you to think only the white press was hostile. *The Chicago Defender* hated it with equal fervor. For primarily the same reasons."

"Oh," Rose repeated. She was glad this wasn't her and Jonas' first meeting. He'd have assumed she was a complete idiot. Instead of merely a periodic one. Mark Twain may have been quoted as saying: *It is better to keep your mouth shut and appear stupid, than to open it and remove all doubt.* But the former Samuel Clemens wasn't the ideal person to turn to when wrestling with the correct response to a matter of racial delicacy, now was he? So, Rose ignored Twain, and compulsively filled the ensuing silence with, "That's a tragic story. For an artist. To put so much of your heart and soul into something, only to have it disappear without a trace."

Jonas nodded thoughtfully. Then changed the subject.

Was it that he didn't wish to discuss the topic further? Or did he merely yearn to end her feeble and meaningless platitudes?

Loath to make a further fool of herself and ruin their meal, Rose waited to revisit the discussion until after Jonas had asked to see the dessert menu. And then the dessert tray. And then request a refill of his coffee. When they finally left, he left the waiter a generous tip. "He did his job. Eventually."

Rose allowed Jonas to help her on with her coat, to hold the door for her as she stepped outside, to escort her through Central Park to Rose's home on the Upper West Side. She might have questioned what exactly it was they were doing, if she hadn't been so eager to establish, "This isn't who I am. I'm not the sort of person who puts up with," she waved her hand in the direction of the restaurant, "that kind of behavior. Like when that other soldier called you…" Rose didn't dare repeat it. "When he suggested you were lying about your war record. Irna's programs are progressive. Not on the surface, but deep down. She's quite subversive. In her way. She gives women a voice. She speaks up for unwed mothers, girls who've made mistakes they can't live down. I hate that we have to keep your face hidden. To sell soap. I'm not a tool of the capitalist machine. I'm a member of Workmen's Circle, since I was in school. I'm on the side of the oppressed. I'm not like… them." This time, her hand wave was all-encompassing.

"What are you like then?" Was he doubting her? Teasing her? Enticing her?

Because, if the latter, then he was doing an excellent job. As they exited the park at 72nd Street, past the waist-high brick walls meant to differentiate the Eden of grass and trees from the concrete jungle, the honking cars, the sudden buildings, Rose couldn't fight the feeling that she could tell Jonas anything. That she should tell him everything. That he, unlike Mama, unlike Irna, unlike the world, would understand and not judge. That he would understand what she'd intended rather than what she'd ended up doing.

But, no, it was still too dangerous. Not just for her, for him, too. Once Jonas knew, he could never claim not to have known.

So, Rose told him the truth. Just not the one that mattered. To his ambiguous query of "What are you then?" she answered, "I'm an almost thirty-year-old woman who loves her job. A job that takes up all my time. Which is good. Because it keeps me from thinking too long or too hard about the things I could—and maybe should—be doing with all that time, which I am not doing."

"What sort of things?" Was he a concerned doctor now? A crusading detective? A hard-boiled reporter? Rose would happily cast Jonas in any of those roles. He was that convincing. Especially when you were dying to be convinced.

He'd maneuvered it so Rose stood against the granite wall, Jonas facing her, his back to the avenue, between streetlamps. Nobody passing by would catch a glimpse of his face, or his hands, which he'd nonchalantly slipped into his pockets. A staging similar to how Hazel posed him to be photographed, all oblique angles, so that only the shadow knows…

It was Rose who made the first move. Rose who leaned forward, Rose who elevated on her toes, something she'd rarely had to do with other men; she and Jonas were almost the same height, but he still did have an inch or two on her. It was Rose who slid a single finger beneath Jonas' chin and Rose who drew him closer. "Things like this."

She could feel his breath on her face. It smelled of the crème brûlée they'd shared after Jonas took his time perusing the dessert menu. Their eyes were level. Nobody was looking down at anybody. His lips parted just the tiniest bit, tongue tapping teeth. It was a relatively mild April evening, yet Jonas' skin charred Rose's fingertip, sending flames down her arm. Flames that somehow transformed into molten weight which plummeted into her stomach, sending not at all unpleasant reverberations throughout the rest of her.

It was Rose who made the first move. And it was Rose who made the last.

It was Rose who lost her courage. Rose who, at the last possible moment, pulled back, withdrawing her hand and placing it against her chest as if saying the Pledge of Allegiance. Or protecting her heart. It was Rose who said, "I'm your boss."

"Yes," Jonas agreed, seemingly understanding what she was trying to convey, yet refusing to budge. Their eyes were still level. His lips still slightly parted. *Stand still and keep quiet. If he is right, time will show it.*

"It would be wrong," she said.

"Would it?"

"It would be difficult," she conceded.

"It would." *Were they still talking about work?*

"It would be… unethical." That was the last arrow Rose had in her quiver.

It was also the one that seemed to get the job done. Jonas blinked. Both metaphorically and literally. He rocked back on his heels. He furrowed his brow. He tightened his lips. *Thank goodness.* Seeing that she'd struck her target, Rose pressed on, "If anyone thought there was something improper going on… you know how actors gossip… you know how jealous they get. It could come off like an abuse of my power. I could lose my job. You could lose yours. You see how it would be… risky… for both of us."

He didn't say yes. He didn't say no. He didn't say anything.

"Please tell me that you understand."

Jonas studied Rose even more closely than he had during the brief moment they'd been connected by a sizzling thread. Whatever he was looking for, he found. Whether or not he was pleased by the discovery remained unclear.

"Only for you, Miss Janowitz."

Chapter Five

June 30, 1952, was the day *The Guiding Light* premiered on television. It was also the day that *Find Your Light*, starring Jonas Cain, debuted in the time slot immediately following its ongoing radio version. In the minutes it took Procter & Gamble to advise that "best costs less than all the rest" when it comes to Ivory soap, the nefarious Edmund Bard magically relocated from Selby Flats, CA, setting of *The Guiding Light*, to New York City, where he could continue wreaking havoc, this time on a much greater (female) population.

It had been Rose's idea to set the show in New York, as opposed to the fictional small towns that Irna preferred. She'd suggested they could mention real locations like restaurants and stores in order to add a sense of authenticity—and generate publicity. She'd also pointed out that, in a cosmopolitan metropolis like NYC, Edmund's provincial villainy wouldn't seem nearly as awful. They didn't want to build a show around a thoroughly bad guy. Edmund needed redeemable qualities, and what better place than the Big Apple for him—and their listeners—to encounter more malevolent threats?

Irna let Rose have her way. She turned absolute control of the new show over to Rose. Except Irna still reviewed Rose's long story proposals, read all of Rose's scripts, listened to every episode—and gave copious notes on each. It was the most power she'd ever ceded to anyone. Lucy Rittenberg, one of *Guiding Light's* television producers, couldn't believe it. She said, "Irna's always telling me: *I'm very fond of you, Lucy, but I can't work with women.* And here she is handing over the keys to the castle to you, Rose!"

Irna wasn't handing over the keys to the castle. She was allowing Rose to house-sit. Because Irna's hands were currently too full with the television broadcast. Not a week went by that Rose didn't hear about some mishap during the live broadcast, whether it was needing to make actors in their twenties look like they were in their thirties by adding white tufts to their foreheads which they dubbed "little gray wings"—and were constantly loosening when they ran their fingers dramatically through their hair, or the Thanksgiving episode when, not only did the prop man forget to put a turkey in the oven, leaving actress Charita Bauer to peek inside, slam it shut and chirp, "I think it needs a few more minutes!" but an actor's head kept getting in the way whenever the camera would track around the festive meal. With each circuit, elderly Theo Goetz was forced to duck under the table. Irna wasn't giving Rose power. Irna was giving Rose an opportunity to play scapegoat if anything went wrong with *Find Your Light* while Irna was focused on the more important parent show.

Not that Rose would ever say so in public. In public, Rose played the good soldier, taking blame and punishment both deserved and not—the buck did stop with her, just like it did with President Truman—smiling, insisting everything was going perfectly, she was fine, thank you, why do you ask?

Most people believed her.

Jonas did not.

Jonas, Rose suspected, hadn't believed her in a while. But, like Rose, he was good at pretending. Since their night in Central Park, Jonas had been pretending it never happened. If he passed her in the hallway, he would tip his hat and say, "Good day, Miss Janowitz." If she came down to the studio floor to give notes, he kept as much of a distance from her as the other actors, only speaking when spoken to, rarely making eye contact. If they should bump into each other when leaving the building—well, that would never happen. Rose still knew his schedule.

Rose also should have known better than to take anything Irna said or did personally. "The show must come first." This wasn't about individuals, it was about the greater good, a sentiment Rose embraced. Nevertheless, it was difficult to keep a stiff upper lip when, for five days in a row, Rose's *Find Your Light* scripts came back with notes scrawled across the top reading, *Lose this*, *In the dark*, and *Quite dim*. Irna seemed to be enjoying her puns a bit more than mere constructive criticism called for.

Rose was walking down the street, leafing through the marked-up script, trying to think of a way to implement the changes Irna demanded without feeling like Rose was a glorified—albeit well paid—stenographer, that she had something to contribute beyond rubber-stamping Irna's vision. Rose was telling herself the tears running down her cheeks were wind chill, when she heard a voice on her left inquire, "Everything alright, Miss Janowitz?"

Dozens of people called Rose Miss Janowitz. Only one said it in a way to make her knees feel like they'd been kicked out from the back.

"Fine," she replied automatically, as she would have to anyone.

Rose wiped her face with the back of one palm, wondering if the gesture smeared her blush, if her eyeliner had dripped, if her lipstick matched the scarf she'd tossed on at the last minute.

Jonas glanced over Rose's shoulder at the script before she had a chance to stuff it into her purse. He was looking particularly dapper in a gray, three-quarter length, double-breasted winter coat with patch pockets. "Are all of Miss Phillips' comments like this?"

"No," Rose reassured, "sometimes they're harsh."

Jonas smiled. She couldn't help smiling back, and the mere gesture of turning up her lips made Rose feel better. Not to mention whom she was smiling at.

Rose indicated that they were a block from the studio. "What are you doing here early?" She realized the query suggested she was familiar with his daily schedule. Well, she had every right to be. She was his boss. Rose had made that clear a few months ago, had she not?

"I was asked to come in early," Jonas said, falling into step beside Rose, "record a few commercials they could run during other shows. Seems Edmund Bard is an expert at flinging mud—then elucidating how it might best be wrung out of clothes."

Rose didn't expect the jealousy that retched through her. There was no reason for it. Of course, Procter & Gamble would want to take advantage of their new sensation to sell a cross-section of products. And, of course, they didn't need to ask Rose's permission. Jonas' contract wasn't with her. It was with P&G. Rose hadn't realized how much pride she took in being the only one to put words in his mouth until learning she wasn't. Some Madison Avenue hack was exploiting that glorious voice to shill detergent. Detergent whose sales paid all their salaries.

"Oh," Rose said, hoping she was the only one who heard the crack. "I see."

Rose entered the studio lobby. She assumed Jonas would head off his way, and she would head off hers. It didn't happen that way. Jonas followed Rose to her office, said good-morning to Hazel at her desk, then closed the door behind them. He asked, "Do you know how movie heroes manage to remain so brave and strong?"

"What? No. How?" Rose was simultaneously distracted from her woes and intrigued.

"They only have to do it for ninety minutes." Jonas rested a hand on Rose's shoulder. "Even the long-suffering ones only have to grin and bear it for two hours."

"I'm not suffering." She wanted to pull away, to dart behind her desk. To protect herself. Instead, she stayed where she was. She dug in her heels. "This is nothing." That part was the truth. Especially compared to what she'd been through prior to setting foot in Irna's queendom.

"I understand," Jonas said. For a moment, Rose allowed herself to fantasize that he did, that he might. But she knew that was impossible. Nobody did. Nobody could. Especially not now, when the world was so different from when she'd committed her folly. When Jonas so much as knowing about it would put his own future in jeopardy.

Jonas took a step back. The spot where his hand once rested prickled with cold. Rose fought the impulse to rub it, to scoop up what remained of his essence before it dissipated like stardust. He said, "I was also raised to pretend."

He turned towards the door. But, before Jonas left, he asked Rose, "What do you think we were doing at the restaurant? My parents, to this day, live the life they should have, not the one they do have; if they just act as if liberation is already here, they can will it into being. No complaining, no suggesting anything is less than ideal. Dignity and nobility. We rise above petty grievances. We turn the other cheek. Always. It's exhausting."

"That's not what I'm doing," Rose challenged.

"No?"

"No." Rose was on solid ground. She knew exactly what she was doing. And it wasn't what Jonas accused her of. Well, not exactly. "I'm a writer. I'm a soap-opera writer." She stressed the distinction. "Not a novelist, not a playwright, a soap-opera writer. I believe that no matter how dire things get, no matter how bleak the situation may seem at the end of Friday, I can always figure out how to engender a happy ending first thing Monday."

"*When life mocks her, breaks her hopes, dashes her against the rocks of despair,*" Jonas intoned, "*Helen Trent fights back bravely, successfully, to prove what so many women long to prove, that because a woman is thirty-five or more, romance in life need not be over, that romance can begin at thirty-five.*"

Rose's first thought was, *does he think I'm thirty-five?* But her second, more offended one, which she spoke out loud was, "That's not one of Irna's shows!"

"My apologies." Jonas' grin matched the merriment in his eyes.

"Are you auditioning for them?" So many issues floating in the ether between them, yet this was the one Rose felt compelled to address first. "Are they trying to poach you? What are they offering? Because, whatever they're offering, I can match it. I can beat it." She was already going over her budget, wondering what she could cut in order to sweeten the pot, compel Jonas to stay with them. With her.

"What are you offering?"

"Anything."

SHE'D FELT MORTIFIED the minute that promise escaped her lips—seemingly with no input from Rose's brain. Jonas, on the other hand, appeared anything but mortified. He appeared amused. He appeared charmed. He appeared… challenged. Rose wasn't sure if that was a good thing. If that was a safe thing.

"I think we should discuss your earlier offer," Jonas informed Rose gravely, entering her office after Hazel had already rushed home and the building was nearly deserted, save for the cleaning crew, security, and, of course, Rose, burning the eight-forty-five oil. "Not here. You haven't had dinner yet." Jonas made the obvious and safe assumption.

"No," she admitted.

THEY STOOD ON THE SIDEWALK, looking right to left, then back again. This was the East Side of Manhattan. Their restaurant choices should have been endless. Their restaurant choices were endless. Except Rose had no interest in a repeat of their last dining experience. She also knew that it wasn't her place to say so.

"How about we try the other side of the park?" Jonas offered, and Rose nodded gratefully.

They made small talk during their walk to the West Side, Jonas asking Rose how she got started in writing soap-operas, and what drew her to the genre. She told him more or less the same thing she'd told Irna at her interview. "Serials offer chance after chance to get life right. You can keep trying, over and over."

"Until you get your happy ending?"

"Exactly!"

"So, you cannot conceive of any scenario where even the most gifted of writers fails at engineering happily ever after?" Jonas looked at her with what she thought might be newfound respect. "You are a most entrancing woman, Rose Janowitz." It was the first time he'd used her given name. It slid ever so enchantingly off his tongue. Then again, what didn't? She mustn't think anything of it. But since when had knowing she mustn't ever stop Rose from charging full speed ahead?

Their reception at a cozy Greek diner on the West Side proved the exact opposite of what they'd experienced on the East. Instead of being ignored and made to wait, the hostess went out of her way to make it clear that she understood they were together—and that she was absolutely delighted by it! She led them to a well-lit table in front of the window, so they might be easily observed by anyone passing by on the street. She handed them their menus and called over a waiter in the middle of taking another order, telling him to make sure he took extra good care of their extra special customers. As they ate, not only the hostess, but the owner stopped by to confirm everything was to their liking. They wanted to stress what a friendly, welcoming establishment they ran, not like some others. Those people were a disgrace to the melting pot that was New York City, and especially the progressive and welcoming Upper West Side. The management hoped Rose and Jonas felt welcome. Did they feel welcome? Was there anything more they could do to make them feel more welcome?

This time, instead of asking for the dessert menu and lingering over his coffee, Jonas didn't even wait for the check. He left enough money on the table to cover their dinners and yet another generous tip, then hurried Rose out.

Still somewhat flustered by the encounter, Rose could only ask—they hadn't had much of a chance to talk over their meal, they kept being interrupted—"Is it often like… this?"

"Not as often as the alternative," he admitted, "but often enough."

"How do you bear it? It feels like being under a microscope, like they're prying you open with a stick. Or like being a performing poodle. They want you to do tricks!"

"Dignity," Jonas repeated. "Nobility. And fleeing the scene as fast as you can."

THE NEXT TIME THEY WENT OUT—and, somehow, they'd both agreed there'd be a next time without either articulating that they'd like there to be a next time—Rose tentatively ventured, "It isn't fair. The previous occasions, you were the one who stood out. All eyes were on you. You shouldn't have to be the one perennially made to feel like you're out of place. Maybe we should go… maybe, tonight, we should go… uptown?"

Rose had countersigned Jonas' employment contact. She knew he resided in Harlem. Sugar Hill, to be precise. The neighborhood got its name because of the "sweet life" it offered those who opted to live in its high-priced apartment houses, complete with elevators and doormen to challenge anything found further south. But she didn't know how Jonas felt about entertaining there. Or about being seen with someone like her.

He hesitated. Rose was about to reassure that he didn't have to, she understood she might be putting him on the spot, that's the last thing she wanted—for a moment she feared she sounded as obsequious as their Upper West Side hosts—when Jonas clarified, "Are you certain that's what you want to do?"

He appeared more worried about her than himself, presumably with good reason. Rose couldn't remember an occasion when, outwardly, at least, she hadn't looked more or less like everybody around her. Growing up on the Lower East Side, it was the rare neighbor who didn't look like a sibling or a cousin, even the Greeks and Italians blended into the same crowd with the Jews. Matters changed slightly once she began working in midtown. If anybody looked closely, yes, then they could obviously see she didn't quite fit in with the golden haired, blue eyed, perfectly nosed, moneyed crowd. But, upon a quick, surface glance, she rarely stood out. That wouldn't be the case in Harlem.

Rose told herself it would be a good experience to have. She'd lived far too comfortably for far too long. It would serve her well to see how those outside her circle lived. Didn't writers require a multitude of experiences to fuel their imaginations? To enhance their craft? This would allow Rose the opportunity to walk around in Jonas' shoes, to discover how it felt for him to, day after day, enter a space where he was the outsider, the one who visibly didn't fit. It would allow her to understand him. To get inside his skin, to see through his eyes, to experience… him.

"I'm certain," Rose said.

HE TOOK HER TO SMALLS PARADISE, an office building on Seventh Avenue and 135th Street. Down the steps to the basement and into a splendor of white tablecloths, crisply printed menus, Art Deco walls and ceilings, and tuxedoed waiters as likely to break into song—and, once upon a time, into the Charleston—as the house band, which also provided music for the floorshow. It felt like entering a fishbowl of sound, heat, and too much vibrating energy contained within too small of a space.

Jonas had suggested it because, "You love to dance."

She'd told him that. She'd told him everything. Almost.

Rose agonized over what to wear before coming. She didn't wish to appear too prim and proper. Yet, she didn't want to seem disrespectful by dressing too casually. She wanted to fit in, yet knew she never would and suspected it would be insulting to try. Most of all, Rose didn't want Jonas to regret bringing her. She settled on a red New Look By Dior dress with short sleeves, a square neckline and a full skirt. Also matching gloves. Because she thought it was a touch of class Jonas would appreciate. Rose's biggest concern was her hair. She wore it up at work. It was professional. It was how Irna did it. Now Rose wore it down, letting it flow past her shoulders, only pinning it with a clasp at the base of her neck. When she met Jonas at the entrance to the nightclub, he paused, looking her over from head to toe, then smiled a smile that told Rose all her agonizing had been worth it.

Jonas filled Rose in on the history of Smalls Paradise before they entered. It had been the only Negro-owned and integrated Harlem nightclub throughout the 1930s and beyond. All the others, including The Cotton Club, once located on 142nd Street and Lenox Avenue, had colored performers, but exclusively white customers. While The Cotton Club and its ilk closed at 4 a.m., Smalls Paradise remained open all night, culminating with a 6 a.m. floor show of dancing girls and waiters serving drinks on roller-skates.

"Don't worry," Jonas reassured. "It's a very respectable place. W.E.B. DuBois celebrated his eighty-third birthday here just this past February. A favor from the owner. The party was originally supposed to be held at the Essex House, sponsored by Paul Robeson, Mary McLeod Bethune and Albert Einstein! But then those Joseph McCarthy fellows told Essex House they were all Communists. Essex canceled the Banquet, so Ed Smalls stepped in and let them have run of his club for a night. What would you have given to be a fly on the wall and watch Doctors DuBois and Einstein kicking up their heels on that dance floor!"

Jonas was still talking, but Rose had stopped listening. She'd begun shaking. She was thankful for the gloves. They made it less obvious that she could barely control her fingers. Her knees buckled. Rose didn't think she'd have made it down the stairs if not for Jonas' arm supporting her elbow. She hoped he'd think she was merely having a difficult time finding her bearings in the dim light.

Was it too late to turn tail and run? Had anyone seen her come in? They were part of a large entering throng. Rose definitely stood out in it. She didn't think anyone was keeping tabs on her. Not for years now. But you never knew who might still be holding a grudge. One wrong word to the right person and… Rose believed Irna could forgive Rose quite a bit. But she could never forgive Rose this. Not Rose putting Irna's precious shows at risk.

It was too late to turn tail and run. Not only because the stairs behind Rose were packed with people, but because there Jonas was, holding her arm, smiling at her. Rose could never turn tail and run from that smile. No matter the consequences.

They were shown to a table with a minimum of fuss. Already an improvement over the East and West Sides. They were served without comment, treated just like everyone else. So, what if Rose couldn't help noticing that, while Smalls Paradise was, as advertised, a mixture of Negro and white faces, each stuck to their own grouping.

They ate, they drank, they danced. And, in between musical numbers, when the noise level dropped enough to make it possible, they talked.

"So," Rose dredged up a query that, had she inserted it into a script, Irna would have been more than justified to dismiss as dim, "do you come here often?"

"When I was a student at Columbia, yes."

"What was that like?" Though her own alma mater, Hunter College, was described as the Ivy League for immigrants, Rose wondered what bonuses a real Ivy might offer. Sometimes, she walked up to the Columbia campus and loitered, mixing with the hallowed students and faculty, pretending she could ever be that self-assured, that poised, that confident her future was that bright… and that guaranteed.

Jonas took a moment to consider Rose's question. "I was… well prepared."

"Academically?"

"Definitely academically. Most of the required reading for my English literature major, my parents made certain I'd covered in advance. I heard Latin declensions in the crib!"

Academically prepared was not what Jonas meant.

"The home training I received," Jonas chose his words with care, walking the fine line between being honest and being truthful. "I was well prepared for…"

"You were mistreated," Rose guessed. And spared him needing to say.

"Not always. Not exactly. Not by everyone. The professors were exceedingly polite. They offered to help any way they could. They only took offense when it turned out I didn't need it."

"Oh," Rose said. "I see."

"My fellow students were equally welcoming. Until final grades were posted."

"And you were at the top of the class," Rose guessed.

"I wasn't raised to be anything but."

"That kind of condescension is infuriating." Rose thought of her and Irna's struggle to be taken seriously by male executives and even underlings.

"I suspect that's why I fell in love with Shakespeare. If I couldn't be angry as myself—it wouldn't do, what would people think, I had to set an example, be unimpeachable, else I would poison the well for all who wished to come after—then I could be angry through *Hamlet,* through *Richard III,* through *King Lear.*"

"Through Edmund the bastard?"

"Exactly." There went that smile again. "And his spiritual descendant, Edmund Bard."

Was Jonas comparing Rose to Shakespeare? That was more of a compliment than she knew how to process. She vowed to recall it the next time she wrestled with a stack of Irna's blue-inked scripts. To cover her embarrassment, and her thrill, Rose asked, "Who do you think is the angriest character Shakespeare ever wrote?"

"Benedick," Jonas answered without hesitation.

"Benedick?" It was the last name Rose expected to hear. "*Much Ado About Nothing?*"

"Benedick," Jonas reiterated. "He's in love with a woman but convinced she could never love him. Benedick is furious with himself for not being the man Beatrice could risk falling in love with."

Chapter Six

"Excuse me." Rose stumbled awkwardly to her feet. She'd only accepted a single glass of champagne, but she felt as unsteady as after a night of revelry. Her head spun, her ears rang, her vision blurred. She was hot. She needed air. She needed to think. She needed to go.

Jonas half-rose when she did, as a gentleman must.

Rose made her way to the ladies' room, sliding into line. Maybe some water would help settle her. Maybe she was just overheated. Maybe she was just overwrought. Maybe she was in over her head. They'd been discussing Shakespeare. Not real life. Hadn't Shakespeare been the one to reassure that *All's Well That Ends Well?*

But that was in Shakespeare.

Not real life.

What did Rose think she was doing? What did she and Jonas think they were doing?

Their situation was impossible. Their situation was illegal. Well, not everywhere. Four years earlier, the California Supreme Court ruled that anti-miscegenation laws violated the 14th Amendment, making interracial marriage legal. New York state never had any laws against it. And why was Rose thinking about marriage? She should be thinking about her job. And Jonas' job. Why was it acceptable for movie studio heads like David Selznick to be married to women who worked for them, like Jennifer Jones, and why was Rose thinking about marriage?

Maybe she had it wrong. The world was changing, wasn't it? Obstacles that once seemed insurmountable were receding. Taboos that once seemed unshakable were being dismissed as old-fashioned. They had modern art, modern dance, modern furniture and modern fashion. Surely, they were due for some modern thought.

Rose felt her shoulders relaxing, her jaw loosening, the gnawing in her stomach turning to a pleasant buzz. She did have it wrong. They were halfway into the 20th century. The rules and mores of the past simply didn't apply. They were free. Men like Jonas had fought a World War to keep them that way.

Rose's optimism lasted up until it was her turn to enter the lavatory. The woman on her way out forcefully banged Rose's shoulder with her own, shoving Rose against the wall, her cheek hitting the plaster. As Rose grappled to remain upright, already turning to say it was alright, despite no apology being proffered, the other woman whispered to her waiting friend, loud enough to make sure Rose heard, "It's only the homely ones who go after our men. Their own kind don't want them."

Rose didn't know if Jonas witnessed the altercation. She felt certain he hadn't heard what was said. Which was why, when she returned to the table and he asked if she was alright—why, did she look shaken? Surely, he couldn't see the mark on her face, not in this dim lighting—Rose reassured him, "I'm fine."

THEY DIDN'T STAY for the 6 a.m. floorshow. Even though it was Friday and neither had work the next day—there was no such thing as a weekend with Irna, but Rose didn't need to go into the office if she didn't want to—they left around midnight.

They left because Rose asked Jonas, "You live around here, right?"

He nodded, unsure of what she was asking.

"I'd like to see your apartment," Rose said.

Sure of what she was asking.

Rose spent the night and most of the next day in Jonas' apartment. The following weekend, they made it Friday night, all day Saturday, Saturday night and all-day Sunday. Rose finally went home in the evening to call Irna and hear the criticism Irna had been forced to pent up for forty-eight hours. Irna didn't ask where Rose had been, and Rose didn't offer any information.

Only at the end of the call did Irna ask, "Are you happy?"

She could have been referring to anything.

But both women knew what Rose meant when she answered, "Very."

"The show comes first," was Irna's penultimate reminder. Followed by, "Good."

ROSE WAS NO INNOCENT, but she was a virgin to the notion that happiness didn't have to be complicated. Of course, matters were complicated. They were more complicated than they had ever been. But, at the same time, Rose could close Jonas' apartment door to the world, to jobs, to nightclubs, to restaurants, to nay-sayers, and it became utterly simple.

There was her, there was him, there was them.

Simple.

The only hurdle still between them, one that Rose had done her darndest to keep behind the shut door, but it kept hammering incessantly when she least expected it, was the business of Rose's past—and how it could affect both their futures.

They were lying in bed, Jonas on his stomach, Rose's head propped up on one elbow, tickling her fingers down his back with her free hand while he smiled sleepily, when she finally gathered up the courage to say, "I never graduated from high school."

Jonas rolled over slowly, facing her with a quizzical expression. "You went to college."

"I took the test. Got an equivalency."

The side of his mouth twitched, trying to remain serious, "If that's the worst thing you ever did—"

"It isn't," Rose cut him off. And the twitch stilled.

He sat up, back against the headboard. He took her hand in his, stroking the palm with his thumb. He looked down to meet Rose's eyes but, when she glanced away, he didn't push. "What is it?"

"I told you I grew up going to Workmen's Circle. Attended their summer camps, sang with the chorus. They're a social-action organization. They taught me to stand up for the rights of the oppressed, call out injustice, fight for freedom. Not just my own, everybody's."

"Sounds like a cause I could support," Jonas said softly, encouraging her to continue.

"I was seventeen. I was sure I knew everything. I was sure I knew better. Certainly, more than my mother did. Certainly, more than anybody who told me to think my actions through did."

"What actions?" No judgment, just support.

"I went to Spain. To fight with the Republicans in the Abraham Lincoln Brigade against the Nationalists."

It was clearly not what Jonas expected to hear.

"I arrived towards the end. We didn't know how close we were to losing. Or we didn't want to admit it, anyway. There were colored soldiers," she recalled, a detail Rose hadn't remembered up till that moment but suddenly saw as significant. "One of them, Oliver Law, I heard about him through this commander I served under, they were both from Chicago. Law led a full machine-gun company on the Jarama front. And for a couple of days, he led the entire battalion while Walter Garland was recovering from injuries. He died before I got there, but he was a hero. Lots of the colored soldiers were."

Jonas nodded, "Langston Hughes wrote about them, the men who volunteered. Said they saw no difference between the Nationalists and the men in white hoods.

"Our forces were integrated. Everyone was equal, men and women, too. Though one time this all-women anarchist delegation tried to attend the National Confederation of Labour Congress they were told their presence would undermine working-class interests…" Rose dropped that train of thought in favor of, "Workmen's Circle, it's a Socialist organization. Except the Socialist Youth of Spain refused to send women to the front lines. Anyone who wanted to participate in the fighting had to switch allegiance to the Communists."

That last word caught Jonas' attention.

"And that's what you did?" he asked cautiously.

Rose nodded, swallowing hard.

Jonas exhaled, briefly closing his eyes and running a hand through his hair. "Then what happened?"

"Then the war ended. I came home." That sounded convincing. Nothing to question. It was even mostly true. "Couple of months later, Stalin signed a pact with Hitler. We had speakers from the American Communist Party come to Workmen's Circle to tell us why we should support it, but I'd had enough. I quit. I went to college and never really looked back. Well, I did work for WEVD, but that was—it was a soap-opera. It was barely political. I work for Procter & Gamble now! It doesn't get more all-American than that!"

"Does Miss Phillips know?"

"No. The one time somebody mentioned the loyalty oath to Irna, they ended up slinking out of her office like The Burghers of Calais." Jonas should appreciate the Rodin imagery.

"So, you're in no danger."

"Not at the moment. But who knows what might happen to-morrow? Phillip Loeb, he was in *The Goldbergs* on Broadway, then on television. *Red Channels* called him a Communist and General Foods insisted Gertrude Berg fire him or they'd drop their sponsorship. Pert Kelton had to leave *The Honeymooners*. Jackie Gleason covered for her, said it was heart trouble, but she was listed in *Red Channels*, too. Lucille Ball only got away with keeping her show because Desi claimed she was too dumb to know what she was doing when she registered as a Communist."

"Any colored folks on that list of theirs?"

"Paul Robeson, Lena Horne, Langston Hughes, Harry Belafonte, Hazel Scott, Canada Lee," Rose rattled off. She hadn't realized she'd been keeping track.

"So, we all can't claim to be too stupid? Hardly seems fair, seeing as how we're judged too stupid to do anything else."

She wondered if Jonas were truly offended, but his laugh quenched that fear.

"So now that you know, if somebody asks you about me—"

"If someone asks me about you?" Jonas shifted his weight to turn towards her, kissing Rose's shoulder, the crook of her neck, her collarbone, the base of her throat, murmuring, "I'll tell them you're a beautiful woman, a brilliant writer, and a compassionate human being. That's all they're going to get out of me."

And that's all Jonas was going to get out of her. Because no matter how smoothly this part went, Rose had no intention of ever telling anybody what really happened in Spain.

"NOT THAT I MIND holing up with you indefinitely," Jonas told Rose after the fifth weekend they spent exclusively in his apartment, living off pre-purchased food, only popping out to buy the Sunday *New York Times*, because that was non-negotiable, "but aren't you getting bored?"

"No." Rose couldn't imagine that happening. She couldn't imagine ever needing more than Jonas—and, well, the Sunday *New York Times*.

"I saw what happened with that woman at Smalls."

"It was an accident."

"It wasn't."

"It's a lot more dangerous for you than it is for me. So, I get jostled a little, so what? You could be…" Rose thought of Billie Holiday singing about *Black bodies swinging in the southern breeze/Strange fruit hanging from the poplar trees.*

"Been thinking about that." Jonas simultaneously intuited her concerns and dismissed them. "The East Side is out; the West Side is out. Harlem is out." Rose opened her mouth to insist that she was fine with… "What about the Village?"

"Cafe Society closed five years ago." It was the first integrated club in Greenwich Village. The founder, Barney Josephson, a New Jersey Jew, founded it in the name of Negro liberation. Billie Holiday sang at his opening in 1938. He was subpoenaed by the House Committee on Un-American Activities in 1947 but received no support from the American Communist Party due to being a Marxist. Back in her Workmen's Circle days, Rose overheard debates among members as to whether Josephson was truly committed to the issue of equal rights for Negros, or whether he just saw opening an integrated club as an opportunity to double his customers and his profits. If it was capitalism which brought about equality for the downtrodden, then Workmen's Circle wanted no part of it.

"Cafe Society was intentionally integrated. Most Village clubs are passively integrated now." Jonas bopped his arm up and down, snapping his fingers. "Jazz, beatniks, poetry, music. Black turtleneck sweaters! Berets! It could be fun. What do you say?"

He looked so enthusiastic, how could Rose say anything but, "Sure. Fun."

THEY OPTED FOR Village Vanguard on 7th Avenue South, ducking in under the red awning which stretched the width of the street and, once again, descending into the basement. This one called itself "the most famous basement in New York City," claiming the low ceilings and limited space—fitting exactly 123 people, not 124 and certainly not 125—made for the best acoustics. Round white tables, each surrounded by more chairs than should have been possible, were barely visible beneath the packed crush of people, men in jackets and ties, women in cocktail dresses—not nearly as many black turtlenecks and berets as they'd expected. In the dim light, made even dimmer by the fog of cigarette smoke, you navigated your way to the restroom by following a red line on the floor, past the kitchen, where it was best not to peek in if you wanted to keep your appetite. A piano stood wedged at the furthest end of the windowless room, a microphone stand, and a tiny performance space set up in front of it.

Jonas and Rose found a spot by the wall. It was presumably the worst seat in the house, granting an obscured side-view of the performers, and muffled sound. As well as anonymity.

In between jazz singers, spoken-word poets, and stand-up comics, Rose told Jonas, covering her mouth to cough, then waving her hand in front of her face to disperse the smoke, "I need to let Irna know about us. It's the professional thing to do."

"You think she'll take umbrage?"

"I don't know. If she thinks this might create friction with other actors or the sponsors…"

"We cannot possibly be the first couple in the history of

commercial radio. With the kinds of hours we keep, when would we ever get the chance to meet someone who isn't a co-worker!"

"Well, yes, obviously," Rose concurred, "but those other couples, they're…"

"The same race?"

"No. I mean, yes. That's not the issue, though. Not the main one. All those other couples, it's the man who's the boss, and the woman who's…"

"The underling?"

"The employee."

"Which makes the relationship more palatable?"

"Yes," Rose said simply. She'd only lied to Jonas about one thing. A lie of omission. And she intended to keep it that way. All the lies she'd told Jonas about being fine didn't count. They were lies she told herself, too. So, she could pretend she believed them.

"You do what you think is best." Jonas signaled the waiter to bring them another round.

They were attended to as efficiently as possible in a space where the service staff felt obliged to squeeze sideways through a throng of bodies, raising their trays over their heads and all but leaning backwards, limbo-style. No one seemed to pay particular attention to Rose and Jonas, either positive or negative. They were just two more customers, two more cogs in the capitalist, profit-making machine. It was strangely comforting.

They sat through a poet who, while scratching one side of his face then the other, offered a list of synonyms for the color blue. He repeated the words "water" and "sky" several times, before moving on to synonyms for the color brown, followed by "earth" and "death."

"Do you understand any of this?" Jonas asked Rose.

"I feel like I should try." This club was the first time she and Jonas weren't on exhibition. The least she could do was thank them by attempting to embrace their ethos.

Jonas sat back, fingers linked across his chest, endeavoring open-mindedness. A woman marched up to the mic. She proceeded to expound, in great detail and free verse, about the wonders of exploring two men's bodies simultaneously.

Rose realized that she was being a prude, illiberal, and, worst of all, a reactionary. But she couldn't help blushing. It was one thing to engage with Jonas in some of the activities the woman was recounting. It was another to hear them described in front of him. In front of a crowd. Her response was that of an old maid. Which, technically, Rose was. But she liked to think of her spinster status as simply a legal condition, not a moral one.

"Excuse me," she rose and fumbled her way to the ladies' room, trying not to inhale too deeply. Rose wasn't such a reactionary that she couldn't distinguish the smell of tobacco smoke from that of its illegal counterpart.

This time, there was no shoving during the wait for the restroom. This time, there was only an older woman—in her fifties, maybe more—beautifully dressed, her make-up just a touch smudged by the heat and close quarters. She learned forward, her breath smelling of bourbon and the mint popped to cover it. She giggled in a manner out of sync with her age and mien, and advised Rose, "I love those colored boys, too."

She winked and drunkenly booped Rose on the nose before moving on. Rose remained where she was, not so much frozen in place as melted into it. She attempted to puzzle out why the words hit her so brutally. What had the woman said that was so wrong? Jonas was colored. And Rose did love him. It wasn't an accusation. It was nothing to be ashamed of.

Rose wasn't ashamed. Rose was incensed. Not because some intoxicated stranger had accused her of loving a colored man, but because she'd made it seem like Rose loved Jonas not for being Jonas, but for his color. She made it sound like a fetish, a kink, a phase. Like Rose was making a political point. Like she was rebelling, but in a boringly run-of-the-mill manner. She was a cliché, part of a movement, not an individual making her own choices for her own reasons. Once, Rose had wanted nothing more than to submerge her individuality into a greater whole. It's what she'd been raised to do, after all. Once, Rose would have been thrilled to be part of something bigger than her own trifling concerns.

But not this. Not Jonas. Rose and Jonas belonged exclusively to themselves. The door to his apartment stood closed specifically because they were not interested in the judgment of the masses—either bad or good. To say that Rose loved Jonas because she would have loved any colored man who crossed her path was to diminish everything Jonas was.

She returned to their table and told him, "I'm ready to go."

He didn't argue.

SHE TRIED TO DO as she'd told Jonas she would and fill Irna in about their relationship. But she didn't feel comfortable dissecting her private life over the phone, and the next time Irna was in New York, Rose walked into Irna's office to find her mentor in a frenzy.

CBS had awarded *Guiding Light* the great privilege of being their first daytime show to experiment with a color broadcast. There would be massive publicity surrounding it, and likely a boost in the ratings. Irna was not pleased. First, because she had no control over how the show would look, and no opportunity for a test run to make certain the results met her standards. And second, because it hadn't been her idea.

When Rose walked into Irna's office, Irna was huddled with Agnes Nixon, her recently hired associate writer, and the only woman Irna seemed capable of collaborating with outside of Rose. Rose couldn't help feeling jealous. She suspected Irna thought the Catholic, Chicago-born, Nashville-bred Agnes was more suitable to writing *The Guiding Light's* white-bread Bauer family than someone of Rose's background.

"What is it?" Irna demanded, clearly displeased to be interrupted.

"Nothing important." Rose decided now wasn't the time to point out yet another way in which she wasn't like the audience they were writing for. Being a New York Jew was alienating enough. Adding Jonas to the mix could well be career suicide. "We can discuss it later."

Chapter Seven

By the time the broadcast day for *Guiding Light's* first color episode came around, Irna had figured out a way to circumvent her problem. She wrote a script in which the entire show took place in a hospital room. The broadcast may have been in color, but the walls were gray, the medical uniforms were white, and Irna had made her point.

Meanwhile, Rose had lost her nerve. It happened after she heard Agnes was lobbying to add a Negro character to *The Guiding Light*. Irna was adamantly against it. Rose figured if Irna's latest pet couldn't budge her on the issue, Rose had no business drawing further attention to it—even peripherally.

That is, until she was faced with no other option.

This time, Irna made a special trip to New York, and she was the one who came into Rose's office. Not a good sign. You came to Irna; Irna didn't come to you.

"Wonderful news," Irna said.

Another ominous sign. Irna never thought anything was wonderful.

"CBS is very happy with your work on *Find Your Light*."

Rose had guessed as much. They never had nearly as many notes as Irna.

"Which is why we'll be following in *The Guiding Light's* footsteps and transitioning its spin-off show to television, as well."

This was, indeed, wonderful news. Television meant a bigger budget, opportunity to try new things. More work but also, most likely, a raise. Television meant…

Now Rose understood why Irna came to her. And why she'd felt compelled to preface with how wonderful this was.

"Edmund…"

"We'll recast." The way Irna said it made clear she'd given the matter abundant thought and concluded that there was no other recourse.

"He's the star. Have you seen how much fan mail he gets? He's not interchangeable!"

"You and Hazel patched an ingenious solution. But you had to know it was temporary."

"Give the audience some credit, Irna. Maybe they're not as backwards as you assume."

"I know my audience." Irna's tone, which had brushed the outer rim of cajoling earlier, was now pure verdict. "We'll recast. I'll let the actors and other staff know. You handle Mr. Cain."

ROSE WAS FORCED TO GO with Irna down to the studio floor for the big announcement. It was still her show. If Irna was hoping for unanimous celebration at her words, what she received was subdued enthusiasm. Radio actors knew their talents didn't always transfer to television. They were too young, they were too old, they weren't photogenic enough. Yet, even as they worried for their own job security, every single one couldn't help sneaking a peek Jonas' way. No matter how precarious their position, his was a thousand times worse.

Jonas, for his part, did what Jonas always did. His face rested devoid of expression. His body language remained placid. He returned no one's gaze.

Not even Rose's.

"WE CAN FIGHT THIS," she insisted. It was a Tuesday night. Rose was in Jonas' apartment. She didn't give a damn anymore.

He finally allowed himself the privilege of expression. Jonas' shoulders didn't so much sag as they surrendered the soldier-at-attention false front. He bent his arms at the elbows and raised his palms to the ceiling, then let them drop. He smiled, but it wasn't one of happiness. It was cynicism. She knew because his dimples refused to make an appearance.

"How?"

"We can go to the sponsors. Sponsors overrule Irna. We can threaten to make a fuss. Procter & Gamble hates fuss. We can turn public opinion against them."

"You think once Procter & Gamble, which can buy time on absolutely any form of media, publishes their story of how they were tricked into hiring a Negro by a scheming Jewess, public option will swing to our side?"

"Well, not when you put it that way!" No matter how upset Rose was, Jonas could always make her laugh.

He sat next to Rose on the couch just as she bounced up to commence pacing. Jonas swiveled his head from side to side, as if watching a tennis match.

He didn't say another word.

"WE CAN TRY TO SELL YOU ELSEWHERE." Rose sprung awake at three o'clock in the morning and shook Jonas until he grunted to indicate he was listening.

"Like down the river?"

"Bad choice of words," Rose conceded, but she was in too much of an inspirational fervor to slow down for long. "*Find Your Light* is a success for two reasons: My writing, your acting."

"And the several dozen other actors, technicians, engineers, press agents," he mumbled into his pillow.

Again, Rose had no time for pausing. "As soon as *Find Your Light* moves to television, other networks are going to be looking for programming to put up against them and steal their viewers. What better to offer them than challenging *Find Your Light* with the team which made it successful in the first place?"

"Rose," Jonas rolled over on his back. "I'm still a Negro."

"And I'm still a scheming Jewess."

ROSE WENT TO IRNA with her proposal first. Rose wanted her to understand what she was risking when she insisted on implementing her plan to recast Edmund. "Why cannibalize your audience when we can have them all to ourselves?"

"You're a very smart girl," Irna told her protégé. "But I'm afraid love has made you very stupid."

"At my job interview, we agreed the wonderful thing about serials is that no matter how bad the mistake, tune in tomorrow offers you a chance to fix anything."

"I am offering you that chance. But you are tragically close to running out of tomorrows. And no one, not you, not even me, will be able to write you out of this one."

ROSE IGNORED IRNA'S ADVICE. With CBS in first place according to the recently established Neilson ratings, she approached their closest competitor, NBC. When they turned her down, she went to ABC. That third-place network was struggling so much in their primetime offerings, they hadn't attempted launching a viable daytime division. Rose argued this could be their chance to do so, and with a hit! She finally went to DuMont. But they were flailing even more than ABC, and informed Rose that instead of expanding their schedule, their strategy was to truncate it in the hopes of bleeding a little less money.

Word of Rose's pitch meetings promptly got back to Irna. Rose had predicted as much. There was no way to avoid it. The Queen of Daytime would always be kept in the loop regarding any attempt to usurp her throne. Rose hoped Irna understood that wasn't what she was doing. Rose hoped Irna understood that all Rose was doing was trying to make clear to Irna just how serious Rose was about keeping Jonas as the star of *Find Your Light*—and thus swaying Irna into supporting her.

Irna fired Rose the Friday before the television version of *Find Your Light* was scheduled to begin production. She didn't do it in person. Irna wasn't expected to arrive in New York until Monday. She didn't do it over the phone, despite the multi-hour-long conversations they'd shared over the years. She didn't even do it via her scrawl across a dog-eared script. Rose received her coldly typed termination notice, hand delivered by Hazel, at precisely five o'clock. There was nothing personal about it. Nothing to indicate their working camaraderie of the past half-decade. Irna didn't even wish Rose well.

There was still so much work to be done before the director called "Action!" on Monday morning. Rose surveyed the papers needing to be approved and signed sprawled across her desk, the list of phone calls demanding to be returned, the schedules and call times begging to be finalized. She stood up, reaching for her coat and handbag and, without a look back, told Hazel, "I know you need to run home, but if you can think of anyone willing to step in at the last minute like this, the Executive Producer job is likely theirs."

"Actually," Hazel said, looking at the pile of work with a hunger she'd never previously allowed anyone—not even herself—to witness, "I can stay."

JONAS HAD RECEIVED HIS NOTICE weeks earlier. He knew it would be his last day on the radio show. A new Edmund Bard had been cast. He was tall, handsome, a strong actor, with a fine voice. Rose bore the man no ill will. She simply knew he wouldn't be up for the job. His take on Edmund was the same as all the candidates she'd rejected during the first casting round. It wasn't what the role called for, and it wasn't what the audience had responded to. But what did Rose care? She didn't work for Irna anymore.

Jonas did his best to comfort Rose. Rose did her best to assure him she didn't require comforting. This was the optimal thing which could have happened for both of them. They were being stifled creatively, shilling for a traditionalist corporation. Soap salesmen couldn't be artists.

"I have one more idea," Rose said.

IT FELT STRANGE to be walking into the WEVD offices again. When Rose had worked there in the early 1940s, their purchase by *The Jewish Daily Forward* had been completed, and the more money they poured into the station, the more their influence was felt. WEVD's political content kept shifting from the left towards the center, with over fifty percent of broadcast time now dedicated to the commercials which allowed them to stay on the air. Sponsors ranged from mainstream, national entities like Campbell's Soup, to local businesses advertising in English and Yiddish. The latter were less than professional, which, some claimed, added to their charm. Rose remembered a comedian named Aaron Chwatt building a whole routine out of making fun of the real-life ads run by Joe and Paul, a Brooklyn, Bronx, and Manhattan clothing chain. The bit started with some cantorial-sounding singing, followed by Yiddish-accented quick-talking salespeople listing their wares, then a series of interruptions for other products, including Alka-Seltzer, castor oil, and cigarettes. When Chwatt changed his name to Red Buttons and made the shift from the Borscht Belt to *The Tonight Show*, Rose kept waiting for him to revive the classic routine. He never did. Not mainstream enough.

The Jewish Daily Forward claimed the preponderance of commercials was imperative to keep the station broadcasting. The Socialist Party disagreed. To protest what they saw as WEVD's bowing down to capitalist interests, they redirected their budget to buying airtime on NBC and other conventional outlets. Which Rose found hilarious. The Socialist Party boycotted WEVD for being too commercial by giving their commercial money to advance socialism to a purely capitalist enterprise.

In Rose's absence, WEVD had purchased an FM station and gotten rid of most of their scripted dramatic programming, including *Mayn Muter Un Ikh,* in favor of public affairs panels debating, "Should New York State Have a Little Taft-Hartley Law?" and discussions on "The Threat to Academic Freedom." A soap opera seemed like the last sort of show they'd consider adding back on the roster. But Rose was out of options.

She framed her and Jonas' situation not as a case of creative differences, but as illegal termination due to racial discrimination and capitalist exploitation of their labor, which a proudly union supporting station like WEVD should be eager to denounce.

The programming director who'd finally deigned to meet with Rose after over a week of near-hourly phone calls and messages which exhausted his secretary, wasn't impressed. His main takeaway from the conversation was that Rose spent half a decade working for P&G

and had relationships with their marketing departments. Did she think she could get them to buy time on WEVD?

It was all the opening Rose needed. "If I get a sponsor, will you put my show on the air?"

A Yiddish shrug, head cocked to the side, palms in the air and a noncommittal, "Nu...."

Close enough.

IT WAS HAZEL who made the match. As Rose had predicted, her walking out on Friday evening—she was still convinced Irna was bluffing and would have rehired her in an instant if Rose just dropped her insistence on keeping Jonas as Edmund—allowed Hazel, the only other person prepared to hit the ground running Monday morning, to step into Rose's producer role. Ike, Rose learned, after a few nights of needing to cook his own dinner, was now permanently snacking on some nurse from his hospital. According to Hazel, "Better her than me." Especially since Hazel's new beau was the tall, handsome actor playing Edmund. Hazel gave credit for her good fortune to Rose and was happy to make the introduction to a new associate in the P&G marketing department, who Hazel thought would be the most receptive to Rose's pitch.

As soon as she stepped into his office, Rose understood why. The name on the door may have read: Mark Lewis, but Rose didn't feel a need to bother asking what it was before. Levy or Levin were her top guesses, but she supposed it could have been Levine, too. In any case, Rose could see why Hazel thought Mr. Lewis might be open to working with WEVD.

"No soap operas," were the first words out of his mouth, even before Rose's back hit the chair. This was destined to be a short meeting. "We have no interest in upsetting Miss Phillips."

"Miss Phillips certainly won't say the same about you." Rose couldn't help her retort as she thought of the screaming phone calls she'd witnessed between Irna and the "suits" as she called them. "She fired your most popular radio actor. That wasn't in P&G's best interests."

Lewis shifted uncomfortably in his seat. "Once we were made aware of Mr. Cain's—"

"Race?"

"Yes," he shrugged, grateful Rose had been so blunt. Now he could be blunt in return. "We supported Miss Phillips' decision."

"Alright. But now I'm offering you the chance to have it both ways. Irna recast Edmund for the television version of *Find Your Light*, but you can still use Jonas on the radio. Keep his old fans while attracting new ones by advertising on a different station."

"WEVD?" Lewis' wrinkled nose suggested he knew exactly who they were.

"You'd have an exclusive on serials. No internal competition. And you could syndicate across the country, bring the voice of Jonas Cain to listeners who miss him as Edmund."

He linked his fingers behind his neck, knocking his elbows together, staring up at the ceiling, thinking. Rose sat patiently, waiting for the brilliance to coalesce. Finally, Lewis said, "Kraft Television Theatre, Philco Television Playhouse, they get all the prestige shows."

Rose nodded. She was familiar with both. Philco's *Marty*, a play by Paddy Chaefsky about a lonely butcher looking for love, had proven so popular during its live airing that there were rumors of it being adapted for a feature film. Kraft's offerings drew so many viewers that the programs aired on both NBC and ABC and featured actors like Anne Bancroft and James Dean, all in the name of selling Cheese Whiz.

"Critics say our Fireside Theatre doesn't measure up."

Maybe that's because while the others broadcast full-scale productions based on original scripts, Fireside Theatre featured public domain tales which only ran a half hour, and sometimes those were broken into two different fifteen-minute stories, Rose did not say out loud.

"Ratings are going down. We're looking for a new host, a new format. Some are starting to suggest television may just be a fad, after all. Nobody wants to sit for hours at a time, staring at a screen. People want to move around, travel from room to room, get their chores done. They don't want to feel like they're being held hostage. Radio is ideal for that sort of freedom."

"Yes," Rose said. Because she'd learned agreeing with people who held your destiny in their hands was never a bad idea.

"So, what I've been contemplating is we combine radio with prestige television, produce full-length plays, but break them up like soap operas. What do you think?"

Rose knew exactly what she was supposed to think. "Sounds wonderful."

And to be honest, it didn't sound bad. Soaps were considered a woman's medium, its writing trite, melodramatic and confessional, fit only for bored housewives. Combining serialized storytelling with already critically acclaimed dramaturgy could be a boon for the genre, earn it the respect it deserved.

"I would love to discuss some ideas for—" Rose began, already thinking of roles she could write specifically to showcase Jonas' vocal range and power.

"Shakespeare," Lewis said. "He's prestigious, right?"

"Y-yes," Rose confirmed slowly, "many would agree with you there."

"So, I'm thinking a little rewrite on Shakespeare, but keeping the important parts, so it still sounds good. Then breaking it up into thirty-minute blocks—commercials only at the beginning and the end, classy—to keep folks coming back. Do you think you could write something like that?"

"Yes," Rose said. Because she'd learned agreeing when someone asked whether you could get a job done was never a bad idea. She'd work out the details later.

"Great. We try it out on WEVD, local market, so if we self-destruct, few people will know about it."

And you can dump all the blame on me, Rose also did not say.

"Let's start with *Othello*. Perfect for your Mr. Cain, right? Like it was written for him."

Othello. Jonas would make a wonderful Hamlet, King Lear, Henry V, Richard III. But, of course, the former Mr. Levy/Levin wanted him to play an angry Moor swayed by his jealousy to strangle the white woman he professes to love. A moral there for everyone. Rose wondered if it would have been more insulting for Lewis to ask her to adapt *The Merchant of Venice*—but classy, commercials only at the beginning and the end; the pound of flesh turned to a pound of

Cheese Whiz. Though Rose realized that no Jewish executive could propose a Jewish-themed show. It would pigeonhole him for the rest of his career. The way Othello pigeonholed Jonas.

Rose said, "I'll speak to the management at WEVD."

THE MANAGEMENT at WEVD said, "No."

Well, not the entire management, just the programming director she'd met with before. "Shakespeare is too hard to understand for our audience."

"I'd rewrite it. It's what they want me to do."

"It's elitist. It's for the hoity-toity types uptown. We're the people's radio station."

"Shakespeare wrote for the people. He wrote for the masses, not the elites. And there were translations of Shakespeare into Hebrew as far back as Vienna in the last century. It's been done in Yiddish in Poland, and right here on the Lower East Side, too. *Ibergezetst un farbesert*, translated and improved," Rose quoted an expression she'd heard her entire life.

"We're the worker's radio station," he amended, seeing as how she wasn't accepting his previous argument.

"And we'll present them with a worker's version of *Othello*. A socialist version." Rose had no inkling how she might do that. But she'd learned that claiming you could get a job done was never a bad idea. She'd work out the details later. After she'd worked out the earlier details.

He didn't appear convinced. So, Rose felt obliged to sweeten the pot, "Procter & Gamble is committed to buying advertising time for three nights a week, for three months, with an option to extend and syndicate down the line." They'd only agreed to the first part, and orally at that.

More details to iron out later.

The programming director stopped shaking his head and began slightly nodding. The nodding became his reaching for a pen and signing his name to the piece of paper Rose brought him, one she could take back to P&G to confirm WEVD's acquiescence to their project. He shoved it across the desk at Rose and gestured for her to shoo.

As she left, she heard him mumbling something about, "Those capitalist bastards…"

WHEN ROSE TOLD JONAS the news, he picked her up, spun her around, hooted and laughed. Then Jonas set Rose down and they both descended to Earth.

"How are we going to do this?"

"The same way the Negro and the scheming Jewess have done everything else."

"By making it up as we go along?"

"By writing our own happy ending."

"For *Othello*?" He couldn't get through the query without laughing.

"For us."

Chapter Eight

═══

"It's so obvious," Rose announced upon her eighth straight reading of *Othello* in three days. "The entire play is a Marxist critique of a capitalist view of the world!"

"Shakespeare was writing about Marxism? Two centuries before Karl Marx was born?"

"Just because the word didn't exist, doesn't mean the concept was unknown. Iago's hatred for Othello is symbolic of the class struggle. Iago is passed over for a promotion because he is of a lower social class than Cassio. Iago's revenge is class consciousness. It's an attack on the cult of individualism. Othello is an individualist, and we are meant to think that he is the hero of the play. But if he is the hero, then why does he have fewer lines than Iago? I counted! Obviously, Othello represents capitalism and feudalism, and Iago is the new, socialist man."

"Obviously," Jonas deadpanned, accustomed by now to Rose's enthusiasm and aware nothing could derail it.

"Class and race bring about the tragedy of Othello. He's as much victim as villain, his suicide proves it. Shakespeare is calling for a classless society, where racial prejudice doesn't lead to murder. What else could he have meant when he has Othello say of Desdemona: *When I stop loving you, the universe will fall back into the chaos that was there when time began?*"

"You've convinced me," Jonas reassured. "Now what about Procter & Gamble?"

ROSE FULLY INTENDED to convince Procter & Gamble. But only after she'd written her scripts. In Rose's experience, executives had a hard time visualizing concepts. It made them want to put their own two cents in, whether they understood them or not. Especially if they didn't. Executives responded better when they had the finished product in front of them. It made for more work for Rose up front, but less problems at the end and certainly fewer games of "read my mind" and claims of, "Oh, that's not what we were expecting. Rewrite it till it's what we were expecting."

Rose claimed an office for herself at WEVD. Though the romantic image of 'Writer' was scribbling in a lonely garret, rarely seeing daylight, merely the muse for company, a decade of commercial production made it so Rose worked better surrounded by the hustle and bustle of others. She preferred feeling connected to the world and she enjoyed having a place to go in the mornings. How could you write about life if you didn't wade out in the midst of it?

Which was why Rose was at the studio when she heard two of the news writers arguing over whether to broadcast whispered reports coming in of USSR Premier Khrushchev's speech at the 20th Congress of the Communist Party of the Soviet Union, where in a private session closed to foreign delegations, he denounced his predecessor, Josef Stalin, exposed his brutal purges of party loyalists, as well as the torture, deportation to Siberia, and execution of millions of innocent citizens.

"We put this on the air," one of the writers contended, "we're giving every Red-basher out there ammunition to get us shut down."

"No. Khrushchev made it clear it wasn't the system that was at fault for what happened, it was one man perverting everything that Marxist-Leninism stood for. Stalin misinterpreted and misrepresented otherwise faultless political thought in order to hold onto his own power."

"You think your average uneducated bozo off the street can make that distinction?"

"It's our duty to report the news."

"Not if it doesn't serve our stated goals. WEVD's mandate is to promote socialist thought and action. How does it serve our objective to report on criticism of how it went wrong in another country? You think our competitor stations report every time capitalism goes wrong?"

It was a familiar argument, though one Rose hadn't felt compelled to join since she'd left Workmen's Circle. Back then, she'd been regularly lectured that sure, Hitler was bad for the Jews, but the international struggle to liberate workers was greater than a tiny ethnic group's temporary discomfort. Breaking ranks with the USSR over their non-aggression pact with Germany and the subsequent division of Poland would hurt the movement overall. Any schism would be instantly exploited by fascists and capitalists eager to discredit them.

Rose had no opinion on what the two writers were debating, but it did prompt her to tell Jonas, "Wouldn't it be wonderful if the United States were to follow the Soviet Union's lead and admit their past mistakes, then promptly rectify them all?"

"Is that what the USSR is doing?"

"Yes! They're freeing wrongly convicted prisoners, allowing censored artists to work again. They're building millions of new homes for those displaced during the war, and they're covering the entire country in corn fields so they can feed it to their livestock and increase both meat and dairy production. Their country is less than forty years old and they're making strides we haven't managed to in almost two hundred!"

"Sounds like the Soviet version of forty acres and a mule."

"You don't believe in government promises."

"I'll believe them when I see them," he swore.

ROSE'S COMPLETED SCRIPTS did exactly what she'd promised both P&G and WEVD. She broke down Shakespeare's *Othello* into thirty-six half-hour radio plays, simplifying the language where necessary, ending each section on a cliff-hanger to make listeners eager to tune in again, and making it clear how the Bard's words applied to modern times.

P&G didn't like it. "Too political," they said, and handed Rose three, typewritten, single-spaced pages of changes.

WEVD which, previously, had dubbed Rose's scripts, "Too egghead," suddenly did an about-face and announced they wouldn't endorse a single change P&G proposed—even those Rose was willing to make.

Both sides dug in their heels.

And, at the end, it was Rose who ended up with nothing.

"WE'LL DO IT AS A PLAY," Rose declared, brushing off Jonas' attempt to comfort her after P&G and WEVD officially washed their hands of their project, capitalist and socialist alike dismissing Rose's months of unpaid labor. "New York is the theater capital of the world. A fresh take on Shakespeare is bound to be a hot ticket."

The hottest ticket currently on Broadway was *My Fair Lady*. It was a musical based on a play by George Bernard Shaw. Theirs would be more like *Kiss Me, Kate*, which was based on Shakespeare's *Taming of the Shrew*. Only theirs would have fewer songs.

And more class struggle.

MEANWHILE, ROSE AND JONAS were facing a struggle of a different kind. Her going into WEVD every day and his continuing to audition for both radio and television roles had kept them busy enough that when they met up at either his apartment or hers at the end of the day it was still possible to pretend they were living separate lives. They'd stopped trying to find a spot they could go out to in the evening where they weren't unwelcome or too slavishly welcomed in favor of nights spent at home. But now that Rose's office was her dining room table and Jonas stopped by several times a day in between appointments, then often spent the night before heading out again, it was growing difficult to pretend that they weren't, in fact, cohabitating—while continuing to pay rent on two separate domiciles. A situation neither was comfortable with. Not due to living in sin. Due to wasting money. Something two currently unemployed people should be attempting less of.

"The practical thing to do," Rose said, "would be to give up one of our apartments, or both, and find a new place."

"The practical thing to do," Jonas said, "would be to get married."

"Well, yes, obviously," Rose dismissed and attempted to hurry onto the next topic, as if a proposal—unconventional; then again, what about her and Jonas was conventional save for everything… and nothing?—was just another item on a list of viable suggestions. "But, as my mother loves to say, a fish may fall in love with a bird, except where would they live? Especially in New York City."

"Rose." He grabbed her hand as she was turning away, forcing her to look at him. "Are you in love with me?"

"Like a fish loves a bird," she all but twittered.

"Rose." Jonas refused to let go of her hand. He cupped it between his palms, brought it to his mouth and kissed each knuckle, refusing to break eye contact as he repeated, "Are… you… in… love… with… me?"

The voice that had snared her, the gaze that compelled her, the question that broke her. Rose couldn't speak. She could only nod in reply.

And then that smile. If she'd been weak before, she was helpless now.

"Do you want to marry me?"

Another nod. Because 'yes' was too feeble a word to encompass everything Rose longed to convey.

He pulled her closer to him, so that not only their hands but their noses and foreheads were touching. She breathed in when he breathed out, his lips were close, so tantalizingly close, but he was still talking. Which he was also quite good at. "Then we'll get married." Rose opened her mouth to protest. Jonas cut her off. "And we'll find a place to rent, and we'll find a place to eat dinner, and we'll find a place to stage your play—"

"Our play." Jonas could render her speechless on a personal basis. She always knew what to say when it came to the professional.

"Our play," he agreed. "We'll find a place to live happily ever after. You wouldn't write it any other way."

WHILE THEY WERE PRETENDING they were living separate lives, it was easy to pretend their relationship was nobody's business. But now that Rose was wearing a ring Jonas bought her and they were searching *The New York Times* daily to see if they could read between the lines and identify a building open to renting to an unorthodox couple, it was growing more difficult to pretend they could keep their secret indefinitely. A situation neither was comfortable with.

"I suppose we'll have to tell our parents," Rose said, adding in the same breath, "which is perfectly ridiculous, when you think about it. We're adults. We don't need their permission, or their blessing, or their financial support."

"Would you prefer to keep lying then?"

She knew what the correct answer should be, so Rose said it, albeit grudgingly. "No."

It was easier for Rose. Now that she'd reached official spinster age, Mama had stopped asking about romantic prospects, and dedicated herself to loudly worrying that, after foolishly quitting her job at *Find Your Light* and obviously doing something equally foolish to lose her position at WEVD, Rose was going to become destitute and die alone in a flophouse.

Jonas' parents, on the other hand, continued introducing him to admittedly beautiful, admittedly accomplished, admittedly available young women. The way Jonas described them, Rose could see why his family couldn't understand his lack of interest.

"They're all so… perfect," Jonas said.

"Unlike me?" Rose wasn't sure if she was fishing for compliments.

"Unlike you," he agreed. And the way he said it made it clear he was giving her one.

"I suppose we'll have to tell our parents," Rose sighed.

THEY DECIDED TO START with his. They decided Geoffrey and Annabelle Moore—Jonas had changed his last name professionally so as not to embarrass the family, and chosen Cain as a sly biblical reference, the sign of God's protection—were less likely to grow hysterical at the news. It would be good practice for facing Rose's mother, who she feared would.

Rose and Jonas spent a delightful evening at his parents' Hamilton Heights townhouse. The Moores took her on a tour, highlighting the individual rooms done in baroque, romantic, and neoclassical styles; wingback chairs, chesterfield sofas, carved bookshelves, ornate drapes, Westwood lamps, artwork by Romare Bearden and Horace Pippin. Over dinner, Jonas' father talked about authors he'd edited. His mother spoke about working as a translator at the United Nations—French to English. They asked Rose about her days at *Find Your Light* and seemed genuinely curious about her ideas for modernizing *Othello,* even making a small pun about their last name and the title character.

At the end of the night, Geoffrey and Annabelle walked Jonas and Rose to the door. His father shook her hand. His mother kissed her on the cheek.

"You are absolutely delightful," his father said.

"So intelligent," his mother said.

"So talented."

"So elegant."

"No," his father said.

"Absolutely not," his mother reiterated.

ROSE'S MOTHER DID NOT GROW HYSTERICAL when she met Jonas. There was no lovely townhouse to give him a tour of, but Mama made up for it with the dinner she served. Chicken soup, potato kugel, beef brisket and rugelach for dessert. She explained to Jonas, in detail, how each dish was made, how her grandmother made it in the old country, including the substitutions they were forced to go with here since food just didn't taste the same, she didn't know why. Jonas complimented Mama on every course and agreed it was a mystery about the different tastes in America. He told stories about traveling to Chicago, to Atlanta, to San Francisco, to Houston and, wouldn't you know it, foods with the same ingredients did have different flavors! Baffling!

At the end of the night, Mama walked Jonas and Rose to the door. She gave him a hug.

"Such a gentleman," Mama said. "So well-read, so well-raised." She turned to Rose and told her, "Absolutely not."

"THAT WENT VERY WELL." Jonas strove for the joke when Rose, for the first time since he'd met her, seemed unable to summon up the energy to deal with setbacks by bolting towards the next plan of attack.

"Absolutely not," Rose said.

And burst into tears.

WEARING AN ENGAGEMENT RING should have made Rose feel safer. She and Jonas were a legitimate couple now. Interracial marriage was legitimately legal in New York state. Instead, it made her feel like more of a target. Whenever they stepped out together, Rose wriggled with an itch between her shoulder-blades which suggested she was being watched. Jonas assured her it was her imagination. This was New York City. Nobody cared about anybody else's business. They were all too busy concentrating on their own lives to hone in on whether Rose wore an engagement ring or wonder if the colored man next to her was the lucky groom-to-be. Yet Rose still felt as if a spotlight targeted her hand wherever she went. Sure, some people smiled at her. Most, like Jonas said, ignored her. But how did Rose know what they were really thinking?

Rose assured Jonas she wasn't obsessing over the issue. She swore to him she barely so much as thought about the issue. Jonas pretended to believe her. Until Rose handed him a stack of freshly typed pages for Jonas to read out loud so Rose could hear how they sounded, and a folded newspaper clipping describing the murder of Emmet Till fluttered to the ground.

Till was the fourteen-year-old Negro boy lynched in Mississippi for flirting or smiling or whistling or saying hello—no one was sure, but did it really matter?—to a white woman. He was from Chicago, another Northern city like New York where nobody cared about anyone else's business, so Emmet didn't expect Mississippi to be different. The men acquitted of his murder beat Emmet, then shot him, then dropped his body off a bridge into the river where he was eventually found. They used cotton seeds to soak up the blood left behind. He was fourteen. A child. A child like Jonas had once been. A child like she and Jonas might one day have.

Rose scrambled to pick up the detritus, crumpling it in her palm and making a move to pitch it towards the garbage pail. "I must have missed this when taking out the trash."

"It's over a year old," Jonas observed levelly.

"So, I missed it a year ago." She refused to meet his eyes.

"Rose…"

"Don't. Please. Please don't tell me again how nobody cares that we're together."

"What do you want me to tell you then?"

Oh, Jonas. Forever the pliant actor, waiting for her to feed him his lines. It was a fantasy, no different than the worlds they created over the radio. Rose understood the daydream of it as surely as she embraced her eagerness to take advantage of it.

"I want you to tell me that things are getting better. Brown versus The Board of Education integrating public schools. Rosa Parks and the Montgomery Bus boycott. Dr. King coordinating those non-violent protests in Atlanta. Tell me all of that means things are getting better."

"Forty acres and a mule," he reminded her. "We've heard promises before."

"Why do you have to be so cynical?"

"Because I'm not the champion you are. I didn't possess the courage to go charging into Spain, prepared to lay down my life if it meant making the world a better place."

"What are you talking about? You fought in the European theater!"

"Not by choice. I was drafted. You volunteered."

"That was over fifteen years ago. What have I championed lately? The world is burning." She smoothed out the wrinkled newspaper story so they could both, once again, look upon the photograph of poor Emmet in his casket, his swollen face with its missing eyes disfigured past recognition, his grieving mother being pulled away as she sobbed. "Children are dying. And what am I doing to make the world a better place? I'm writing a goddamn play! I'm pretending that words—if I could only find the right words—that words might somehow make a difference."

"You championed me." Jonas slid the picture out of Rose's hands. "You championed us."

"I will never stop doing that," she swore.

"Which is why," he leaned in to kiss her, "that is the one promise I will always believe."

Chapter Nine

"You have a letter," Jonas told her. "From Mr. Khrushchev."

Letters. Rose was buried in letters. Letters of rejection from theater companies to whom she'd sent her revisionist *Othello* script. There were traditional theater companies, and avant-garde ones. Off-Broadway, and Off-Off-Broadway. There were basements of clubs and attics of private homes. Rose had great hopes for The Harlem Negro Theatre, resuscitated by a handful of members after the shuttering of the American Negro Theatre a few years earlier. But their *no, thank you* came so quickly, Rose couldn't believe they'd even had time to read her submission.

"My parents are longtime donors," Jonas offered by way of an explanation.

Neither Jonas' parents nor Rose's mother had gone into hysterics. They hadn't gone into much of anything. They continued phoning their respective children, discussing a variety of topics, from their professional prospects, to current events, to books read, to which neighbor was sick, dead, or moving to Florida (the latter was primarily Rose's mother). What they did not discuss was their children's engagement, which should, theoretically, lead to marriage. They didn't acknowledge the other person at all.

It was terribly civilized.

And terribly frustrating.

At this point, Rose was more likely to believe she'd received a letter from the Soviet premiere than that she'd heard confirmation of her existence from Jonas' parents. Except when it came to making sure Rose's play starring their son wasn't produced on their turf.

Especially when it was true.

The letter wasn't from Nikita Khrushchev personally. It was from the International Preparatory Committee of the 6th World Festival of Youth and Students to be held in Moscow, USSR during Summer 1957 under the coordination of the Komsomol and the Communist Party of the Soviet Union. All that information was in the letterhead.

Rose read it through once. Then she read it through a second time to make certain she understood it the first time.

Rose told Jonas, "They're inviting me—us—to put on our version of *Othello* at this festival. They've had it before. In Prague, in Budapest, in East Berlin, Bucharest, Warsaw. It's supposed to represent global youth solidarity for democracy, against war; all war—nuclear war, especially, and against imperialism. This is the first time it's being held in the USSR."

"The USSR is throwing a pro-democracy festival?" To Rose's ear, Jonas wasn't so much as attempting to disguise his incredulity.

"The USSR is a democracy!" Rose bristled. "They have elections at all levels, and 100 percent citizen participation! Not like America, with their poll taxes, their literacy tests, grandfather clauses, gerrymandering. Everyone votes in the Soviet Union."

Jonas held up his hands, a combination of surrender and a plea for peace—appropriate under the circumstances. "They want us to participate in this festival?"

Rose nodded, picking up enthusiasm with every bob of her head. "They said they'll provide us with a theater, English-speaking actors, technical staff, anything we need. They want you to star. And they want me to direct."

She'd never thought about directing. It was one thing for women to write. That was considered adequately ladylike—as long as they stuck to ladylike subjects. But directing was a whole other matter.

Rose strongly suspected that while The American Theater Wing may have created the Antoinette Perry Awards for Excellence in Broadway in 1947, naming them after the actress, producer, director and co-founder of the organization, that didn't mean they approved of more women following in her footsteps. Agnes DeMille might occasionally direct a musical—as long as it was mostly dance and she was primarily a choreographer. Margo Jones could help Tennessee Williams and William Inge develop their plays regionally at her groundbreaking Dallas theater. But once their work made it to Broadway, it was time for the men to step up and direct each properly.

"Do you want to do it?" Jonas asked. "You were so worried about anyone finding out that you'd gone to Spain. This seems so much riskier."

"That was before." Previous non-stop rejection had inoculated Rose against getting her hopes up. She felt a breakthrough infection coming on. "That was while Stalin was alive, and McCarthy was holding his damn witch-hunts. Everything is different now. The USSR isn't what it was. It's a free society again, Khrushchev saw to that with his speech. This festival just confirms it. And ever since Edward Murrow humiliated McCarthy on television and the Senate censured him, well, nobody takes his nonsense seriously anymore. That's all over."

She wouldn't do it if Jonas didn't want her to. Rose understood he'd be taking the bigger risk. If the issue came up, Rose could employ the Lucille Ball defense. Lucy claimed she only registered as a member of the Communist party "to appease an old man," her grandpa. When asked about sponsoring a Party member for state election, the comedienne swore she didn't remember doing so—she was just a dizzy broad, how could she possibly be held accountable for her actions? For Jonas, however, a trip to a left-wing youth festival could prove the perfect excuse to keep him from future jobs—among those who bothered coming up with any excuses.

This couldn't be exclusively about Rose. This had to be about both of them. It was such an amazing opportunity. Jonas could finally perform one of Shakespeare's classic roles. He could demonstrate what he was capable of outside the shackles of American commercial production. They could demonstrate what they were capable of together. On an international stage, before the next generation. This was their chance to affect the future for couples like them. It was their chance to change the world. It was their chance to matter.

But only if Jonas agreed.

Rose tried to keep her face neutral. She tried not to let Jonas see how much this meant to her. She didn't want to influence his decision. She didn't want to be selfish. She tried to slow down her heartbeat, lest he hear it. She tried to level her breathing. She suspected she was failing. Miserably.

Jonas pulled the letter out of Rose's hands. He skimmed it once, then also did a second read. He looked down at Rose's unbiased, objective, disinterested face.

He asked, "When do we leave?"

THE PREPARATORY COMMITTEE asked Rose and Jonas to arrive a month before the festival was scheduled to kick off on July 28, so they'd have plenty of rehearsal time prior to opening day. Ten nightly performances were scheduled for the duration of the two-week event. Rose and Jonas didn't tell their families where they were going. They didn't tell anybody where they were going. They bought separate seats on their connecting flights to Moscow, with a stop-over in Vienna, Austria. They didn't want any trouble.

Rose and Jonas were told there'd be someone to meet them at the airport. They didn't expect a delegation; a young man and two young women, dressed in their Komsomol, All-Union Young Communist League uniforms of dark brown with bright red scarves and matching Lenin pins, each bearing a bouquet of flowers. Behind them stood a photographer, and behind him yet another young woman, this one dressed in an ethnic Russian national costume, colorful skirt, embroidered blouse, and an ornate headpiece shaped like the tops of Red Square with ribbons trailing down past each ear. She held forward a wooden cutting board atop which sat a round loaf of bread, its center hollowed out to encompass a pile of salt.

Rose and Jonas were hugged and kissed heartily on each cheek. Rose and Jonas had flowers pressed into their hands. Rose and Jonas were urged to break off a piece of bread, dip it in the salt and take a bite "to build great friendship between us!" The photographer circled them, snapping bright flashes into their eyes.

They were ushered into a gray, limousine-shaped car, Rose and Jonas in the back with the photographer, the bread bearer and the three Komsomolniks in the front. A leaping deer hood ornament decorated the bonnet, yet every other spot on the chassis where a label might have gone appeared to have been ripped clean.

Noticing Rose looking, the Komsomol girl with the golden braids crisscrossed over her head proudly explained, "No more Molotov."

"Like the cocktail?" Rose blurted the first association that came to mind. She realized it might have been less than a wise choice. That weapon was developed by the Axis-allied Finns to use against the Soviet Union—Molotov being their Foreign Minister—during the last war. She blamed the slip on jet lag. And stupidity.

At least her hostess laughed, then explained, "This car, it is first made in factory named after Molotov. We call it ZIM. The M is for Molotov. But now, he is against Comrade Khrushchev making great changes, so we no longer honor him. No more street names, no more ships, no more factories. Car is now called GAZ. We remove all former markings. We are waiting for new ones to put on."

"Isn't that wonderful!" Rose exclaimed. "In America, we keep our statues of disgraced politicians up." She spent the remainder of their ride enlightening everyone about how Southern states still displayed monuments to their insurrectionist—and losing—generals.

"How most disrespectful," her hosts agreed.

They drove through the rings of Moscow at dusk and into the center of the city down Mir Street, newly renamed to honor peace.

"We make new roads, new parks, new sports center for athletic demonstrations, all for festival," the boy Komsomol boasted.

"What was there before?" Jonas wondered.

"Also, Hotel Ukraina. Is tallest hotel in USSR. In Europe. In world, also. Two hundred and six meters! One thousand and twenty-six rooms! You are to be staying in this."

"What was there—" Jonas tried to repeat politely. Rose flashed him a warning look. There was no need to aggravate their hosts. What used to be didn't matter. Only what was there now, and what would be there in the future. It's why they were in the USSR, wasn't it?

"Our Youth Festival will also be biggest," Boy Komsomol recited. "Thirty-four thousand people coming from 131 countries! You will have many audience for your show."

Rose, once again, struggled to keep her face unbiased, objective, and disinterested, but, inside, her heart expanded and sped up until she could hear the pounding in her ears and feel it vibrating throughout her body. Not unlike when she'd first met Jonas. This was all she'd ever wanted. An audience. Not for herself, but for the progressive ideas she was lucky enough to be tasked with presenting. She was a conduit. A cog in a machine. But not a capitalist, exploitative machine. A machine to serve the people. She was nothing. The message was everything.

Despite Rose's unbiased, objective and disinterested face, Jonas understood what this meant to her. He slipped an arm around Rose's shoulders, smiling, and leaning over to give her a kiss on the temple. All three Komsomols and the ethnic garb girl made a point of discreetly looking out their respective windows for the duration.

They arrived at Hotel Ukraina, where Rose and Jonas were ushered to the front desk and given keys to two separate rooms on two separate floors. Once again, Jonas opened his mouth to ask—Rose knew exactly what he was going to ask, he was going to ask for them to room together. Once again, Rose shut him down with a single look.

Not because she thought their Soviet hosts would object to an unmarried couple sharing a room. The USSR was much more progressive about such matters than puritanical, provincial America. A few years earlier, a Czechoslovakian sexologist conference had decreed that women in Socialist countries enjoyed more fulfilling sex lives due to their countries' social and cultural context, which offered complete equality among the sexes. Naturally, feminists in the West had objected, attempting to discredit the Eastern Bloc's achievements by claiming that because they weren't established via independent women's movements but imposed from the top down by a committee of males, they were somehow inferior. That was the West for you.

Completely failing to realize that artificial distinctions between men and women was just another ploy by capitalism to keep the masses from realizing they were all workers engaged in the same struggle. It was yet another division tactic, nothing more.

And, of course, Rose didn't for so much as a moment consider that she and Jonas might be condemned for being an interracial couple. Just like gender discrimination, the Soviet Union had long moved past such silly, superficial differences.

The only reason Rose quickly and almost imperceptibly shook her head to keep Jonas from asking his question was because she didn't want to make extra work for the Komsomol members who'd greeted them. She was being courteous and polite. She was most certainly not being a coward.

"We will need your passports, please," still smiling, one of the girl Komsomols held out her hand.

"Why?" That question came instinctively from Rose. Once again, she blamed jet lag and stupidity.

"Is procedure." Her smile never wavered. "For safety. Your safety."

Jonas tapped the outside of his inner jacket pocket. "We're fine. Thank you."

"Is procedure," she repeated. Her hand never wavering, either.

"Of course." Rose told herself she was continuing to be courteous and polite. She was certainly not being a coward when she handed over her documents.

Jonas hesitated. Rose told herself she didn't blame him. Unlike her, Jonas wasn't familiar with the way things were done in Socialist countries, for the good of the whole rather than the individual, with the understanding that the best interests of the collective trickled down to each member of the masses. It wasn't Jonas' fault he'd been brainwashed into believing in individualism, or the propaganda he'd been force-fed about the dangers allegedly lurking behind Winston Churchill's boogeyman of an "iron curtain." Considering how horrifically Jonas' people had been treated by the US government, of course he found it impossible to recognize an administration that existed solely for his welfare. But he would learn. That's what they were here for. To learn.

In the meantime, Rose told herself she was still being courteous and polite, that it wasn't fear of public embarrassment and a possible withdrawal of her festival invitation which prompted her to look pleadingly at Jonas, wordlessly begging him to go along, to not make a scene. Please. For her.

Jonas received Rose's unvoiced message.

He didn't look thrilled, but, after a long beat during which the five of them stood trapped in a game of freeze tag, Jonas reached into the same pocket he'd tapped earlier, withdrew the only official document listing him as an American citizen, and handed it over to the same girl who'd already palmed Rose's passport.

Only for you, Miss Janowitz....

ROSE HAD DONE HER RESEARCH before coming. She understood that her *Othello* would face competition, at least in memory, from previous Soviet productions. The poet and novelist Boris Pasternak had translated it, employing a colloquial, modern Russian vernacular. But as he was now out of favor due to that year's Italian publication of his non-social realist, anti-Soviet fiction, *Doctor Zhivago*, Rose pretended she'd never heard of it, the same way the rest of the USSR was currently doing. There was also the Sergei Yutkevitch film, which won the Director's Award at the 1956 Cannes Film Festival. Rose completely understood the point Yutkevitch was trying to make by casting a Slavic actor in the title role. In his reading, Othello was oppressed not due to his race, but due to his class, a more appropriate topic for Soviet audiences, as the former was not a problem in their country, while they must always remain vigilant for the emergence of the latter. Class had been the point of Rose's reimagining, as well. It's how she'd pitched it to all the outlets that had turned her down. She was in complete agreement with a Socialist reading of the text. Yet, she couldn't get past the conviction that removing Othello's race from the equation demeaned and dismissed the entirety of his motivation. And, by extension, it demeaned and dismissed the lived experiences of actors like Jonas.

But Rose couldn't quite come out and say so. It would be discourteous and impolite. So, when asked what made her staging different from those which came before, Rose stressed her mounting of a Shakespeare play in its original English, to give audiences from around the world a taste of its poetic language without sacrificing the anti-capitalist message. She didn't dwell on the subversion of casting a Negro in the lead. Except when asked by Soviet reporters about the racism Jonas faced in America, and why he could not have played the role there. Jonas being a Negro was not relevant to the story Rose was telling. Except for when it was.

Rose thought she wouldn't be able to sleep at all the night before their first rehearsal. Much to her surprise, her eyes were closed before she tried pulling the hotel blanket up to her chin, struggling when all she was able to grasp was a handful of starched duvets, unused to the lack of top sheet. Rose slept the entire night through. Tormented by dreams where she couldn't communicate with her actors or crew, not due to the language barrier, but because, when they looked at her, they could see the inexperienced fraud Rose really was.

In some ways, reality proved a letdown from the night terrors. Rose had been so looking forward to working with her Soviet colleagues. She relished the opportunity to collaborate in an environment where every worker was an equal, and not the capitalist model, where the fat cat who paid the bills, or, at best, the class traitor overseer deputized by the fat cat who paid the bills, was presumed to always be in the right creatively, because, as they said, whoever paid the piper picked the tune. This wouldn't be a repeat of Irna and her pen of doom. Everyone's ideas would be listened to, evaluated, and only the best ones implemented.

Or so Rose imagined. Once work actually started in earnest, she was surprised by how quickly and meekly her instructions were followed. The actors stood where she told them to and delivered their lines in the manner she instructed. The set designer approved her sketches without a peep. As did the costume designer, the lighting designer, and the audio engineer. There were no questions, no discussions, no dissent. It was the most peaceful, harmonious production Rose had ever been involved with. She should have been ecstatic. Wasn't this what she'd abandoned America for? The chance to be creative without the interference of networks and sponsors? Why then, did it feel so... dull?

Rose wished she could discuss it with Jonas. But opportunities for private conversation proved non-existent. On the one hand, Rose felt thrilled Jonas was finally being feted like the star he was always meant to be. Other actors deferred to him. The crew double-checked that everything was to his liking. There'd already been several glowing features on him in *Pravda*, with photos. Rose had been assured their opening night review would be a rave. She couldn't imagine such things happening in the States.

On the other hand, they were both so busy, Rose hadn't said a word that wasn't about the show to Jonas in days. While actors periodically had downtime when a set was being moved, a light adjusted, a music cue finessed, Rose was involved in every technical aspect, too. She ate while listening to her craftsmen explain their latest obstacle—though she knew Mama would describe such slovenly behavior as uncouth. She drank the cups of tea she was constantly being handed while sitting in the audience, trying to gauge how her efforts would look to customers. She used her time in the lavatory to scribble stage directions in her scripts. Rose didn't want to know how Mama would feel about that.

The only chance Rose had to come up for air was at the end of the workday, when she and Jonas were driven around to see the sights of Moscow by the same three Komsomolniks who'd greeted them the first day. They visited the Kremlin and Red Square. They saw Lenin lying in state in his mausoleum, looking as small as a ventriloquist's puppet, only not quite so lifelike. They marched through Gorky Park and sped through the Tretyakov Art Gallery. At the end of each evening's excursion, Rose and Jonas were deposited back at their hotel, where he was escorted to his room and she to hers. Rose supposed they could have snuck out and met up after their hosts had left for the night. But creeping down the darkened hallways while the matron who sat by the elevator doors watched her disapprovingly was an uneasy prospect.

The one day Rose and Jonas got off from their feverish work was for the opening ceremonies of the festival. Held in Lenin Central Stadium, Rose thought it put any Olympic festivities to shame. She couldn't possibly count how many thousands of cheering young people were packed into the stands, or how many proudly strode around the running oval, holding up their countries' flags, wearing their national costumes, performing their ethnic dances, and waving to spectators who included no less than Nikita Khrushchev himself! There were Chinese dragons and African drums, Arab robes, Spanish headdresses, and even Americans bearing flowers right alongside Soviet hammers and sickles. Balloons flew into the blinding blue sky. Forty thousand specifically bred white doves were released in the name of peace. Finally, as the sun set, hundreds of performers swarmed the field, forming swirling, geometric shapes. At the end, they picked up placards which first created the silhouette of a nuclear bomb, then flipped them over to display the universal symbol for "no," and, as a last, indelible image, spelled out the word, MIR, PEACE, PAXIS. Boys and girls of all colors, all nationalities, religions, castes and classes were dancing and hugging and laughing and crying and, more than anything, Rose wished she were down there with them, while also grateful that she was at least there to witness it. She turned to Jonas and grabbed his hand. This was how life could be. This was how life should be. After witnessing such unity and brotherhood, such indifference to race, class, gender and all those other categorizations they'd been taught were not just necessary but inevitable, how could they ever return to the divisiveness of the United States?

"I'D LIKE TO SHOW YOU SOMETHING." The afternoon of their premiere, the one afternoon they'd had off in weeks in anticipation of the work they'd be doing that evening, Jonas managed to catch Rose at the theater during a moment when she wasn't surrounded by associates or reporters or their Komsomol shadows. Everyone was wiped out from the blood they'd poured into putting this production on its feet, not to mention vibrating with nerves over how it might be received—despite the already promised *Pravda* rave.

"When?" Rose startled. "Where?"

"Now," Jonas said. He gestured past the door of the theater. "Out there."

Rose looked around nervously. "I don't think we're supposed to leave on our own. We... we might get lost."

"I know where I'm going," Jonas reassured.

"We should tell someone…"

"No." On this he was firm. "Not this time."

"It would be rude," she began. But Jonas cut her off.

"For me, Rose," he said. "Please do this for me."

It didn't feel right. No one had told Rose she wasn't allowed to venture out on her own. She knew she was free to do so, anything else would be ridiculous. So why did the prospect of stepping out unaccompanied make her so anxious? She didn't fear for her safety. The streets of Moscow were much less dangerous than those of New York, for Pete's sake. The USSR had no murderers, no perverts, no purse snatchers, not like in America. There was no drive to commit crime when all your needs were provided for by the state, and gratis medical care made it so no mentally ill people were left to their own devices. They were all safely in hospitals.

Rose had no reason to be scared.

While she had every reason in the world to tell Jonas, "For you."

Chapter Ten

Jonas walked Rose towards Red Square following the same path they'd taken when with their Komsomolnik friends. If possible, the streets were even more clogged with people now that the festival was officially underway than it had been during the run up. It was impossible to take a single step without bumping into a group of citizens and visitors in the midst of some convivial activity. Within a span of just a few minutes, Rose glimpsed a girl with Ukrainian ribbons in her hair handing a girl with an Indian dot in the middle of her forehead a bouquet of flowers from a basket carried by a dog in matching festive attire; a man in a turban playfully rubbing the head of a man in a colorful tunic with hair identical to Jonas', and a boy in a three-cornered hat pulling a girl in a smart business suit not unlike ones Rose would wear to the office, out of a crowd and into his dance while those around them clapped and cheered. They put a white scarf on the ground, both knelt, and the boy kissed the girl on both cheeks in a ceremony Rose didn't understand, but fervently wished she could be a part of. It was Rose's greatest regret that, despite having arrived in Moscow ahead of most visitors, she hadn't had the chance to experience the festival. She'd been locked inside the theater, working on her own project. She'd been forced to hear second-hand about the bonfires on the water, the American jazz concerts, the English brass bands, the French chemists' demonstrations, the International Exhibition of Fine and Applied Modern Art, and, of course, the song, *Moscow Nights*, which was being sung and played everywhere, translated into foreign languages on the fly. As with many other things in her life, Rose still felt like an outsider, standing on her tiptoes, bobbing between taller heads, trying desperately to peer into what was happening at the center of the action.

As if to drive home that point, Jonas led Rose toward the front entrance of Lenin's Tomb. A crowd of hundreds, maybe as many as two thousand, gathered around a lone man, medium height, stocky, dark-haired, Jewish, if Rose had to guess. She'd been hearing Russian for so long that it took Rose a minute to realize he was speaking English, New York accent with just a touch of Boston. Harvard, if Rose had to guess again.

"No," Rose shook her head and backed up, a task made impossible by the fact that, as soon as they'd arrived, more Russians swarmed in behind them, an impenetrable wall of bodies. "I heard about this—him. Eleanor Roosevelt even commented on it. She said Americans who visited other countries should consider themselves guests. They shouldn't go out of their way to antagonize and provoke."

"Eleanor Roosevelt," Jonas repeated, amused. "Didn't you call her husband a Fascist for refusing to accept Jewish refugees, and for his internment of the Japanese?"

"Yes," Rose confirmed emphatically, then, just as emphatically added, "This is different." With growing horror, she gasped, "Have you been coming here to listen to this man?"

"I'm hardly the only one. Look around. It's fascinating. Soviets have so many questions about the outside world. I've seen him standing here, ten, twelve hours, just answering whatever anyone throws his way. The other day, somebody wanted to know: Is there much of a difference in America between the workers and the bourgeoisie?"

"And what did he say?" Rose was curious in spite of herself.

He said, "In America, the workers are the bourgeoisie!"

Rose crossed her arms, "That's not funny. Or accurate."

  Alina Adams

Grinning, Jonas continued, "They ask him about his family, about law school, about how much money he's going to make, where he lives, what New York looks like. We've espoused the brotherhood of man in theory, but this is it, right here. No censors, no press, no government, no gatekeepers, just people talking to one another."

"Why did you bring me here?"

"I thought you'd find it interesting. How could a writer not find this interesting? It's an incredibly literate crowd. Yesterday, someone brought up the author Howard Fast, how he was a proud American Communist. George—the speaker, his name is George, by the way, George Abrams, he's a Harvard student."

"So, he is Jewish, then," Rose confirmed, mostly for herself. She appreciated the chance to be in the right whenever possible. Especially when confronted with potentially being in the wrong.

"George had to tell them how Fast quit the Party last February, after Khrushchev revealed everything Stalin did in its name. They didn't believe him. They heckled him. But, at the end of the night, after he'd been here so long the Metro trains stopped running, a bunch of people chipped in so he could take a cab back to his hotel." Jonas was practically beaming. "Isn't this amazing? It's everything we're always talking about. Self-organizing, mutual cooperation. And today—wait till you hear what happened today! There was a huge argument yesterday about the Hungarian uprising. The crowd insisted the Hungarian government invited the Soviet Union to come in and help them quash a Fascist rebellion and restore the People's Government. When George referred to the United Nations' report contradicting that, he was shouted down. So, he said he'd come today and read the entire report out loud. It's a historic moment. I wanted to share it with you."

Even as Jonas spoke, Rose could see the crowd doing what he'd said, they were self-organizing, splitting into four groups. At the head of each one stood a young man or woman. As George began to read the UN report out loud in English, each of the four translated it in Russian for the people in front of them.

From deep inside the crowd, a voice cried out in English, "It's true, it's true. What he says is true. I work for the railroad. After the revolution, I found bottles that had been dropped along the tracks. There were notes inside from Hungarian students. They said they'd been protesting the USSR's control of their government. They wanted our Army gone from their land; they wanted self-determination. And now they are on their way to Siberia for it!"

"No." Rose pivoted and pushed her way through the mob, Jonas in hot pursuit, their abandoned spaces quickly and gratefully filled in by those who wanted to draw closer. "We can't stay here. We can't keep listening to this."

He waited until she'd broken free, until Rose was no longer trapped amongst the tightly packed bodies. As she gulped for air, Jonas gently asked, "What's wrong?"

"Don't you see?" She gasped as if she'd just run up all the flights in St. Basil's Cathedral. "Can't you see what they're doing? That man, he's clearly a provocateur. Sent here deliberately to spread misinformation and discredit the Soviet Union. What other reason would a person have for exposing a government's actions than to cause trouble and dissent among the citizens?"

"Like those troublemakers riding buses down in Alabama?" Jonas asked innocently. But Rose could hear the real question behind the guileless one.

"No. Oh, no." Rose grabbed both of Jonas' hands, looking him in the eye, willing him not to misunderstand. "Not like that at all. Dr. King and the rest, they're forcing the Americans down South, all Americans, really, to confront the ugliness of Jim Crow. Dr. King is fighting for positive change. He's fighting to make our country a better, less racist place. This man—this man is just here to inflame and turn Soviet citizens against their country. Segregation is happening right now. The Hungarian Uprising is over. What good does it do to autopsy the past? We should be looking forward. That's what this whole festival is about. Youth… the future…"

"He's telling the truth," Jonas said softly. "Doesn't that matter?"

"So, what if he's telling the truth?" Rose demanded, hearing her voice growing shriller but feeling helpless to rein it in. "So what? There's a reason I don't work in news, Jonas. There's a reason I work in fiction. I am so tired of hearing about how the world is. I know how the world is. I see how the world is. I saw it in how you were treated. I saw it in how we were treated. What I want, even if it's just for a moment, I want a world where everything isn't the way it is. I want a world where everything is better. Where everything is calm, and perfect, and safe, and decent. I want a world where I'm not always looking over my shoulder, wondering what horrible thing is creeping up to jump me from behind. I want to just breathe. Is that such a terrible, selfish thing to want? One single, solitary breath during which I'm not worried about the future or guilty about the past, or too frantic to even notice the present? Where I know what I know, and I believe what I believe, and it isn't constantly being challenged and turned on its head. So what if he's telling the truth? Can't the world just stay," she fumbled for an adverb and only managed to come up with, "still? Can't the word just stay *still* for one minute?"

He listened to her rant. He indulged her rant. He even smiled at her rant. And then Jonas noted, "A world that stays still is a world that isn't progressing. It's a world that isn't improving. Could you ever truly be happy in a world like that?"

THEIR KOMSOMOLNIK HANDLERS were waiting when Rose and Jonas returned to the theater; the two girls who'd greeted them the first day, along with a heavily mustached man who looked old enough to be their father.

"We heard," the first one began, "that you were caught up in our shameful happening in Red Square today, on accident." The way she posed the final two words made it clear that Rose and Jonas were being offered an out. And that they'd be wise to take it.

"Yes," Rose nodded, the expression growing more fervid as she went on. "We wanted to take in some of the Festival's sights. It's our first free afternoon since we arrived. We had no idea that—"

"The boy from America, he is speaking all lies," the second one said, her demeanor as cheerful as if reciting a celebratory poem. "We know you would wish to hear truth. So, we bring you head of Hungarian delegation to Youth Festival. He explain what is honest."

"Youth?" Rose heard Jonas blurt out. She didn't have to turn her head to know he was struggling to suppress a smile. The gentleman who stepped forward was clearly in his mid-30s if not older. The overflowing mustache was turning gray just beneath his nose.

"We prepare, for Americans," he said, barely able to keep the sneer from his voice as he shoved a pair of books, one in each of their hands, "in English. So, you can understand."

Rose gingerly opened to the first page, where she instantly spied the phrases, "events of past October" and "fascist counterrevolutionaries."

"Also photographs." Both girls were smiling now. They showed Rose and Jonas a horrific black and white photograph of a half dozen Államvédelmi Hatóság, Hungary's Secret Police, officers lined up against the wall of their station as rebels opened retributionary fire. "In *Life Magazine*," they said. "Your American *Life Magazine* shows this."

Rose nodded. She'd seen the images when they came out the previous year. Before the uprising was quickly crushed by Soviet tanks.

"This is he," the girl said, pointing to the mustached man. "He is AVH officer. This is him in photo. He survive this attack. He will to tell you what truly happened, who to attack him and his beloved home country."

"They are nationalists," he droned, reciting from memory without any variation in tone, even as Rose flinched at the word. Had he said it deliberately to get a reaction out of her? No. Because how could he know? There was no possible way he could know about Rose's past.

"They are hooligans, criminals, fascists from The Great War, who wish to overthrow our democratically elected government. They use Molotov cocktails, shoot women and children in street, march into villages and rip them apart. They call strike to cripple and starve us. Almost 3000 people dead. We cannot let our people suffer like this. We beg Soviet Union to come and help us to retake our country. USSR is our great hero."

"You are great hero," one of the girls said, patting his arm as she beamed at him. She told Rose and Jonas, "It is miraculous he survive shooting attack. He is much venerated in his country."

"Thank you for telling us." Rose attempted to hand back her book, but the man stared straight ahead, refusing to acknowledge her actions.

"Are gifts for you," the second girl explained. "Hungary to bring many boxes of books in many languages so they can to show truth for those who ask questions."

"You've certainly thought of everything," Jonas said.

"Yes," the girl agreed, then, in the same cheerful chirp, advised, "You should think of everything, too."

IT WAS HOURS LATER, when Jonas was getting into his costume for the night's performance, and Rose stopped by to wish him luck, that they were left alone long enough for her to whisper, "What do you think will happen to that boy from America?"

"He'll be fine." Jonas was an excellent actor. Very few people could tell when he was putting on an act. Rose was one of them. "The Soviets won't want to make a scene. Not while throwing a festival to demonstrate how open and non-repressive they are. They'll probably just send him home and prevent him from ever coming back."

"What about those who were listening to him?"

Jonas was an excellent actor. But even he couldn't hide the concern on his face.

THE SHOW MUST GO ON.

Rose hadn't learned the sentiment from Irna, but it was Irna who'd turned it into an edict to live by. Personal problems, physical obstacles, philosophical concerns, political conundrums, nothing was more important than the show.

And Rose was in Moscow to put on a show.

Once the curtain went up, nothing else mattered.

She watched from the wings, standing where she wasn't in the way of the sets being carried on and off, or the actors rushing back and forth to change costumes. She stood where Jonas couldn't see her. She didn't want to distract him. Rose watched what had lived in her mind for years and had taken weeks to pull into something resembling the perfection she'd imagined.

Of course, it wasn't perfect. No show could ever be as perfect as that initial dream. But it came close. So, so close.

Jonas was magnificent. Rose had known he would be. His glorious voice, his dignified movements. The way he made each member of the audience feel like he was sitting beside them, arm encircling their shoulders, whispering in their ear, only for them, all for them. Rose doubted every spectator understood English, especially not Shakespeare's archaic variety. But that didn't matter. The language was beside the point—no matter what Rose had said to the reporters. Jonas' visceral performance was about feeling. It was about love, it was about passion, it was about brotherhood as much as it was about jealousy. And it was about rage. Rage at the class system, as promised, but also rage at being marginalized for the sin of living in a dark skin.

When the curtain came down, before its edge reached the stage, the patrons erupted. Rose had never experienced anything like it. She'd been to plenty of theater, to opening nights of Broadway shows that went on to become record-breaking hits. Even there, the spectators' reaction hadn't come close to the reception her and Jonas' *Othello* garnered. Rising to their feet was the least of it. Clapping was the prelude. They shouted—no, they screamed, "Bravo! Bravissimo!" They'd brought buckets of flowers which they rushed the stage to deliver, flinging the roses, the carnations, the multicolored lilies at Jonas' feet.

After five curtain calls, Jonas stepped into the wings, seized Rose's hand and pulled her out with him, bowing deeply in her direction, palm pressed to his chest. The cheers continued, somehow growing louder instead of dying down. The raucous enthusiasm followed Rose and Jonas backstage.

A party had been set up just outside the dressing room area, with champagne, wine, and vodka Rose hadn't previously seen stashed anywhere emerging alongside crystal serving dishes of black and red caviar, enamel black trays painted with bright red and white floral designs stacked with rolls of pork and beef cold cuts, pickled tomatoes, pickled beets, sauerkraut and pickled, well, pickles, as Rose and Jonas were urged to try the local *zakuski*.

The hallway filled up with well-wishers. Not just the rest of the cast and crew, their family and friends, but seemingly the entire audience, ranging from youth speaking a smorgasbord of accented

English—Rose thought she heard everything from Eastern Europe to Africa to Latin America represented—to elderly people leaning on canes, stumbling to remain upright in the jostling throng. Rose saw military uniforms and dashingly tailored suits, women in evening gowns and Arabic men in thobes. There were visitors even darker than Jonas, and ones who could have been the relatives of those Rose had worked with at WEVD. Everyone wanted to talk to her. Everyone wanted to congratulate her. They said they loved the show. They said it was the best production of *Othello* they'd ever seen. They handed her the (as promised) glowing review in *Pravda*—Rose wondering how their critic had managed to write and publish it so quickly; they'd wrapped less than an hour ago!

Between undiluted shots of vodka, the expanding multitude of well-wishers wanted to talk to Rose about America, how awful life was in America, how awful it was that Rose couldn't have staged her version of *Othello* in America, how she couldn't marry Jonas in America, but that wasn't a problem in the Soviet Union and how to cement the spirit of the Youth Festival and international brotherhood and true love and freedom and brotherhood—wait, did they already say that?—wouldn't it make perfect sense for Rose and Jonas to tie the knot right now, right here, in front of everyone who'd just witnessed their great artistic conquest and who would bear witness to the triumph of their love over any and all capitalist obstacles?

Rose's head spun from the vodka. Her breath quickened from the stuffy heat of so many people packed into such a small and windowless a space. Her heart swelled from the attention and compliments. But she nonetheless liked to think she was fully in control of her faculties, mental and physical, when Rose glanced across the room, caught Jonas' eye, thought how unbearably handsome he looked out of his costume, wearing the slacks of Othello, but his own, skintight white T-shirt, which emphasized the width of his shoulders, the smoothness of his chest, and the chiseled definition of his arms, when Rose said, "Why not?"

AFTER THAT, Rose felt like when she needed to look over a piece of film and, in order to get to the section she was searching for, asked the projectionist to speed through everything which came before. As soon as Rose agreed to the impromptu civil wedding, her hosts raced off to appraise Jonas of the situation. It came off somewhat like they were the ones asking him to marry her, rather than Rose herself. It threw her briefly, before Rose opted to chalk it up to yet more joyous communal spirit. She hoped Jonas would feel the same way. For just a moment, he appeared taken aback. But then, equally as affected by the vodka and the heat and the flattery, though, like Rose, still enough in control of his faculties to give informed consent, Jonas also acquiesced, "Why not, indeed!"

At which point the world lurched into accelerated motion.

A space was somehow miraculously cleared for Rose and Jonas to stand in. A bouquet of flowers was hastily assembled from multiple earlier bequests and thrust into Rose's hands. His dresser ran to get a dinner jacket for Jonas. The stylist attempted to make something of Rose's damp, frizzled fair. They were introduced to Tatiana, who worked at ZAGS, *Zapis Aktov Grazhdanskogo Sostoianiia*, the citizens marriage office, and was qualified to perform the ceremony. "Everyone will be witness, not just two!" she pronounced.

Words were said. Vows, Rose supposed, though, in the din, she had trouble following both the Russian, and the translation whispered to them by the same woman who'd been hired to facilitate communication between Rose and her crew. Papers were signed, Rose wondering how they'd managed to acquire some so quickly; the suggestion for her and Jonas to wed had only been proffered that evening!

Rings! They needed rings! Unlike the *Pravda* review or the marriage license, those weren't instantly available. It took the improvisation of a stagehand to yank on the cloth they'd used to fashion curtains and remove two of the dozens of metal loops holding them up, handing one to Jonas and one to Rose with a grin and a courtly bow.

Rose slipped the facsimile onto Jonas' finger. He did the same for her. The pit musicians struck up Mendelssohn's *Wedding March*, and their horde of witnesses broke into thunderous cries of "Gorka! Gorka!"

Rose knew this one! *Gorka* meant *bitter.* Friends and families shouted it at weddings so that the couple would kiss in order to chase the bitterness away.

She turned to Jonas, her heart beating madly—though it was not due to over-excitement or heat or even intoxication. Her heart was beating hard enough to knock both of them over because Rose was terrified of looking into Jonas' eyes and seeing… what? Amusement at her folly? Anger at being coerced into putting on a minstrel show for strangers? Exasperation with Rose and her romantic, irresponsible, impractical need to concoct a narrative that fit what she wanted to be true, not what actually was true? Would Jonas be judging her? Condemning her? Worst of all, humoring her? Rose saw none of those things.

When Rose looked into Jonas' eyes, she saw complete and utter acceptance. There was adoration, sure. There was bemusement. There was even, as always, love. But the acceptance was what moved her most. Jonas knew who Rose was. Not who she pretended to be for others, but who she really was. The idealist, the dreamer, the world builder. He didn't just tolerate those parts of her. He actively embraced them. Jonas loved all the things about Rose that she disliked about herself. No vodka shots could be more intoxicating than that.

She obeyed the orders of "Gorka!" and kissed her new husband.

How was it possible that, in this instance, Rose felt as if they were both the only people in the world, and a part of every human being who'd come before them, not to mention who'd come after. Children she needn't worry about sharing a fate with Emmett Till. Fellow citizens who didn't resort to violence or, at best, turning away when they spied Rose and Jonas coming, nor patronize and trip over themselves to exemplify how brave they found Rose and Jonas for simply existing. Everyone who'd witnessed their vows accepted Rose and Jonas' marriage the way Jonas accepted Rose, wholeheartedly and without conditions, as they also cheered for them as artists, as intellectuals, as comrades.

It wasn't the vodka, it wasn't the heat, it wasn't even the flattery, which, as they stood at the center of a cheering, laughing, loving audience moved Rose to pull back from their kiss, grab Jonas' hand the same way he'd seized hers to pull Rose on stage with him earlier and, yelling to be heard over the cacophony, though it felt like the most intimate of whispers, ask the man she'd vowed to spend the rest of her life with, "Why don't we stay here? For good?"

Part Two: Moscow

Chapter Eleven

Graphic: *The Phil Donahue Show*
Airdate: December 21, 1985
Episode Title: *A Citizens' Summit*
Show Transcript

Announcer: This is Moscow, the capital of the USSR, and this is Baltimore, Maryland, just outside of the United States capital, Washington DC. Today, citizens from the Soviet city and citizens from the US city will talk by television satellite on *A Citizen's Summit.* Hosted in the US by Phil Donahue and in the USSR by his journalistic counterpart, Dennis Kagan, with a trio of special guests. Rose Janowitz and her husband, Jonas Cain, were born in New York City. But after they were unable to marry in the States, they came to the USSR, where they decided to make their home and raise their daughter, Emma, for the past twenty-eight years. The Cain family joins us today to offer Americans a unique perspective on the two countries. Participants in *A Citizens' Summit* are free to discuss whatever they wish; no subject will be off limits. The Soviet and American audiences are men and women who work in factories, schools, hospitals, and their own homes. They are students and fishermen, farmers and physicians, and, like the Cains, artists and intellectuals. They'll meet each other face to face thanks to the wonders of modern technology—next on *A Citizen's Summit!*

Donahue: Welcome, welcome, everybody, to our historic conversation. I'm Phil Donahue, and my counterpart is Mr. Dennis Kagan, well-known television personality across the USSR. Hello, Dennis! How is everything with you this evening in Moscow?

Kagan: It is a warm evening in Moscow, only a few degrees below zero. How is your Maryland this afternoon?

Donahue: It is one PM in the afternoon here on the East Coast, eight PM in the evening in Moscow, and may I extend a very special welcome to your in-studio guests, Mr. and Mrs. Cain, Miss Cain, it's wonderful to see all three of you.

Rose: Thank you, Mr. Donahue.

Jonas: Pleasure to be here.

Emma: Hello.

Donahue: We understand that for the last almost thirty years, ever since you defected to the Soviet Union at the conclusion of the 1957 World Youth Festival, that you have been living as honored guests in your adopted country.

Rose: This is incorrect. We are not guests. We are Soviet citizens, no more or less honored than any other working person.

Kagan: Yes, Phil, I am afraid you are confusing the USSR with America. Celebrities like the Cains receive no privilege unavailable to any Soviet citizen. All are equal in the USSR.

Donahue: And that is why you chose to defect, is it not, Mr. and Mrs. Cain? Because your interracial marriage would not be recognized in the United States in 1957? This would be prior to the US Supreme Court decision of Loving v. Virginia in 1967.

Rose: It's no concern of mine what the United States does or does not recognize. It is a concern of mine that my husband and our daughter would be treated as full-fledged human beings, with all the rights pursuant to that, and not as three-fifths of a person.

Donahue: And have you found that to be the case in the Soviet Union?

Rose: Of course! In the USSR, Jonas was able to play the great roles of Shakespeare denied to him in the US. He's played not just Othello, but Hamlet, Richard III, Benedick, Romeo, Henry V, Shylock. This was not only in the theater, you understand, but on television, too. We are given free rein to adapt American classics like *Huckleberry Finn, Native Son, Up from Slavery*, for a Russian-speaking, and very appreciative, audience.

Donahue: Do you agree, Mr. Cain, with your wife?

Jonas: Do you, Mr. Donahue, ever disagree with your wife?

(Studio laughter.)

Donahue: Only when she is mistaken. Which is rarely.

Jonas: Then there's your answer.

(Studio laughter.)

Kagan: As the Cains and I have made clear, it does not matter whether you played Othello at the Bolshoi Theatre, or if you are in charge of sweeping up its floors. No one working citizen receives privileges above another. Perhaps we can shift now and allow some others in our audience to ask questions.

Donahue: Excellent point, excellent point, Dennis. But I am compelled to let you know that there is a good deal of skepticism in the US about the integrity of the statements that you will make. Not a few Americans believe that you are not really able to speak from your soul for fear of reprisal from Soviet government authorities. There are even some people in this country who feel you will all serve as mouthpieces for the official party line because to do otherwise might earn you a visit to a psychiatric hospital or perhaps a prison. This is not to say that all Americans believe that, this is not to say that you are dishonorable people. It is rather to honestly share with you the perception that millions of Americans have about life in the Soviet Union and the inability to speak one's mind.

Audience Member: We express our opinions from the heart, and we listen to our government with joy because it is right in all things. None of us here believe that you can't say what you truly think, why do you think that about us?

Donahue: What about dissidents like Andrei Sakharov?

Audience Member: Sakharov has slandered the Soviet Union. He is a traitor. Traitors should not be treated liberally.

Donahue: Why, because someone dissents from Soviet policy, are they immediately called a traitor? That is offensive to America's understanding of free speech.

Audience Member: Unlike America, we have laws in the USSR which forbid propaganda of war and hatred. Since 1917, we legislated peace with all people. Sakharov encouraged America to begin war against us. The government sent Sakharov to where there are no foreign consulates so he could not spread propaganda against the Soviet Union.

Donahue: Millions of Americans view the lives of Soviet people as restricted. This is especially an agony within the Jewish community in the West who believe there are thousands of Jews in Russia who cannot emigrate simply because they are Jewish, or because of some unjustified Soviet reasoning.

Kagan: Phil, Phil, listen to what you are saying. How can what you are saying be true? I, myself, am of the Jewish nationality, as is Rose Janowitz, as is her daughter. We are right here, and, as you can see, we are not suffering, we are free. Why do you have such bitter experiences, where do they come from? Why do you only have negative experiences, where are the positive experiences? You assume that we only have a country consisting of so many millions of unhappy people. You say Jews can't leave the country because they are Jews? Jews are the main immigrants. It is easier for them to immigrate.

Donahue: Why would 250,000 Jews want to emigrate from the Soviet Union?

Kagan: Where did you get that number? Did you hold a referendum in our country? Have you, yourself, spoken to a Jew in the USSR? Have you asked them?

Rose: Have you asked me? I know you didn't. Because if you had, you would have heard me tell you that, as a Jew, as a woman married to a Negro, I have been treated better in the Soviet Union than I ever had been in the United States. Look at my daughter. When my Emma was born, in 1958, do you know what kinds of names she would have been called in America? In 1958, in America, under your Jim Crow laws, she would not have been allowed to go to school with white children. She would not have been allowed to drink from the same water fountain. She would be forced to sit in the back of the bus and kept out of the best universities. None of that was an issue in the USSR. Not one, single thing. My daughter went to school with children who did not notice different skin color, different hair texture. Negro, Jew, woman… none of that is harped on here like it is in the United States. Everyone is equal here, that is true freedom.

Donahue: Was that your experience, Ms. Cain?

Rose: Ms.! There, you see, there's a new word you had to make up in America, because in America, you needed an entire movement for Women's Rights. Your wife, Mr. Donahue, she's a major force in this movement, isn't she?

Donahue: She is, indeed.

Rose: Did you and your wife ever discuss why there was no need for a Woman's Movement in the USSR? It's because Soviet women have had equal rights since the first day!

(Audience applause.)

Donahue: Ms. Cain, we didn't get a chance to hear your answer. Did you truly, as your mother claims, grow up in a country that didn't notice differences in race or ethnicity or gender roles?

Jonas: Do you, Mr. Donahue, ever disagree with your mother?

(Audience laughter.)

Donahue: Never!

(Audience laughter.)

Emma: I grew up in a country which is very proud to say they do not notice differences in race, ethnicity, or gender roles.

Donahue: You speak excellent English, Ms. Cain.

Emma: Thank you, Mr. Donahue.

Donahue: Did you study it formally at school, or merely learn it at home?

Emma: My parents always spoke English to each other and to me. They gave me books to read by Mr. John Steinbeck, Mr. Upton Sinclair and Mr. Theodore Dreiser so I would have a clear view of American life, rather than what Western propaganda would like the world to believe.

Donahue: And did you, as a native-born daughter, help your parents have a clearer view of Soviet life?

Rose: Emma would translate for us sometimes, I admit it. Jonas and I did our best to learn Russian, but we'll never be perfectly fluent speakers, not like our Emma, I'm afraid.

Kagan: Alright, Phil, you have heard from the entire Cain family. As you can see, they are free to speak their minds, even in front of judgmental Americans.

Donahue: You know, Dennis, another example of America's most beloved freedom, that of free speech, is that, outside our studio at this moment, are gathered several protesters. What you see here is America's free speech in action. They believe that they should have been entitled to access this program to complain about human rights violations that they claim to have evidence of in your country. This is to offer you evidence of the widespread belief that the Soviet Union's interest in peace is significantly undermined by the treatment of many of its people. One of our largest newspapers has condemned this program, claiming that this audience is rigged, and so is yours. So, if, to you, we appear preoccupied by the issue of human rights, it is because we are reflecting the interests of the American people.

Kagan: They are protesting our friendly talks? And there are children I see there? What do they understand? Doesn't it seem that someone is paying them to do this? I have a question for the Americans: To whose advantage are these children, are these protesters speaking?

Audience Member: What I think Americans don't understand when they talk about free speech and free speech means you must protest your government, is that we choose our government so that our government can carry out our will. I don't understand how I could be in disagreement with a person who is doing what I want them to do. If I were to ask someone to do something and he did that, then I can't disagree with that. I took part in a protest meeting, a protest meeting protesting not my own government, but against international militarization. We all fully agreed with the policy of our government against militarization. We do have demonstrations, and we demonstrate our views openly and frankly.

Donahue: You are against international militarization, yet the Soviet Union invades Afghanistan and Poland.

Audience Member: We don't have to justify ourselves on Afghanistan and Poland because, unlike you, we believe in our government with equanimity. We believe, most of all, that it is our government. It was our government which stated that it has committed itself to never, ever attack anyone first. Can one fail to trust such a government and such a state? This is why we are perfectly calm regarding the steps the government has undertaken. We have problems, we have a great many problems, economic and social problems. You ask us about Afghanistan, we ask, why did you begin a war in Vietnam? Why did you help Israelis destroy Arab people? Why are you concentrating forces in Lebanon? Why did you destroy Grenada? Why are you helping South Africa in their fight against Angola? Why have you used your forces to attack Nicaragua? Why do you all feel you are so right, and don't give us the benefit of the doubt?

(Audience applause.)

Donahue: We think what you do in your country is your business. But we ask you to believe that millions of Americans see the crushing of Solidarity in Poland as an autocratic move against the will of the people, they see the invasion of Afghanistan similarly. The difference is that we argue our foreign policy decisions and you do not. We cannot overstate how discouraged Americans are to realize that we have such a powerful, enlightened nation of over 260 million people who appear to be intimidated by a select few about where Soviet influence will be felt without any concern about how their own people feel, thereby denying yourself the wisdom of your own populace.

Audience Member: Look at our newspapers, we have criticism, real criticism, general criticism, of our government and our social organizations. We make use of the same democratic rights as you do. I have exactly the same rights as any other citizen of our country. I have the right to be elected to our government, and I have the right to vote, too. Freedom of speech is wonderful, but if no one is listening, what use is it? We don't get the feeling that your protests against the policy of militarization really result in serious reaction on the part of your government. So, what good does it do?

Rose: And is it really freedom of speech, or is it only freedom of speech you agree with? For instance, there were stories printed in the American press after Jonas and I decided to relocate to the Soviet Union. I read them in the newspaper. Yes, American newspapers are allowed in the USSR. Are you surprised to hear that? Not a single one of those stories asked Jonas or my reasons for doing what we did. They simply all railed against us and inferred our motives.

Kagan: What would you have told them if you'd been given the chance?

Rose: I would have told them that, contrary to Western propaganda, for me, my husband, and our daughter, America wasn't the land of opportunity—the Soviet Union is. Jonas was fired from his job on the Procter & Gamble soap opera, *Find Your Light*, when it transitioned from radio to television because corporate, capitalist interests feared they'd lose money putting a Negro front and center. I was fired for standing up for him. We were not allowed to mount our production of *Othello* due to fears of miscegenation and the raising of workers' consciousness. That is why we left the US. In the USSR, I'm allowed to write and produce any shows I want. I'm allowed to cast my husband alongside actresses of any color. Our daughter attended Moscow University. The best, most prestigious university. A woman. Colored. With Jewish ancestry, no less. She studied microbiology. Now Emma works in an elite laboratory. Tell me that would have been possible in America. I'll take the true freedoms of the Soviet Union over anything Americans write in their so-called free press.

(Audience applause.)

End Transcript.

Chapter Twelve

<hr>

At the conclusion of *A Citizen's Summit* broadcast, the audience was quickly shuffled out of one door, while Rose, Jonas, and Emma were personally escorted into the back of the studio by no less than Dennis Kagan, himself. He unclipped the microphone from his suit jacket's lapel, handing it to a technician, and accepted a hand towel from the make-up artist to wipe away the sweat-smeared powder, blush, and eyeliner. He shook his head, making his sepia hair fly every which way, before settling into a more natural spike than his previously meticulous coif. Based on his high position at Soviet Central Television, Emma assumed Dennis was in his late 40s, maybe even a well-preserved early 50s. Now, however, she doubted he was more than in his late 30s, at most.

"Thank you so much for doing the show," Dennis said, addressing Rose, Jonas, and Emma, in nearly flawless English. "You gave terrific answers."

"My wife always gives terrific answers" Jonas slipped a prideful arm around Rose's shoulders, "as long as you ask her the properly inciting questions."

Dennis grinned. "I don't think our Mr. Donahue knew what hit him."

Emma was surprised by the colloquialism. Since she and her parents spoke English at home, she was used to being the only one familiar with slang unavailable to those who learned the language from textbooks or tutors educated at Oxford. Then again, Emma felt certain all her expressions were out of date, severed as Mom and Dad were from post-1950 American idioms.

"How I feel around Rose, perennially." Jonas gazed adoringly at his wife. She returned his gaze. If Emma were still thirteen, or fifteen, or even twenty, she might have rolled her eyes. However, by twenty-seven, she barely noticed it anymore. That was just the shape her parents' faces naturally fell into.

"There's a car waiting outside to take all three of you home." Dennis gestured in the direction of the back door. As Rose and Jonas turned to go, he rested a hand on Emma's elbow and politely inquired, "Perhaps you might be free to have dinner with me tonight?" He assured Rose and Jonas, "I have a car, I will make certain she gets home safely."

Was he asking her parents or her for permission? Considering the outsized shadows they cast, Emma was accustomed to Mom and Dad taking center stage, even when she was ostensibly the subject under discussion.

To her credit, Rose looked to Emma, both eyebrows raised. Jonas, also, declined to speak for her. Which meant everyone was waiting for Emma's answer.

As a rule, she avoided accepting invitations from men who appeared more enraptured by her renowned parents than by her. But, on this particular occasion, Emma had nothing more interesting on her calendar than returning to the two-bedroom apartment she and her parents shared, reading, drinking a glass of milk, and going to bed. Besides, Dennis Kagan was, arguably, more regionally famous than her parents. Which made it less likely he was using Emma to get to them, for a career or a political boost.

"Sure," Emma shrugged. "Why not?"

HE TOOK HER TO THE PRAGA RESTAURANT on Arbat Street. Emma wasn't surprised. If you wanted to show off in Moscow, your choices were either Praga, or Seventh Heaven. The latter was the highest restaurant in the Soviet Union, rotating 330 meters above the ground in the Ostankino TV tower. It could only accommodate eighty people at a time and required a ticket to enter. Officially, one cost seven rubles. Unofficially, ten rubles slipped to the host could get you in any time. Seventh Heaven was fancier than the Praga, but the food was simpler. Sandwiches, salads drenched in mayonnaise, and maybe a breaded patty. The reason for the basic fare was that cooking wasn't permitted in the tower due to fire safety, so everything was prepared off the premises and only warmed up on site. The Praga may have been located on the ground level, but the food was more palatable. Especially if you qualified for the rooms catering to VIPs and foreign guests—meaning you had hard, non-Soviet currency to spend—and so had your choice of veal filet with champignon mushrooms, pork cutlet Slovak style, or caviar with toast and butter. Dennis, naturally, had the access—and the hard currency.

As he escorted Emma to their table, he guessed, "I'm sure you've been here before."

"When my parents first came to Moscow, they stayed at the Hotel Ukraina. But lots of other delegation members were housed at the Intourist next door. They came here to celebrate their marriage. They've been coming back for their anniversary every year since."

"Soviet egalitarianism at its finest," Dennis observed, leaving Emma to wonder whether he was kidding, sincere, or something even more sinister. With an average salary of about 150 rubles per month, few citizens could afford to eat at Praga—even if they managed to wrangle a reservation—when the veal, for instance, cost thirty rubles a serving, and the caviar fifty-four rubles per patron. Was he testing Emma with his provocative quip?

Emma took her seat and, while unfolding the white linen napkin onto her lap, made as noncommittal a sound as she thought she could get away with.

Dennis asked if she preferred wine, brandy, or cognac.

"Not vodka?" she teased, unsure of what her objective was, but refusing to let him be the only one potentially having fun at her expense.

"Vodka is for everyday occasions. We're celebrating."

"Celebrating what?" Emma asked as she let him order them both a glass of merlot.

"A great show. We will take the two hours we filmed, cut them down to about forty-five minutes both our censors and their censors will find acceptable, then air on the same night in both countries."

"Which parts will be cut out?"

"Afraid of losing your moment in the spotlight? You barely said anything."

"Mom is the family spokesperson. The rest of us are there for background. She's Diana Ross. Dad and I are the Supremes."

Dennis laughed. "What could a good, Soviet maiden like you possibly know about such a decadent, American singing group?"

Figuring a man who had access to The Praga's VIP foreign currency room lacked the standing to judge them for a much smaller transgression, Emma confessed, "My parents got all the latest records from America. Not just the Supremes. We got Beatles, Rolling Stones, David Bowie, Billy Joel, also the scandalous Broadway albums like *West Side Story*, and *Hair*. I would wake up at night, and there they'd be in the living room, volume so low you could barely hear it, dancing. They love to dance. Well, Mom loves to dance. And Dad loves Mom, so there they always were, dancing—cheek to cheek, like the song says—to *Age of Aquarius, Ob-La-Di, Ob-La-Da, Heroes, You're My Home*. They said they kept the sound down so not to disturb the neighbors. I was pretty sure it was because they didn't want the neighbors knowing they were listening to subversive music."

It was a risky confession but, again, Emma was gambling he'd done the same, if not worse.

"Mom said we weren't doing anything wrong. She and Dad were artists. They had to keep up with the latest creative trends. They got all their records from official, government sources, not on the black market. She said it was OK for them to listen to that kind of music, because they're from America, so they wouldn't be fooled. They knew the songs were full of Western, imperialist lies. The reason the music had to be banned for others, was because more impressionable people might actually believe what they heard. And that might destabilize a socialist society. So, it was for everyone's own good it be outlawed."

Dennis took a sip of wine. He waited for the server to step away before asking Emma, "Do you believe that?"

"What?"

"All of it. Everything we've been taught from the cradle. That this," he gestured past the exclusive restaurant, into the world they'd have to return to, "is, to paraphrase Voltaire, the best of all possible worlds?"

She'd been toying with him before. Mostly out of boredom. Emma rarely met people who lived as privileged of a Soviet life as her family did, so it felt fun, and a little transgressive, to step outside their prescribed boundaries and drip a few crumbs past what they'd been trained to say, what they were expected to say, what they were allowed to say. This parlay, however, was drifting dangerously towards the potentially incriminating.

Dennis must have recognized her reasonable apprehension because he went first, as insurance to allay her fears. "My parents were Jews. I told Mr. Donahue the truth. They were doctors. Serving bravely at the front during The Great Patriotic War. Unfortunately, that wasn't enough to protect them during the subsequent roundups. My parents were arrested as part of Comrade Stalin's Doctors Plot in 1952. Maybe they had a show trial, maybe they didn't. They did sign confessions. Both signatures in the exact same hand, can you imagine that? Then they died. Maybe shot in the head in Leforto-vo Prison, maybe frozen to death in a gulag, maybe somewhere in between those two customary fates. None of those details matter in the end. I was sent to an orphanage for the children of Enemies of the People. Made what Mr. Dickens wrote about his *Oliver Twist* feel like, well, like The Praga. It's where I was shown my parents' signed confessions. To make clear how worthless I was. That was also where, and this likely was not a part of my tormentors' plan, I learned my own worth."

She was intrigued in spite of herself. Emma had begun their exchange assuming she and Dennis were equals. She was beginning to suspect he was way ahead of her in an aspect she hadn't realized was in play.

"And what are you worth, exactly, Comrade Kagan?" Emma kept her tone light. This could all still turn out to be a trap, albeit a cleverer one than usual. With better wine.

"To the Soviet propaganda machine? Quite a bit. Once Comrade Khrushchev made his speech denouncing Stalin and embarked on his tour to show the West how non-threatening the Soviet people were, I… well, I may not have been the first child of two enemies of the people who realized how useful I could be as a symbol of the new, forgiving USSR, but I'm pretty sure I was the first to do something about it. I began writing school compositions about how grateful I was that, even after what my parents had done, the Soviet Union still clothed, fed, educated and raised me. I let one of my teachers think it was his idea to send that essay to the newspaper. I let the newspaper man who came to speak with me about it afterwards think it was his idea to have me read the composition at a May Day celebration. After that, it was just a matter of letting more and more people think they had the idea to make me their poster child for everything that was noble and moral about the USSR. I make excellent speeches. If you've never heard one, I suggest tracking down a children's record I was able to squeeze out before my voice changed. Very touching. I highly recommend it."

Emma didn't know whether to laugh, commend him for his ingenuity, or immediately turn Dennis in for making his libelous statements—before he turned her in for listening to them and not doing anything about it. This could still be some kind of trap. Emma wasn't being modest, however, when she wracked her brain trying to guess what Dennis wanted from her. She was nobody. Her parents were maybe worth entrapping. Not her.

"Why are you telling me this?" Emma hadn't grown up in the USSR without picking up rudimentary skills in asking a question that could mean a variety of things, depending on the context. She was already mentally preparing her defense, should the conversation take a turn too dangerous to continue indulging. Though, she also had to admit, this was the most intriguing conversation she could recall having in… ever.

"I watched you. During the broadcast." Was Dennis answering Emma's question, or preparing a defense of his own? This was what was making this conversation so intriguing. Usually, Emma could figure out what a person wanted, or at least what they wanted her to think they wanted, almost instantly. She had no idea what was happening here. Or what the ultimate objective was. Not just intriguing, it was exciting. Exhilarating. Intoxicating. That's what she had to be on the alert for. And not merely from the wine.

"Not only did your mother cut you off when it appeared you might be so much as considering giving a less than politically proper answer, but every time she started one of her patriotic speeches," Dennis noted, "I saw you grip the edges of your chair and stare at the floor. Like you were trying to prevent yourself from storming off the set, or rolling your eyes, or groaning out loud."

"She's my mother," Emma shrugged. Was that the best he could do? What a letdown. "Doesn't everybody feel that way about their mother once in a while?"

"I wouldn't know," Dennis reminded. He mimed the signing of a confession, and a gun to the head. Complete with a "psheeew" noise.

"I'm sorry," Emma said. In lamenting the privileged upbringing she'd received, Emma sometimes forgot other people might have missed what she took for granted.

"Would you care to guess what all the women I go out with have in common?"

Had her insensitive lament driven Dennis into a complete non-sequitur? Once again, Emma felt lost in conversation, though, once again, it was not a completely unpleasant experience.

"They all want to be on television?"

"Besides that…" He clearly bounced back quickly from offense. When Emma didn't wager a follow-up guess, Dennis did it for her, "They all think they understand me. They see me on the air, and they assume I am what I appear to be. A good, staunch, loyal party member and citizen. Or somebody who's pretending to be one in order to move up the ranks. It doesn't really matter which. Even in this *Perestroika* free-for-all Comrade Gorbachev has thrust us into, you still need to be one or the other if you intend to get ahead. Either way, they think they know what I want—no, they think they know what I need—in a partner."

"And they're wrong?"

"They are wrong."

"So, what do you need?"

"You," Dennis said.

AS HE'D PROMISED HER PARENTS, Dennis dropped Emma off at home at the end of their evening. He gave her a gentlemanly kiss on the cheek, then a less gentlemanly one on the lips. She did not refuse either. He waited until she'd made it from his car to the front door of her apartment building, then up to the fifth floor. He only drove away after she'd waved to him from the bedroom window to demonstrate she was safe.

She'd grown up in this apartment, in this room. This was the residence her parents were assigned to when they first immigrated, and they saw no reason to ever ask for a change. They were already living better than almost everyone else in Moscow. While some were stuffed nine, ten families to a single apartment, five, six people to a single room, children sleeping in drawers, teens sleeping on windowsills, elderly parents in walk-in closets, sharing kitchens, bathrooms, or making due with a public bathhouse when the basic facilities were lacking, the Cains had three rooms for three people, a living room, a bedroom for Mom and Dad, and a bedroom for Emma, not to mention their own kitchen, their own bathroom—even if there was no tub, only a shower.

Just like with the contraband Western records, Mom explained that, of course, all people should be equal, and all people in the USSR already were equal, this was the law of the land, so how could it be any different? The reason they had grander living quarters than so many others was because the Cains were regularly visited by overseas delegations, which meant the foreign press, as well. If they did not live in such relative luxury, why, then, the reporters might go back to their countries and write scathing editorials on how one of the most venerated couples of the Soviet theater had been reduced to poverty and squalor. Wouldn't the Americans have a field day then? How would Rose and Jonas be able to drive home their point about the terrible racial conditions in the US and why they'd been forced to flee them if their circumstances in the USSR were no better? Of course, Rose and Jonas, and Emma, too, knew that superficial details like the number of rooms they occupied didn't represent the moral advantages the Soviet Union had to offer, but Americans weren't educated enough to understand that. They saw material things as a sign of how respected you were. So, to drive home how generously Rose and Jonas had been treated since Day One in the USSR, they were forced to live in conditions the Americans would consider adequate. It was unfortunate, yes, but they were doing it for the common and the greater good. Which, as Soviet citizens, was their primary duty.

She'd said as much to Dennis. He'd laughed. And then he complimented her mother's mental gymnastics. It was a shame it wasn't an Olympic sport, he said. Because then Soviets would dominate that event even more than they did the artistic one.

When Emma asked Dennis why he thought she was so different from all other women he'd dated—at a certain point of the evening, they'd both agreed this was, in fact, a date—he explained, "I am looking for a woman who sees the world the way it is. Not the way we keep being told it is, and not the way that she thinks I want her to see it, but the way that it really is."

"Why?"

"Because that is the only way for a couple to be truly united. Sexual compatibility is a wonderful thing. But that can be worked on, that can be developed. A shared sense of cynicism, though, that's the true kismet."

If he was setting a trap, then, kudos, he was doing it impeccably. Alas, like her mother, Emma was a sucker for an intelligent man.

Dennis looked around, and then he leaned in. Emma thought he might be meaning to kiss her, but, no, Dennis had something much more intimate in mind. "This hasn't been made public yet, but it will be in the next few weeks. I am leaving Moscow. I am being sent to America. One of their networks, not a major one, a small one, on what they call cable television, they are giving me my own show. Once a week, for an hour, no commercials, I am to explain the Soviet Union to American viewers. Can you believe it? Can you imagine one of our television stations turning over an hour a week to an American to spew propaganda non-stop? There's precedent for it. As part of Khrushchev's rehabilitation campaign, he did allow a magazine called *Amerika* to be distributed in the USSR in exchange for a magazine called *Soviet Life Today* being sold in the US, but those were difficult to find here. You had to know it existed, you had to know the few newsstands where it was being sold, you had to have permission to purchase it, you had to be able to afford it. Television is everywhere! And I will be the Americans' Soviet face of it!"

"That is exciting," Emma cheered sincerely. "Congratulations."

"Come with me," Dennis said.

"What did you just say?"

"They will love you in America. They love Negroes now, I am told. Though the proper term is Black. Or is it African-American? They cannot seem to make up their minds."

"I don't think that's accurate. If my parents were certain of one thing, it was that they do not love Negroes in America. I believe history backs them up."

"This will be different. Your story will fascinate the US press. The US press loves to be fascinated. They are like cats with shiny objects."

Why did he keep making her laugh? Especially when what he was saying was quite serious? As in life changing.

"You want me to come with you to America…?"

"We'll need to get married, first, it's the only way you'll get permission to leave."

"You're asking me to marry you?"

"Not right away. There are still a few weeks before I leave. Get to know me. If you like what I have to offer, yes, let's get married and go to America together."

"You're insane."

"I am not. This is the USSR. All insane people are safely tucked away in asylums. The fact that I can walk the streets freely is the government's seal of approval on my sanity."

She was at some point beyond laughter now. She was now in silent incredulity.

"Can I at least think about it?" Emma managed to choke out.

"Think quickly."

"Why? Are you afraid I might quit being cynical? Or a Negro?"

"No." About this, Dennis appeared most sincere. "I am afraid this window of opportunity, this openness of Gorbachev's, might close as quickly as the one after Khrushchev's removal from power. I would much rather be in New York than Moscow when it happens."

SO, EMMA THOUGHT ABOUT IT. She thought about it all night as she lay in the bed she'd been sleeping in since nursery school. She thought about the life she had. And about the life Dennis was offering. The life she had was the life she'd wanted—up till now. Thanks to her parents' position, Emma had been eligible to attend the most prestigious school in Moscow, Number 25, where the students were reminded that Josef Stalin's daughter had once been a pupil, as had Paul Robeson Jr., son of the great American singer, recipient of the Stalin Peace Prize, who told his fellow Americans his child would be educated in the USSR because, there, he would not be discriminated against. Each time the teacher stressed that point, everyone in the class would turn and look at Emma.

Thanks to her parents' position, Emma could have attended a specialized music school. It was assumed that since her parents were artistically talented, then she must be, too, so no audition necessary. Emma declined. Thanks to her parents' position, not only was she accepted to the USSR's top college, Lomonosov Moscow State University—it was assumed that since her parents were brilliant, then she must be, too, so no entrance exams necessary—but advised she could focus on whatever subject she wished, no quotas would be in effect for her. Traditionally, there were only as many university spots available as the government intended to create jobs for in that field via the upcoming Five-Year Plan. But Rose and Jonas Cain's daughter should have no trouble getting a job! Would she like to study literature? Journalism? Political science? Math? Physics? Those were the most difficult majors to get into. Emma declined. She picked microbiology. She refused to explain why.

Emma had no complaints about the laboratory job she'd been assigned. She researched the microbes that helped with food production. An honorable endeavor, her parents assured her, though Emma could tell that not only did they not understand what she did, they were baffled why anyone would want to spend their days alone, staring into a microscope, when they could be on stage, or at least, telling the people on stage what to do. It was assumed that, eventually, Emma would meet somebody and marry. Her parents would arrange for the newlyweds to be assigned an apartment, one large enough for them to raise children in, one they wouldn't have to share with anyone else. Emma wondered how Mom would justify that entitlement. It's not like the foreign press ever stopped by to interview and photograph her.

Emma had no objection to following the life plan set out for her since before birth. She just hadn't seen any point in rushing towards it. Yes, there'd been boys, in secondary school and at university. And there had been men afterwards. Colleagues, important enough to have been allocated single rooms of their own, so they and Emma didn't need to have sex in her childhood bedroom, making awkward conversation in the kitchen with her parents before and after. Emma prioritized avoiding awkward conversation over ignoring the judgmental looks and knowing smirks from communal apartment neighbors as she came and went. She could've married one of those men. There was nothing much wrong with them. There also wasn't much right. Emma understood that marriage meant taking a step from one small room into the next, hearing the door lock behind her, limiting her options moving forward even further.

Dennis was offering her options she'd never dreamed of. Going to America. What would Mom and Dad think of that?

She supposed she'd get the chance to find out.

Because, the following morning, Emma called Dennis and told him, "I'm in."

Chapter Thirteen

Mom didn't get hysterical. Then again, Emma had never seen her mom get hysterical, so she wasn't sure why she'd expected it to happen now. Maybe because, up to this point, Emma had always done what was expected of her. So, what reason would either of her parents have had to get hysterical?

All Rose wanted to know was, "Why?"

"I've never been outside of the Soviet Union. I'd like to see the world."

"I've seen it. There is nothing for you out there, trust me. Your father, he saw the world, thanks to Uncle Sam and Adolph Hitler. He saw the world through the periscope of a tank. Ask him how he enjoyed it."

"The outside world isn't Moscow," Dad said. Emma couldn't tell if he thought that was a good or a bad thing. "People will look at you, Em, and they will act based on what they see on the surface."

"They will act based on the color of your skin," Rose clarified, though Emma was so much lighter than Dad that, when her hair was straightened and people didn't know who her father was, they asked if she was Arab or Indian or Spanish or Gypsy. So, there were quite a few potential reactions there. "Here you are treated no differently than anyone else. In America—"

"Stop it, Mom." Emma figured if she didn't spit it out now, she might never get up the courage again. "You've always said that. It's never been true. From the time I was little, other kids; adults, too, they'd come up and want to touch my curls, or my skin to see if the brown rubs off. In school, if I ever wore my hair out of braids, they pulled it and called me Angela Davis. At least it was better than when they called me a monkey or a savage and made animal noises as I'd walk by. They used to flick slivers of soap at me from under their nails and tell me to go wash so I can be clean like them."

Mom stiffened, crossing her arms. "You never told me this."

"You never wanted to hear it. All you ever talk about is how much better it is here for Dad and me than it would have been in the States. Any facts that don't fit your position, you toss like it's an excess scene from one of your teleplays."

"Some people," Dad mused, "see things as they are and ask why? Your mother dreams of things that never were and asks, why not? She has that in common with Robert Kennedy."

"How can you stand it?" If Emma was about to flee the continent—and she was growing more certain of that course of action by the minute—she might as well get everything out in the open now. "How can you put up with her living in this perpetual dream world? She took you away from your family, from your home, from everything that was familiar to you. She insists it's all for the better, it's all great. I know it's not all great. I see how people stare at you in the street. I hear what they mutter when we pass by. You can never walk anonymously into a room. You always stand out. I know you do. Because I do, too."

"And why is that a terrible thing?" Rose challenged.

"You wouldn't understand. You can disappear if you want to. Not that you'd ever want to. You have to be the center of attention. Rose Janowitz Cain and her oh-so progressive family. *Look at me! Aren't I fascinating?* Well, that's your choice. Dad and I didn't choose to constantly have people sneaking peeks at us, or asking why we're there, where we're from, what we want. You're not treated like some exotic creature from another planet, or an animal in the zoo they can't wait to dissect, see if it's normal on the inside."

"Stop," Jonas commanded calmly. For a man who projected his voice to the rear of a cavernous theater without seeming effort, his whisper came off more ominous than any shout. He could have yelled. He deliberately chose not to. "You will not speak to your mother this way."

Right. Of course. Dad would always defend Mom. Emma had been a fool to not even so much as believe but to hope that could ever change.

"You are, however, correct about one thing," Jonas conceded to his daughter. "Living in the USSR has not been as effortless for me as your mother would like to believe. As she insists on believing."

"Jonas? What? You never said…" A baffled Rose looked from her husband to their daughter. "You didn't… How was I to know? I… You never said!" Was that a modicum of doubt in Rose's voice? Of self-reflection?

"You know what it has been, though, Em?" Jonas may have been addressing Emma, but he turned to face his wife. Of course, he did. "It has been the adventure of a lifetime. Yes, your mother took me away from my family, from my home, from everything that was familiar to me. But you know what else she took me away from? She took me away from a life that had been preordained for generations, a life of no surprises, just the monotony of going through the motions. Twenty-eight years ago, I took your mother's hand, and we leapt off the edge of a cliff, into the abyss, together. Did I expect what happened next? Could I have predicted it? Did I know I wanted it? No. No to all that. But am I sorry? Do I regret it? Do I wish I'd done things differently? Also no. Never. Not once. Your mother didn't take my life from me. She gave me a life. One bigger and brighter and bolder and… and *ballsier* than anything I could have dreamed of. Because your mother taught me what it meant to really dream."

There were tears in Rose's eyes. There were tears in Emma's eyes, too. Emma suspected her mother's were there for different reasons.

Emma told her parents, "That's what I want, too. My life here, it's fixed. If I go to America with Dennis, anything could happen."

"That's what I'm afraid of," Rose said. But she never raised another objection.

HER PARENTS MET DENNIS, this time as her intended, rather than merely the host of a television show. Her parents were charmed by Dennis. She didn't blame them. Emma was charmed by him herself. Did that mean she loved him?

Not really. But she liked him well enough. And there was plenty of time for more down the line. Dennis' position in America was guaranteed for at least two years, with an option for two more years at the conclusion of that. This would give them the chance to really get to know each other, maybe even fall in love, who could say? Besides, Dennis made it clear that wasn't a priority. His priority was being with someone who saw the world the same way he did, who could be as cynical as him, yet dispassionately strategic about exploiting it.

For instance, as part of his charm offensive, Dennis did what he claimed he didn't want the woman in his life to do, and allowed Emma's parents to assume they knew who he was and what he stood for.

Mom told him, "As long as Emma is determined to go to America, I'm glad she's going with you. I listened to what you said during our show with Mr. Donahue. You truly understand the differences between the USSR and America. You won't let Emma get deceived by their... their nonsense. Their pretty words, their spectacles. They're good at staging spectacles in America. Did you see the Olympics last summer in Los Angeles? Their spectacles are designed to fool you about what's really happening. Madison Avenue was created for that purpose. I know. I was one of those shills tasked with selling nonsense housewives didn't need so they'd be too distracted to focus on the class struggle, sexual liberation, the race problem, anti-Semitism, all of it. Progress betrayed and traded in for shiny trinkets!"

"Don't worry, Mrs. Cain." Sometimes, Emma thought Dennis' English was better than hers. It was certainly slicker. "Emma and I recognize America for exactly what it is. There will be no fooling us. We'll be the ones doing the fooling."

THERE WAS NO TIME to plan a wedding. Emma and Dennis decided to just have a small ceremony at the local ZAGS. Emma didn't want a veil. She didn't even want a sole-occasion white flowing dress. It was February. She went with a long-sleeved gray wool jacket and skirt suit, which could be reused, together and separately. Mom didn't object.

"I didn't exactly have a conventional wedding ceremony either," she said, wistfully.

Dad was the one who admitted he was disappointed not to have the chance to give Emma away. But there would be no aisle. Just Emma and Dennis signing papers, surrounded by her parents, a few friends of hers from work, a few friends of his from the studio, and the photographer sent by *Pravda*. Emma had gone from having celebrity parents to a celebrity husband. She tried not to dwell on the implications of that.

The other thing Emma tried not to dwell on, even as she was penning her name to make their marriage legal, was Dennis boasting to her, on the night they met, how good he was at getting people to do things… by making them think it was all their idea.

THE EVENING BEFORE Emma and Dennis were scheduled to fly out from Sheremetyevo International Airport to JFK, Mom took Emma aside and, when she was sure Dad couldn't hear, shoved a piece of paper into her hand.

"This is my mother's address. Your grandmother. Bluma Janowitz. It's on the Lower East Side of Manhattan. I don't even know if she's alive, but, please, if you could check… Tell her," Rose hesitated. "Tell her I named you after my father. His name was Emil."

"I thought you named me after Emma Goldman, the anarchist."

"That's what I told your father," Mom said.

ROSE AND JONAS WERE LEAVING Dennis' apartment after having said their final good-byes to him and Emma. While Mom went to grab her coat from the radiator where they'd laid it out on to dry from the melting snow, Dad took Emma aside and, when he was sure Mom couldn't hear, shoved a piece of paper into her hand.

"This is my parents' address. Your grandparents. Geoffrey and

Annabelle Moore. It's in Harlem. That's Upper Manhattan. I don't even know if they're alive, but, please, if you could check… Tell them," Jonas hesitated. "Tell them I named you after my granny. Her name was Emmaline."

"I thought you named me after Emma Goldman, the anarchist." Emma felt like she was in a most peculiar loop of déjà vu.

"That's what I told your mother," Dad said.

IT TOOK EMMA BARELY A WEEK to recognize that, for better or worse, life in New York City wouldn't be too different from Moscow. Just like her parents had been assigned an appropriate home when they immigrated, Emma and Dennis taxied straight from the airport to an apartment on Central Park West, on Manhattan's Upper West Side, which had been procured for them by Dennis' new employers but was being paid for by Soviet Central Television. It was a fourteenth floor, furnished two-bedroom, two bath with bay windows and a terrace looking out over Central Park itself. A doorman worked the desk downstairs. A cleaning lady came by twice a week.

Dennis took in the wood clad walls, the vertical blinds, the leather lounges, the crimson carpet, the remote controlled television, the stereo with speakers, and the matching mahogany dining room table and chairs—the very latest in interior design fashion—and deadpanned to Emma, "No reporters will be writing scathing editorials on how one of the Soviet Union's most venerated journalists has been reduced to poverty and squalor."

"Superficial details like how grandly the USSR can afford to house their overseas staff doesn't represent the moral advantages the Soviet Union has to offer, but Americans aren't educated enough to understand that," she agreed.

"We are forced to live in conditions Americans would consider adequate. It's unfortunate, yes, but we are doing it for the common and the greater good."

"Which, as Soviet citizens, is our primary duty."

The last two pronouncements were delivered punctuated by bursts of laughter.

"Give my best to your mother," Dennis bid as he set off for his first day of work.

With Dennis gone, and no job or housework to attend to, Emma set about exploring the city that, if matters had played out differently, would have been her hometown. The similarities between New York and Moscow were the tall buildings, the sprawling museums, the elegant theaters, and the constant noise which barely ebbed during nighttime hours. The differences were you didn't need to buy a ticket for restaurant access, their metro was filthy and devoid of towering, patriotic artwork like bronze monuments to revolutionaries, partisans, workers, the writer Maxim Gorky, athletes, Romulus and Remus, fertility, and dogs, the latter of whose nose gleamed brightly due to thousands of commuters rubbing it daily for luck.

But the main difference between New York and Moscow was that when Emma walked down the street, she didn't stick out. At all.

After a lifetime of seeing exclusively white faces, with a sprinkling of Asiatic ones from Eastern republics like Kazakhstan, Uzbekistan, and Tajikistan, it was a shock to Emma's system to observe so many different flesh tones zipping past. There were men and women as dark as the Congolese Patrice Lumumba, whose photographic visage Emma spied outside The Patrice Lumumba Peoples' Friendship University of Russia named in his honor. Others were closer to Dad's shade, like the Pepsi-Cola drinks Mom felt compelled to set out whenever foreign guests visited, while still others matched Emma, with skin the color of Roman mushrooms, so lightly tan that only the fullness of their lips, or the near blackness of their eyes suggested all was not as it appeared.

And, of course, there was the hair. So much variety of hair, so much variety of styles. Growing up, Emma exclusively observed the short, tight curls of the Africans', like her father's. Then there was the stalk straight, nearly white blondeness of the ethnic Russians. Emma's hair was neither. It was closest to Mom's looser, thicker curls, technically ebony, but a shade or two lighter than her daughter's. The texture was completely different. Mom's hair might tangle in the wind, but you could pull a comb or brush through, even if she cursed while doing it. Emma's hair was too thick for that, as well as uneven. Soft in some parts, wiry in others. When Mom braided it, instead of lying flat down Emma's back, it curled in the middle, looping up like a fish-hook.

Naturally, Mom braided it. All good Soviet girls had long plaits, sometimes one, sometimes two, sometimes dozens, in the Asian style. It didn't matter that Emma's hair wasn't right for it. She was still forced to wear braids all through school. Her sole alternative was to cut it short. But that came out too curly. The one time she'd tried, the other kids called her hedgehog and pretended to prick their fingers on the spikes.

Emma never realized plaited and cropped weren't her only options. Until America.

Long, short, chemically straightened, braided close to the scalp, twisted, colored, waist-length, shoulder-length, even shaved bald! In New York City, Emma was the one blatantly staring in public at the spectrum of humanity on display. She'd assumed it would make her feel more comfortable to blend in with the crowds, but reality proved the opposite.

In Moscow, Emma didn't have to wonder which group she belonged with. She knew. She didn't belong anywhere. Here, the choices were nearly infinite. And just as exclusionary. She clearly wasn't African-American, even if she did learn to use that designation over Negro, which she'd been advised was no longer in fashion and, in fact, offensive, as it sounded too close to a slur. Emma was neither African nor American, while the Jews she saw coming out of their basilica-like synagogues looked nothing like her. Strangers may have spoken Spanish to her on the street, surprised when Emma only shrugged dumbly, but she certainly knew she didn't belong among them, no matter the surface resemblance.

Emma had heard that new Soviet immigrants, especially those who'd arrived in the late 1970s, had a tendency to faint in grocery stores, overwhelmed by the abundance of choices in produce. Having grown up shopping in emporiums reserved for high-ranking party members and other citizens of importance, Emma wasn't impressed by expensive wares. What fascinated her was the abundance of cheap, disposable trinkets. She haunted pharmacies, marveling at one-time-use razors, paper towels, floss, plastic plates, juice boxes, numerical birthday candles, tropical drink umbrellas, and bendy straws.

Wandering from Duane Reade to ninety-nine cent store, Emma understood that she was stalling. The pieces of paper her parents had slipped into Emma's hand prior to her departure were still there, tucked into the back pages of a novel she finished reading on the plane. (*Lucky*, by Jackie Collins. Dennis said the bestseller would give Emma an insight into the kind of country they were headed for. Plus teach her lots of new and colorful English words.) At least once a day, Emma took the addresses out and glanced from one to the other. She'd looked up both on a map. She'd researched which subways would deliver her. She'd found a brand-new telephone book on her doorstep one morning and looked them up. Neither Bluma Janowitz nor Geoffrey and Annabelle Moore were listed. Emma wondered if her parents were responsible for that. Because, in addition to her shop visits, Emma had also dropped by the main branch of the New York public library in midtown, the one with the majestic, carved marble lions out front.

She'd pulled a chair up to the microfiche machine, and, optimizing the known dates of the 1957 World Youth Festival, scoured *The New York Times* for any mention of Rose Janowitz and Jonas Cain. She found it at the end of the celebration's coverage—after the write up of the young American reading from the UN report in Red Square, and Eleanor Roosevelt's genteel condemnation of him for it. The story of Rose and Jonas' marriage and defection made the front page, albeit of the Arts section. They used the same photograph her parents had shown her in *Pravda*. It was from Opening Night. Dad center-stage, in Othello's costume—scarlet regimental coat and braids, white trousers, high-top black boots and metal dragoon's hat—holding out his hand with the grace of a dancer. Mom stepping out from behind the curtain to join him. He was looking at her, she was looking at him. The rest of the world might as well not exist. That tracked with Emma's experience.

The article underneath, however, was hardly the laudatory tribute published by *Pravda*. Her parents were called a series of names, of which *traitor* and *Judas* were the least offensive. Paul Robeson was invoked. Also, the Rosenbergs. That did seem to cover both angles nicely. Mom's old boss, Irna Phillips, who had just, coincidently, been named one of *TIME Magazine's* 100 Women of the Year, was quoted reminding the public how wholesome and all-American her shows were, and denouncing Miss Janowitz and Mr. Cain. Irna said she could barely remember either one working for her. She was based in Chicago, you know, and had very little contact with the New York office.

Mr. and Mrs. Geoffrey Moore of Harlem, NY would only refer to their son's stellar war record and his summa cum laude from Columbia. Mrs. Bluma Janowitz insisted a mistake had been made. Her daughter "wasn't like that. Not anymore. She promised me. She's a nice girl."

There was also a statement released by her parents. If you'd watched Rose on *A Citizen Summit*, you'd already heard everything she had to say on the subject.

As they'd both admitted, neither Mom nor Dad had any notion if their respective parents were still alive. There'd been no contact between them for twenty-eight years, not even gossip passed on by third parties. It sounded like Rose and Jonas didn't expect Emma's grandparents to know she existed.

Her parents had both begged Emma to rectify the situation.

No more stalling. It was time for her to try.

Chapter Fourteen

She decided to try Mom's mother first. The way Dad talked about them, his parents sounded a lot more intimidating. Without a phone number in the book, Emma was left with no choice but to head down to the Lower East Side. She took a taxi. If her grandmother happened to look out the window, Emma wanted her to see Rose's daughter arriving in style. She didn't want her grandmother thinking her child had been reduced to poverty and squalor. It's the least Mom would expect Emma to do.

There was no Bluma Janowitz listed along the buzzer on the apartment building's front door. The name next to 6F read: Chin. Emma waited until a woman about Mom's age stepped outside, leading a tiny dog outfitted in a pink, hand-knitted sweater-vest on a leash. Awkwardly blocking the woman's way, Emma asked if she might know of anyone named Janowitz who lived there, or maybe had lived there at one point, but then moved? If so, did she know where to?

"There was a Mrs. Janowitz on the sixth floor when I moved in—"

"Yes! That's her."

"Oh. Well, she died a couple of years ago."

And there went that. "Thank you," Emma said, wondering if she should ask where her grandmother was buried, if that was information Mom might want to have.

"Are you a friend of the family, dear?"

"I'm her granddaughter. Her daughter's daughter."

"How strange," the woman frowned, struggling to figure out who might be the liar in this scenario. "We were neighbors for years. She never mentioned having a daughter."

EVEN HER GRANDPARENTS' HOUSE was intimidating. Emma stood at the foot of a dozen brick lined stairs, peering up at the second-floor oak paneled door, one hand clutching the banister, the other nervously tapping her thigh. So, this was Harlem. Well, Hamilton Heights, technically. But Harlem, just the same. Everything Emma had been told about the storied neighborhood led her to expect, well, poverty and squalor. Gangs, purse-snatchers, rapists, all the consequences of a capitalist society which life in the USSR had guarded her from. Yet, save for recurring piles of garbage on the sidewalk—garbage which, to Emma's eyes, spoke of affluence, not poverty; garbage like discarded dining room sets, refrigerators, and televisions larger than any Emma had seen in even the wealthiest Moscow homes—Hamilton Heights was lovely. Elegant townhouses, row houses, and brownstones, all with extensive porches and windows framed by colorful plant-boxes and tasteful drapes. Sure, there were black metal bars on those windows, and snatches of graffiti on some stairs. But there was a dignity to it, a sense of pride, and, as a result, an atmosphere of grandeur. Her grandparents lived in a lovely neighborhood. If they still lived there. If they were still alive.

Emma rang the bell, listening to its ominous echo. A woman wearing an apron answered the door. Too young to be Emma's grandmother. Emma asked if this might be the home of Mr. and Mrs. Moore.

"Mrs. Moore," the woman confirmed in an accent Emma was learning to identify as Spanish. Back home, all Emma needed to know was that Muscovites said "sh" where those from Leningrad would say "ch," and that the capital had rounder o's while in Lenin's namesake city they were more precise with their p's. Everyone else was an uneducated peasant. It wasn't nearly as simple here. Here, even the highly educated spoke in a mish-mash of dialects.

Emma rushed through an explanation of who she was and what she wanted. The woman studied her suspiciously, then, having judged Emma acceptable, or, at least not much of a threat, beckoned her inside. She led Emma through the foyer, past the parlor, and into a small sitting room. Light streamed in through the window, illuminating an elderly woman who, nonetheless, sat perfectly straight-backed on a wingback chair below a Westwood lamp, framed on either side by paintings Emma was unfamiliar with, but could tell, at a glance, were valuable.

The woman stared at Emma curiously, yet with an automatic veneer of politeness and welcome. How old must she be, Emma wondered. Early eighties, most likely. Her hair was gray, neatly brushed and pulled back. She wore a skirt which skimmed the floor, and a blouse with a cameo brooch featuring a Black silhouette at the collar.

"I—I'm… I'm Emma Cain. My father is—"

"Jonas?" Her voice quavered. She instantly got it under control. "My Jonas?"

Emma nodded.

Her grandmother gestured towards the chesterfield sofa. "Sit down."

Emma did as she was told.

The woman studied her intently before finally pronouncing, "You look like your mother."

Emma couldn't tell if it was a compliment or not. She could think of numerous reasons why it wouldn't be. So, she said nothing in return.

"Emma…" her grandmother stretched the name into multiple syllables, assessing if she liked it.

"Dad said it was after his Granny Emmaline," she rushed to make the offering.

"Not after Emma Goldman, the anarchist?" A sly smile twitched along the older woman's lips. It was the same smile Dad got when he was teasing.

Emma smiled back. And shrugged innocently.

"How is he? My son. How is his life? Is he happy?"

"He is." Emma thought of Dad's passionate defense of her mother and the adventure she'd led him to and felt confident in her appraisal. "He's a star. He performs in several plays a year, in Moscow and on tour. Also, television. My mother writes them, and he acts in them. He's done almost all of Shakespeare." Emma hoped that would impress.

"Does he ever talk about us? Does he ever wonder if we're happy?"

Emma wasn't sure how to answer. Yes, Dad did talk about his parents. It's how Emma knew enough to feel nervous approaching them. He talked about growing up in Harlem, and his life from before. He always did it outside of Mom's earshot, though. Not because he feared her disapproval. Because he feared her thinking he missed it. So as far as Mom knew, Dad never thought about his former life at all.

"Does he know what happened to us after he left?"

That Emma honestly didn't have an answer to. She suspected not, since he apparently wasn't aware that his father had died.

"Does he know that Geoffrey was fired from his job? That I was fired from mine? We can't have the parents of a subversive working here, they said. All the boards we used to serve on, all our friends… gone. Even the ones who sympathized, even the ones who agreed, those so-called fellow travelers. They couldn't risk standing up for us, couldn't risk being associated with us. A lifetime of work, generations, proving we were trustworthy, proving we were as good as anybody else, proving we deserved to be here, we were good Americans. All of it gone. Blink of an eye—and all of it gone."

"I'm sorry," Emma said. Because she couldn't think of anything else to say.

"Why?" Her grandmother dismissed. "None of this is your fault."

Emma couldn't think of anything to say about that, either. She could, however, suspect whose fault her grandmother did think it was. She felt an urge to apologize for resembling the culprit.

"How are you in New York?" Annabelle asked. "I thought you weren't allowed out."

That wasn't precisely true. Her parents were allowed to leave the Soviet Union. The only stipulation was that they had to leave Emma behind. As insurance to make sure they returned. Mom and Dad had every intention of returning, so that wasn't a hurdle.

"The opposite, actually." Emma wasn't specifically keen on defending the USSR. But she did feel obliged to defend why her parents had never visited their families. "They were afraid that, if they came back to America, they'd be arrested, and their passports taken away. Then they'd be stuck here, and I'd be left behind. It happened to this American couple in the 1930s. Eugene and Peggy Dennis. They left their son, Tim, in the Soviet Union while they returned to the US, and then Eugene was put into prison, so they couldn't go back for Tim."

"What was this Dennis creature sent to prison for?"

"Calling for the violent overthrow of the American government," Emma mumbled.

"Hm," her grandmother said. Then she asked, "So why wasn't the boy sent back to live with his parents in the States? His mother wasn't in prison, was she?"

"I don't know," Emma admitted. "But that's why the singer Paul Robeson..."

Emma had hoped that invoking the internationally-esteemed figure would demonstrate for her grandmother that, despite growing up across the world, Emma had been educated about important African-American figures in history. Instead, she could feel the contempt radiating off Annabelle Moore after Emma prefaced Robeson's name with his profession. As though the older woman might not know who he was.

Deciding to quit while she was behind, Emma raced through the remainder of her tale. "It's why Robeson was advised not to leave his son in a Soviet boarding school while he came back to the US. And that's why Mom and Dad never took the risk."

"But you're here. You took the risk."

"It's different for me. My husband has a job here. One officially sanctioned by the Soviet government. He will be hosting a television show."

"Will your father come and visit you now?"

"I don't know," Emma admitted. Everything from meeting Dennis, to marrying Dennis, to preparing to move to America with Dennis had been such a whirlwind, Emma hadn't been left a moment during which to consider the possibility—much less discuss it with Mom or Dad.

Inspiration struck. "Dad and I, we were on American television a few weeks ago." She didn't need to add that Mom had been there, too. "It was your Mr. Donahue, and my husband Dennis. They hosted this conversation between Soviet and US citizens. Would you like to see it? I'm sure I could get a recording of—"

"No." Her grandmother shot down the proposal so quickly, Emma didn't even have time to complete it.

She couldn't help it. She had to ask, "You're not even curious? You don't want to see your son? After all these years?"

"If my son wishes to see me, he can do the same thing you did, just ring that doorbell."

"He misses you." Dad had never said as much to Emma. But she knew it was true, all the same. Mom's pretending to the contrary couldn't change that.

"I miss him," her grandmother felt no qualms confessing. Just like she felt no qualms adding, "But he made his choice. Now all of us need to pay for it. Including Jonas."

EMMA LEFT AFTER AN HOUR. She told herself it was because she could see Annabelle was growing tired, but truth to be told, Emma's energy was the one flagging. It's not that she found it difficult to watch what she said. That habit was as autonomic for Emma as a heartbeat. It was that, at home, she knew what was expected of her and what reaction to her words was equally as expected in return. Emma had no idea what Annabelle wanted to hear or how she might respond. How did people do it? Engage in conversations without a concrete script, not knowing what might inadvertently offend, or what was required to curry favor? How did average Americans survive dozens of different interactions within any given day, needing to first feel out or, worse, guess where the other stood on a multitude of political, social, and personal issues, then adjust their conversations accordingly? It was as if you were required to become a different person depending on who you were talking to and what you wanted from them. How did this not induce some sort of multiple personality disorder? No wonder she'd heard that all New Yorkers saw a psychiatric analyst on a regular basis. But even within the medical office, how could you know the right thing to say to them to avoid a diagnosis of antisocial personality and a risk of forced institutionalization?

The more time she spent in America, the better Emma understood why Dennis had wanted her to be the one to accompany him.

He'd been right. Sexual compatibility was a wonderful thing, but that could be worked on. They were, in fact, fine in that department, no complaints. But a shared sense of cynicism, that was, indeed, the true kismet. And they were more than fine in that respect. At the end of every day, Dennis and Emma reconvened to share notes on what they'd done, whom they'd met, what they'd learned, and what they'd said versus what they'd really meant. Also to laugh about the performances they'd put on.

It was during those twilight hours that Emma felt like her marriage came the closest to her parents'. She'd never expected to match them in their mutual admiration society. The way her parents adored each other was, frankly, a bit unseemly. Why would you ever yield that much control over your personal happiness to another person? Worse, why would you let them know you'd yielded that much control to them?

But Emma had hoped to at least come close to Mom and Dad's sense of comfort with each other. That no matter what happened outside their apartment's doors, inside was a place where they would always be accepted, supported, and agreed with. Home was where you hid from the world. Home was where you practiced your act, but didn't need to put it on.

Emma thought she had that with Dennis. Well, she came close. In their apartment, they could make fun of the people they were forced to become outside of it. They reassured each other that they were the sane ones, everyone else was crazy. It was a very pleasant feeling.

But was it love?

Did love matter?

Those were the two questions Emma applied great effort into never asking herself.

Obviously, she didn't love Dennis the way her mother loved her father. But that, as she might have mentioned previously, was an unseemly amount. And ridiculous. And dangerous. Also impossible for people who saw the world realistically, like Emma and Dennis did, rather than through the rose-colored glasses her mother jammed onto Jonas and Emma's noses and refused to ever let them take off.

But did Emma love Dennis at all?

She loved talking to him. Especially behind other people's backs. She loved being with him, especially when they could catch each other's eye over the heads of a crowded room and know exactly what the other was thinking. She loved the lifestyle he'd introduced her to, and one Emma intended to become accustomed to as soon as possible. And if he disappeared tomorrow, she would definitely miss him, not just the lifestyle.

Yet Emma couldn't help thinking that the way in which she'd miss him wasn't the way a wife should miss her husband. Emma would miss Dennis like the co-worker you ate lunch with every day gossiping about the institution which employed you. One that you were happy to grab a drink with after work, meet up for a movie, invite to your Christmas party. A co-worker that, if he were transferred to a different position on a different floor, you'd think about fondly, visit once in a while and wish he'd stuck around; it was kind of dull without him. But you would survive without him.

Emma suspected that couldn't be said about her parents.

She suspected she knew what it said about her and Dennis, too.

BUT EMMA NEVER THOUGHT about such things. It was pointless. And unproductive. And, most importantly, boring. From the moment she set foot in the United States, Emma preferred to never be bored. Boredom was what allowed the unwelcome thoughts to come creeping in.

Which was why she was delighted to come home from her visit

with her grandmother—she hadn't asked Emma to call her grandmother, to call her anything, in fact, so Emma stuck to the older
woman's full name, even in her own mind—to find Dennis dressed
in a tuxedo.

Her husband was one of those men who looked particularly
dashing in formalwear. He was so tall and thin, regular clothes emphasized his lankiness, like an adolescent who woke up one morning
in possession of gangly limbs he had no notion how to operate. Formalwear, on the other hand, smoothed out the jutting lines, granting
an elegant wholeness to his movements.

If Dennis was dressed in a tuxedo, that could mean only one
delightful thing.

"We've been invited to a party. And you won't believe what this
one is for!"

Chapter Fifteen

They took a taxi to the event being held on Riverside Drive, even though it was less than twenty blocks northwest of their own apartment. Emma thought it was a silly expense when they could just walk. Dennis said it was expected of people like them.

"Who are we?" Emma wondered.

"The dancing monkeys," he grinned.

The doorman smirked when they announced who Emma and Dennis were there to see. The elevator operator discreetly rolled his eyes as he pulled the lever to transport them to the duplex penthouse. Emma was sure they didn't expect her or Dennis to notice. But she'd spent a lifetime being studied surreptitiously. She knew when she was being judged. And mocked.

The elevator doors opened into a narrow, mirrored foyer with a coat rack. A second door led straight into the duplex. In a two-steps-down sunken living room, what looked to be over one hundred people in a variety of tuxedos, sports jackets, gowns, and cocktail dresses mingled from buffet table to full-service bar. Sunset through the twelfth-floor windows overlooking the Hudson River bounced off the crystal chandelier and the assortment of diamond jewelry, not to mention the guests' flawless, sparkling teeth.

"This," Emma whispered in Dennis' ear, "is the Socialist Workers Party of New York?"

"You don't recognize the oppressed masses when you see them?" he marveled, before smoothly turning, arms outstretched to heartily shake hand and elbow, in the American politician style, of the man stepping forward to greet them. "Emma, I do not think you've met. This is Larry. He owns the network which broadcasts my program. Larry, this is my wife, Emma."

"It's a pleasure to meet you," Emma said to the man who owned the means of production at a Socialist workers meeting.

"Your husband is doing terrific work. His first show ranked third overall for the week. We can't wait to see what he comes up with next!"

"That is very kind of you," Emma said to the man at the Socialist workers meetings who was raking in advertising revenue based on her husband's labor. Though Dennis' actual show had no commercials—Soviet Central Television had insisted on it—there were ads at the beginning and at the end. Soviet Central Television had insisted on splitting the profits.

"You're Emma Cain, aren't you?" A woman stepped up to discreetly pull her aside while Dennis and Larry continued discussing how wonderful it was that they were getting the word out about labor uprisings around the globe. One of the first things Dennis had told Emma about his new employer was that while the majority of NYC's television workers were unionized, Larry had managed to get an exception so that his didn't need to be.

"I wrote my master's thesis at Barnard about your parents," the woman trilled.

"Then you must know more about them than I do," Emma replied sincerely.

It triggered a twitter of merriment in response.

"I focused on the repressive racial climate of 1950s America which made it impossible for your parents to stage their *Othello* here, and why they had no option but to immigrate to the USSR in order to achieve their full artistic expression. I can't imagine how wonderful it must be for them to perform without fear of reactionary backlash, like in our commercial sphere."

"Yes, they couldn't stage *Othello* the way they wanted to in America in 1957."

"Would you believe the United States is still banning works of art they don't agree with? This wonderful little Canadian film, *If You Love This Planet*—it urges nuclear disarmament for the US and the Soviet Union, it advocates for peace, what could be controversial about that?—this lovely little film was banned by the Canadian Broadcasting corporation, and the US called it foreign political propaganda! Only the London Socialist Film Co-op was brave enough to screen it! Why, if it hadn't won the Academy Award for Best Documentary Short a few years back, no one would have even known it existed!"

"A movie banned in America won an American movie award?" Emma double-checked.

"Yes! When the director accepted it, she thanked Ronald Reagan for the extra publicity his condemning it had gotten her. Isn't that absolutely radical?"

"What happened to the director?" Emma wondered how long US prison terms for such infractions were. A data point Dennis, and she as his wife, would be well-advised to calculate into all their decisions moving forward.

"Oh, don't worry. She just finished a film about women anti-war activists and she's shooting a new one about the nuclear age. She's a warrior like your parents. She won't let American Fascist repression stop her."

"has it been immensely difficult? Picking up and switching countries the way you did?" As soon as one woman decided she'd monopolized Emma's time enough—or maybe she grew tired of Emma failing to understand what she was saying, it must be a language barrier—another was happy to glob onto her in between the hors d'oeuvre trays.

"Oh. No. It's been fine. Everyone has been very kind and welcoming. Americans are so friendly! They smile at you. Even strangers on the street."

"I try to imagine the world through your eyes. It must be heartbreaking, coming from the USSR, seeing the homeless on our streets, the blatant racism. You want to assist, everyone in this room does. Though it's such a tightrope to walk. My mother always had African-American household help. Colored, they called it in those days, can you imagine? But I refuse to go down that path, absolutely refuse. So condescending, don't you agree? As if Blacks were put on earth to serve whites. What kind of message does it send to my children, seeing that day in and day out? The exploitation stops with me. I only hire white servants. To set an example. Sometimes from South America. As long as they can look white. You are so lucky, Emma, to never have to even think about such things where you're from."

"DO YOU PREFER BEING CALLED Black or African-American?" This time it was a man, dressed less formally than some of the others, who'd decided to chat Emma up. She wasn't sure who he was, only that he wore several colorful buttons along his lapels featuring slogans like *Labor is entitled to all it creates*, *Direct action gets the goods*, and *Kickin' ass for the working class*!

"I don't know," she admitted, panicking. "I've never given it any thought." She'd only recently stopped saying Negro!

He nodded sympathetically. "Issue probably never comes up in the Soviet Union, racism being outlawed. Here, we wrestle with it every damn day. Don't want to offend, say the wrong thing. That's why I was excited to see you. I thought you might know." He looked glumly about the room, "There's nobody else to ask."

Emma hadn't noticed. She was so accustomed to being in the minority wherever she went that this gathering looked no different from any other.

"I am so in awe of your father," the man went on. "Most astute of him to realize that the USSR was the only place for a man like him. He was highly educated, right?"

"He graduated from Columbia University."

"Maybe that's what made the difference. You would not believe what a difficult time we have here, convincing the lower classes that Socialism is their path out of persecution. They're so brainwashed by capitalist rhetoric, television, movies, comic books. It's like talking to a brick wall. Maybe if more of them were as highly educated as your father… It's tragic how they can't see what's in their own best interests! That puts the onus on us. It's a grueling responsibility. I'm exhausted." He handed his tumbler to a passing servant.

"I AM SO IN AWE OF YOUR MOTHER." A woman who Emma would eventually recognize as an actress playing the role of Mother on what Dennis explained was a very popular television situation comedy, confessed to Emma, "I wish my parents had been as smart. My grandparents came over in 1905. It made sense then. The pogroms, the Czars, that unpleasantness. They were devoted Socialists. My parents were the original Red Diaper Babies! I swear, there wasn't a left-wing summer camp they didn't attend. I understand why my grandparents left, but what I cannot fathom is why they didn't turn right around and return to the Soviet Union the minute the revolution triumphed? It makes no sense, right? Everything they wanted had finally come true, and they were still planted in this backwards country?"

Emma had nothing to say to that. Not that her participation was necessary. This was clearly a monologue. She'd been raised by performers; she knew the drill.

"Maybe my grandparents were afraid. You know, after everything they'd lived through. They probably didn't dare let themselves believe that the USSR was for real, or that it wouldn't be undermined by Western forces. But what was my parents' excuse? They could have gone at any time, just like your mother! They made noises about having careers, friends, a life here. But your mother didn't let that stop her. She was so brave. If only my parents had been brave like yours, I could have avoided this American rat-race, this endless competition to earn the most money, the biggest home, the fanciest car, keeping up with the Joneses… I'm trapped, Emma. And I could have been free, like you."

"YOU MUST VISIT OUR SCHOOL." Tag team, a married couple took their turn welcoming Emma. "Both our children attend. It's called The Little Red Schoolhouse. We've been at the forefront of progressive education since the 1920s! We encourage cooperation, activism, social justice, and acceptance. The Meeropol boys are alumni. That's the adopted name of those poor Rosenberg orphans." They assumed Emma knew about Julius and Ethel Rosenberg, put to death for the crime of passing radar, sonar, and atomic secrets to the Soviets. Mom told Emma about them, including that Julius attended the same Lower East Side high-school as she had, graduating right before she started. "Oh, and, of course, Angela Davis." Their coy smiles made it clear why Emma should feel a particular affinity with the activist. She unconsciously ran a hand along the back of her hair, newly straightened for the occasion. "We took her in during her junior year of high school. Poor thing was absolutely stagnating in Alabama. Why, if we hadn't extended a helping hand, who knows what might have happened to that brilliant mind!"

"That is very nice that New York City is supportive of such a progressive school."

"Oh, please! That couldn't be further from the truth. They pretended to be supportive in the beginning. We started as a public-private partnership, where the Department of Education gave us money to operate. But then, as soon as the Depression hit, they used the lack of funds as an excuse to shut us down! We transitioned to a private school and have been independent ever since. No government bureaucrat will keep us from teaching our collective values!"

"So now the school is paid for by the Socialist Workers Party?"

"In part. And, of course, everyone pays their fair share in tuition; we're very cooperative."

"In America, you pay for school? How much does it cost?"

"A few thousand dollars a year, we do our best to keep tuition as low as possible, so that the children can interact with peers from all walks of life. That's very important to us."

"They do not have free schools in America? Government schools?"

"I realize this is difficult for you to understand, coming from a classless society, but, the government schools, they're called public, they are terribly... oh, how can I explain—they're just terribly middle-class. They teach children bourgeois values like individualism. No surprise, they were established to perpetuate an oppressive, colonialist, capitalist way of life. The only way we can be certain our children value an egalitarian community where all are respected not based on how much money they have but on what they contribute to the greater whole, is by removing them from the brainwashing of our government. We need to protect them from any ideas which might prevent their growing into true revolutionaries, untainted by status quo pablum."

EMMA DIDN'T GET A CHANCE to speak with Dennis all night. They were constantly being tugged in separate directions, here to meet a publisher who'd just released a compendium of Chairman Mao's quotations, like *The Little Red Book*, but not quite so political; or there to say hello to a banker who'd visited the USSR as a Yale student and was just enchanted by the Soviet system of no-cost medical care. He'd been considering becoming a doctor, but once he realized how inequitable American medicine was, he wanted no part of such injustice.

The next time Emma saw her husband, he'd been pressed to the front of the room and introduced by Larry as their guest of honor. Larry thanked Dennis and Emma for joining them tonight. He hoped he'd helped them see that not all of America was greedy and materialistic. That there were people like them out there, fighting the good fight, supporting the USSR in their struggle for workers' rights, an end to racism, and liberation for the Third World. Larry nudged Dennis to make a speech. Emma's husband never shirked from the spotlight.

He held up his champagne flute in a toast. The audience followed. Dennis thanked the assembled for their warm welcome. He thanked them for showing him the true heart—and the true power—of America. He thanked them for being free-thinkers rather than meek, obedient sheep. He thanked them for instilling him with confidence about the future. There could and there would be peace between their two countries, if men and women like them could gather in friendship, as they had tonight. He thanked them for being them. He drank a toast to them being them.

When the group spontaneously broke into a rousing chorus of *L'Internationale*, first in French, then in English, then in Russian—the gentleman who'd rushed over to accompany them on the Fazioli grand piano looked like someone Emma might have seen in concert in Moscow—she finally caught her husband's eye. His expression, just for her, said: *This is only the beginning.*

AND HE WAS RIGHT. Dennis' program wasn't just a ratings winner in its third week. It kept on going. His initial two year contract was extended for two more years, and then for two more years after that. As his network signed up more and more subscribers, Dennis grew more and more famous. He was recognized on the street. He was asked for his autograph, a ceremony Emma failed to understand. What value did Dennis' signature have? Was it contractual proof of a chance meeting?

He was invited to lecture at universities across the country. He appeared on TV shows outside his own, on more popular networks than his own, explaining the USSR's perspective on whatever happened to be the topic of the day. Dennis talked about himself: poor orphan, son of disgraced enemies of the people, and just look at what heights he'd been allowed to achieve! Who needed the American Dream when the Soviet one was so much more cinematic?

Dennis also talked about Emma. Emma's parents, mostly. Rose and Jonas' story had once been buried by the US press. Now it was tabloid fodder. A book was pieced together by an author who'd never met Rose or Jonas, reached out to Emma, or run the manuscript by any of them. It was an embellished rehash of the handful of newspaper stories which had been allowed to hit the wires in the early days of the Cains' defection, before it was decided that writing about them might encourage others to follow in their footsteps. There was even a Made-For-TV movie, though, like Dennis' news program, it ran on cable. The rumor was that Procter & Gamble, wary of how they might come off regarding Jonas' firing from *Find Your Light*, had threatened to pull advertising from any network which dared broadcast such slander. This kerfuffle only served to increase awareness of the telefilm and raise its ratings.

Having heard Emma's retelling of the censored documentary short which won an Oscar, Dennis wondered if they should thank Ronald Reagan, as well.

"We should thank Mom and Dad," Emma said.

They'd only gone back to visit her parents in Moscow once. They brought along a VHS tape of the TV movie about their lives. Mom and Dad admitted they had a video-cassette player. It was vital, if they were to see what sorts of films and teleplays were being written in the West. The four of them watched together. When it was over, Emma waited for Mom or Dad to say something. She had no idea how they might react to this trip through a parallel universe.

Finally, Jonas deadpanned to Rose, "You could have written it better."

"You could have acted it better."

"It's a good thing—" he began.

Mom finished Dad's thought, "Irna isn't alive to see it."

"She would definitely have notes."

"For both of us."

To Emma's surprise, neither parent asked many questions about her life in the United States. Which was good. Because Emma had spent the bulk of the flight worrying about what she would tell them. Her America was nothing like the lives her parents described. Emma realized it was a different time and she was in a very different position. But she also understood, if on a subconscious level, that Mom wasn't interested in hearing how things had gotten better for people like them. That wouldn't fit Rose's narrative. She'd rather go on pretending.

Rose hadn't even asked if Emma did as she requested and looked up her grandmother. Emma was the one who brought up her attempt to fulfill that promise. And report that Rose's mother had died. Mom didn't even thank Emma for the information. She nodded her head to indicate she'd heard and walked away.

Emma was able to give Dad better news. His father was gone, but his mother was still alive. She wanted Jonas to visit her.

"You can do it now," Emma prompted gently. "It's different under Gorbachev. People are allowed to travel back and forth without fear of not being able to go back."

He looked as sorely tempted as Emma had ever seen him by anything. Ultimately, though, Jonas shook his head, "Your mother wouldn't like that."

Who cared what Mom thought, Emma wanted to scream. *Why was it always about her, why was it always about cosseting her feelings, maintaining her delusions?* But Emma knew the time for such questions had long passed. Jonas had made his decision, like Emma had made hers. His life was shackled to Rose's, the same way Emma's was to Dennis'.

And like Dad, Emma could claim no regrets. She enjoyed a life where her parents were famous, her husband was famous, but she was famous adjacent. Sure, she was recognized when she was with Dennis, and every once in a rare while, on the street by herself. But, overall, Emma was anonymous in a city which made that happy state easier than most.

After it became clear she and Dennis were in the US for the long haul, Emma advised her husband that she didn't intend to spend the bulk of her days waiting for him to come home and take her to yet another party. She was happy to go to parties, she understood how crucial they were for his position. But she wanted a life of her own. Which could best be accomplished via a job.

Initially, Emma's visa was solely as Dennis' wife. She had no right to seek employment. But after Emma vocalized her feelings, back-channel phone calls were made, and what do you know, Mrs. Dennis Kagan now had a microbiology research position at a lab affiliated with Columbia. It was doing clinical trials for weight loss medication instead of looking for ways to increase food production—America already had plenty of the latter but never enough of the former. That was fine with Emma. She appreciated the silence of the lab. So different from the non-stop words being generated at home.

The only time Emma's name came up in public was during Dennis' show. Whenever he had a guest on who challenged Dennis' spirited defense of the Soviet Union and their practices by bringing up anti-Semitism, Dennis would parry with himself as an example. He was the son of two Jews who'd been executed by Stalin and look at how high he'd been able to rise! Look at his wife! Her Jewish mother had chosen to leave America for the USSR. Would she have done so if there was still anti-Semitism there? If his challenger accused the

Soviet Union of racism toward its non-Russian population, Dennis would suggest they look at his wife! Again! Her Black father had chosen to leave America for the USSR. Would he have done so if there was racism there?

Dennis' counterexamples worked to silence nearly everyone. Even loud and loquacious conservatives like William F. Buckley and George Plimpton pronounced Dennis a delightfully well-read and witty fellow, if terribly misguided, but considering his tragic back-story, who could blame him? The only ones not charmed by Emma's husband were the demographic living in Brighton Beach, Brooklyn. Whenever Dennis said something they believed to be particularly, egregiously wrong about the merits of the Soviet Union, these Russian-speaking recent refugees from all the republics had a tendency to descend on his midtown studios, picket-signs in hand. It was Dennis' favorite part of the job. As soon as he saw even a handful of protesting bodies beneath his thirty-eighth-floor office, Dennis would grab a microphone and a camera crew and head downstairs for a chat.

He loved listening to their rants, letting them exhaust themselves yelling and sputtering, before asking when they'd left the Soviet Union.

Nineteen seventy-seven, came the answer. Nineteen seventy-eight, seventy-nine, eighty.

"Why, that was over a decade ago," Dennis would exclaim, as if this were the first time he'd heard such a reply. How could they speak with confidence about what things were like in the USSR now? Who was the viewing audience supposed to trust, ten-year-old memories, or Dennis, who'd been back last summer? Who spoke with Moscow every day!

As there was no adequate rejoinder to that one, most critics stopped and slunk away, mumbling under their breaths, but no longer at the camera. For those who persevered, who insisted they were also in touch with people still living in Moscow, in Leningrad, in Odessa, in Kiev, in Alma-Ata, too, so, yeah, Buster, they knew what was really going on in a way Dennis refused to admit, Dennis would ask who was paying them to say these things?

After all, Dennis reasonably pointed out, he was being transparent in broadcasting that he was being paid by the USSR to offer his commentary, so who was paying them? Everybody knew nothing in America came for free; they had to be someone's employees. Why were they afraid to admit who they were working for? Dennis wasn't afraid. And here Dennis was the one they claimed came from a repressive regime!

Just like the question of when one stopped beating one's wife, it was a tricky charge to defend. Dennis usually won on those rounds, too.

And thus, life went comfortably on for them both.

Until August 19, 1991, when Dennis got an emergency phone call at home, telling him to hightail it to the studio for a live broadcast. As he was throwing on his clothes, tying his shoes, and trying to comb his hair in case there wouldn't be time to do it before he was thrust on the air, Emma turned on the bedroom TV.

And watched their world flip upside down.

Chapter Sixteen

There were tanks in Red Square. How could there be tanks in Red Square? Sure, Emma had watched them lumber past the Kremlin on holidays like May Day and Victory Day. She'd sat on Dad's shoulders and feverishly waved her little red flag along with every other child privileged to warrant such a close-up view of the parade. But she'd never seen tanks on the street during a regular weekday. Except this wasn't a regular weekday.

There were tanks in Red Square. There were tanks near the Russian Soviet Federative Socialist Republic's Parliament Building, nicknamed The White House, lest the Americans think they were the only ones allowed to have one. Warships anchored at the port closest to Mikhail Gorbachev's *dacha*, and the local airport had been ordered closed. Freedom of the press was officially dissolved by the newly formed State Committee on the State of Emergency, headed by the Vice President, the Premier, the Interior Minister, the Defense Minister, the Chairman of the KGB, the First Deputy Chairman of the Defense Council, the Chairman of the Peasants' Union, and the President of the Association of State Enterprises. Every hardliner who'd been against Gorbachev's reforms. They wanted the General Secretary gone. This was a coup.

This wasn't like Khrushchev. Emma had been almost six years old in 1964, when she'd heard Mom and Dad discussing how the man who'd made the Soviet Union open enough for the Cains to move there had been voted out of office. The Central Committee blamed him for various failed economic policies, including giving more power to local provinces at the expense of centralized Moscow control. They derided him for his botched handling of the Cuban Missile Crisis, when he gave in to the Americans and removed Soviet weapons from the allied island, followed, even more humiliatingly, by his withdrawal of the IL–28 bombers. They accused him of voluntarism and immodest behavior. Mom stressed how wonderful it was that, in the USSR, an ineffective leader could be promptly removed by a simple, efficient vote of the ruling council, instead of America, where they either had to wait for the next, cumbersome election cycle or attempt a recall, which was time-consuming and allowed the bungling politician to keep causing damage while each vote from every polling place in the nation was tediously counted.

But this wasn't 1964. This was a military takeover. Gorbachev was under house arrest. And there were tanks in Red Square, and in front of The White House.

There was one more reason why this wasn't like Khrushchev in 1964. There were people in the streets. Dozens of them, hundreds, thousands. And they were converging on the tanks, on Red Square, on The White House. Her whole life, Emma had been told that the USSR was famous for its spontaneous demonstrations of support for the government, one organized by the people. The boast had come up during Donahue's program. What had one of the audience members testified to? "I took part in a protest meeting, protesting not my own government, but against international militarization. We all fully agreed with the policy of our government against militarization. We do have demonstrations, and we demonstrate our views openly and frankly."

Why then did Emma feel like she was only seeing her first such gathering now?

Most of them were young people, dressed in jeans and T-shirts and sneakers and light windbreakers. And they were climbing up on the tanks, over the tanks, towards The White House. And there was Boris Yeltsin, the President of the Russian Federation. Yeltsin was also climbing up on a tank, his silver hair blowing in the wind. Yeltsin in his brown suit with a brown tie, too fat to button it properly, but he was climbing up on a platform; the Russian Federation flag, not the Soviet one, but the Russian Federation flag behind him. And he was reading from a proclamation declaring the coup illegal, calling for a general strike in protest. His security detail tried holding him back, but Yeltsin promised, "They will not shoot their President!" He advised the armed soldiers who claimed they were only following orders, "Here is an order then: take your equipment and go back to base."

The crowds cheered. Yeltsin grabbed the arm of the head of the Tamanskaya elite forces after the commander announced his soldiers would be joining the rebellion. Yeltsin pulled him up on stage and handed him a Russian Federation flag to wave. Yeltsin held up his fist in defiance.

Emma asked Dennis, "What is happening?"

For the first time since they'd met, her husband mumbled, dazed, "I don't know."

BY THE TIME DENNIS MADE IT onto the air—no make-up, sweat dotting his hairline from the mad rush to midtown—US President George H.W. Bush had condemned the coup. Soviet Vice-President Gennadi Yanayev announced that Mikhail Gorbachev was ill and would be staying at his summer home for the time being. Lithuania's president encouraged passive resistance, miners across the eleven time-zone nation went on strike, and Yeltsin proclaimed himself the legal head of Russia.

Dennis was reading the news live as it came in. Emma had never seen her husband so pale—and it wasn't the lack of make-up. His hands were shaking, rustling the papers he was holding. He stumbled multiple times trying to keep up with the teleprompter. His accent, usually barely perceptible and prompting coos of, "You speak English so well, Mr. Kagan," was out now in full force. He turned his Ws into Vs, rolled his Rs, growled his Ks particularly hard. He was breaking down in front of their eyes. Viewers at home attributed it to worry about his homeland. But Emma knew better. Dennis was worried about himself.

Emma was worried too. For him, for her, but also for Mom and Dad. She'd dialed their home number multiple times, never expecting to get an answer, unsurprised when it simply rang and rang. She tried friends from university and her former job. She even tried calling Soviet Central Television, hoping Dennis' name might get her answers denied to everyone else, but nothing was getting through.

He stayed on the air for almost twelve hours straight. He reported that President Bush had called the coup leaders to negotiate for Gorbachev's reinstatement. Bush then called Yeltsin to offer his support. Emma guessed Bush's phone connection was stronger than hers. Dennis reported on the mayor of Leningrad condemning the coup, on the Ukrainian and Moldovan parliaments condemning it. He reported that the President of Kazakhstan had resigned from the Politburo and the Central Committee in protest. That Estonia was declaring its independence from the Soviet Union and that the Army's Baltic commander had declared control over not just Estonia, but Latvia and Lithuania, as well, followed by Yeltsin announcing he was now in control of Russia's military forces.

Emma couldn't breathe. She couldn't eat, she couldn't sleep. She couldn't think. What was happening? How could it be happening? The protesters kept coming. In Moscow and in Leningrad primarily, but in other parts of the country, as well. They were setting up barricades, braving not just the tanks and the machine guns, but the consequences of what might happen to them after everything had died down, after order was restored, after the Soviet Union was the Soviet Union again. Because this was not the Soviet Union. Emma had no idea what this was. She'd never seen anything like it before.

Dennis' voice began giving out as he entered his fourteenth hour of broadcasting. He was constantly clearing his throat, needing to make an effort to swallow, choking on even the water he was sipping during commercial breaks to keep from sounding like a lifetime smoker.

By the time he finally got home, Emma expected Dennis to

collapse into bed and sleep for at least the next few hours. She was prepared to continue watching the news so she could keep him posted on what had happened while he rested. But instead of stumbling in exhausted, Dennis was wired. He couldn't stop pacing, couldn't stop talking.

"What are we supposed to do? I don't know what we're supposed to do. If I side with the coup plotters and they lose, I won't have any credibility with this government anymore, much less with the American people. You know how they love their revolutions and their underdog stories. It's in their DNA. But if I side with Gorbachev and Yeltsin and they lose, that's it, I'm done. They'll call us back home. Who knows what will happen to us then, how they'll punish us. And hardliners always win in the end. Always. Look at Khrushchev. His reign was an aberration, just like Gorbachev's will be. The logical thing to do is to back the coup. But what if I'm wrong?"

"We don't have to go back," Emma offered tentatively. "Even if you're fired. We could stay here in America."

"And do what? I told you, if I back the wrong cause, I'll be ostracized. Nobody will want to hear anything I have to say." He strode to the window, gazing over Central Park, muttering as much to himself as to Emma, "How did this happen? How can I not know what to do? I always know what to do. They made it so easy, so clear, so obvious. Why is it different now?"

"The Emergency Committee didn't expect this level of resistance. Did you expect it?"

"Hell, no. Who could have expected this? We're Soviets. We're programmed to take a kick in the back, hit the ground, and let the tanks roll over us, if that's what our government tells us to do. But they're fighting the tanks. Did you see? They're standing up to goddamn tanks in goddamn Red Square!"

"I tried to call Mom and Dad." Emma wasn't sure if changing the subject would calm him or fan the flames. "No answer."

"Oh, shit, and that's another thing. You say if things don't work out, we could stay here. If we're on the wrong side, what do you think will happen to your parents? If they can't punish us, who do you think they'll make an example of, instead?"

"No," Emma shook her head. "No. Mom and Dad, they're celebrities in Russia. They're very important people. They wouldn't dare… besides, Mom and Dad didn't do anything wrong. I don't think."

"Stop it, Emma. You're talking to me. We both know what happens to very important people who cross the Soviet government, especially very important artists, especially very important Jewish artists. The Night of the Murdered Poets? Mikhoels beaten so badly they couldn't even hold an open casket funeral for him, despite claiming his death was an accident? How many writers sent to gulags? How many composers, painters, filmmakers?"

But that was the problem. Emma didn't know. Dennis just assumed she did. While the events he referenced may have been whispered around kitchen tables in the middle of the night in cramped Soviet apartments, Emma's parents—rather, Emma's mother—deliberately avoided any references to murdered poets, or to tortured Yiddish actors. Brutality didn't fit the narrative she'd constructed around their new homeland.

"What are we supposed to do then?" Emma wasn't used to Dennis asking questions. She was used to him having all the answers. It's why she was with him. So, she didn't have to be responsible for doing either.

"I don't know," he screamed in frustration, voice cracking and devolving into a parched cough. "I don't have any fucking idea!"

BY THE TIME DENNIS slid back on the air for the evening broadcast, he'd sprayed his throat with enough analgesic to sound raspy, but intelligible. He'd showered, re-combed his hair, put on a fresh white shirt and dark suit to bespeak the seriousness of their crisis, and dabbed at the bags under his eyes with concealer. Dennis was calm and in control, everything he hadn't been at home, everything the American public expected from their earnest, charming guide through the intricate world of Soviet politics.

An even-keeled Dennis briefed the Western world that Emergency Committee members were starting to resign—for health reasons. Nonetheless, the army was charging the barricades in front of the Russian Parliament building.

Protesters, numbering in the tens of thousands now, pushed back, setting two tanks on fire, even as a dozen others headed straight for the makeshift barricades, despite the clusters of people sitting atop them. Dissenters on the ground linked hands to form a human chain to keep the deadly machines at bay. Emma suspected they were thinking of China's Tiananmen Square pro-reform uprising of two years prior. They were remembering the lone youth with the shopping bag in each arm, facing down a convoy of tanks. Emma suspected they were not thinking about the hundreds of thousands massacred or wounded in the six weeks which followed. They were not thinking about the pro-democracy advocates arrested, exiled, and executed. They were not thinking about the civilians murdered in riots outside the square. If Emma were still in the USSR, she might not have known either. But she'd watched it unfold nearly live in the US. So, she knew, even if the Soviet young people on her TV now didn't.

Shots rang out in front of The White House. In the smoke and the debris and the camera operators doing their best to dash madly from place to place and capture everything, it was near impossible to tell what was happening, who was hit, who was advancing, who was retreating, or who, in fact, was in the right.

Emma heard screams, she heard curses, she heard orders to stand down, and cries of defiance. These were all people she might know. Ones she'd gone to school with, worked besides, maybe gotten drunk with at parties. Now they were there, and she was here. Which one of them was on the right side of history?

There was no escape now, no end in sight. Another civil war, the pundits were predicting, just like in 1917, when the Reds battled the Whites, with the anarchists, the separatists, and the non-ideological green parties sometimes fighting one, sometimes the other, sometimes among themselves. It lasted for six years and resulted in twelve million casualties, including civilians. Those who weren't killed in battle or executed, died of disease, frostbite, or suicide. And, as Dennis pointed out earlier, the hard-liners always won in the end.

But, somehow, it felt different this time. The spontaneous demonstrations actually felt spontaneous. The political positions seemed sincere, not merely calculated. And the people. Emma couldn't stop staring, mesmerized, at the people. She'd spent large chunks of her life amongst crowds at Red Square. Mom never could resist a parade. It fed her love of drama, of pageantry. Those crowds were always orderly, always calm, always… resigned. Could such a word be used to describe a crowd? The crowd was there because they knew they were supposed to be there. They'd known they were supposed to be there for so long that they'd long forgotten why.

This crowd was different. It was loud, chaotic, and unruly. Everyone looked like they'd been abruptly awakened from a dream they hadn't realized was a nightmare. And they'd be damned if they'd ever be lulled into sleep again. This crowd was disobedient. This crowd was disruptive. This crowd was alive.

The only question now was how long they'd be allowed to stay that way.

EMMA KEPT WATCHING THE NEWS, even when a visibly exhausted Dennis was, once again, taken off the air with the promise that he'd be back soon, so don't you dare change that dial! Emma presumed he was on his way home for a stolen nap and another change of clothes. She watched as, the morning of August 21, Gorbachev reportedly refused to return to Moscow as commanded by the coup's leaders, and Yeltsin just as emphatically refused to travel to Crimea to fetch his one-time superior and forcibly return Gorbachev to the capital.

She kept watching even as the phone rang. It had been ringing non-stop since the start of the mutiny, a combination of fellow travelers dying to hear Emma's take on events, and press corps members fishing for a quote from Dennis they could run in their own stories. Emma had let the machine answer them all.

She did the same with this one, expecting more of the same. She didn't expect Mom's voice to break through the reverie, which was why it took Emma a moment to realize who it was, much less what she was saying.

"They killed him!" Rose was practically in hysterics; a state Emma could never remember seeing her in. Mom never got hysterical because Mom would never admit anything was dreadful enough to require it. "They killed your father!"

Chapter Seventeen

"Mom?" Emma snatched up the phone, shaking from shock. When she'd been unable to reach Moscow, she'd assumed Moscow would be equally as stymied in reaching her.

"They killed him," Rose repeated. "Those bastards, those hooligans, those ingrates!"

"Who? Mom, what happened? What happened to Dad?"

"They jumped him. There must have been five, six, seven of them, who could tell? They all jumped him. They had boards and pipes, pieces from the barricade."

"You were at the barricade? In front of The White House?" Of course. Mom could never resist a demonstration. And Dad could never resist Mom.

"They called him a collaborator! Can you believe it? After everything we've done!"

"A collaborator? With whom? Who attacked Dad? I don't understand. Why would the soldiers target him?" Dennis was right. Dennis was right. Dennis was right. Choosing the wrong side could prove deadly.

"It wasn't the soldiers. It was the crowd. Children. They were all children. What do they know about anything?"

"Why would the protesters jump Dad?"

"They blamed him for the coup! Have you ever heard anything more ridiculous? They said he was part of the old guard, trying to keep young people like them from making progress. They said he was part of the system that oppressed them. A confederate of the regime, a tool of the dictatorship. There were thousands of people there. Tens of thousands. You couldn't tell who anyone was or what they stood for. Except Jonas. He stood out in that crowd. They recognized him. So, they made him a scapegoat. All their anger for the past seventy years, they turned it on him. How could they? How dare they?"

"They killed Dad?" Understanding shriveled Emma's voice.

"They beat him to death." Mom's seething bitterness was also new. Was this rancor what happened when Rose was finally forced to confront a reality she couldn't happily-ever-after her way out of? "There was nothing the hospital could do. Not that they tried hard. It didn't matter, everything we've done for them. Even medics decided we were the enemy."

In school, Emma had learned about what happened to traitorous Soviet citizens who'd collaborated with Nazis during The Great Patriotic War. In Ukraine, which had been occupied by Romanians and Germans, those who'd joined the enemy's military, their auxiliary police, or the SS, as well as those who'd worked as guards at local concentration camps, or served as civilian administrators, all were either sentenced to exile and decades of hard labor, or to public hanging, including a decree to leave bodies on gallows for multiple days in order to make it "obvious for everyone what a person who collaborates with the enemy can expect."

And now her distinguished, loving, loyal, wonderful, brilliant father had suffered the same fate. Because, as far as the dissidents advocating for a new, freer USSR were concerned, Dad was a collaborator with the apparatus which had tyrannized them for over seventy years. But what had he done, exactly? He'd pledged his loyalty to the Soviet Union. He'd moved there, he'd worked there, he'd married and raised his child there. Every production he'd ever appeared in had been explicitly sanctioned and funded by the Communist government. He never criticized them. Which meant he approved of them.

So many others had done far worse. But they were anonymous faces in the crowd. Dad stood out. Dad always stood out. And now that had gotten him murdered.

"How could you let it happen?" Emma demanded of her mother. Blaming the protesters or the coup plotters or Gorbachev himself was too nebulous. Rose was right here.

"I tried to stop them. I tried to get between them and him. I didn't think they'd hit an old woman. What did their parents teach them? I screamed at them to stop. I begged…"

Emma believed her. Dad could never resist Mom, true. But Mom would also do anything for him. No matter how incensed it made her, Emma believed the butchery had unfolded exactly as Mom reported. "Are you okay? Are you hurt? Did they get you too?"

"Nothing major. Some bruises, some broken bones."

"Mom!"

"Bruises fade. Broken bones heal. He's gone, Emma. They took him from us. How could they? How dare they?" Mom repeated her questions as if any answer was possible.

"Don't do anything rash," Emma ordered, worried Mom had already done just that. "Don't go back out there, do you hear me? Go home. Stay home. It's not safe."

"I can't leave him here. You should have seen how they treated his body. Like it was nothing. Like *he* was nothing. He was *everything*, wasn't he? Wasn't he, Emma?"

"Yes," Emma whispered. He was Mom's everything. "But there's nothing you can do for him now. Dad would want you to take care of yourself. He wouldn't want you getting hurt further. Not to avenge him." The daughter of a Shakespearean actor, Emma heard herself launching into Shakespearean pretension. She only hoped it got the job done with Mom. "Promise me you'll just wait this out. Don't even leave the house until everything is over."

"And when will that be?" Rose demanded as if her daughter were the one in charge.

Dennis walked through the door. And Emma repeated the primary phrase she'd heard from him over these past three, fraught days. "I don't know."

SHE'D PLANNED TO TELL HIM about Dad after Dennis had gotten some rest. But he could tell from Emma's tone of voice that something harrowing had taken place.

"Shit!" Dennis raged at the heavens as represented by their ceiling. "Goddamnit!"

Emma knew this wasn't all about Dad. Dennis had liked her father well enough, but Jonas' execution was just another component of Dennis' perennially processing equation.

"It's over," he raged. "They've won."

"No. Look at the people in the streets. Look at the Emergency Committee members already resigning. I don't know if you heard, they announced it right before Mom called, maybe you were already on your way home, but there's a rumor the coup planners have fled Moscow. They didn't win. They're in retreat."

"It doesn't matter. Even if Gorbachev is reinstated, he's done for. He's still associated with the Party. Even with all his reform plans, he's still one of them. This is the second coup attempt, you know. They covered up the other one. Why do you think Gorbachev suddenly up and decided to hold an election for President in 1990?" If something could be called an election when there was only one candidate and the vote was not by the people but by the Congress of People's Deputies, a body Gorbachev himself created in 1989 and was head of. "He knew the Central Committee was preparing to vote him out, Khrushchev style, so he created a new job for himself."

"But that's good." Emma clutched at straws. "It proves how resourceful Gorbachev is. How difficult to get rid of. He's like a rat. Or a cockroach."

"No. No, no, no." Dennis was pacing again, his legs the turbine powering his mind, driving it to think harder, further than he'd ever had to before. "The people in the streets, they're lumping Gorbachev in with the Old Guard. It's why they turned on your father. He's associated with all of them. Khrushchev, Brezhnev, those two, doddering idiots in the middle—Andropov, Chernenko; nobody even remembers their names. Gorbachev, too. They're all the past. And the past is what the kids want to wipe away. They don't trust Gorbachev to do it for them. They want someone new. I thought it mattered who came out on top, Emergency Committee or Gorbachev. I see now it doesn't. I could side with either of them, and still lose. Your parents were perceived as comrades of Gorbachev. So am I. Everything I have is thanks to him. Gorbachev sanctioned my position. He's sat for interviews with me dozens of times. I'm going to be seen as his stooge. I'm going to be seen as part of the problem. There's no right answer here, Emma. How can there be no right answer? There's always been a right answer before."

"What are we going to do?" Emma asked.

And there it came again. "I don't know!"

DENNIS SEEMED NO MORE CERTAIN of his plan of action when he left the house a few hours later than he had been when he'd arrived. He'd slept, he'd showered, he'd gone through his set grooming routine. But if any of it came with enlightenment, he was giving Emma no indication.

Emma realized that her tenuous position paled in comparison to the people still in Moscow, in all of the USSR. They had no idea if the next few hours would bring a martial law crackdown, complete anarchy, a return to the terror of the 1930s, the tentative openness of the 1950s, the stagnation of the 1970s, or the non-stop reconstruction of the 1980s. They didn't know if they'd have food, homes, jobs, or basic human rights. Emma was worried whether she'd be allowed to keep living on Central Park West. Oh, and whether she and her husband might be kidnapped off the streets of New York, smuggled back to the Soviet Union, and publicly hanged from gallows. So maybe her concerns weren't as trivial as all that.

After two straight days of Dennis on the air alone, reading the news as it came in, somebody at the studio must have decided to liven up the format. Viewers were growing bored. And that was worse than any coup attempt. The next time Emma tuned in, her husband was still at his announcer desk, but now he was talking by satellite hook-up with the same Phil Donahue whose Citizens' Summit had upended Emma's life six years earlier. Mr. Donahue looked deeply concerned. But then, as Emma recalled, Mr. Donahue always looked deeply concerned.

They started their discussion with the latest updates: Several coup principals had been arrested in Bielorussia. The Supreme Soviet's Defense Committee had declared the emergency over. The Soviet Parliament abolished the Emergency Committee's instructions and restored Gorbachev to power, followed by the Supreme Soviet announcing Gorbachev was President of the Soviet Union once again.

Mr. Donahue perked up quite a bit. "This is certainly wonderful news, isn't it, Dennis? Now the Soviet Union can return to the neoteric nation it had been before this criminal attempt to regress it back to the bad, old days of Stalin and company."

"Yes, Phil," Dennis said. And then paused. Maybe those watching at home didn't notice. Emma did. It couldn't have lasted more than a heartbeat. In that heartbeat, she saw something inside Dennis change. Was it the way he shifted in his chair, sitting up a smidge straighter? Was it the way he cleared his throat, swallowing the rote sentiment? Was it the way his eyes, which, since the beginning of the coup, had been nervously shifting side to side, suddenly locked into place, focusing on some point beyond the prescribed perimeter? It could have been all of it. It could have been none of it. But Emma knew. Whatever Dennis said next would determine the course for the next stage of their lives.

"Yes, Phil," Dennis repeated. His tone didn't budge. He sounded the same as he always did. "The Soviet Union can return to the nation it had been. A nation where megalomaniacal and blood-thirsty leaders like Josef Stalin can kill ten million people through unholy policy, as well as the deliberate targeting and elimination of anyone perceived a threat, or, worse, a nonbeliever. A nation where surveillance of its citizens is the norm. Where freedom of the press and speech is suppressed at any cost. Where thousands of Jews are taunted that they'll never belong yet are forbidden from escaping. Where a man like Mikhail Gorbachev can be heralded as a reformer, yet he covers up environmental disasters like the meltdown of a Chernobyl nuclear plant, props up terrorists in Libya and Syria, signs trade agreements with China, and, when faced with losing his position, creates byzantine layers of bureaucracy to circumvent the true will of the people."

Mr. Donahue looked deeply concerned again. Also perplexed.

And, in an unprecedented development—speechless. Emma was right there with him.

"I want to tell you a story," Dennis went on. Emma could only imagine what was going on behind the scenes in his control room. If this were the USSR, he'd have been pulled off the air by now, the screen cutting abruptly to black, like what happened when the US hockey team beat the Soviets at the 1980 Olympics. The next morning, Emma heard a teenage boy whispering to another on the Metro, "Did you hear? We nuked Lake Placid!" But this wasn't the USSR. Dennis was allowed to continue. Emma wondered if his producers were as breathlessly eager to hear what Dennis might say next as she was, and so had forgotten their obligation to Soviet Central Television to silence him if Dennis went off-script. "It's the story of my father-in-law."

Emma startled. With the ongoing crises, she'd managed to compartmentalize her grief over Dad, promising she'd return to it shortly, that she'd mourn him as he deserved—in a little while. But not now. It was self-serving and it was self-deceptive. It was all she could currently handle. Dennis bringing Jonas up smacked Emma in the bowels with a gut-wrenching reminder, at the same time as it infuriated her. Sure, Dennis had invoked her family before for a variety of politically expedient reasons. It was the consensus of their marriage that such references were not only acceptable, but they were also necessary and a key part of their partnership. She had no right to be angry or even surprised. Yet she managed to be both.

"My father-in-law, Jonas Cain. The African-American actor. A man who believed in civil rights, a man who believed in civil liberties. A man who literally gave his life to the Soviet cause. Because do you know what happened to Jonas Cain earlier today? Jonas Cain was beaten to death on a street of Moscow. Why? Because he stood out. Because he didn't belong. Because of the color of his skin, and his marriage to a Jewish woman who, like him, believed in a cause greater than herself. My wife's parents didn't just talk the talk, they walked the walk—misguided though they might have been. Rose Janowitz and Jonas Cain threw their lot in with the Soviet government. And how were they rewarded? Jonas Cain is dead. He's dead because that's how the Soviet Union treats anyone who is different. They turn on them, and they annihilate them. Stalin, Gorbachev, they're the same. This coup has proven it. This is who they are, this is what they do, and, yes, with the return of Gorbachev to power, the USSR can, once again, be the nation it has been. Except that, starting right now, with our eyes at long last open, the world should refuse to stand for it."

EMMA WAS THE ONE PACING when Dennis got home. Not because she was trying to jumpstart her brain, but because it was the only way she could keep herself from throwing random objects at the wall, starting with her and Dennis' wedding photo.

"What have you done?" she demanded before he'd even removed his shoes.

"I bought us time."

Chapter Eighteen

The phone never stopped ringing. If Emma thought the press was interested in speaking to Dennis during the coup, that was nothing compared to what a hot ticket he became after he'd more or less bitten off the hand that had fed him for over forty years. And, on live television for all to witness, no less. Whether *The New York Times*, *The Washington Post*, or *The Jewish Daily Forward*, Dennis hit his same talking points.

"Yes, I believed in the USSR. But I was a child raised in a Soviet orphanage. What choice did I have? I was completely cut off from the world and indoctrinated by experts. Yes, I believed in Gorbachev's reforms. It's why I was happy to come to America and help spread his message. However, after the attempted coup, after what happened to my father-in-law, I saw that the system was moribund. You can't reform something that, at its core, is fundamentally evil. And you can't build a new nation under the auspices of a leader who came to power under the old. Gorbachev isn't the root problem. Even the Soviet Union isn't the root problem. The root problem is Communism. And until that's abolished, the Russian people, and all the republics yoked to it by force, will never truly be free."

  Alina Adams

The people in whose living rooms Emma had once clicked champagne glasses with, the ones who'd praised Dennis' intelligence, his insights, who thanked him for sharing his life experiences—as there was nothing more valuable than first-hand knowledge—now excoriated him. They wrote angry *Letters to the Editor* calling him an imbecile, uneducated, ignorant; a perjurer who twisted a single, aberrant occurrence and acted as if that could be extrapolated internationally. The more generous of them clucked sympathetically about his childhood trauma, suggested he seek psychiatric help, and pointed out how, under the circumstances, his opinion couldn't be taken seriously. He was obviously mentally ill. They'd watched him have a nervous breakdown on live television. Clearly, seeing the country he loved nearly come apart at the seams had done the same to his psyche. They'd have prayed for him but for that opiate of the masses metaphor, which forbade loyal Marxists from doing any such thing.

On the other hand, those who'd once picketed Dennis' studio, dubbed him an apologist, brainwashed, deluded, and a prevaricator, were delighted by how astute he'd grown overnight. The man whom they once accused of either grossly misinterpreting history or being deliberately misleading about it was now a Messiah. Not only were his facts finally unimpeachable, but his veracity and sincerity were unassailable.

Dennis' network fired him, issuing a press release about how they could not, in good conscience, stand behind a man willing to alter his values after a change in circumstances. Why should new facts trigger a shift in opinion? His flip-flopping was confusing for their viewers. They were seeking consistency, not complexity, at the end of a long, hard workday. Their cable rival extended Dennis a job offer before the end of that same day. They even agreed to continue underwriting their rent, so Mr. and Mrs. Kagan wouldn't be inconvenienced by a move, and Dennis could get straight to work for them.

Emma would have found it all hilarious. If it weren't also terrifying.

"How am I supposed to go back to Moscow for Dad's funeral?"

"You can't," Dennis answered practically, as if her question had been about logistics, and not utter bewilderment at the precariousness he'd thrust them into—without consulting her.

"I am not missing my father's funeral."

"It's too risky. You could be arrested the minute you set foot in Domodedovo Airport."

"I'll be fine. They wouldn't dare make a scene. Not while Gorbachev is still determined to demonstrate how open and non-repressive he is." Emma had no idea how close she came to echoing Jonas' reassurance to Rose about the boy reading from the UN report in Red Square.

But, in the end, it wasn't Dennis who kept Emma from honoring her father one last time. It was Mom. When Emma called Rose with the details of her flight, it was Rose who said, "No. You can't be here."

"Why the hell not?" Emma understood her mother was likely in shock. She'd just lost her husband, the undisputed love of her life. But Emma had just lost her father. And, after the past few days of bedlam, she was too emotionally drained to pussy-foot.

"We know what your husband did. We saw clips of it here. You think Americans are the only ones with freedom of the press? You should hear what they're calling him."

"I've heard."

"It's disgusting. Him exploiting your father's tragedy like this."

Emma didn't disagree. "Dennis won't be there. Only me."

"That's just as bad. If you're there, you and he become the center of attention instead of Jonas. He deserves better."

Emma didn't disagree with that, either. But this was Dad… "I'll stay in the background. I won't call attention to myself. I won't even speak. Please, Mom…."

"Don't you care about the trouble you could cause me? There'll be important people from the theater there. Government officials, neighbors. How am I supposed to explain what you've done? There could be repercussions. Did your Dennis think about that?"

"He doesn't want me to come, either," Emma admitted.

"Good. He hasn't lost all his sense."

"I want to say good-bye to Dad." Emma's voice cracked as she struggled to not make a complete fool of herself by bursting into tears.

At that, something in Rose cracked as well. Though she did a much better job hiding it. "Come after. Not to the cemetery, to the house. After everyone has left. The next day would probably be best. Just make sure nobody sees you."

STEPPING OFF THE AEROFLOT PLANE, down the creaking metal stairs, onto the tarmac, Emma half-expected Dennis' prediction to come true—for her to be arrested the minute she set foot in Moscow. A perverse part of her even wanted it to be true. That would show Dennis! Of course, knowing her husband, he'd be happy to spin it to his advantage, the way he'd leapt on Dad's death. So, no, Emma didn't want to be arrested, after all. Mostly out of spite.

But nobody seemed to care who she was. Her ticket said Emma Kagan, which was a much more common name than Emma Cain. Unlike Dennis, she'd done her best to stay out of the camera's spotlight. Neither the stewardesses nor Passport Control glared at Emma any more than they did at anyone else gauche enough to expect them to do their job. She took a taxi from the airport. No one followed her, as far as Emma could see. She did as Mom asked and arrived after dark, creeping up the backstairs to the place she'd once called home.

Rose opened the door just as Emma was raising her arm to knock. She must have been watching from the window and through the peephole. Rose rushed Emma inside, finger to her lips. Despite her wrist being packed in a cumbersome plaster cast, Rose took extra care to close the door gently behind her, so you couldn't hear the lock click.

Emma expected a hug, a peck on the cheek, some expression of their mutual grief. Mom only studied Emma at arm's length before appraising, "Treason looks good on you."

"Oh, please." Thirty-three years of her mother's penchant for dramatics had made Emma immune. "You've just lived through an attempted coup. Dennis isn't even in the top one hundred offenders, much less me."

"The Emergency Committee may have been misguided in their methods, but at least they were fighting for a USSR they believed in. Dennis leapt on the first opportunity to discredit everything we spent our lives fighting for."

Emma didn't disagree in theory. In practice, though… "It's over, Mom. The Soviet Union you moved for is gone. And what's taken its place is at death's door."

"Thanks to people like your husband!"

"Sure. Fine. Have it your way. But if everything is so great, Mom, if everything is as great as you spent my entire life telling me it was—despite evidence I could see with my own eyes to the contrary—why did I have to sneak home under cover of night?"

"Because I'm embarrassed! Because I'm ashamed of what my daughter has become."

As Rose had never made an effort to hide what a disappointment she found her only child to be—why was Emma so unambitious? Why was Emma so apolitical? Why was she uninterested in the things that Rose and Jonas valued the most?—this was hardly the revelation Rose might have expected it to be. And it wasn't a deterrent.

"Bullshit." Living in America had boosted Emma's profanity. She'd picked up a few words growing up, but Dad didn't like Emma swearing. He said it was unladylike. He'd never forbidden her, of course; that wasn't Dad's way. But Emma acknowledged his distaste, censoring herself around him. Except she'd never be around Dad again. And Emma knew whom to blame for that.

"You're scared. You're terrified of a knock at the door, a police-man with no warrant or anything equally decadent, dragging you outside, throwing you in the back of a Chaika limousine, locking you up in Lubyanka prison, where you'll be interrogated day and night, kept awake, beaten, tortured, until you sign whatever confession they order you to sign, declaring yourself an Enemy of the People. You'll disappear, never heard from again. That's what happened to Dennis' parents. That's what happened to millions under Lenin, and under Stalin, and yeah, under your precious Khrushchev, and Brezhnev, and all the rest. It's happening right now to the coup plotters, and to anyone who's suspected of being a coup plotter, and to anyone who, at some point, did anything to piss off those in charge of rounding up the coup plotters. Now that I'm living a life outside the lines you worked so hard to trap me in, you're petrified your blasphem-er daughter might get you arrested. And still—still!—you refuse to admit that this is the regime you freely volunteered to support!"

"You sound like those delinquents who killed Jonas!" Rose did a good job keeping her emotions in check when she could direct all her bitterness at Emma and Dennis. Now that she'd been forced to relive the reason for Emma's impromptu visit, her daughter recognized that all remnants of Rose's self-control were gone.

"They got the wrong person," Emma heard herself saying out loud words she'd barely allowed entertainment since learning the cataclysmic news. "It should have been you."

She expected Rose to explode. She expected Rose to berate. She expected Rose to defend. But all Mom said was, "You're right."

THERE REALLY WASN'T ANYWHERE a conversation could go from there. Mom turned away from Emma and strolled into the kitchen as if nothing out of the ordinary had taken place. Emma considered not following her. Emma followed her. What else was there for her to do?

"How was the funeral?" she asked, voice calm. If there was one thing Emma had three decades of practice in, it was acting as if everything was just fine.

"Beautiful." Her mother's head bobbed up and down, a wistful smile fighting the urge to weep. "We played a recording of Paul Robeson singing the *Monologue* from *Boris Godunov*."

They'd often trumpeted the Mussorgsky opera around the house, so Emma could quote from memory, "*From Heaven upon the tears of Thy true servants / And send on him whom Thou hast loved, whom Thou / Exalted hast on earth so wondrously.*"

Mom nodded. "And a video from our production of *Othello*. We had it transferred from the film shot opening night."

"Which part?" Emma started to ask, before realizing the answer was obvious. "*When I stop loving you, the universe will fall back into the chaos that was there when time began.*"

"I'm having that engraved on his tombstone."

"It's perfect," Emma conceded. Dad would have loved it. "Did anyone ask about Dennis and me, like you were worried they would?"

"They were too polite. It was a funeral."

"And how long do you expect that to last?"

Mom plopped a cup of coffee in front of Emma. She and Dad never developed the Soviet taste for tea, and, as a result, neither had Emma, though she would drink it when offered, so as not to offend. Soviet coffee was made of chicory, oats, and nobody dared ask what else. New York was where Emma discovered what real coffee was supposed to taste like. Nonetheless, she drank Mom's pale imitation. What else was there for her to do?

"Until I step out of that door again. Sooner, if you do it."

"It's over," Emma repeated, more gently this time. "Dad is gone. Your dream of a Soviet Union is gone. Why are you still clinging to it?"

"You would prefer I be like your Dennis? Modify my beliefs to accommodate whichever way the wind may blow?"

"You're doing Lillian Hellman?" How many times had Mom quoted her fellow playwright to Emma? Hellman wrote, explaining why she wouldn't testify before the House Committee on Un-American activities: *I cannot and will not cut my conscience to fit this year's fashions.* "Did you know Hellman was sued because it turned out her memoirs of an anti-Fascist, revolutionary past were actually somebody else's stories that she stole?"

Mom took a sip of coffee, staring at Emma with renewed interest. "This is not how your father and I raised you. When did you become so cynical? Why? Or is the answer: Who?"

"Dennis didn't make me cynical. Dennis was the first person who made me feel that it wasn't just natural, but that it was mandatory to feel cynical in the USSR. Otherwise, you'd constantly be questioning your own sanity."

"It sounds like a very sad way to exist, not having a cause to die for."

"I'd rather have something to live for."

"And Dennis is that for you?"

"Dennis made me feel like I wasn't losing my mind, growing up in this house, seeing one thing, being told it was something else. Dennis showed me that there was a world outside of the Soviet Union. There are people with differing opinions, and lifestyles, and, oh, yeah, skin tones. And hair! Do you know how many different ways there is to do my hair? You lived in New York, you had to know it. And you still kept forcing me to wear those stupid braids."

"May that be the worst thing that ever happens to you," Rose deadpanned.

"It's a metaphor," Emma shot back, as if she had to explain figurative language to her writer mother. "With Dennis, I can say what I mean. He doesn't censor me, and he doesn't judge me. He lets me be myself, not someone he wants me to be. It makes for a nice change of pace."

"Dennis doesn't ask you to be who he wants you to be?" It was amazing any of Rose's words made it to Emma's ears, bathed as each was in irony.

"That's not the same thing." Emma leaned back, crossing her arms.

"Is that so?" Emma swore there was no coffee left in Mom's cup. She simply lifted it to her lips for the drama. Like it was included in her stage directions.

"I don't mind it with Dennis. We're not at cross-purposes. We're on the same team. We both want the same thing."

Just as Emma had leaned back, Rose now leaned forward across the table, studying her daughter in a fashion Emma couldn't remember her endeavoring to before. "You don't love your husband, do you?" It wasn't an accusation. More of a surprise discovery which intrigued Rose so much she wanted to share it.

"How is that relevant to what we were talking about?"

"You don't love him," Rose repeated, confirming it for herself, not for Emma. "You admire him. You appreciate him. I'd even say you enjoy him. But you don't love him." Emma might as well have been one of her own specimens under a microscope.

Emma really needed this conversation to end. Sooner rather than later. "Not everybody, Mom, spends their life in a mutual admiration society where they think the other is the most amazing person who ever lived."

Rose shrugged. "They should."

"COME BACK TO AMERICA with me," Emma begged after Rose had

taken her to see the spot of earth in Novodevichy Cemetery, fellow final resting place of writers Chekov, Mayakovsky, Gogol, Bulgakov, famed acting teacher Stanislavski and visionary film director Eisenstein, where Dad's tombstone, complete with Shakespearean inscription would eventually go up. "There's nothing left for you here."

"Jonas is here. Always will be."

"You said you didn't raise me to be cynical. You did raise me atheist. You know Dad isn't here. He isn't anywhere. He's gone."

"You're very selective with what you absorbed from my parenting."

"I also learned to hear only what I wanted to hear."

Mom actually smiled at that. Being here, so close to Dad, mellowed her out. As usual. "You were such an easy child, Emma. Why did you have to become a difficult adult?"

"I was lulling you into a false sense of security."

"One thing my mother will never say about me."

Were they actually having a pleasant conversation? Emma decided to press her luck. "I'm scared for you. You're scared for you. You've never admitted that before."

It was clearly the wrong thing to remind Rose of. "You go back to America. Settle into your new life there. I'll be fine here. As soon as I disassociate myself from you."

IT KILLED EMMA that Mom couldn't see it. No matter how many times and in how many ways Emma strove to point out the scarcity of logic in continuing to believe in a system where your personal safety depended on publicly repudiating your child for uttering something which went against the grain—even then, Mom's security wasn't guaranteed; who knew what tomorrow might bring?—Rose refused to hear it.

So, Rose stayed, and Emma left. She didn't bother contacting any old friends while in Moscow. They likely felt the same way Mom did. Even if they agreed with what Emma and Dennis had done, they would never risk associating with them.

Arriving at the airport four hours before her flight's scheduled departure—a combination of wondering if there might be trouble with her paperwork and needing to get away from Mom—Emma

                    Alina Adams

did wonder if the reason entering the USSR had been so easy was because they had no intention of letting her leave. She still had a Soviet passport. Anyone who needed to know who she was and where she was, already did.

She went through passport control with minimum fuss. Sure, the official stamping it growled at her. But he growled at everyone. And, sure, they opened her suitcase, riffled through every item, then threw each back inside with no regard for how it had originally been packed. Emma considered herself lucky they only confiscated as illegal to take out of the country the Kodak camera she'd brought for this purpose and hadn't bothered to take pictures on. And, finally, sure, the woman who checked her ticket spoke in a monotone, as if programmed with a stock set of phrases which she employed repeatedly, no matter the question. In her defense, the DMV in New York was no different.

Only when Emma had gotten through the Soviet checkpoints and was heading towards the plane itself, inside the terminal this time; it was being flown by Delta, not Aeroflot—Dennis had insisted on it for the return flight, to be extra safe—and she caught sight of the Hispanic head steward, his name tag identifying him as: *Santiago*, did she permit herself to quit trying to look as small and inconspicuous as possible. Emma raised her chin. She straightened her shoulders. She smiled at Santiago and told him sincerely, "I am so happy to see you!"

"Yeah," he grinned, understanding completely. "I get a lot of that on this flight."

EMMA TOLD DENNIS not to bother meeting her at the airport. She'd take a cab home. But there he was, anyway, waiting for her even before Emma made it down to baggage claim. That was odd. And rather ominous.

"What's wrong?" Emma asked, forgetting about her circling suitcase.

In lieu of an answer, Dennis told her, "We should have a baby."

Chapter Nineteen

<hr>

Dennis had rational and logical reasons for his proposal. Emma wasn't surprised. Dennis had rational and logical reasons for everything he did. He enumerated them in the cab during their ride home from the airport. They all came down to: It would be good for his—their—image.

"Family values." He elaborated, "They like those."

Emma understood everything he was saying. Emma also hadn't slept for close to twenty hours and had just come back from visiting her father's grave and arguing with her pig-headed mother. Emma was not in the best place to be making life-changing decisions.

Emma asked, "Can I think about it?"

"Of course," Dennis replied, rationally and logically.

DENNIS' POLITICAL ABOUT-FACE did little to alter their social schedule. There were still parties to attend, though now they were more likely to take place in a penthouse overlooking Central Park on the Upper East rather than the Upper West Side. Now, there was no concern about the optics of hiring Black servants. A mixture of hues milled about, some darker than Emma, some lighter, offering drinks and appetizers off silver trays, as well as discreetly removing Wedgwood soup bowls and Christoffel spoons before serving the next course.

To Emma's surprise, the chit-chat remained disturbingly similar. Now, instead of being lectured on how public schools brainwashed revolutionary children with bourgeois middle-class values of individuality, she was treated to arias regarding how they were hotbeds of Communist indoctrination designed to incite class warfare. Either way, the solution was to remove their own offspring from government influence via private institutions whose principles matched their own.

Now, instead of hearing about how in awe they were of Emma's mother for her bravery in leaving America for the USSR, Emma heard about how in awe they were of her mother for Rose's creative achievements. A woman who told Emma that she worked for Procter & Gamble gushed, "Rose Janowitz was truly a pioneer. She and Irna Phillips created an entire genre. The advertising industry and commercial television would look completely different today if it weren't for women like her."

Emma nodded politely, refraining from contributing how Rose felt about commercial media these days.

"She is just such an inspiration. Such a role model. Proof positive that anybody with enough talent and drive can succeed in America. I bet your mother never complained about being kept down because she was a woman, or a Jew. Your mother just pulled herself up by her bootstraps and got on with doing what needed to be done. She didn't ask for hand-outs or demand the government step in to support her. I so wish more women today were like her."

Even if Emma wanted to contribute everything Rose would have to say on that subject, there wouldn't be nearly enough time to unpack it all during the course of a single evening.

Now, when it came to her father, instead of hearing how astute it was of an educated man like him to realize the USSR would serve him better than America ever could, Emma heard from a professor at Dad's alma mater, "Jonas Cain, now there was a man to emulate. Columbia graduate, student of the classics, master interpreter of Shakespeare. Your father made his own opportunities in life, rather than waiting, hat in hand, for someone to extend him an offer. He was smart enough to understand he wasn't a victim; thinking of yourself as one only demoralizes a man. Why, he was one of the earliest examples of color-blind casting, wasn't he? On that little radio program of your mother's? Proof positive that this obsession with race is needless. There is plenty of opportunity for everyone!"

But the thing that shocked Emma most was how quickly Dennis had been accepted by the people who, only a few months—months? No, weeks!—earlier, he'd been publicly denigrating. Nobody questioned the sincerity of his conversion. Nobody questioned his motives. They took it for granted he'd just come to his senses one day—well, the coup obviously helped, as did the convenient murder of his father-in-law—and decided to defect to the correct side.

Did it never cross their minds that he might be a plant? A spy? A saboteur? Americans were so adorably trusting! They took it on faith that their opinions were the only right opinions, so how could anyone possibly disagree?

"It's the same game we've always played," Dennis confirmed. "Just different teams."

The only group exhibiting a healthy amount of skepticism towards Dennis' U-turn were the residents of South Brooklyn. The same people who once protested him. The same people he regularly eviscerated on live television. They weren't falling for his charade. Emma respected them for it. They came to protest him at his new place of business. Accusing Dennis of being a fifth columnist, out to bring their beloved America down from the inside. They were wise to his tricks! They were Soviet hustlers, just like him.

Once again, Dennis went down to speak with them. Once again, he was rational and logical. He pointed out that, once upon a time, they'd been children in the USSR, had they not? And, once upon a time, they'd believed the propaganda they were being fed, did they not? Well, yes, they were forced to admit. But that was a long time ago!

Dennis complimented them on having come to their senses faster than he had. They truly were sharper than him, congratulations! But they had families, mothers and fathers who raised them and taught them right from wrong, did they not? Pity poor Dennis, who had no such nurturing childhood. He accepted responsibility for taking longer than them to open his eyes to the realities of the evils of Communism. But could they not, under the circumstances, spare him some compassion? America had given them a second chance. Could they not grant him the same? What better way to express their love for their new country than to practice its greatest virtue? Could they not fill the roles of the loving, forgiving parents Dennis never had?

It didn't work right away. But it did work eventually. Nobody could resist Dennis for long. Emma knew that better than anyone. Now, in addition to discreet, dignified gatherings on the Upper East Side of Manhattan, Dennis and Emma were also regular guests at the nightclubs which dotted the boardwalk of Brighton Beach, Brooklyn. There was nothing discreet about any of them. Here, the walls were mirrored—where they weren't covered in red damask. Every table boasted caviar, herring, cold cuts, stuffed mushrooms, stuffed cabbage, calf's foot jelly, and pickled… everything. There was wine, there was schnapps, and there was, oh, so much vodka. The ceiling strobe lights never stopped. Neither did the band, pumping out covers of everything from the pop hits of Alla Pugacheva to techno versions of *Hava Nagila*, to an English language disco ditty dedicated to Rasputin, where Emma learned that the man who helped bring down the Czarist empire was also, apparently, Russia's "greatest love machine." Who knew?

The first time she and Dennis danced to it, they weren't sure how seriously to take it. All around them, couples were bouncing up and down with abandon. So, they did, too, breaking into hysterical laughter by the end. Mom was right. Emma did appreciate and admire her husband. She also enjoyed him. Why did Rose make it sound like there was anything wrong with that?

The visits to South Brooklyn became more frequent once local Republican party leaders, determined to break the Democratic chokehold on NYC at the grassroots level, decided to run Russian-speaking candidates in their communities. They thought Dennis' presence would help with the turnout at their campaign events.

Sometimes these bombastic happenings were held in public parks, sometimes in Russian restaurants, sometimes in synagogues, and sometimes in private homes. At each one, whoever stood up to make a rousing, recruitment speech sounded exactly, at least in vocabulary and cadence, like every speech Emma had ever heard growing up in Moscow. The sentiments may have been different, but the language was the same—as was the cognitive dissonance. Candidates running for election in districts where the majority of Russian-speakers were on food stamps and welfare, warned them to vote Republican, else Democrats would give food stamps and welfare to shiftless bums who refused to work, opting to mug and rob instead; not to mention any illegal who crawled across the border. They'd let murderers and rapists out of prison to sell drugs to children. They'd give unions free reign until the only way to get a job would be through someone you know. Vote for someone you know to ensure that can't happen!

One of the organizers confided to Dennis, "They're so used to being told who to vote for, it never occurs to them to question it. Genuine choice overwhelms them. They're grateful to us for making their lives easier. We hand them a card with the names to check off, and they vote a straight ticket. Thank you, Great Stalin, for turning your expats into terrified sheep!"

As a result, the gatherings were more parties than political meetings. There were people Dennis and Emma's ages, as well as some elderly, who'd been tutored to pass citizenship tests so they could vote for "their" candidates. And there were children. Babies, toddlers, pre-teens, even teens. Dragged against their will, surly and uncommunicative, but there. That was the difference Emma noticed between native-born Americans and Soviet newcomers. Americans talked endlessly about children. Their eating, their sleeping, their schooling, their extracurricular activities. They talked about boosting their children's self-esteem and quality time. They talked about the dangers of violent video games, pedophiles, and sexually explicit song lyrics. But their children were rarely present. Any event Dennis and Emma attended appeared to be Adults Only. At the ex-Soviet parties, even in the nightclubs, parents might complain that their children didn't eat enough, didn't study enough, weren't respectful of their elders enough, watched too much television and needed a good smack periodically to keep them in line. But the kids were also everywhere. They were expected to mind their manners when eating at the same table as adults, but they were also expected to entertain themselves while grown-ups discussed grown-up things. They were forbidden from interrupting, but they were free to run around, out of the room, up the stairs, even outside if the weather wasn't too bad, and, even then, *just put on a coat, for God's sake!* No one worried if they felt validated for their feelings and opinions. No one hesitated to tell any child—not merely their own—that they were acting like a hooligan and, if the child failed to fall in line, call them expletives. No one looked at their watch, grabbed their purse and mumbled apologies; they had to go, it was past the child's bedtime. It was as-sumed that if the child was tired, they'd find a warm pile of coats to snuggle down in, until their parents came to carry them home.

Dennis was now in his element. Not just with peers who'd finally come around to accepting his metamorphosis, but with the older people, too. Emma supposed life in an orphanage made pleasing his elders a Pavlovian response. But he was also good with the children. He mugged at babies, tossed a ball for toddlers, held serious dis-cussions dissecting *The Legend of Zelda* and *Terminator 2* with the school-age crowd, and slipped cigarettes to the teens, which might not have earned him a break from their all-inclusive sneers, but did elicit the briefest nods of the head, "You're OK, man."

Dennis may have told Emma that having a baby would be good for their political image, but she also got the impression he'd gen-uinely enjoy being a parent. He'd be good at it. Emma wished she could confidently say the same thing about herself.

Observing the wildly contrasting manner in which American and Soviet parents viewed their roles and obligations made Emma feel even more ambivalent about becoming a mother. She didn't know what sort of mother she wanted to be. Because she didn't know how she felt about the mother she'd had.

Rose loved Emma. She'd provided for Emma. She'd made sure Emma had the best of everything, even when it meant going against her communal values—not that Rose would ever admit that's what she was doing. Rose had also made clear, in deed if not in word, that Emma was not her priority. Rose's priorities ranked as:

First: Dad.

Second: Rose's work with Dad.

Third: Rose's work without Dad.

Fourth: Emma.

Or maybe the worldwide ascension of socialism.

That would put Emma in fifth place.

From what Emma could see, in America, your child had to come first. And she wasn't sure if she could do that. She wasn't sure if she wanted to do that.

She really wasn't sure if she wanted to do it with Dennis.

Like Rose, Dennis never hid his priorities. First) Dennis. Second) Dennis' work. Third) Emma?

Sure. Let's pretend Emma was in third place.

Would a child move her down to fourth? Did she care? Would the child?

Luckily, between Dennis' new job, their social obligations, applying for US citizenship—important calls had been made by immigration officials so their applications moved to the head of the line; it's not as if they needed to prove they could speak English and wouldn't be a burden on society—there was very little time for Emma and Dennis to revisit the baby issue. Especially in light of the rapidly disintegrating situation in the USSR. Dennis, as always, had been right. Despite his return to power, Gorbachev was a lame duck.

"Game over, man," Dennis quoted the Marine from *Aliens* when, after the withdrawal of the Baltics in September 1991, Russia, Ukraine, and Belarus signed the Belovezha Accords that December, recognizing each other's independence, and announcing that these three countries would establish the Commonwealth of Independent States to replace the Soviet Union. All the remaining republics, save Georgia and the Baltics, agreed to join them on December 21, as part of the Alma-Ata Protocol.

On December 25, Dennis reported to work as others were enjoying holiday celebrations at home, to cover Gorbachev's resignation and the turning over of his presidential powers—including nuclear launch codes—to Yeltsin, now president of the Russian Federation. As he had during the coup, Dennis stayed on the air through the next day's lowering of the USSR flag from the Kremlin, to be replaced by the Russian one, and until the Supreme Soviet's upper chamber formally dissolved the union… and themselves.

Emma wondered how many people felt like they were watching the unthinkable. She certainly did. Dennis might as well have been reporting that the sun failed to rise or that men now flew and birds could breathe underwater.

She'd tried calling Mom for hours. When she finally got through, Emma found herself at a loss for what to say. In a way, this was worse than Dad's death. No matter how much you dreaded it, you accepted that everyone had to die eventually. The Soviet Union was supposed to reign forever. It was supposed to subsume the world, not the other way around. As they'd covered during Emma's visit, Rose had lived for Jonas. But she would have died for her beliefs.

"Are you… OK?" was Emma's pathetic attempt at a question.

"Your husband is enjoying himself," was Rose's captious reply.

"People enjoy being proven right."

"It'll be civil war. Same as before. Thousands will starve. Thousands will die. And your new compatriots will find a way to make money off it."

"You can't always write a happy ending, Mom. Why won't you admit that? You've led an amazing life. Everyone agrees with that, even those who don't agree with how you did it. You took chances, you achieved great things. But not everything you touch is going to turn to gold. No matter how many times you insist it already is."

When Rose only harrumphed from half a world away, Emma continued, "Nothing that's happened today is an affront to you. Nothing that's happened today has anything to do with you, frankly. You taking it personally is a bit… narcissistic. Don't you think?" Emma didn't add that this was reality, not one of her mother's scripts. Rose wasn't God. Or a studio head. She didn't get the final edit.

Emma's mother said, "Everything that I came here for is gone."

"I know. And I am truly sorry. For you. Do you believe me?"

Emma wasn't sure why it was important to her that Rose believe her.

"It doesn't matter." When had Rose ever given up so easily? When had Rose ever given up at all?

"Come back to America," Emma pleaded. "We'll take care of you." And then, because she knew how her mother's mind worked, what really motivated her, Emma flipped the script. She'd learned how from a master. Emma said, "Come back to America, and you can help take care of me. I'm going to have a baby."

Chapter Twenty

Her daughter was born a week before Halloween, less than a year after the collapse of the Soviet Union. When Dennis made up his mind to do something, Dennis did it with maximum efficiency. He'd come home from close to forty-eight hours straight of live broadcasting to find Emma waiting for him with two announcements: her mother was moving to the United States, and Emma was ready to have a baby.

Dennis' reaction to both was, "Perfect."

She wondered if he would still feel that way once Mom arrived.

Emma assumed the process would take months, maybe years. Mom and Dad had given up their US citizenship decades ago. Once again, phone calls were made, strings were pulled, and Rose was on a flight, Moscow to New York, by Martin Luther King Day. Which offered so many levels of dramatic irony Emma didn't dare begin unpacking them all.

She stressed over how Mom might react to Dennis. It would be their first meeting since her husband's reactionary reversal. As it turned out, both opted to pretend nothing had changed. They greeted each other courteously, then pointedly avoided any potentially incendiary topics. It left Emma feeling like she was the crazy one, worried for nothing. Everything was obviously fine. She'd grown out of practice with Mom's gaslighting. Now that Dennis had joined her, Emma had no choice but to play along.

She'd ensconced Mom in the guest bedroom and assured her she could stay with them as long as she liked. Even forever. Rose nodded absently. After she'd had time to get over her jetlag, Emma asked Mom if there was anywhere in particular she wanted to go. Maybe visit her old neighborhood? Her mother's grave?

Rose said, "We should go see Annabelle."

Emma hesitated. "She hasn't been well. The last year or so, she hasn't remembered who I am."

"She'll remember who I am," Mom predicted. She sounded anything but happy about it.

They took the subway to Harlem. Mom insisted. Emma couldn't recall Rose claiming taxis were "too decadent" in Moscow. She carried a plastic shopping bag. She refused to show Emma what was inside.

On the platform, Emma watched her mother drinking in the atmosphere. Compared to Moscow's underground, NYC subways were filthy, with rats dashing between the rails, pecking at garbage thrown directly onto the tracks. They were either freezing cold when winds swept in through one access point and out another, or sweltering in the overheated cars, especially with dozens of bodies pressed tightly against each other. They smelled of human waste, cigarette smoke, and marijuana. Saliva and vomit dotted the ground. There were certainly no inspirational political slogans painstakingly tiled onto the walls. But that wasn't what seized Mom's attention. She was mesmerized by the people. Like Emma had been at the beginning, Rose couldn't get over the variety of skin tones, of hair styles, of languages spoken. She'd been gone too long. She'd forgotten. It was the International Youth Festival all over again. Only every day. And not nearly as sanitized.

Once in Harlem, every time a man of Dad's approximate build and complexion passed them during the three-block walk to the Moores' house, Mom instinctively swiveled her head in their direction. It'd been so easy to find Dad in a crowd in Moscow. She still expected every man of Jonas' height and color to be him.

Annabelle's housekeeper greeted Emma warmly. They were old friends by now. But when Emma explained who Rose was, the woman looked like she was debating between shutting the door in Rose's face or punching her there first. She ultimately did neither. She stepped aside and graciously welcomed them both. That's how things were done here.

As Emma had predicted, her grandmother didn't recognize her. Annabelle spent her days in bed now. She was too frail to make it downstairs to her favorite chair. But her hair was still impeccably brushed, her housecoat freshly laundered, her nails neatly manicured.

Unlike what Rose had predicted, Jonas' mother did not appear to recognize her, either. Even when Rose introduced herself with her full name, "Rose Janowitz Cain." If Emma were Annabelle, she'd have blocked it from her mind, too.

Rose didn't let that stop her. Rose was incapable of letting anything stop her. So, what else was new?

She pulled up a chair to Annabelle's bedside. She reached into her shopping bag and pulled out one of the many scrapbooks Emma remembered from her childhood. It was filled with pictures of Dad in performance, his reviews, his show programs. Rose spread the album out across Annabelle's lap and began talking her through them all. "This is Jonas as Othello. This is him as Pushkin, as Dumas. We did a production of *Huckleberry Finn* with Jonas as Jim, but not in stereotypical dialogue, that would be demeaning. Here is him performing the speeches of the Reverend Martin Luther King. We toured the entire country with that production."

Annabelle's chin bobbed politely. It was plain she hadn't registered what Rose was trying to tell her. Her eyes moved from photo to photo without stopping to peer deeply at any of them. The Cyrillic text framing it occupied her attention as much as her son's image did. Rose didn't let that stop her. Rose, as previously noted, was incapable of letting anything stop her.

Back into the shopping bag she went, this time pulling out a mini tape-recorder. She clicked the Play button. Jonas' sonorous voice filled the room. He was reciting the St. Crispin's Day speech from *Henry V*. Mom had been true to her word. After Dad's triumph in *Othello*, she'd made sure he had the chance to play Hamlet, Richard III, Benedick, Romeo, even the Merchant of Venice.

"*Old men forget: yet all shall be forgot,*" Jonas proclaimed from one of his favorite passages. "*But he'll remember with advantages/What feats he did that day: then shall our names/Familiar in his mouth as household words...*"

Annabelle's shoulders began to shake, followed by her hands, then by her entire body.

"Mom!" Emma reached for the tape recorder. "Stop. You're upsetting her."

But Rose held it out of Emma's reach, closer to Annabelle.

"Where is he?" Anabelle's head swiveled, her eyes desperately sweeping from corner to corner. "Where's my boy?" She clutched Rose's wrist. "What have you done with my boy?"

"He's right here," Rose cooed. "Jonas is right here with you. Listen. Listen, he's talking to you. He's right here. Jonas is right here by your side."

ROSE LEFT THE TAPE RECORDER with Pilar. "I have my own copies. Please play them for Mrs. Moore whenever you get the chance."

Pilar made a noise suggesting she might, she might not, she hadn't decided yet. But she didn't look as eager to punch Mom in the face this time around.

As they walked back towards the subway, Emma observed, "Still insisting on writing your happy endings, aren't you, Mom?"

"No. I don't believe in those anymore."

THE DAY AFTER THEIR VISIT with Annabelle, Rose informed Emma she would be moving out. She was looking for an apartment to rent in Harlem.

"How?" Emma wondered. "You don't have any money." Rampant inflation had taken care of whatever savings Rose had managed to accrue in Russia. Emma and Dennis had needed to pay for her plane ticket.

"Money," Rose snorted.

"How do you expect to pay for your own apartment without it?" Emma realized this was a conversation usually held in reverse, with the mother chastising her dreamy, rebellious daughter.

Rose didn't let that stop her. Rose was incapable of letting anything stop her.

The next morning, Emma's mother hit the streets, a list of organizations that she thought would fit her requirements tucked into Rose's purse, and a fistful of subway tokens. By the end of the day, she'd secured volunteer positions writing fundraising copy for Planned Parenthood, Act Up, and The Actor's Temple. By the end of the week, they'd all hired her for freelance work. By the end of the month, she'd earned enough for first and last month's rent on a 143rd Street studio, with a view of the highway and the South Bronx.

"Your mother is a born capitalist," Dennis cheered.

Emma did not pass on his compliment.

She'd confirmed her pregnancy by then, making the lie Emma told Rose to get her to come to America, the truth. If Rose noticed that the timing didn't match, she declined to mention it. There was a true beauty in consistency.

She did appear excited by the idea of a grandchild. Like Emma, Rose assumed the baby would be a boy. They'd call him after Jonas. It made so much sense narratively, they never even considered the alternative.

It wasn't as if Emma was against having a daughter. She just wasn't prepared for one. Especially when it came to picking a name.

Mom suggested Joanna, Joan, Jean, Jan, Jody. She may have raised Emma an atheist, but the Jewish tradition to use the first letter of a deceased's name ran deep. None of them felt right to Emma. It should be Jonas, or nothing at all.

There, Dennis put his foot down. He would have been fine with Jonas for a boy. But, in the circles where he now swung, a more traditional girl's name would be fitting. Dennis even suggested they name her Rose. Emma's mother would be obliged to feel flattered, and if she brought up the Ashkenazi Jewish superstition about not naming children after the living because then the Angel of Death would get confused, well, that would be funny in its own right.

After twenty hours of labor, Emma was not in the mood to be amused.

She was, however, in the mood to compromise. When Dennis floated the name Liberty—what could be more perfect for his current persona?—Emma agreed. On the condition that her middle name be Jonas. Dennis' compatriots wouldn't need to know. But Emma would.

Mom approved of Jonas as a middle name. But she absolutely hated Liberty. Even the nickname Libby didn't pacify her. She thought it was pretentious and pandering. Mom advised Emma and Dennis that she would be calling her granddaughter, Lubov. It was a Russian name which meant Love. Luba, for short. Actually, Lubochka, which was the Russian way of making a diminutive nickname longer than the actual name. Which told you everything you need to know about Russian logic.

And Rose did love Libby, there was no denying that. From the time she was in the crib, Rose sang Libby Russian lullabies and Socialist protest songs. She played her recordings of Robeson singing Russian lullabies and Socialist protest songs. She took her to demonstrations and strikes. She regaled Libby with tales of parasitic capitalists and workers of the world uniting as she walked Libby from her private school to her private music lessons to her swim classes at a private club.

Emma thought Dennis would be incensed. But, as with all things Rose, he found the development hysterical. "Everybody knows kids rebel against whatever they're taught to think. Your mother is ensuring Libby grows up to become a neocon."

That designation was working out very well for Dennis. With Yeltsin appointing Vladimir Putin as the new prime minister of Russia, Dennis' rhetoric that this federation was no different from the Soviet state, played beautifully across every television channel in America. He pointed out that Putin had been trained under the old system, that he'd been a lieutenant colonel in the KGB, and later, ran the Federal Security Service, the KGB's successor. How could you expect anything new to come out of the old? Those who thought the Cold War was over and they could let down their guard were making a lethal mistake. Merely because Putin wasn't banging on a podium with his shoe, threatening to bury the United States, didn't mean he wasn't covertly planning the exact same thing.

Dennis told Emma he was making real progress, getting important people in government to take him seriously and to act accordingly, when, about a month before Libby's ninth birthday, the worst thing that could possibly happen to Dennis' career exploded onto their TV screens.

A pair of airliners crashed into The Twin Towers of the World Trade Center.

Chapter Twenty-One

Mom may have quoted Malcolm X's remark regarding the assassination of President Kennedy, the one about chickens coming home to roost, but Dennis was no longer amused by her nonsense. The instant al-Qaeda took credit for the September 11 attacks, Dennis discerned his own relevance dissipating in the same hoary puffs of smoke which swallowed the South and North Towers of the World Trade Center.

Within hours, no one was interested in discussing the Russian threat. News became all Middle East, all terrorism, all weapons of mass destruction, all the time. First the debates and testimony about invading Iraq pre-empted regular television programming, including Dennis' show, then the actual bombing and march on Baghdad took him off the air. For the first time since arriving in America eighteen years earlier, Dennis' input on a foreign affairs controversy wasn't solicited… or relevant. Dennis sat at home, watching new faces, experts on US-Islamic relations, assume the pundit chairs Dennis once claimed as his own. They were the ones being called for comments. They were the ones being rushed to the studio to cover breaking news.

Dennis' show got moved to the Friday night death slot. His ratings dropped on a weekly basis. When President George W. Bush parachuted onto the flight deck of the USS Abraham Lincoln and announced that major coalition combat operations in Iraq had officially concluded as of May 1, 2003, Dennis hoped that this blip in his career trajectory was equally at an end. On that front, he was sorely disappointed.

Saddam Hussein's capture in December, followed by endless suicide bombings, civil and religious clashes, and photographs of prisoner abuse at Abu Ghraib continued to dominate the news cycle. Even debate over the design of the Iraq Interim Governing Council's flag warranted coverage. Why did it look so much like the flag of Israel? Why did it look so little like other Arab national flags? A disgusted Dennis called it immaterial minutia. Not just to Emma at home but live on the air.

His show was canceled the following week. The Powers That Be said it had nothing to do with his outburst. It's just that they couldn't ignore his sagging ratings any longer. Viewers weren't interested in what Dennis Kagan had to say anymore.

Neither were the hosts whose homes Dennis and Emma had been welcome guests in for over a decade. The anti-Communists were too busy supporting the invasion of Afghanistan. Heck, they were feeling some sympathy for their old enemies. Maybe the Soviets had been onto something when they did the same thing back in 1979. Maybe they had tips and tricks to share!

It's not that Dennis and Emma were uninvited, exactly. It's just they weren't the center of attention anymore. Emma, for her part, didn't care.

Dennis cared. And his frustration spilled over onto Emma. Without a job, political rallies, or parties to attend, they'd never spent so much time together. Without other people's hypocrisy and naivete to snicker and roll their eyes over, they had nothing to say to each other. They tried using Libby as a buffer, asking her endless questions about her day, school, friends, *Veronica Mars* and Beyoncé. Unused to being the focal point of her parents' attention, to them wanting to know what she was interested in rather than drowning her in their interests, Libby's eyes shifted suspiciously from one to the other. She answered in monosyllables, then retreated to her room. Emma wished she could utilize her mother. If Rose and Dennis could get into it over their wildly divergent political convictions, hurl dates and statistics at each other, caterwaul over who killed more people, where, and in the thrall of which immoral ideology, it would take the pressure off Emma to contrive alternative conversation topics. Alas, thirteen years post her return to the US, Rose and Dennis continued to tenaciously skirt any incendiary topics, clinging to their facade of domestic tranquility, no matter what it cost Emma. They thought they were doing it for her sake.

At least she had work to escape to. Dennis also withdrew into his home office, making phone calls, looking up former contacts, submitting editorials to lesser-known publications, and sending emails. He spent hours there now. Emma never wondered what he was doing, as long as he was engaged and out of her way.

In the summer of 2004, the thought crossed her mind that maybe she should've taken more of an interest when, out of nowhere, Dennis told Emma and Libby, "We're moving to New Hampshire."

DENNIS HAD RATIONAL and logical reasons for his proposal. Though it was less a proposal, more of a mandate. "It's called the Free State Project. The idea is for 20,000 liberty-loving," he said, winking at his daughter. Libby remained stone-faced. "For 20,000 liberty-loving Americans from all walks of life—Republican, Democrat, Independent, Libertarian, Anarchocapitalists, Pacifists—to relocate, en masse, to a town already in favor of low taxes, limited government, and personal freedom. We'll have the critical mass to take over the local administrations, both city and state, and to create a truly independent community where everyone is free to live as they please."

"This utopia is in New Hampshire?" Emma felt like she was a step behind.

"It is the *Live Free or Die* state. The town we voted for is called Corinth. Not the one in Vermont or Pennsylvania. This Corinth's current population is barely 2000 people."

"And 20,000 pilgrims are going to descend on it? You'll overwhelm the citizens already living there. Where would you stay? The place will explode!"

"It's not going to be 20,000 people right away. That's the long-term goal, and it's for the whole state. Right now, the plan is a maximum of 5,000 new residents in Corinth. Only about 300 have made the move so far."

"You want us to make it 303?"

"It's an amazing opportunity," Dennis gushed. "They want someone to be the face of the Free State movement. To publicize it. Newspaper op-eds, on-line videos for their website, talk shows, TV appearances, the works. And they've offered me the position!"

"Oh." Now, at least, it made sense. Even if it did little to raise Emma's enthusiasm. "This is about you getting back on the air."

"It's perfect, don't you see? Our mistake was putting our trust in the government. Right, left, it doesn't matter. They were both going to abandon us in the end. That's what governments do. They don't care about people. They care about holding onto their power. The solution is to take government out of the equation. That's what this project intends to do. It's about personal freedom. It's about you living your life, me living mine, nobody judging anybody else or imposing their values on their neighbors."

"It's about you getting back on the air," Emma repeated.

"What's wrong with that?"

"Nothing. I want you to do what you love. I want you to be happy." If Emma couldn't make that happen, the least Dennis deserved was a political movement which picked up his wife's slack.

"I don't want to move to New Hampshire," Libby interjected.

"How long is this supposed to be for?" Emma asked Dennis.

"Hopefully, forever."

"Mom!"

Emma held up one hand to pause Libby's reasonable objections. She turned to Dennis. "We can give it a try."

"Thank you."

"You were right about us moving to America. You were right about us cutting ties with Gorbachev. You've earned your shot to prove that you're right about this."

TO EMMA'S SURPRISE, Mom was intrigued by the concept. "It's a commune."

"It's the exact opposite of a commune. It's hundreds of individuals living in proximity of each other while proclaiming total independence. It's an oxymoron."

"It's a commune. It's an experiment. It's a chance to create something new for the benefit of all. I will visit you there," Rose said, sounding a great deal more enthusiastic than Emma felt.

LIBBY, ON THE OTHER HAND, was the definition of unenthused. "I want to stay in New York. I want to stay at my school, with my friends."

"This is important for Daddy," Emma pleaded, selling the move to Libby much harder than she was selling it to herself.

"He can go by himself."

"He wants us with him."

"Why?"

Emma suspected the answer was the same as when he'd proposed their having a baby: Because it would be good for his image. But she didn't say as much to Libby. Instead, she told her, "Almost fifty years ago, your grandfather turned his back on his life, on his career, on his family, to follow your grandmother to the Soviet Union."

"I know. Grandma told me. But it wasn't just for her. It was both of them. It was so that they both could have better lives, better careers."

"He did it for her." Emma said what she'd always believed. "He did it because he wanted to support her, because he loved her, and because he wanted her to be happy."

"If Daddy loves me, then he should want me to be happy. And I'm happy here."

"Everything that we have today," Emma indicated Libby's bedroom, decked out with her computer, her television set, her DVD player, the corkboard littered with pins of tickets from Rush, Pearl Jam, and Justin Timberlake concerts, "is thanks to your dad. I wake up at night, terrified, thinking about what might have happened to us if we'd been forced to stay in the USSR. You know what happened to your grandfather. We owe Daddy this."

"I won't like it there." Libby crossed her arms defiantly.

"You will." Emma heard Rose's echo in her words.

EMMA HAD NO PROBLEM with giving up their apartment. Since Dennis lost his job and the housing subsidy which came with it, she saw no reason to be paying for so much space. Emma felt a twinge of regret at putting their furniture in storage, since it wasn't financially practical to ship it, but she agreed it was the sensible thing to do. Emma was stunned when Dennis informed her that since Corinth was so small, there was no available housing to be rented or purchased. The Free State immigrants were responsible for fabricating their own living accommodations. One had already acquired a former church that was being used as a barn and was in the process of transforming it into a public meeting house. Another had bought a multi-acre swath of empty farmland within city limits and was inviting new residents to set up housekeeping in his fields however they saw fit. Not that Dennis expected Emma and Libby to live with him in a field. Dennis had enough of sleeping on the hard, cold ground after being shipped to the countryside, where loyal, Soviet young people served their mandatory volunteering tours, helping farmers bring in their crops. Instead, he purchased them a motorhome! State of the art! This model came with a queen-sized bed for them, a twin for Libby, desks they could work on, a full kitchen with oven and stove, a bathroom with shower, a satellite entertainment system, exterior storage compartments, a generator and a freshwater tank. It was better than what most families had in the Soviet Union.

Emma agreed. And then reminded him that was why she'd left the Soviet Union.

"It's not like we'll be trapped inside for days on end. We'll have miles of fresh, unspoiled outdoors to explore. The camper is only for sleeping. We don't even have to eat there if we don't want to. And it's so practical. If we don't like the spot we parked in, we'll pick up and drive off somewhere else. It's the definition of freedom!"

Emma asked Dennis how much it had cost. She didn't particularly care, she was merely curious. She and Dennis rarely talked about money. His erstwhile earnings more than covered monthly expenses, leaving Emma to bank her much lower salary. Even after Dennis was fired, she hadn't worried, since they had plenty saved to live on and could manage on what she made for a while if they had to. But the way Dennis ducked the question, talking about the fees they'd save in the long run with this up-front investment, prompted Emma to inquire, "How much are you being paid for this?"

"That's not how it works."

"You're not being paid?"

"It's a Libertarian project."

"Libertarians love being paid. For everything."

"I'm not somebody's employee. I'm working for myself."

"Fine. How much will you make for this?"

"It depends."

"On what?"

"How everything plays out. I expect there'll be a market for newspaper articles, and for television shows. I might get a book deal out of it."

"*Expect*," Emma said. "*Might*. I'm not hearing *will*. I'm not hearing *earn*."

"Damn it, Emma! It's an experiment. Nobody knows exactly what will happen. That's part of the adventure! And since when do you care so much about money?"

"I care about feeding my kid."

"You think I'd let Libby go hungry?" Dennis kept his expression neutral, yet Emma still caught sight of the helpless orphan beaten by older kids, his meager ration of food stolen out of his hands and spitefully consumed in front of him.

"Of course not."

"Then trust me. It's all going to work out. We'll be fine."

"We'll be fine," Emma agreed. She heard Rose's echo in her words.

EMMA DIDN'T KNOW how to drive. It was too complicated to get a license in Moscow. You didn't only have to prove you knew the rules of the road and how to maneuver your vehicle, but also recite how its mechanism worked. It wasn't worth the effort, not to mention un-affordable for most wage-earners, even ones as exalted as Dennis. In

New York, there was no need. They had cabs, subways, buses. Plus, everything was walkable. For their trip to New Hampshire, though, the Cains insisted Emma learn. She took lessons in New Jersey. No road in Manhattan was broad enough for their behemoth-sized new home.

The day they finally took off, Mom came to say good-bye. She exchanged a few words with a sulky Libby. Emma thought she overheard dictums like, "No fears, famines or perils can break a spirit until you break it yourself by surrendering," and "It takes a revolution to make a solution." Oh, good, as long as Mom wasn't putting Libby in the wrong frame of mind.

To Dennis, Mom intoned, "There will never be real freedom as long as there is no freedom for women from the privileges which the law grants to men, as long as there is no freedom for the workers from the yoke of capital, and no freedom for the toiling peasants from the yoke of the capitalists, landlords, and merchants." *Thank you, Comrade Lenin.*

Emma wondered which Communist slogan she'd be favored with. But all Mom said was, "This is the most interesting thing you've ever done." A compliment? In Rose's world… probably.

"It's what Dad did for you."

"I hope you're as happy as we were."

"That's not possible."

"I know," Rose sighed.

EMMA HADN'T GROWN UP watching American television, nor was she particularly enamored with it now. But she'd lived in the US long enough to pick up on common cultural references like, "They loaded up the truck and they moved to Beverleeeeee," as well as Lucy, Ricky, Ethel, and Fred heartily singing in their convertible on the way to Hollywood. Emma hadn't expected their estimated five-hour drive from New York, New York, to Corinth, New Hampshire, to resemble either of those adventures. But neither had she expected their actual arrival in town to mimic a scene from *The Grapes of Wrath*. Mom and Dad had shown Emma the black and white Henry Fonda movie. The novel was required reading in Soviet schools. They learned that the Joad family's wretchedness was a prime example of capitalist exploitation, and that the book's author, John Steinbeck, was a loyal Communist dedicated to exposing America's degeneracy. It wasn't until years later that Emma found out Steinbeck was equally as critical of Communist agitators who exploited the workers for their own ends as he was of the owners and bankers who did the same. Living in New York, Emma had little reason to think of either the book or the movie on a daily basis. But, as Dennis maneuvered their camper down a dirt road abutted by forest on either side and glanced over his shoulder to alert Emma and Libby that, "We're here!" Emma couldn't help noticing the similarity.

Dennis parked in an open field, where Emma spotted a few other trailers. The majority of the housing appeared to be hastily assembled lean-tos made of planks and boards seemingly torn from other structures, or tents with sputtering fires in front of them, surrounded by discarded cans, glass bottles, and paper wrapping. In *The Grapes of Wrath*, the Joads had no choice but to live in squalor. Were the Kagans' new neighbors opting to do it voluntarily? Emma assumed so. After all, it's what she and Dennis were doing.

Catching sight of Emma's repulsed expression, Dennis assured her, "It's temporary. Most of these people are in the process of either buying or building houses closer to town."

"Where is the town?" Emma tottered down the RV steps and looked to all four cardinal directions, pretending her view wasn't blocked by the behemoth they'd arrived in. She saw pastures, trees, and sky. She could hear a creek in the distance, the barking of dogs, the chirping of birds and crickets, the buzzing of insects.

"A couple of miles down that way." He pointed in the direction they came. "It's walkable." Emma's husband also took a full circle look around. He appeared to be drawing a very different conclusion than she had. Dennis put his hands on his hips. He took a deep breath. He grinned. "We're finally home."

Chapter Twenty-Two

Emma didn't cook. Rose hadn't either. She claimed she'd been taught to by her mother but got out of the habit while working for Irna. Those days were simply too packed to do anything but grab a quick bite on the go. Then, in Moscow, despite insisting that they lived average lives no different from any other Soviet, Rose didn't have the time to stand in line after line in the hope that some produce or cut of meat might still be available by the time she made her way to the front. Rose and Jonas worked evenings and slept in mornings. Their schedule just wasn't conducive to shopping or cooking or anything domestic. The hired woman who cleaned their apartment purchased their groceries at the specialty stores designated for party members in excellent standing, and cooked their meals, leaving plates in the refrigerator for when the Cains got home. When Emma asked her mother why that woman regularly stole a fraction of what she bought for them if everyone in the USSR had what they needed, Rose said it wasn't stealing—she'd given her permission. But why did she need permission? Why couldn't she buy the same food on her own? Mom said they all needed to share their good fortune with others, it was the Soviet way. But if everyone had what they needed, why did anyone need to share? Mom told Emma that, in America, nobody shared and Emma should stop acting like such an American.

In America, the hired woman who cleaned Emma and Dennis' apartment bought their groceries at whichever store she liked, and cooked their meals, leaving plates in the refrigerator for when the Kagans got home. If she stole, it was never so Emma noticed. On her days off, they either went out or ordered in. In Corinth, neither appeared to be an option. While Dennis grabbed his newly purchased digital camcorder and set off to document the promenade to freedom, Emma assessed the pantry of their mobile kitchen and concluded that if they wanted to eat anything other than oatmeal, tuna fish, pasta, rice, or Jell-O in the foreseeable future, she and Libby would need to make the trek into town for supplies. She expected Libby to be resistant to the slog. Her daughter surprised Emma by grumbling, "Beats staying here," as she hit the trail first.

Dennis proved right. The distance was walkable. It took less than an hour for Emma and Libby to make their way out of the field, past a smattering of one-story cabins and a handful of two-story houses, and into what would be considered Corinth proper. They recognized they'd found the town because the buildings were closer together, the roads were paved and cars were parked neatly at meters, instead of looking like they'd been abandoned mid-trip. They passed a gas station, a diner, a pharmacy, a police station, a movie theater, and a hardware store before locating a small grocery. There were five people inside. A teenage girl with a nose-ring worked the register. A teenage boy with a buzz cut was stocking the shelves. An elderly couple were by the produce, tapping on watermelons. A woman about Emma's age was perusing her cigarette options. The minute a door chime broadcast their entrance, every pair of eyes turned in Emma and Libby's direction. They didn't say anything. They watched Emma browse the refrigerator section, searching for ground turkey, settling for ground beef. They watched her pick up a loaf of bread, a packet of American cheese and a bunch of bananas. They watched as she brought her haul to the register, Libby following so closely, she bumped into her when Emma stopped abruptly.

"You're the new people," the Virginia Slims smoker pronounced. It wasn't a question.

Emma nodded anyway, as if it were.

"You're a cult," the girl ringing up Emma's purchase decreed just as definitively.

"A homo cult," the boy clarified.

"Not a lot of women and kids there," the older man explained, in case Emma and Libby had joined the wrong sect.

"Enough for a pedo cult," his wife amended.

The girl handed Emma two paper bags. "Have a nice day."

She seemed to mean it.

"Did we join a cult?" Libby asked Emma on their way back towards the grasslands.

"Yet again," Emma sighed.

"MOM..." Libby whined almost twenty-four hours later, when Dennis was off somewhere doing something, and the novelty of cleaning their miniscule home, followed by frying up some hamburger to throw atop a plate of spaghetti and garnish with a dollop of ketchup had worn off—not to mention taken up barely any time. "There's nothing to do here."

Neither had ever been faced with nothing to do. Emma's life at Libby's age had been days filled with school and nights accompanying her parents to the theater. Her life as an adult had been work and accompanying Dennis to... a different kind of theater. Where she was also a prop. Summer, for Libby, meant no school, but definitely camp. Libby didn't know what to do with her free time, either.

Dennis had promised them a plethora of outdoor activities. Hiking, fishing, berry picking, mushroom hunting, flower gathering, hunting, meat curing, whitling... None of those particularly appealed to either of them. Growing stir-crazy in a home where you could see one end while standing a few feet away at the other, Emma and Libby stepped outside purely out of desperation. They were greeted with sunlight piercing directly into their eyes, mosquitos smelling fresh blood, and an odor that could only be described as marijuana-smoke-open-sewer. Emma made a mental note to ask Dennis what those who didn't have toilet facilities in their campers (like they did) were using for latrines.

Emma had described Corinth to Rose as "hundreds of individuals living in the proximity of each other while proclaiming total independence." Her sarcasm hadn't been far-off. As Emma and Libby wandered through the individual campsites, nobody paid them any mind. They were reading or sunbathing, cooking over fires and hot plates, smoking or drinking beer, while looking through Emma and Libby at the horizon. Emma realized they'd be offended by the comparison, but the tableau reminded her of every statue of Lenin she'd ever passed in Moscow, particularly the ones of him gazing unfalteringly into their bright, Communist future. Maybe he'd also been stoned?

Emma and Libby were almost to the creek, gingerly looking where they stepped lest their sneakers end up in a pile of excrement they sincerely hoped were dog, deer, fox, or even bear, when they spotted what, for a change, didn't appear to be a single man, but two women, and a whole gaggle of children, ranging from toddlers to Libby's age.

Emma was not one for marching up to total strangers with aspirations of friendship. What she liked best about New York was how people minded their business and left each other alone. But as another American pop-culture reference taught her: *They weren't in Kansas anymore.*

The women appeared pleased to see Emma and Libby approaching. Well, Emma was approaching, Libby was dragging. They waved heartily and introduced themselves as partners, Tammy and Ronnie. The kids were River, Sky, Lark, Willow, Summer, Winter, Autumn. Emma hoped there wouldn't be a test where she'd be obliged to match season to child. Though their meaningful monikers did prompt Emma to introduce her daughter as "Liberty," which she hardly ever did. Libby scowled. Tammy and Ronnie nodded approvingly. They explained that they'd met on a USENET message board—before such e-friendships became commonplace—for mothers determined to give their children the most natural lifestyles possible. They were both worried about the chemicals which were being dumped into their drinking water, the pesticides coating their food, the mercury in vaccines, and, worst of all, the blind acceptance of it all. After corresponding for a few months, they met in person, discovering that not only were their values compatible, so were they! For the past four years, they'd crisscrossed the country, searching for a community which would accept their lifestyle. Oh, no, not their being a couple. They didn't give a damn what people thought about that; hardly anybody blinked at that anymore, it was the twenty-first century. They were on the hunt for a community that wouldn't legislate injecting poison into their babies' bodies, stop them from feeding their children fresh milk, eggs, and juice the way nature intended, rather than pasteurizing the nutrients away, or herding them into government reeducation camps where they'd be brainwashed into believing such pernicious efforts were for their own good. Tammy and Ronnie wanted their children to learn to think for themselves. Which was why they'd come to Corinth, where everyone thought that way.

"Does that mean you don't go to school?" Libby extracted what she believed was the most crucial part of their manifesto.

"We homeschool," Tammy announced proudly.

"You should join us," Ronnie urged. "We're reading and writing free responses to John Stuart Mill's *On Liberty* right now. It's perfect for you!"

"Oh," Emma watched her daughter's enthusiasm deflate. "Homeschool has homework."

"THIS IS SO EXCITING." Dennis double-checked that the rechargeable batteries for his camcorder were at full capacity. "We're finally going to get the chance to see true by the people, for the people governance in action."

Flashlights in hand, they maneuvered down an otherwise pitch-black road for a meeting at the refurbished church Dennis had told her about in New York. Emma clutched his elbow, trying not to trip over an obscured tree stump or step on anything dead. Or, worse, alive. She used her other arm to slap the mosquitoes feasting on the back of her neck, as if the bug repellant Emma had slathered on earlier was simply a challenge for them to try harder. Dennis had wanted Libby to come along. As a young person who would one day inherit this libertarian utopia, she should be a part of its birth process. Libby passed. Dennis had spent money on a satellite dish for their camper. She would stay home, watch TV, and make sure they got their money's worth. Wasn't that also part of a libertarian utopia?

Emma thought their daughter's riposte pretty clever. Dennis appeared less amused.

He perked up as they approached the meeting place, and Dennis was greeted by name by those who recognized him from not just his recent reporting in the area, but from his time on TV. Dennis stopped to chat, shake hands, listen and nod sagely. Emma let him be, slipping into the back of the former church, so she wouldn't be in the way, and could remain unnoticed.

It was a smaller turn-out than Emma expected. She was used to either money-studded soirées on the Upper West and East Sides of Manhattan, or boisterous Brooklyn blow-outs. This was a few dozen people scattered across a handful of wooden pews, and exactly four Corinth city council representatives sitting along the furthest wall, behind what had once likely been an altar, but was now a makeshift podium. Emma recognized a few faces from the field and waved in response to Tammy and Ronnie's greeting. All the New People, as she'd learned they were called—which still beat Cultists, Homo Cultists, and Pedo Cultists—gathered towards the front. In the back, Emma spotted the cigarette-smoking woman from the store, surrounded by locals who did not seem particularly pleased to be there.

The meeting was called to order over objections that it should only be for those who'd lived in Corinth their entire lives, not those strangers who'd come to take them over. They didn't need immigrants here. Especially not perverts; fingers pointed at Ronnie and Tammy. Especially not ones with accents like his; fingers pointed at Dennis. This remonstrance was countered by a dramatic reading out loud of the town's bylaws, which specifically stated anyone residing within the county's borders was entitled to a vote.

Tammy kicked off the proceedings by asking why her family was forced to pay a public-school tax when their children didn't attend public schools? And while they were on the subject, why was she being coerced to pay for other people's children to learn values she fundamentally disagreed with?

A motion was made to slash the public-school budget. The motion was passed by the majority. It wasn't just the Free State contingent, Emma noticed. Several of the elderly locals also raised their hands in support.

Next was the question of why there was a monopoly on garbage pick-up? Why should everyone in the county be compelled to use the same service? Why couldn't people decide for themselves how they wanted to handle their trash? Those who wished to stick with the status quo could pay out of pocket for it. The rest of them would make do on an ad hoc basis.

That motion also passed. This time, it was the Free Staters and the younger locals who voted for it. Garbage, it seemed, was exclusively an old fogey concern.

A member of the city council brought up the topic of adding more streetlights. He noted that with so many newcomers living on the outskirts of town, there were enough folks trafficking up and down the side roads that those warranted nighttime illumination, too.

"What for?" Dennis spoke up.

"Well, so that you all don't hurt yourselves, that's what for."

"Why is my personal safety your concern?"

"Not just your personal safety, sir. Personal safety of everyone who uses those roads."

"My safety is my business. If I'm afraid of the dark, I can bring along a flashlight." Dennis held up precisely that tool. "So can anyone else who chooses to walk that way. Why should the men and women of Corinth see money taken out of their pockets to provide for the welfare of people you don't even want here in the first place?" He turned to the crowd. "Wouldn't you rather keep that tax money for yourself? If I go out at night, trip, fall, break my neck, shouldn't that be my problem, not yours?"

The motion to prevent installing any more streetlights was passed nearly unanimously.

By now, the next year's budget had been slashed by over a third, with the subsequent tax refunds promised accordingly. There was still one major issue left for Ronnie to present, while Dennis filmed from the side.

"Why does Corinth need a police department?" she asked. "Is there any substantial crime in this county?"

"Well, not substantial, ma'am, but there is some."

"Not enough to warrant a full-time police chief, three officers, and two squad cars. Why, with what goes on here, surely, one man and one car could get the job done."

"Well, now, since you brought it up, our crime rate has spiked since you all got here."

"Are the crimes happening on our property?"

"That they are."

"Then why not let us handle them?"

"Trust me, ma'am, when shit hits the fan, you want trained professionals on your side."

"And how exactly are paramilitary fascists preferable to us handling our own problems?"

"You defund the police, missy, you see what happens to you and those brats of yours."

"I thank you for your concern. I'll also let you know that when we had a problem a few weeks back, one of our own residents taking too close of an interest in my children—" Emma's head swiveled Dennis' way. He hadn't mentioned this when he sold her on the utopia that would be Corinth. Now the accusations of being a Pedo Cult made more sense. Dennis, eyes glued to his viewfinder, ignored Emma's glare. Ronnie went on, "We ameliorated the trouble on our own, with no need to call the police, by employing a baseball bat. We can take care of ourselves. We do not require paternalistic supervision. You've made it clear we're not wanted here. We intend to stay, nonetheless. But we do not wish to be a burden on your municipality. Don't claim you require an increased police force on our account. What do you care if we murder each other? You'd probably prefer it. So why not leave us to our own devices?"

The motion to slash the police budget passed.

That was the final item on the printed agenda. But, before they adjourned, a man Emma hadn't seen before stood up and declared that he had one more issue he wished to discuss with the council.

"I would like to present," he began, "the case for consensual cannibalism."

THEY WERE WALKING BACK, trusty flashlights in hand, along the road which Dennis had kept from being illuminated at taxpayer expense. This was the part of the evening Emma traditionally loved best. The part where they could drop the acts they'd been putting on all night, and whisper to each other the snide comments they'd otherwise kept inside. When they could roll their eyes freely and feel utterly superior to not just their clueless hosts, but the rest of the world at large. They'd done it in the USSR. They'd done it on the West Side. They'd done it on the East Side. They'd done it in Brighton Beach. It was when they were most united, most in sync. It was when Emma's marriage to Dennis came closest to replicating what she'd seen with Mom and Dad. Theirs was the opposite, of course. Rose and Jonas were bound by love and by passion. For their work, for each other. Emma and Dennis were bound by disdain, and a self-aware sense of smug superiority. Emma suspected it wasn't what her parents dreamed of for her. But it was still what made her feel the most confident about the life choices she'd made.

Emma waited for Dennis to kick off the proceedings. He always did. Since Dennis was the center of attention wherever they went, he had access to interactions Emma missed. He knew how much she enjoyed his debriefings, with their obligatory sarcasm.

Dennis was uncharacteristically quiet tonight. Emma didn't understand it. The stillness was making her uncomfortable. She was familiar, in theory, with feeling a compulsion to babble in order to fill up an awkward silence. But Emma had never experienced it in practice. Her life was filled with people where getting a word in edgewise was the challenge.

She was experiencing it now. The further they walked, the less Dennis talked, the more Emma felt it her responsibility to say something, anything. Was her body the only one filling with tension? Was her chest the only one tightening? Was her mouth the only one somehow both drying and drowning in saliva? Why wasn't Dennis fulfilling his part of their bargain? What was wrong? What had she done wrong?

"Consensual cannibalism," Emma blurted out, lunging for the most ridiculous part of the evening, unable to imagine even this new, muted Dennis having no opinion on such lunacy.

He stopped in his tracks, pivoting toward Emma, his flashlight spinning around, the beam hitting her in the face like a suspect. He did not look amused. He looked annoyed. And not with the potentially consensual cannibal. With her.

"Damn it, Emma, grow up," Dennis scowled, before stomping away, leaving his wife to find her own source of illumination if she intended to make it home safely.

Chapter Twenty-Three

<hr>

Emma heard about the bears before she actually saw one. Barely a month into their grand experiment, the sightings began. It was, she supposed, something to break the tedium. In Corinth, every day was more or less like another. She woke up, she eked some water out of a shower barely wide enough to turn around in, she tucked away their beds to make a living area, she poured cereal into a bowl while Dennis and Libby did the same. She stared at the tiny cupboards and tried to think of something to make for lunch. She went to the store, she ignored being ignored, she came home, she tried to talk Libby into taking a walk in the hope they might discover a patch of nature they hadn't already explored numerous times. She read one of the books she'd ordered from Amazon, wondering how many more she could get away with buying before they ran out of room to store them. She turned on the TV, flipped through the channels and determined there was nothing to watch. She composed emails to her mother which never left Emma's drafts folder because she couldn't think of anything to tell Rose that wouldn't trigger her disapproval. She listened to Libby whine and told her daughter, "Stop complaining, it's not that bad. Grow up, Libby." Then they waited for Dennis to come home so he could tell them how much progress was being made on the revolutionary front.

That was all on sunny days. On rainy days, Emma and Libby stayed inside. And fought.

When Libby complained, "I'm bored, there's nothing to do here," Emma told her, "You're fine. Boredom is good for the developing brain. It forces you to think outside the box and come up with creative solutions instead of reverting to familiar archetypes." At least, that's what the parenting magazine Emma subscribed to claimed. "You'll thank us for this opportunity we've given you. Someday."

When Libby complained that the "seasons kids" were weird and she didn't want to hang out with them, Emma tramped down her instinctive feeling of relief that her daughter wouldn't be spending an excessive amount of time with children whose mothers didn't believe in vaccination and told her, "You're fine. It's good for you to be exposed," perhaps an unfortunate selection of words, "to people whose worldview is different from yours. This isn't New York, where everybody spins in their own narrow-minded bubble and never gets out of their comfort zone. You'll thank us for this opportunity we've given you. Someday."

Libby complained about the garbage everywhere, the smell of rotten food, the flies it attracted, not to mention the wildlife that came to scavenge at night. While some responsibly set out compost bins—which also reeked, but at least you could justify them as serving a noble purpose—or dragged their refuse to the city dump themselves, proudly eschewing any taxpayer funded collection service, others simply left their detritus to molder where it fell.

"You're fine," Emma said. "It's their property, they can do whatever they want on it. Just keep your distance. You have no right to tell other people how to live their lives. This isn't the Soviet Union. Freedom is why we moved here. It's why everybody moved here. We can't expect others to leave us alone if we don't do the same for them."

Emma recognized that she should apply the same argument when Libby, more reticent than usual, ventured that she felt uncomfortable with the men who chose to parade around the campgrounds naked. She didn't know where to look when they were out there, squatting to cook their food or stretching to construct their lean-to, every-thing swaying freely in the breeze. Libby also didn't like the way they looked at her while they were doing it. They tried to meet her eyes. And whether she did or not, she said they made her feel ashamed for choosing either option.

Emma willed herself to stay calm as she clarified, "Did any of them try to touch you?"

Libby shook her head. Emma thought of Ronnie expounding how a similar problem had been solved via baseball bat. Could Amazon do one-day shipping on a baseball bat?

"Did they do anything else besides look at you?"

"No," Libby admitted. "They're just… creepy."

"There's nothing creepy about the human body." The parenting magazines insisted on that, too. "Being uncomfortable with someone else's actions isn't a valid reason to demand they stop doing it. How does them being naked hurt you?"

Libby opened her mouth to answer, then changed her mind and abruptly shut it. She looked down at her hands and shrugged.

"Have they hurt you, Libby?" Emma repeated. She softened her tone. "You can tell me."

"Nobody hurt me," Libby said, refusing to meet her mother's gaze. Emma lifted her child's chin with one hand and forced her to. She knew it went against the bodily autonomy they preached here, along with spiritual, emotional, and mental autonomy. Screw it. "Nobody hurt me," Libby reiterated more firmly. "I just don't like it, that's all."

Emma understood where Libby was coming from. If she were honest, she didn't like the exhibitionism either. Sagging balls, graying chest-hair and wrinkled asses were not a beautiful sight first thing in the morning. Or at any time of the day. But Emma's distaste was, as Dennis made clear, a "her" problem, not a "them" problem. She agreed, in theory. There were people who found the sight of Tammy and Ronnie together uncomfortable. There were people who found the sight of Emma's parents together uncomfortable, not to mention Emma's existence an abomination. Emma certainly didn't want to throw her lot in with those people. Which she would be doing if she judged her neighbors' lifestyles the way bigots judged others. So even though Emma sympathized with her not quite eleven-year-old daughter's distaste for being leered at by naked men, all Emma told her was, "You're fine."

The bears seemed like much less of a threat, in comparison. Libby hadn't even seen one. She'd just heard about them. Settlers on the far reaches of the property, those closest to the woods, claimed bears were coming out at night to rummage through their trash, looking for food. Those who didn't appreciate the development started picking up after themselves. Which, Dennis pointed out, was a perfect example of how an anarchist libertarian society was designed to work. Without being commanded or coerced, people acted in their own best interests which, in turn, benefited the rest of the community. People left out garbage, garbage attracted bears, people disposed of garbage. Cause, effect, gain—with no government intervention necessary.

Except that not everyone was getting with the program. Some people, sure, were taking steps to keep the wild animals off their property, while others were actively encouraging them to visit. Libby said that Summer said that River said that one man was deliberately laying out raw meat in the hope that a bear would shuffle by so he could shoot it. Another woman announced that, like the Little Prince and his fox, she was determined to tame the 400-pound black bear who sniffed around her property. She intended to trail food closer and closer to her house, until she could get him to eat straight out of her hand. Donuts were her lure of choice.

As a result, Libby was more terrified of leaving their trailer for fear of encountering a hungry predator, than she'd ever been of a wayward penis. Emma saw her point here. The difference was, this time, she actually went to Dennis about it.

"This isn't a personal freedom issue. The bears aren't part of the Free State project."

He was barely listening to her. Dennis' days now were filled with shooting video, editing video, uploading video and promoting video. In his spare time, he pitched articles, wrote articles, and promoted articles. Sometimes he did radio interviews by phone, and sometimes he hitched rides to Manchester or Concord, or Burlington in Vermont, or even back to NYC, to appear on a local talk show or a nationally syndicated special.

"These aren't pets. These are wild animals, Dennis."

"Just tell Libby to stay out of the woods."

"Who's going to tell the bears to stay out of our houses?"

"Bears have learned how to unlock doors now?"

"They're strong enough to burst right in! Libby says that's what happened at one place. The bear just pushed against the door, and it snapped right off its hinges. Owner came home to find their kitchen ransacked."

"Libby saw this happen?"

"Summer told her."

"Summer saw this happen?"

"Summer heard about it from River."

Dennis actually looked up from his computer long enough to wrinkle his lips at the corner. "We're playing telephone now? Rumors? Hearsay? This community is based on facts. Reason. Logic." He pointed at the screen. "What would happen if I started reporting rumors?"

"You'd be no different than any other media outlet."

Once upon a time, Dennis would have at least smiled at that. Once upon a time, he'd have been the one to say it. Now, he simply ignored Emma's barb. "Doesn't Libby have anything better to do than help spread ridiculous gossip?"

"Actually, Dennis, no, she doesn't. She doesn't have a school to go to. You, Tammy, and Ronnie saw to that. She doesn't have any clubs or leagues or teams to join, because we're in the middle of nowhere. She's watched all the DVD movies she brought, and the satellite dish keeps coming in and out. Sticking close to home means being surrounded by naked men and venturing any further risks getting eaten by bears. So, she's stuck in the house all day. We're both in the house all day. And it's not even a house. It's a glorified hallway. So, no, Libby doesn't have anything better to do. And she's getting pretty sick of it."

"Too fucking bad," Dennis snapped. He spun around in his desk-chair, facing Emma for the first time in she couldn't remember how long. "Maybe if you didn't coddle her, maybe if you didn't spoil her, she—and you, too—would appreciate what I'm trying to give you. I am trying to give you freedom. Do you know what I'd have done for that at her age? Not to be constantly told where to be, and who to be, and how to feel, and what to think? I am trying to save all of us from a life of serfdom!"

If his eruption was supposed to cower her into submission, it had the opposite effect. When Dennis was being calm and reasonable, Emma felt obliged to respond in kind. But if Dennis was going to yell, then Emma was damn well going to yell back.

"Libby doesn't care about your politics! She wants a normal life!"

"What's a normal life? Who had a normal life? Did you? Did I? Neither one of us had any choice in how we were raised. Did you enjoy being paraded around like a trained monkey? And, yes, monkey is exactly what they called you and your father. You know it, I know it. I certainly didn't ask to be branded an Enemy of the People at two years old. But I survived, you survived, and Libby will survive. I am trying to create a world for her where she can be whoever she wants to be. Where she doesn't have to obey blindly, like you and I were compelled to."

"But that's exactly what you're doing." Emma's righteous indignation faded into genuine confusion. Surely, Dennis could see the contradiction in what he was saying. Dennis had always been the first to identify hypocrisy, the first to call it out, if only to her. "You're forcing her to live where you want, how you want, why you want. How is this any different from your orphanage?"

"You're a fool." A frost settled over Dennis' words, dousing the fire, leaving only dry ice behind. "Your parents let you think the world revolved around you. That you could do whatever you wanted, like they did, and everything would go your way, like it did for them. I'm teaching my daughter how life really works. I want Libby to learn how to put up with shit for as long as she needs to, in order to get what she wants in the end. I am demonstrating to Libby how to always prepare for the worst, to be flexible, to be cunning. She is

     Alina Adams

going to learn that getting your own way means making your own way. Because no one hands you anything, they only rip out the rug from underneath you the minute you feel like you're getting anywhere. My daughter is going to be a fighter and a survivor. She's not going to be like you."

THE BEARS KEPT COMING. As expected, there was no consensus on how to deal with them. Some were thrilled with the opportunity to bring out their completely legal firearms. Others set traps. Still others sprinkled cayenne pepper on their garbage to discourage late-night snacking while another contingent lobbed lit firecrackers at the intruders.

"Mom!" Libby came running home one day, cheeks crimson and covered with tears. "Mom, Mom, Mom," she could barely get the next word out. "The k-k-k-itten!"

"What kitten? Summer's kitten?"

Libby's ambivalence toward hanging out with Ronnie and Tammy's brood had mellowed recently, when the moms gifted each of their children a kitten from a feral litter. Summer had been the most generous with visitation rights, and now Libby went over there nearly every day.

"What happened?" Emma scanned Libby's bare arms and legs for feline scratches. She suspected that women who refused to get their children vaccinated were even less likely to do so for household pets.

"We were… we were… we were…." Libby struggled to articulate her distress in between sobs. "We were playing, with the kitten, by the stream. She likes to drink from the stream. It's so cute. She scrunches up her face when water goes up her nose."

"Did the kitten drown?" Emma's heart sank at the thought of her daughter experiencing such trauma, even as she wondered what Ronnie and Tammy's views were on water safety. For kittens. And for children. Were they all playing in the creek unsupervised?

Libby shook her head so violently, her hair whipped from side to side. "A bear," she whispered. "It came right out of the woods. Right at us. It grabbed the kitten and it… and it… and… it put it right in its mouth!"

Emma's stomach churned. This was worse than she could have

possibly imagined. She focused on the one thing she could control. "Are you alright?"

"It ate her, Mom!"

"Is Summer OK?"

"We ran. We ran away as fast as we could. But the poor kitten. It chewed her up alive!"

"I'm sure it didn't feel anything." Emma could hear herself babbling, but also could think of nothing else to say. "It was so quick. I'm sure it didn't hurt."

"It was awful, Mom. I could hear its bones crunch. And then it spit out a part of its head. And then…" Emma hugged Libby tightly, partially to comfort her, partially to stop the torrent of details. Emma didn't want to learn anymore.

But she also knew it was her responsibility to find out.

EMMA LEFT LIBBY AT HOME, the door locked and with Dennis' reassurance, "Bears can't unlock doors, baby." She headed to Tammy and Ronnie's, where she found Summer equally tear-stained, but a great deal more serene.

"Valerian root." Tammy pointed to a beaker of dark brown liquid on their kitchen cabinet. "Great for calming, and all natural. I can pour you off a dose for Libby."

"No, thank you." Emma was familiar with Valerian root. In the USSR it went under the brand-name *Valeryanka*, and was distributed in lieu of otherwise unavailable medication for cramps, insomnia, anxiety, and menopausal symptoms. It was, to Emma's microbiologist mind, quackery with a dash of placebo. She pulled Tammy and Ronnie aside and whispered, "What are we going to do about these bear attacks? This has gone too far!"

The women exchanged glances. "The bear was just acting on its natural instincts. Who are we to interfere with nature?"

EMMA PREPARED to interfere with nature.

She took advantage of Libby feeling terrified to leave their trailer, to head into town alone. Emma claimed it was to pick up groceries. It was actually so she could make a call in private, in a location where

she was guaranteed reception. Emma looked the number up in the
Yellow Pages chained to a phone booth outside their police station.
She called the New Hampshire Fish and Game Department.

It was, she understood, the ultimate betrayal, her turning to a
government organization for assistance with a problem the Free State
movement had brought upon itself. Dennis would never forgive
Emma if he found out.

"Yup, yup," the woman who answered the phone chirped when
Emma filled her in on the crisis. "We've gotten a couple of phone
calls about Corinth already. I must say, the local citizens aren't very
happy with you all."

"Yes," Emma jumped on the opening. The Department might be
hostile to helping a band of interlopers, but, surely, they cared about
their local population. "It's gotten completely out of hand. You have
to step in."

"Yup, yup. Now, tell me, when the bear came up out of the forest,
was there, maybe, pot roast being cooked?"

The image of a giant beast masticating a kitten proved incongru-
ous with that same beast sniffing at a kitchen stove, à la Yogi Bear.
"No! This was outside! Nothing was being cooked. Two little girls
were playing with a kitten!"

"You really should be careful with cooking too close to their hab-
itats. Can't blame a bear for wanting a taste!"

"Right, natural instincts, I know." Emma struggled to remain
calm. "Your department, you're not just in charge of keeping people
safe, right? You're also in charge of protecting the bears? So, they
don't become endangered?" Emma had no idea if that was true. It
felt like it should be.

"Yup, yup."

"Well, ever since they started coming closer to people, a lot of
them are being shot."

"It's illegal to hunt bears without a license."

"Sure." Emma could just imagine how well being forced to sign
up for gun licenses would play in Corinth. But that was yet another
problem for another time. "So, shouldn't you come and do something about it?"

"Can't, I'm afraid." Where had all the "yup, yups" gone?

"Why not?"

"No money for it. Allocating funds for wild animal sustainability projects isn't very popular in New Hampshire."

Based on the city council meeting Emma witnessed, she shouldn't have been surprised.

"Besides, it's a bigger problem than just your garbage. All across the state, we're seeing drier summers. That means droughts. And warmer winters. That means less plants and animals to eat. Bears looking for food and water have no choice but to come into the cities, especially as the cities keep sprawling out into their woods."

"So shouldn't the Fish and Game Department be doing something about it?" Emma repeated dumbly.

"Soon as we get the funding," she agreed. "Yup, yup."

A BEAR WAS LOOMING over Libby. The entire world shrank down into just that pinprick of Emma's vision. A bear the height of a professional basketball player and the width of a hockey player was towering over her child.

Ever since the attack on Summer's kitten, Libby had refused to leave the camper. Taking counsel from the same parenting magazines which advised Emma to be penis positive and that boredom was good for a developing child's brain, Emma resolved to help Libby face her fears via the process of gradual, repeated exposure. She accompanied her outside for slightly longer and longer periods each day. After a week, they'd made it to the edge of the field. Which was when the bear came charging out at them.

Libby didn't scream. Libby didn't run. Libby didn't do anything.

She stood frozen to the spot. She covered her face with her hands, like a much younger child, who believed that if they couldn't see the threat, then it didn't exist.

After her extremely unproductive conversation with that representative of the Fish and Game Department, Emma had rented a PO Box in town and wrote a letter straight to the head of the commission. What she received in return was a single brochure, entitled, *Something's Bruin in New Hampshire—Learn to Live with Bears.*

The non-response made Emma livid. But, nonetheless, she'd read the instructions, which included *Tips on Avoiding UnBearable Conflicts*, a *Black Bear Fact Sheet*, *Preventing Poultry Loss by Bears*, *Protect Your Agricultural Investment*, and an introduction to *The Black Bear Society*. It also came with a sheet on: *What you should do if you encounter a black bear.*

The official literature advised: *Stand your ground and slowly back away.*

So, naturally, Emma went charging straight for it.

Chapter Twenty-Four

A bear the height of a professional basketball player and the width of a professional hockey player was towering over her child. And Emma was going to protect her.

Disappointed by the lack of useful instruction in her state's brochure, Emma had scoured the internet looking for more applicable advice. Thanks to Google and Yahoo, Emma now knew that, when facing an angry black bear, she should: 1) Play dead. 2) Definitely not play dead. 3) Kick and punch at the bear's face, using rocks and branches if available. 4) Make loud noises and wave her arms to seem bigger. 5) Avoid direct eye contact. 6) Don't run.

Emma ran. She ran for the bear, screaming. Her screams shook Libby out of her stupor. Libby dropped her hands, opened her eyes, and stared at Emma in shock. Then she ran.

To keep the bear from chasing Libby, Emma picked up a rock and hurled it at his flank. The bear turned around slowly, curious. But not so curious that he couldn't still return to Libby.

Emma looked him straight in the eye, to make certain that wouldn't be happening.

Now, she had his complete attention.

Emma now had a bear's complete attention.

This was not her best thought-out plan ever.

But it didn't matter. Because now the bear was focused on her, not Libby.

Now the bear was focused on her.

Should she halt or should she wave? Charge or retreat?

Emma dropped her gaze. She took a step backwards. The bear watched her, impassive. She took another step. He appeared even less interested. It was almost insulting. These bears had grown so accustomed to people, a human not carrying donuts was apparently not even worth interacting with anymore.

Emma inched backwards until she found a tree she could duck behind. She counted to one hundred, then counted to one hundred again, terrified that what she imagined to be the sound of a bear lumbering away was actually him circling to find her. One more hundred count, and Emma dared peek. No bear. No Libby.

Emma hightailed it back to the camper.

"YOU'RE FINE, YOU'RE PERFECTLY FINE." Emma arrived home to find Dennis rocking Libby on his lap like he hadn't since she was a little girl. "And look," Dennis pivoted Libby so she could see the door. "Here's Mom. She's perfectly fine, too, just like I promised. See? All good."

"Mom!" Libby leapt up to wrap her arms around Emma's waist. She hadn't been doing a lot of that lately.

Dennis grinned in relief. Despite his promises to Libby, Emma could tell he'd been at least a little worried. But now that she was here, unscathed, his certainty returned in full. "What did I tell you? Nothing to worry about!"

Dennis looked to Emma for confirmation. Her instinct was to give in to him. Yes, of course. Of course, she was fine. Of course, there'd been nothing to worry about. How silly of Libby to make a fuss. Didn't she know everything was wonderful?

"We almost got attacked by a bear!" Emma heard herself saying, as much to her own surprise as to Dennis'.

"But you're fine," he repeated, more firmly this time.

Cheek against Emma's chest, Libby looked up at her mother. Her lashes were still clumped with tears. Emma saw scratches on Libby's arms from where she must have gotten scraped by loose branches while blindly running away.

"Tell Libby you're fine," Dennis instructed, his undercurrent suggesting this was not a suggestion. "Tell her you're both fine, no harm done."

Emma kissed the top of her daughter's head. She tapped the cuts on her arms with a finger and told Libby, "Go take a shower, wash those out, and I'll put some Neosporin on them later. We don't want you getting infected."

Libby peered questioningly at Dennis. He shrugged. "Do what your mother says."

They both waited for the water to start running before resuming their conversation.

"Are you alright?" Dennis asked, managing to sound both concerned and perfunctory.

"You've already declared that I am."

"No reason to upset Libby."

"Libby has been upset since the day we got here!"

"She'll be fine."

"You keep saying that. Maybe one day it will even be true."

"I'm sorry about what happened, OK? I'm sure it must have been terrifying for you."

"Only I'm not allowed to admit it."

"Admit it all you want. Admit it to me, admit it to your mother, admit it from the rooftops. Just keep Libby out of it."

"She was there. She saw what happened. Do you want me to pretend otherwise?"

"I don't see the point of dwelling on it."

"And I don't see the point of sweeping it under the rug. No," Emma corrected, "scratch that. I see the point. I see your point; I see Mom's point. Keep repeating your version of events enough, and eventually it becomes the official version. I believe that was Lenin's point, too."

"So, I'm Lenin, now? Or am I your mother?"

"You all employ the same blueprint. Stalin, too."

"Could you, at least, pretend, Emma?" He was using her choice of words. Either as a peace offering. Or as a threat.

"Pretend what?"

"Pretend to be on my side?"

"Are you kidding me? I've been on your side since the beginning. I left Moscow with you. I went to all those ridiculous, Socialist performance-art parties with you. And then, when you did a 180, so did I. I came here because of you. I live in a trailer because of you. My daughter got attacked by a bear because of you!"

"You got to leave Moscow because of me. You got to live in America because of me."

"I never denied that."

"You never thanked me, either."

"That's what this is about? You want a thank you note?"

"Fuck your thank you note. You act like everything I gave you was your due. Like it just happened. All the work I put in, all the work I'm still putting in, the least you could do is support me!" She'd known Dennis for nearly twenty years. She'd thought she understood him. She'd thought she'd seen his true self during those frantic days when he was trying to figure out how to come out on top post-coup. The Dennis berating her now was either a total stranger, or, finally, the unadulterated man she'd married. "Not everybody, Emma, gets to be born a celebrity. Some of us have to fight for every crumb of bread, for every breath, merely to claw from one day to the next."

"I know." She could feel her conviction wavering. Nobody had to tell Emma that she'd lived her life in a cosseted cocoon. No matter how many times Mom insisted they were just like anybody else, no special privileges for the Cains of Moscow!

"You don't know anything. You couldn't survive for a minute in the real world, without your Daddy and Mommy, without me. This is my last chance; do you understand that?"

"No. Dennis. Don't be ridiculous. This isn't life or death. Nothing is."

"Everything is," he corrected. "I should have been executed with my parents. I should have starved in the orphanage. I should have drunk myself to death like literally every other stray I grew up with. I should have been discarded with Communism. Instead, I bought myself second chance after second chance. I won't go back to being nothing."

"But you don't really believe this nonsense, do you?" Where had the man gone who'd wooed her with the credo: *I am looking for a woman who sees the world the way it is. Not the way we keep being told it is. A shared sense of cynicism, that's the true kismet.*

It was a different Dennis, a stranger Dennis who replied, "My critical mistake was believing a political philosophy could protect me. Any political philosophy. They're all just smoke and mirrors. Pull back the curtain and they're all exactly the same. Propagating the cause means sacrificing the individual. Damn the man, save the empire. I thought I was surviving because I'd attached myself to the *cause de joure*. I got it backwards. The only reason I've survived this long is because I was looking out for myself. The collective was hindering me, not helping me."

"Yes," Emma felt like they were having two different conversations. Dennis' charge of her failing to support him had stung. As had his allegation that she couldn't survive without him. Even if both were untrue, she presently felt it wise to agree with him. At least until he'd calmed down. "You're right. Everything you've achieved, you did on your own."

"That's why this," Dennis' sweep of the arm encompassed not just their trailer or the field out beyond it, "is perfect. It's all about the individual. This is exactly where I should have been all along. My life, my success, my survival is in my hands, no one else's."

"But that's not true." Emma's agreeableness appeared to have a shelf-life of barely a few minutes. "Come on, Dennis, you can see how untrue that is. Sure, you're you, and I'm me, and Libby is Libby. We can all do our own thing, but someone else leaves their trash out, or doesn't vaccinate their kids, or decides that feeding bears donuts is a cool thing to do, and we all still feel the effects of it. You can't possibly believe what you're saying!"

She kept stressing that final point. Emma and Dennis were together because they saw the world the way it was. Cynicism had brought them together; cynicism had kept them together. If that disappeared, what remained?

"It's our last chance," he repeated. "Can't you at least try?"

She thought she had been trying. And, maybe, if it had just been her, Emma would have been willing to continue trying.

"I can't do this to Libby. I can't tell her that everything is fine when we both know it isn't. I can't keep telling her to ignore what she sees. I can't order her not to trust her own judgment."

"I am not your mother. This isn't the same thing."

"I can't go on pretending," Emma said.

EMMA CALLED A CAR to drive them to Durham Station. She and Libby rode the train into Grand Central, then the subway to Mom's apartment in Harlem. It was walking distance from Columbia, where Emma had already arranged to get her old job back. The plan was for her and Libby to stay with Rose until Emma found a place for the two of them. They'd get their things out of storage. They'd resume the life they'd left, though without Dennis. He hadn't fought Emma on leaving. That would go against his individualistic principles. He'd said good-bye to Libby without a fuss. He told her she was welcome to visit him, but he wouldn't force it. Just because she was a child, that didn't mean she'd given up her right to self-determination.

"I couldn't do it," Emma told Mom as they were making up a bed for her and Libby on the couch. "I couldn't be like Dad, give up my whole life for a cause."

"Jonas did it for me," Rose corrected.

Was that possibly the beginning of an admission?

"I couldn't be like you either." Emma confessed the shame which had been nagging her from the moment she'd made up her mind to abandon ship. "I think about you, closer to Libby's age now than you were mine, heading off to Spain, into a war zone. I try to imagine the noise, the shooting, the blood, you must have been terrified. Hell, you stuck it out under fascism, and I couldn't handle garbage and nudity. You were fighting Franco. I got scared off by a bear."

"Revolution," Rose sighed, "isn't for everybody."

She wasn't even pretending not to be disappointed.

Part Three: Rojava

Chapter Twenty-Five

2012

Libby's email read: *I'm going, Mom. Please understand.*

Whenever Libby asked her to understand, she meant: *Agree with me.*

Whenever Libby said she was going, she meant: *I already went.*

Emma closed her laptop, pulled on her sneakers, and took the 2 train from her home on the Upper West Side of Manhattan to Harlem. She used her phone to show Rose what Libby had written. She told her mother, "She's doing this because of you. So, you're the one who has to bring her back home."

"Me," Rose repeated, managing to stretch the word out into three, doubting synonyms. "Only me? Not Dennis?"

Libby hadn't seen her dad in the almost ten years since they'd left Corinth. They kept in touch through email and video chat. Emma made a point of leaving the room and closing Libby's bedroom door to give them their privacy. Though she couldn't help overhearing phrases like "an alternative vision to the nation-state model," "libertarian municipalism," and names like "Abdullah Öcalan" and "Murray Bookchin." Were these normal conversations for a teenage girl to pursue with her father? Since they weren't that different from the ones Emma endured growing up with her mother, she had to assume so.

Emma periodically popped on to say hello to her husband. Yes, he was still her husband. When Emma floated the idea of divorce, Dennis responded with a two-page diatribe against government having a say in relationships between consenting parties. He managed to invoke the 13th Amendment, Loving v. Virginia and The Defense of Marriage Act to back up his position. The bottom line was *No*. Emma let it stand. She wasn't interested in getting remarried, and Dennis didn't take advantage of their status to demand money from her—that, too, would be against his individualistic principles. He sent child support for Libby. Even if Emma suspected he had little to spare. Though Dennis became a major name in Libertarian circles, once again invited to parties and rallies and to comment on national events in major newspapers, without a television show, his actual income was negligible. He'd monetized his YouTube channel and some other platforms, but he continued living in the same camper they'd bought in 2003. It's what ended up killing him.

In early January, a fire broke out in his encampment. Nobody was sure how it started, but under the circumstances Emma remembered, the fact that they'd avoided a similar inferno for a decade was a miracle. Residents not caught in the flames were felled by smoke inhalation. Thanks to their constant voting to keep taxes low, Corinth was down to only one firetruck, and it couldn't even get to the blaze, as its tires had been slashed in some unspecified political protest months earlier. The budget didn't allow for replacements.

"Libby may miss her dad. I know she misses her dad. She brings him up so much more to me now than she ever did when he was alive. But you will also notice that, at no point over the past ten years, did Libby express a desire to visit him, much less stay with him. Maybe Dennis' death is what spurred her to take off now, rather than doing something silly like waiting until after she'd finished college, or at least the conclusion of the semester. Nonetheless, Libby made it very clear that she had no interest in living the way Dennis did. She had enough of that the summer we spent in Corinth. You're the one who filled her head with romantic tales of fighting Nationalists in Spain, of charging off to save the world. She wants to be like you, not like Dennis. That's why she's gone to Goddamn Rojava!"

Rojava. Emma began hearing about the Kurdish region of Syria and their battle against ISIS, the Islamic State of Iraq and Syria, just as Libby started her freshman year at Middlebury College. Libby chose the Vermont school based on their celebrated International and Global Studies program. She wrote her application essay on her father and her grandparents, how she intended to continue their proud tradition of activism. Emma suspected she didn't come up in her daughter's statement unless it was as an example of indolent apostates who refused to engage in insurgency. Libby's infatuation with Rojava suggested to Emma nothing more than that her daughter was enjoying her classwork. And Emma had to admit, the topic was certainly interesting. After their Worker's Party was banned in Turkey, some Kurds immigrated to Syria, primarily the area known as Rojava. There, they founded the Democratic Union Party.

So far, so Revolution 101.

What really captured the imagination of not just Libby, but multiple dreamers around the world, was the phenomenon which came to be known as the Women's Revolution.

Syria's civil war opened the door to not only a revival of the Kurdish liberation movement, but the chance to create, from scratch, the concept of democratic confederalism. They wouldn't merely push back on President Bashar al-Assad, they wouldn't merely battle to eradicate ISIS. They would, in the process, establish a society based on democratic autonomy, gender equality, feminism, and environmentalism. Rojava would be governed by elected councils, commissions, and coordinating bodies. These four levels of autonomous, self-organized councils would be connected through a bottom-up pyramid. Communes would extend through neighborhood and district levels, followed by People's Councils to represent each canton. Power was structured to arise from the lowest level, where each resident was free to be involved in all decision-making. The goal of such a grass-roots organization was to be non-hierarchical, non-discriminatory, and to make a state of any kind unnecessary.

But that wasn't all. Every level of commune, council, commission or court was mandated to be occupied by two democratically elected co-chairs, one of which must be a woman. In any mixed-gender institutions, democratically elected women were required to make up a minimum forty percent. This was in addition to separate women's communes and women's councils in every district specifically designed to advance women's interests.

Among those interests was the banning of child marriage, as well as any kind of forced marriage, polygamy, dowry payments, and honor killings. Rape and domestic violence were decreed illegal, while abortion was permitted. To ensure these principles were carried out, the justice system was also non-hierarchical, with consensus taking priority over a formal vote when it came to passing judgment. Security forces were trained in feminist theory and non-violence before they were issued weapons.

Furthermore, in 2011, Rojava introduced the concept of *jineology*. This Kurdish feminist movement aimed to correct the absence of women in the writing of history and science. Women and men received training and education in jineology and the history of oppression. Rojavan men were taught how to overcome gendered, stereotypical, and oppressive behavior, with the goal of creating a new type of man, alongside the freely liberated woman.

Emma agreed with Libby. It all sounded absolutely wonderful.

But Emma had grown up surrounded by a philosophy that also sounded absolutely wonderful. And she had seen how that played out in reality.

Emma foolishly assumed Libby had learned that same lesson after Corinth. But apparently, it either hadn't sunk in thoroughly or, like every American Socialist Emma had ever met, the working assumption was that the USSR had failed because Marxist principles hadn't been applied correctly. When they were in charge, they would apply them correctly.

And the subsequent society would be absolutely wonderful.

Emma would have been embarrassed by her child's naivete—not to mention her conventionality. Libby was asserting her individuality by thinking and acting just like everybody else her age. But there was no room for embarrassment while Emma was consumed with terror for Libby's life.

"How does she even intend to get there?" Emma raged at Rose. She hated to think that Libby might have confided in her grandmother over her mother. On the other hand, she'd be grateful if Rose knew something more about Libby's plans than Emma did. "It's not like you hop on a direct flight and there you are. Isn't this one of those plane, train, automobile, trek through the hills kind of deals? My God, it makes crossing the Mexican border with a coyote feel like an all-expense paid royal cruise in comparison."

"There are emissaries to help volunteers get across. Luba will not be the only one. They are avidly recruiting fighters for the People's Protection Units. They have all-women units."

"So that's what she's doing? She's volunteering to fight a guerilla war against ISIS?"

"I presume."

"You presume, or you know?"

"I'll find out," Mom promised.

AND THE IRONY WAS, Rose did. Thanks to her work in the non-profit space since returning to America, it only took Rose a half-dozen phone calls before she was able to confirm that Libby and a group of other American, British, Italian, and German students had taken off for the Middle East in order to join the International Freedom Battalion of the US-backed People's Protection Unit, the YPG. The United States was sending those Kurdish fighting forces warplanes, drones, artillery, weapons… and young people. Volunteers. Like the ones who'd decamped for Spain in the previous century.

"I'm going to get her," Emma said.

She expected Mom to fight her. She expected a lecture on how Libby was simply doing no more, no less than what Rose had done back in the day. She expected to be told that her daughter was a grown, nineteen-year-old woman and Emma should let her make her own decisions and take her own risks, especially when it came to such a noble cause.

But all Rose said was, "I'm coming with you."

Now it would have been Emma's turn to fight. To lecture on how, unlike Libby, Mom was a 90-something woman. In 1939, she might have been up to bumpy plane trips, doorless jeep rides, and slogging through miles of mud under gunfire. But this was 2012. Emma questioned her own odds of coming out alive. Rose's prospects, anyone could see, were even more dire.

But, in the end, Emma had no choice in the matter. Everyone she turned to for help in transporting her halfway across the globe and into Rojava, pleaded ignorance of how anybody might possibly accomplish such an endeavor. Rose proved to be the one with the connections.

So, Rose proved to be the one spearheading their expedition into a war zone.

EMMA WOULD HAVE ASSUMED even the first leg of their journey would be too much for Mom. They couldn't fly into Turkey. Their border with Rojava was closed. As a result, Emma and Rose were forced to take the twelve-hour flight from New York to Damascus. Mom arranged for their Syrian tourist visas, and she was the one who charmed their way past the border guard who wanted to know why they were in his country.

"To see the Al-Azem Palace in the Old City," Rose replied as smoothly as if she'd been asked her name. Her 91-year-old mother who, as far as Emma could tell, hadn't slept a wink on the plane, came off sharper than her 54-year-old daughter. Emma couldn't stop yawning, picking at the dry skin around her lips and eyes. She could barely remember where they'd landed, much less why. She certainly didn't possess the wherewithal to construct a cogent lie about it, though she'd had the entire flight time to do so. "I'm told it's among the best architecture the Ottoman Empire had to offer."

"It is the best," he clarified.

"The best," Rose agreed, and offered him a smile that managed to be both flirtatious and utterly old lady harmless.

"Have a wonderful visit," he said, stamping their passports, and waving Rose and Emma in.

The next logical step would be a flight from Damascus to

Al-Qamishli in northeast Syria, along the Turkish border. But that would require waiting two days, then still finding some means for crossing into Rojava. Emma wasn't enthused about either option. She didn't want to spend any more time in Syria than she absolutely had to. Even if they couldn't tell by looking at her that Emma had a daughter who'd just volunteered to fight against them, they could certainly tell all sorts of other things by looking at Emma and Mom's faces, not to mention their names.

"How well do people named Janowitz and Kagan do wandering around Syria?"

"Relax," Rose advised, "they haven't publicly hanged a Jew since 1965. And he was an Israeli spy, so it wasn't just a random execution." In response to Emma's unamused expression, Rose shrugged. "What? I read."

"Did you read about it while living in Moscow?" Emma's curiosity got the best of her.

Rose nodded.

"And you agreed with what the Syrians did?"

Rose nodded again, a little less certainly.

"You didn't feel even the smallest twinge. Him being a Jew, you being a Jew…"

"I renounce any kind of tribalism."

"Good. You can tell them that if we're arrested. I'm sure it'll carry a lot of weight."

"I don't intend to stay in Syria long enough to risk arrest."

"So how do we get out of here?" Emma whispered, though no one was paying the least bit of attention to them as they crossed the airport.

"The same way as Luba."

ROSE HAD MADE A CALL to someone who made a call to someone who forwarded an email to someone who made a call to someone who sent a text. Within five hours of getting off a plane in Damascus, Rose and Emma had been picked up by a car who took them to the outskirts of what appeared to be a completely deserted airfield. They were instructed to wait. And then the driver took off, his headlights the final bit of fading illumination. Even the moon didn't feel like engaging tonight.

They were two women, each clutching a rucksack, standing alone, in the dark, in the middle of Nowhere, Syria. Even Mom didn't tell Emma to relax this time.

"At least we know they won't hang us," Emma offered. "There's no public around to watch."

It was Rose's turn to look unamused.

There was nothing for them to do. There was nowhere for them to go. If this was a setup, there was nowhere for them to run, nowhere to hide. So, Emma and Rose simply waited. At least it wasn't cold. Nighttime outside of Damascus was actually quite delightful. If you weren't paralyzed by fear. And trying your darndest not to show it.

Almost an hour after they'd been dumped and abandoned, Emma heard the buzz of what sounded like a small plane growing closer. She couldn't help thinking of the crop duster scene in Alfred Hitchcock's *North by Northwest*. She wondered if they should take cover. Unlike Cary Grant, they didn't have a handy cornfield to duck into. So, they stayed where they were, watching what did, indeed, prove to be a light aircraft, glide and touch down without turning on their lights. That didn't seem safe.

The plane bounced to a stop, the pilot's side door opened. A male voice ordered, "In."

Was he talking to them? Was there anyone else for him to talk to? In English, no less?

Emma and Rose exchanged looks. Then, without a word, both moved in his direction. It's not like they had any better offers.

If they were taken aback by the sight of their unexpected deliverer, that was nothing compared to the disdain which crossed his face once he'd laid eyes on Rose and Emma.

"Volunteers only."

"We're volunteers." Once again, Rose's ability to become whoever she needed to be in that instant came in disturbingly handy.

"Kids," he specified.

"Oh," Rose reached to pull herself up on the first rung of the rope ladder he'd tossed out before getting a good look at them. "I lied."

EMMA WONDERED if the pilot was just going to sit there, watching as her mother struggled. It might have been perversely entertaining, but she also suspected they didn't have all the time in the world. Men who flew into abandoned airstrips with their lights off to pick up anonymous passengers tended to not be following prescribed flight plans.

"Will you help her, please? Otherwise, we'll be here all night."

Seeing Emma's point, he reached out, slipped his hands under Rose's armpits and swept her from the ground, into the cabin. Emma followed behind on the ladder, eager to prove that she, on the other hand, could manage on her own. The pilot did the same to her. She couldn't blame him. Emma was the one who'd pointed out they were in a hurry.

He gestured for them to move to the back, where the cargo hold was filled to the ceiling with wooden crates and overstuffed canvas bags. He didn't say what they were, and Emma knew better than to ask. She hoped they weren't the artillery and drones the US was supplying. And, if they were, she hoped they weren't the kind which exploded on their own.

"Hold on," he advised, without suggesting onto what. A moment later, they were back in the air. Rose propped herself against the wall, arranging the softer canvas bags as a barrier between her and the crates. Emma did the same, squeezing in beside her mother.

"You've done this before?" she guessed.

Rose shrugged. "Some things, you never forget."

Emma expected a bumpy flight. Who knew what sort of loop de loop maneuvers they might need to do to avoid radar detection or, worse, anti-aircraft fire. Which was why she was surprised when, less than an hour after they'd taken off, she heard the creaking sound of wheels descending, followed by the soft bump of hitting the earth and gliding to a smooth stop.

"Air Force training," Rose identified. "Special Warfare unit. They need to be able to fly in without being noticed, and land without making a sound."

Who knew Emma's mother was such a fount of specific and

obscure knowledge? Emma supposed she might have known. If she'd bothered to ask.

Emma rolled over onto her knees, crawling towards the cockpit and straightening up in preparation for exiting. When she noticed Rose wasn't budging, Emma turned back and held out her hand, asking, "Need help, Mom?"

Emma, once again, considered the folly of taking a nonagenarian into a war zone. Had Rose given any thought to what they would do if she got sick or hurt?

But Rose ignored Emma's overture, eyes fastened on the plane's rear doors which, sure enough, in the time it took their pilot to jump out and walk around, were opened not only by him, but by a dozen young people piling in behind him, each grabbing a bag, a box, and proceeding to haul them outside. Only then did Rose climb to her feet and follow. She gestured for Emma to do the same. Not that Emma couldn't figure out the next steps on her own. She was just a little thrown off. Momentarily.

But not nearly as thrown off as in the next moment, when, among the khaki-clad men and women helping to unload cargo, Emma spied Libby.

She'd anticipated needing to look for her, going door to door with a photo, trying to make herself understood. She'd weighed the possibility of exposing Libby to danger in case she was in hiding… or something. Emma had no idea how things worked here. How much danger was her daughter actually in?

And yet there Libby was. Tall and slender like Dennis, her hair a light brown, straight like his, too. Only her eyes were pitch black. Darker than Emma's. Darker than Mom's. They were Dad's eyes. They didn't exactly fit with the pallor of her skin, but Emma and Rose had marveled over them since Libby was a newborn. It gave them a thrill to see a part of Jonas looking back at them.

Stunned, Emma didn't know what to say. Mom never suffered from such malady.

"Lubochka!" she cried, startling not just Libby, but her fellow combatants, who appeared shocked to hear Rose's Russian.

At least Libby had the decency to look as astonished as Emma felt, nearly dropping her end of the grain sack she was helping to maneuver outside. "Grandma?" And then, with even more disbelief, "Mom?"

Emma tried not to take it personally that her daughter thought Rose more likely to pop up in these mutinous mountains than her own mother.

They scrambled to keep up with her and the rest of the troop who kept sneaking curious, unabashed glances at what the proverbial cat had dragged in. But only Libby, once she'd loaded her freight onto one of the half-dozen open-backed trucks lined up waiting for them, demanded, "What the hell are you doing here?"

"Your mother was worried about you," Rose replied, as if Emma had dropped into Libby's dorm ahead of parents' weekend, not traveled halfway around the world.

"Are you nuts, Mom?"

"Heading out!" A girl barely older than Libby called from the head of the convoy, and everyone jumped into either the cabin or the back of the truck they were standing closest to. Libby moved to do so as well, then hesitated, looking from the vehicle to Emma and Rose, and back again, paralyzed with indecision.

Rose opened the cabin door. She painstakingly but efficiently climbed inside, scooching over to make room for Emma.

"Heading out," Rose confirmed. And slammed the door definitively behind her.

Chapter Twenty-Six

Their ride to base camp took almost as long as the flight from Syria had. And it wasn't nearly as smooth. Sometimes there was a road through the mountains. Sometimes it was just well-worn tracks made by other transportation. Sometimes, it was no more than a cliff-face on one side, a drop straight down on the other. Whatever path they were taking, it was obviously not the shortest distance between two points. They meandered from mountains to countryside to concrete encampments that looked as if a giant child had tried to build a series of buildings but got frustrated and knocked off all the roofs with one, furious swipe. Some structures were missing their front facades, continuing the illusion of multiple dollhouses. Only doll houses were rarely charred by mortar fire. The only signs of life were the graffiti. Most of it was in Arabic. But Emma did spy a huge, red, spray-painted hammer and sickle. She swiveled her head to try and catch Mom's reaction to the bygone symbol. But either it was too dark in the cab, or Rose was deliberately keeping her expression neutral.

To Emma, there was no marked difference between the fifth concrete compound and the four they'd bypassed previously. But this was where they stopped, everyone jumping out just as efficiently as they'd clambered in, to unload their trucks. Emma climbed out. She helped Rose do the same, though her mother made a point of not needing assistance. Emma recalled her first glimpse of Corinth which she'd deemed *Grapes of Wrath* level squalor. This made New Hampshire look like paradise. What had Gertrude Stein condemned Oakland as? *There is no there, there?* In Rojava, Emma felt hard pressed to find *here.* She saw a maze of white stone bunkers, some missing facades, some missing roofs, most with barely hanging on doors and shattered windows. The only light had to be from candles, maybe one barely functioning generator. Barren land on all four sides. Some trucks, some smaller cars, maybe a tractor, maybe a tank, and, in the distance, what appeared to be a series of scarecrows but, when she saw Emma's confusion, Rose whispered, "Shooting range."

More camouflage-clad bodies spilled out of the dilapidated buildings to help put away what they'd brought. Some wore red, green, and yellow scarves wrapped around their heads. Emma saw patches from American and other military units. She saw green triangles with red stars. She saw the letter YPG.

"People's Defense Units." Libby came up behind Emma and Rose to translate. "The yellow is for all. The green is for the Women's Battalions."

Ever since hearing Libby's email ping into her inbox, Emma had been picturing what would happen when she set eyes on her again. She envisioned herself shaking Libby, she envisioned herself shouting at Libby. But now that the moment was finally at hand, all Emma could do was hug Libby. And then she shook her. And then she shouted, "What the hell do you think you're doing?"

Libby looked around her, embarrassed, as if Emma had shown up on the first day of middle school and made Libby look uncool in front of the girls she hoped would be her friends.

"I'm helping." Libby looked to Rose for affirmation. "I'm making the world a better place."

Emma genuinely didn't know what to say. Was she supposed to forbid her nineteen-year-old daughter from pursuing such a noble goal? Emma certainly wanted to. She, at least, wanted to ask why making the world a better place required Libby to put her life in danger? Didn't Libby understand that the world was a better place with her in it?

Taking Emma's silence as assent, Libby pressed her luck, gushing as she gestured around her, "It's awesome. You have no idea. A true community. Volunteers from everywhere. Syria, Turkey, Iran, the US, England, France, the foreign legion. Arabs, Muslims, Christians, Westerners, even Native Americans. Communists, Socialists, anarchists, all working together towards the same goal."

"20,000 liberty-loving Americans from all walks of life," Dennis had said, *"Republicans, Democrats, Independents, Libertarians, Anarchocapitalists, Pacifists."* All working together to achieve a common goal. Emma remembered how that had turned out. Didn't Libby?

Their cargo unloaded; the young people gravitated towards the ramshackle buildings. Libby joined them. Emma and Rose had no choice but to follow.

"Shouldn't we," Emma wasn't quite sure how to put this, "check in or… something?"

Libby laughed. "It's not a Holiday Inn, Mom."

"I understand. But we're volunteers. Shouldn't we let someone know we're here? Who's in charge?"

"Nobody," Libby chirped, delighted. "That's what makes this place so special. Everyone is equal. Nobody's in charge. It's a communal effort."

"We choose our government so that our government can carry out our will," the audience member at that long-ago Donahue/Kagan summit had said. *"I don't understand how I could be in disagreement with a person who is doing what I want them to do. If I were to ask someone to do something and he did that, then I can't disagree with that."*

Libby showed Emma and Rose how they could glide their hands along the wall so they might navigate unlit stairs. Libby took Rose's other arm to guide her up. After three flights, they entered a common room the width of the entire floor. The glassless windows were boarded up. A kerosene lamp illuminated each corner. Sleeping bags and bundles of blankets lay scattered about the floor. Libby led Rose to one burrow, pulling back a green knitted blanket to reveal what might once have also been a blanket underneath. "You can take my bed, Grandma. Mom and I will find another spot."

As with the hammer and sickle insignia, Emma couldn't tell if it was just too dark to see, or if Rose was deliberately keeping her expression neutral.

"Just like old, Spanish times, huh, Mom?"

"Yes," Rose nodded after a longer pause than Emma expected. "Very similar."

Emma immediately felt guilty. If she was ready to collapse from exhaustion, how must Rose feel? She gestured for Libby to take her grandmother's left elbow, while Emma reached for the right. Together, they settled Rose on the pallet. Libby offered to bring her water. She pulled a granola bar out of her fatigue pocket and asked Rose if she was hungry.

Her daughter was a good girl. Emma had to remember that. Even when she was doing something phenomenally reckless, Emma should remember Libby's impulse was noble.

Rose declined both offers. She waved Libby and Emma away and was asleep within minutes. The kerosene lights being extinguished suggested her daughter and granddaughter had best do the same.

In the near darkness, Libby dragged Emma to an unused sleeping bag. "We should both be able to fit in here."

"What about the person it belongs to?"

"We don't have personal belongings here. If you need it, you use it."

"Fine," Emma clarified. "What about the person who usually uses it?"

"She's dead," Libby said, before closing her eyes and turning her back on her mother.

EMMA EXPECTED SOME KIND of reveille wake up call. She'd been up since dawn, bracing herself for what she presumed would be a horn blare or a door-to-door drill sergeant. She was so tense with anticipation, she startled, heart speeding, at the slightest noise. A snore, a body turning over, footsteps on the stairs.

No such clarion came. Instead, as hesitant beams of light edged their way in past the covered windows, first one figure stirred, then another. The noise woke up other sleepers, who sat up in their bundles, stretched, and greeted their comrades.

"Good morning, Friend Libby."

"Good morning, Friend Ameena."

Libby explained to Emma, "We always address each other as Friend, to remember that's what we are."

"I got that," Emma said.

The last few sleeping holdouts were gently nudged awake, not unlike the way Emma used to pry Libby out of bed before school. They helped Rose rise from the floor. Emma noticed she didn't protest their assistance nearly as much this time.

"We start the day by meeting," Libby expounded as they made their way down the stairs, still needing the wall for guidance as no sunlight could penetrate that deeply into the interior. "This morning, we will discuss last night's operation; what went well, what could have gone better. Everyone will have the chance to speak and offer suggestions on how others might improve."

"Oh." Emma knew how to play this game. "*Samokritika.*"

Emma couldn't count the number of such meetings she'd attended in the USSR. Starting in first grade up through high school, university, and any place she'd ever worked, citizens were expected to gather and call out their comrades for failures adhering to proper Socialist behavior. Crimes could range from refusing to share colored pencils during drawing time to challenging a teacher's interpretation of a text to criticizing the efficiency of their workplace. The accused was then expected to admit their wrongdoing, perhaps throw in a few other, previously unmentioned infractions to prove their sincerity, and grovel for the group's forgiveness, accepting whatever punishment was doled out with gratitude.

"Oh, no," Libby recoiled. "It's not like that at all. *Samorkritika* was intended to humiliate and penalize people. It was a form of government control. Our meetings are the exact opposite. We want to bring out the best in everyone, in order to strengthen the collective as a whole."

"*We express our opinions from the heart,*" the other audience member at the summit had sworn, "*and we listen to our government with joy because it is right in all things.*"

"It's been so helpful to me." Once again, because she sensed she couldn't win Emma over, Libby focused her paean on Rose. "For instance, I learned that my form of feminism is rich, white woman, western feminism. It's way too focused on the individual, rather than on the group. I'm working hard on changing my mindset here. On other imperialist notions also, like queer theory, since that comes directly from capitalism. They offer daily classes on *jineology*. That's the correct, cooperative form of feminism. The reason we're able to have true equality in Rojava among races, religions, and genders, is because only when women are liberated, can all people be truly liberated."

It was Emma herself who told Dennis decades earlier, "*I grew up in a country which is very proud to say they do not notice differences in race, ethnicity, or gender roles.*"

After a breakfast of flatbread coated with a fig marmalade reçel— Libby informed them that both were produced by women-owned cooperatives with no interest in profit, so they were able to sell their goods for less than what was available in the general marketplace; they offered it for free to those without financial means and to volunteers fighting to defend their homeland—Emma and Rose tagged along to the self-criticism meeting. Libby noted that nobody ordered them to do it, it was simply what the group—which now included Emma and Rose, there was no criteria for joining or any kind of citizenship test or loyalty oath—agreed to at this time.

The meeting was held out in the open, in the shadows of the figures Emma had mistaken for scarecrows but which now, up close, she saw were wooden figures riddled in bullet holes. Everyone sat in a series of circles upon the ground, though before Rose could settle next to Emma, Libby came to lead her grandmother to a group of older women who were perched upon a series of rocks, around which the circles had formed. Offered no such privilege, Emma plopped down on the outskirts of the gathering.

A lone figure stood to shout something Emma didn't understand.

"She is asking, in Kurdish: *Do you have any problems, friends?*" Libby translated before leaving Emma to take a seat closer to her unit.

When did Libby learn Kurdish? Emma wondered. And then she remembered the magic of the internet. Her daughter had been preparing for her adventure much longer than Emma had been the wiser. For all she knew, it was what Libby and Dennis had been discussing with the door closed.

One of the younger women stood up to say something. When she sat down, another stood up to speak. The first stood up again to counter. The second stood up to rejoin. Then a third party had something to contribute. The first had something very specific to say about that. This went on for almost ten minutes. Having no idea what was being discussed, Emma amused herself by looking past the convocation, studying the barren landscape; mostly rocks with a few pathetic plants trying to break through the coarse earth. She was surprised to note, a few feet away from her, also more on the outside than in, the pilot who'd delivered them to Rojava. He appeared to be a few years younger than Emma, which marked them as the outliers, neither the youthful rebels, nor the venerated older women. He sat, elbows propped on his upraised knees, eyes closed, either listening intently, or not listening at all. Unlike the soldiers, he didn't wear a uniform, opting for jeans and a tan shirt, which Emma could see had been repeatedly patched under the arms and along the collar. The face, neck, and hands that peeked out were the color of tree bark which had been oversaturated with sunshine, then dragged some distance. His hair was cropped close to the scalp. Emma recalled what Mom had conjectured as his past Air Force experience. Emma inched closer. If asked why, she wouldn't have been able to say. Boredom, most likely. And a strand of curiosity.

He heard her approach and lazily opened first one eye, then the other.

"Hello," Emma ventured. She figured it wasn't colonialist racism of her to assume he spoke English, since she'd heard him use it the previous evening.

A nod in greeting.

Okay, so he wasn't the chatty type. Emma pointed to the group who obviously were chatty, popping up every few seconds to assert their positions. "Do you understand what they're saying?"

Another, even more reluctant, if possible, nod. But when Emma kept expectantly staring at him, he deigned to reply, "She's accusing her comrade of coming to Rojava to kill Muslims, instead of building a society based on the revolutionary principles of Abdullah Öcalan."

Ah, there was a name Emma had actually heard of. Dennis had presumably introduced their daughter to the Turk who, at one point, was considered so dangerous he was the sole inmate held at İmralı prison for the crime of founding the Kurdistan Workers Party and leading the PKK into battle against Turkey. In jail, Öcalan wrote numerous books, including the foundational text on Jineology. Originally a Marxist-Leninist with just a touch of Stalinism for good measure, the freedom fighter converted to libertarian socialism and social ecology. The latter was influenced by the philosophies of American Murray Bookchin, who combined urban planning and studying how individuals respond to the environment around them and how these interactions affected society, with what he saw as the best of socialist, anarchist, and libertarian thought. After Dennis read several of Öcalan's manifestos, he pronounced, "It's simply classical libertarianism, with the word socialist left in so he wouldn't lose his deluded Lefty followers." It was one of the few times Dennis sounded honestly impressed with anybody. Emma figured that game recognized game. And Libby had grown equally enamored, as a result.

The mutual finger-pointing in front of them came to an abrupt stop as one of the older women Rose had been seated amongst pushed up from her perch and proceeded to lecture both parties.

"What's she saying?" Emma whispered.

The pilot's visible disdain for playing the role of Google Translate triggered Emma's memory of making the exact same face every time Mom or Dad would have trouble following what was being said and turned to her for help. Though Rose and Jonas had enthusiastically set to learning Russian, their language skills never came close to the kind of thoughts they were capable of expressing in English. If the speaker was rattling too quickly, or if they couldn't find just the right word for a soliloquy Mom was writing or a speech Dad was enlisted to make, they would ask Emma to assist. And she resented it every time. Just like she resented having to be there when they stumbled through their mis-gendered, mis-tensed words in public. It was bad enough Emma's family looked different from everyone else's and could be instantly picked out as abnormal in a crowd. Did they have to sound so different, too? In a society where conformity was paramount, Emma was persistently confronted with just what an oddity she was. She'd expected Libby to feel the same. While Dennis and Emma's English was above average—"We actually studied their grammar, we speak better than Americans do," Dennis had crowed—they still sometimes made small mistakes, such as dropping an article, or pronouncing Ws like Vs. Libby maintained that she didn't mind. "I like being different." In the USSR, you gained social capital by fitting in. In America, you did it by standing out. Why then, had her daughter chosen to come to a place which appeared to espouse the exact opposite?

"She's quoting Öcalan: *Resolution to the problem exceeds the importance of revealing and analyzing it.*"

"What does that mean?" Emma figured he was already annoyed with her. Did it matter if she made him more annoyed?

"It means, they're out."

As he spoke, two of the girls who'd been part of the accusation were being told to pack their things and go. Emma didn't need to speak Kurdish to understand. Their body language—not to mention the body language of those who were banishing them—was crystal clear.

"I thought there was no criteria for joining or any kind of citizenship test or loyalty oath?"

A shrug. Then his eyes drifted shut again.

EMMA ASKED LIBBY about it as the gathering disbanded, some drifting back towards the compound, others remaining in the field, heading for the stockpile of weapons left out for target practice. Libby wanted to flex about their amazing demonstration of restorative justice, where conflicts didn't need to go to the courts but were settled peaceably and amicably amongst the people themselves, with wise, older women being the ultimate arbitrators of what was optimal for their communities.

"But didn't you say everyone was accepted here? That gender, race, nationality, religion, political affiliation was irrelevant, as long as you were all fighting for the same cause?"

"Don't be naive, Mom. We don't want fascists here, or sadists, or racists. Why do you think you had to fill out that online form before you were allowed to volunteer? The questions are designed to weed out reactionaries and other mentally ill people."

"I didn't fill out any—" Emma began, then caught sight of Rose's deliberately innocent looking expression. "You filled out the form for me, Mom?"

"You would have done it wrong."

LIBBY INVITED HER MOTHER and grandmother to stay and watch target practice. She even proposed they give handling the armaments a go. Rose had the good sense to turn that down.

But she did, the minute their conversation could be covered up by the rounds of gunfire, snap at Emma, "Are you not even going to try?"

"Try what?" Emma took her hands off her ears as they got away from Libby's platoon.

"Try to understand what it is about this place which calls out to Luba? Why she wants to be here?"

"She's nineteen years old. Her father died a few months ago. What calls out to Libby is the romance of fighting the good fight. The belief that she's on the right side of history. And the reason she wants to be here is because she wants to be like you."

"And what drew Dennis and me to our causes? Did you ever try to understand that?"

Emma had several answers to that question. All of them sarcastic, several quite rude. So, she held her tongue.

Which only prompted Rose to continue, "You've always been like this. Always, even as a little girl. Standing on the outskirts, looking down on anyone who, in your exalted opinion, was foolish enough to believe in something. To believe in anything."

"How am I supposed to believe in anything when you, Dennis, Libby—you wax poetic about how smoothly everything works here, and I can see with my own eyes that it's a crock!"

"You're so perfect that you get to call out anything and anyone that isn't?"

"I'm not perfect. I am so Goddamn far from perfect. But I'm also not blind. What did your belief in a cause get you? It got you Dad, dead and buried across the world."

"The only reason you were listening today was so you could point out all the contradictions to Luba later."

"She should be able to see them for herself. They're obvious."

"What makes you think she doesn't? What makes you think she doesn't notice every single bit of hypocrisy and inconsistency, but still chooses to stay, to overlook what's wrong, to fight to make it better?"

"Like you did, Mom? How did that work out for you?"

"I was happy, Emma. Our years in the USSR, with Jonas, I was truly happy. Can you say the same? About any period of your life?"

"So, you didn't mind if anyone else was suffering? Just as long as you were happy?"

"Your argument is intellectually dishonest."

"And yours is emotionally manipulative."

"Isn't it nice," Rose observed, "that no matter where we go, we're still who we are?"

Emma felt compelled to smile at that. She could accuse her mother of many faults. Not being clever wasn't one of them. "Libby is going to end up like Dennis. Like you. Completely disenchanted, demoralized. Or, worse, living in a dream world, refusing to see what's right in front of her."

"You can't wait for Luba to grow cynical like you. It's what connected you and Dennis. It certainly wasn't love."

"His cynicism wasn't enough to protect Dennis. Poor cuckold ended up buying what he was supposed to be pretending to sell. For the last decade of his life, he was miserable. I want to spare Libby that."

"Try to see it through Luba's eyes." Rose wasn't giving orders now. She was pleading. Which wasn't like her. "Stop looking for flaws and seek out the virtues. It's the only way you're going to get through to her. She'll never listen to you if she doesn't believe you've given Rojava a fair chance."

"And how am I supposed to do that?"

"Get involved! Don't just watch—participate!"

"Fine. Fine, Mom, you win." Emma looked around. Was she supposed to grab a rifle, go plant crops, clean up rubble, scrub the filthy floors?

Emma caught sight of their pilot. He was loading up a truck with some of the bags which had been driven here last night. Which seemed to defeat the purpose.

"What are you doing?" Emma asked, partially out of curiosity, partially because a plan was forming in her mind.

He narrowed his eyes, unused to being questioned. "Deliveries."

"Perfect," Emma said. She helped him heft the final sack onto the truck-bed, then walked around and took a seat in the cabin. "I'll come with you."

Chapter Twenty-Seven

It's a good thing hierarchy and patriarchy had been eradicated in Rojava, Emma thought. Otherwise, she might have been required to ask permission for her spontaneous tag-along. And there might have been the possibility of her being refused. But as it was all bottom-up planning, Emma couldn't imagine there was anyone more at the bottom than she was.

Libby caught sight of the truck as they were pulling out and ran to catch up with them.

"You're going with Coop?" Libby shouted through the open passenger side window.

Oh. Was that his name? Good to know.

"Yes," Emma said, "I'm going with Coop." She turned to face him. "Right?"

He shrugged without taking his eyes from the road.

The last thing Emma saw was Libby's face, looking a great deal more flummoxed than Emma imagined the scenario required.

What in the world had Emma gotten herself into?

DRIVING. That's what Emma had gotten herself into. Endless driving. The sun stayed stubbornly overhead, making it impossible for her to tell if it were morning, midday, or afternoon. Not that she knew how to do that. But it would've been nice to pretend. Like it would've been nice to have something to entertain herself with, even solar speculation.

Coop wasn't much of a conversationalist. He hadn't said a word to Emma since stepping on the gas. The truck had no radio. Even if it had, Emma doubted there'd be much to listen to. There certainly wasn't anything to broadcast from. Behind her, in front of her, to the left of her, to the right of her, was nothing but patchy desert. Not the sandy, *Lawrence of Arabia* kind; more like stretches of California. Heat-cracked land, the occasional shrub, a scrawny tree, a random fence keeping in/keeping out nothing. Emma grew excited, leaning forward in her seat, when she spotted some protrusions in the distance. It offered the outline, or at least the shadow, of a town, maybe even a city. She expected they'd be there shortly. Anything to break the monotony.

What Emma hadn't considered was the flatness of the countryside. It was the kind of flat which, like many car-mirrors warned, made objects appear closer than they actually were. There was nothing in between to suggest scale or distance. It had to have been another forty minutes before they arrived at the outskirts of a settlement somewhat different from the ones they'd driven through last night. This one looked like it might have once been a bustling capital, possibly a seat of government. The bullet-scarred buildings looked like they might have been grander structures. Flags, wreaths, and political posters added splashes of color. Emma spied stores, a petrol station, a trio of outdoor tables like a cafe, a movie theater with a blank marquee, and citizens strolling the streets not dressed in military garb. She saw children scurrying in packs, women with baskets slung over their arms, old men planted in wicker chairs staring critically at anyone who walked or drove by.

One hand on the steering wheel, Coop leaned over Emma and tugged at a shade above her window, yanking it down. He switched hands and did the same on his side. He also did the opposite of what Emma would have expected entering an obvious residential area. Instead of slowing down, he sped up.

"What's going on? Why did you do that?" Emma hoped he'd give her credit for all the times she'd wanted to speak up previously but had gotten his hint to stay silent by answering this suddenly incredibly pressing question. Even if he had no way of knowing how close he'd come to being forced to listen to her babble in the preceding hours.

"ISIS."

"ISIS?" What Coop had managed to make less than a syllable, Emma stretched into four. "I thought you'd gotten rid of ISIS. Wasn't that the whole point of this independent region?"

"Some stayed," Coop said. And drove faster.

He stopped in front of what, from the front, looked like it might have been a government building, though the gold-plated official writing on the walls had been scratched out, new words carved in their place. Coop climbed out of the cabin. Emma did too, though he hadn't asked her. A young man, possibly no older than Libby, exited and offered Coop an effusive greeting. Coop only nodded in return. Nice to know his taciturnity wasn't limited to Emma. She might have started to take it personally.

Coop unlatched the back of his truck-bed, pointing to a half-dozen canvas bags, which the young man and the handful of compatriots who came out after him grabbed enthusiastically and proceeded to drag inside the building. Coop didn't follow, so neither did Emma.

He got back into the cabin. So did she.

"What was that?" Emma came along to do what Mom said, not just watch and seek out flaws but participate and understand. Would be nice to understand what she'd participated in.

"Bread. Every citizen gets a loaf a day, rationed. Syrian prices are too high, so co-ops sell to local administrations to distribute."

It was the longest sentence he'd spoken so far. Emma felt encouraged to follow up, "These are the guys in charge of distributing? How do you know the stuff you bring ends up in the hands of people who need it, instead of on the black market?"

The Emma who'd grown up in the USSR couldn't imagine any other end result.

In lieu of an answer, Coop revved his engine and kept driving.

EMMA EXPECTED TO BREATHE a sigh of relief once they were out of the city and the chance of an ISIS fighter popping out from between ravaged buildings with a machine gun or bomb had diminished. But that meant they were back in the desert. Sun overhead, horizon desolate, her entertainment options even more so.

She'd put up with the stifling heat previously because she'd assumed they'd shortly get wherever they were going and stop. She'd even imagined water might be a possibility. Now that Emma understood that had been a pipe dream, she was forced to acknowledge how the jeans she'd stupidly worn were sticky with sweat beneath her thighs, her bra was filling up with liquid between her breasts, and her hair was clinging to her neck, like spiders rappelling in an arachnid Olympics. She'd been swallowing saliva to quench her thirst for hours. There wasn't much left. Emma ordered herself to look on the bright side. With dehydration imminent, she wouldn't need to ask Coop to pull over so she could pee. Not that Emma could imagine where she might find a spot of privacy to do so.

As if to mock her attempt to stay positive, Coop took a swig from the canteen sitting on the seat between them, then passed it over for Emma to drink her share. She did so eagerly, toilet situation be damned.

What had Emma gotten herself into? It never crossed her mind she might be embarking on an odyssey. She thought they were going out for the morning, maybe the day. The roasting sun was finally making some gesture towards giving it a rest, yet they were still driving. Emma couldn't decide what galled her more, feeling that she was slowly decomposing in a crock pot, or the ongoing silent treatment. Deciding she had more control over one than the other, Emma, in the friendliest tone she could summon, asked Coop, "How long were you in the Air Force?"

That got his attention. He actually turned his head to look in her direction, appearing if not impressed, if not intrigued, at least not as irritated as before.

"The way you flew. Well, the way you landed. Like you were coming in under radar. That says military training." Emma didn't feel the need to add that Mom had figured this out, not her.

"Army," he corrected. "Aviation."

"Did you like it?" Yes, it was a stupid question. Yes, it was the best Emma could come up with. She hadn't expected a response.

"Sometimes."

Was this almost a conversation? "Did you come to Rojava as a soldier then?"

Coop hit the brakes.

WHEN EMMA STEPPED OUT of the truck for the second time that day, all she could see in the dusk was a smattering of tents at the far end of land a bit greener than the other stretches they'd driven past. There might also have been neatly dug rows, like furrows waiting to be planted. She followed Coop as he moved towards those tents, waiting for her eyes to adjust and resume recognizing color amongst the browns and grays. Emma winced as her muscles complained that they'd just gotten used to their cramped seating position. Why try to walk now?

At the shuffle of their approach, the tent flaps opened and out came spilling wave after wave of women, followed by children. It might have looked like a clown car, except that Emma had to wonder just how many people were stuffed into each domicile. The number she came up with was way higher than could have been comfortable.

They gathered around Coop, chattering in what Emma assumed was Arabic or Kurdish, making Emma feel as stupid and helpless as she had at the meeting that morning. Coop smiled, first with one half of his mouth, then the other. Children grabbed at his hands. He let them drag him into one of the tents. Some women noticed Emma and gestured for her to follow.

They all ended up in a space packed with people sitting on the floor and reclining along canvas walls. It smelled of yeast and spices, earth and sweat. The air inside was stuffier than outside. It clogged Emma's nostrils, making her lightheaded, prompting her to all but collapse where she stood, hitting the ground in a less than graceful manner and attempting to arrange her limbs into what Libby's pre-school teacher had called crisscross-applesauce, a phrase even Emma's American-born mother had found baffling. What did applesauce have to do with the sitting?

Exhausted from the heat and disoriented from the drive, Emma allowed the conversation to wash over her, until a young girl, twelve or so, wedged herself into the space between Emma and another woman to shout over the din, "I am Awira. I speak English."

Emma didn't possess enough English words to express how grateful she felt for that. "Hello, Awira." She coughed to clear her throat, desiccated from her involuntary vow of silence. "Nice to meet you." Wanting to keep the talk going, Emma added, "How did you learn English?"

The girl beamed, thrilled to be asked. "My mother teaches me. She studied English in Oxford when she is a young woman."

Oxford. Emma looked around. It was a long and questionable journey from Oxford to a tent in the middle of nowhere, sitting in the dirt.

"My mother is married to important man in ruling of Syria. But he is not good to her. He is hitting." Emma startled. She assumed the man Awira was referring to was her father. And yet, instead of being embarrassed by the family shame, Awira came off proud to report, "After our revolution, he runs away. But my mother, she takes me and my sisters and she comes here. We are safe place for women and children of Rojava."

Emma had noticed that Coop was the only man in sight. But in her Western, capitalist, imperialist—she was channeling Libby now—xenophobia, she'd assumed the men were away working somewhere, or serving in the armed forces. It never occurred to her that this might be a woman's only settlement.

"We will grow fruits and vegetables and olive trees with the seeds you have brought us," Awira announced. "Very little of this in Rojava. Very hard to get after embargo. We will grow food to feed ourselves, then to trade with others, then to sell in the market, then to sell in the world."

"Oh," Emma said, realizing that the seeds this community was counting on to prosper, she and Coop had left in the truck. "We should go get your supplies then. Can't leave them unattended. Someone might steal them."

Awira stared at Emma, first in bewilderment, then with a fit of giggles. "The seed you bring belong to everyone. Why would we steal from ourselves?"

Everyone kept talking. Everyone kept handing Emma and Coop food. A pizza-looking flatbread drizzled with cheese flakes and zaatar, bulgur wheat with yogurt, roasted lentils, and enough cups of tea to make a Russian hostess feel inadequate. When the temperature dropped enough for Emma to assume the sun had at long last paused its oppression, Coop rose to his feet and bid what Emma fervently hoped was good night.

It seemed to be, but when Emma attempted to follow him, he held up a hand and shook his head. "You've been invited to spend the night here with the others. I'll sleep in the truck." Coop's tone made it clear this was not an invitation Emma had any right to refuse.

She sighed and sat back down.

With Awira and her mother as translators, Emma's hosts wanted to tell her all about their plans for the future. This cooperative was merely one of many planned for Rojava. While they focused on agriculture, others were gearing up to raise livestock, prepare dairy products, and produce locally sourced textiles. The plan was to sell their wares at below current market prices in order to drive up demand. But these wouldn't be capitalist, profit-based objectives. These would promote labor's independence from the exploitative wage-based patriarchal system in the service of developing ideological consciousness!

Emma nodded. Emma was so used to nodding that the gesture came automatically.

Yes. Yes, of course. It all sounded wonderful. Yes. Yes, of course. It all sounded doable.

And yes. Yes, of course. Emma wished she could believe them.

They all seemed so sincere. So resolute and purposeful and steadfast. So happy.

Emma truly wished she could be like them. And she was trying. Not just so she could tell Mom that she had. Emma really and truly wanted to recognize what Libby saw here. She wanted to be able to listen to these beatific women without judgment, without cynicism, without a Cassandra complex which made it painfully obvious what would go wrong, when, and how.

This, as Libby would say, was a her—Emma—problem, not a them—Rojava—problem. Emma was the problem. She understood that. She always had, no matter what Mom thought. Her hosts were joyful. Emma was miserable. Any sensible person, given the choice, would opt for the former.

She kept listening. She kept nodding. She kept waiting for her politically Grinchy heart to grow three sizes that day. Night fell, and it still hadn't happened.

Emma waited until everyone else had fallen asleep before sneaking outside. She knew it would be perceived as rude, but she had to get out of there. It wasn't just the stifling air or the hardness of the ground. It was that Emma knew she didn't belong. She needed to extract her toxicity before she tainted these good people's hopes and dreams. The way Mom and Libby and Dennis accused Emma of tainting theirs.

The weather had cooled down enough that Emma could take a deep breath, stretch out her arms and feel like she'd dodged a bullet, even as she knew it would be coming 'round again by daybreak. She thought about just laying down on the ground to try and catch however many hours of sleep were left in the fresh air before remembering that she was fifty-four years old, and her previous night spent in such a manner had hardly been restorative. Emma headed for the truck. Maybe she could convince Coop to let her sleep alongside him in the cabin. Maybe, like with letting her tag along, saying no would be upholding the patriarchy. Or something.

To Emma's surprise, Coop wasn't sleeping in the cabin. He'd stretched out in the back, atop the bags of what she now knew were seeds. It actually looked pretty comfortable. Certainly, softer than the ground. Without asking permission, Emma crawled in, too.

Coop startled awake at her first movement. Emma questioned her decision to sneak up on a trained soldier. She was lucky she didn't get her head blown off. Especially since, as soon as Coop's eyes snapped open, he instinctively reached for the firearm at his side.

"Don't shoot," Emma whispered in what she hoped was a jokey yet convincing manner. "It's just me."

Coop pulled his hand off his gun as quickly as he'd gone for it, splaying his fingers to ensure he didn't tap the trigger on accident.

"Thanks," Emma said, for not shooting her, and in advance for letting her bunk with him.

Coop shifted to make space. Emma collapsed in it gratefully. Now she understood why Coop hadn't handed over his delivery right away. It still had a purpose to serve.

Coop didn't ask what had driven Emma out. She told him anyway. She felt compelled to explain herself. To defend herself. Even when she knew Coop didn't care enough to judge her, Emma still cared to not be judged. Especially when she knew she deserved it.

"I just can't do it," she said. "I can't pretend everything is going to be fine. Nothing is ever fine. There's no such thing as happily ever after. Not politically, not personally. Even the greatest love story in the world comes to a tragic end. Somebody dies. Always."

Coop looked at her for a long moment.

"It's fine now," he said, rolling over and going back to sleep.

THEY TOOK OFF BEFORE SUNUP the next morning, leaving the bags of seed by the edge of the field. Emma was proud of herself for not asking whether it was safe to do so. Why would anyone steal from themselves?

She'd stopped trying to figure out which direction they were headed in, but she had become used to the rotating scenery of barren desert, struggling farmland, and bombed out, patched together towns. Their next destination was different.

It looked like a town, but instead of buildings, Emma saw tents. Not the square, canvas ones erected by the women's cooperative, but long, narrow, and white, barracks, side by side like a series of vacuum cleaner tubes. She saw electric generators, roads scraped in the sand, piles of garbage. She saw children kicking a soccer ball, women carrying buckets of water. And all around the encampment, which stretched in multiple directions like an overly creative child's train set spanning several football fields, Emma saw barbed wire. And armed guards.

"It's a prison camp," she exclaimed. "I thought Rojava didn't believe in prisons?" This time, she wasn't being negative or argumentative, she was genuinely curious.

"No prisons for domestic crimes," Coop said. "This is ISIS."

"We're going to an ISIS prison camp?" Had Emma's voice just gone an octave higher?

"No."

Emma wondered why they were still driving in that direction then. She could hear it now, the rumbling of thousands of people living on a too-small patch of land. And she could smell it. Unwashed bodies, their detritus and their excrement left to fester in the sun.

About half a mile from the camp, Coop turned, driving parallel to the wire, into a patch of faded greenery which couldn't exactly be called a forest, more like uncleared bush with minimal tree cover. He stopped the truck and sat back, palms on his knees, waiting.

"What are we delivering here?" Emma wondered. They didn't have enough bread to feed everyone, and she couldn't see any space designated for planting or harvesting.

"Medicine."

"To ISIS?"

"Women and children. Families of ISIS fighters held in other camps. Sanitary conditions are atrocious here. They need help. They're people."

"People who'll use our medical supplies to get well enough to murder people like my daughter!" When Coop didn't respond, Emma pressed, "Tell me I'm wrong. Tell me the children in these camps don't grow up to attack the refugees we distributed bread to? Tell me the women in these camps aren't as zealous as their husbands, that they wouldn't love to burn the women's cooperative we visited to the ground, given the chance?"

"They need the medicine now," Coop said.

"Then why aren't we driving up to the gates and handing it out in the open? Why are we hiding? Are you distributing this stuff on your own?" Emma was stunned she hadn't seen the obvious before. "Are you the black market?"

"I sell medicine to people who need it, to pay for fuel to bring volunteers to Rojava to distribute bread and seeds to people who need it."

He made it sound perfectly reasonable. Inevitable, even. He wasn't asking for Emma's blessing or even her agreement. He was simply answering her question.

Except she had a lot more questions. Except she never got the chance to ask them.

Before Emma could open her mouth, both cabin doors were ripped open.

Hands grabbed Emma by the shoulders and flung her to the ground, doing the same to Coop on the other side. She fell on her hands and knees. A kick to her lower back sent Emma sprawling, face down into the dirt. She rolled over instinctively, wiping her mouth and shading her eyes with her palm.

To spy the barrel of a gun pointing directly at her.

Chapter Twenty-Eight

Her back throbbed where the heel struck it. Dirt dribbled out of Emma's lips and nose. Bruised fingerprints embedded into her shoulders. Sunlight nearly blinded her. None of that mattered in comparison to the gun less than a yard from her face. Or maybe it was a rifle. For all of Dennis' late in life embrace of the NRA, Emma had no idea what differentiated them.

Did it matter? She knew both shot bullets. Bullets that could reach her skull in a fraction of a second, and that would be that. What did it say about Emma that her immediate thought was, *won't Mom and Libby be sorry then*?

The young man—was everyone in Rojava Libby's age?—with a red and white checkered scarf covering his head and shoulders, silently held Emma at gunpoint. His partner on the other side shrieked at Coop. Emma may not have understood the language, but she recognized an order. Emma heard Coop dragged to his feet, then shoved towards the back of the truck. The second teenager—was this one even younger than Libby?—gestured for Coop to unlock it and hand over the merchandise. The child keeping an eye on Emma slowly backed up to help, while leaving the gun trained in her direction, lest she get any ideas.

Emma didn't have a single idea.

Coop did as he was bid and unlocked the truck bed. She noticed that his own gun was missing, presumably the second weapon in their hijacker's hands. He handed over the bags of medical supplies without protest. The boy nodded approvingly. Smugly. *God, teenagers really were the same wherever you went.* He wasn't a terrorist. He was a child playing at being a terrorist. Which made him even more terrifying.

He held out his palm and gestured at Coop's keys. He wanted the truck.

Up to this point, Emma's dominant sensation had been shock. Everything happened so quickly. She wasn't scared, she was numb. She watched the proceedings like it was unfolding on television. She was curious about what would happen next but detached. As if the denouement didn't really affect her.

Now, she finally registered exactly how it would affect her. If Coop surrendered the truck, they'd be stranded in the middle of nowhere. No. Not in the middle of nowhere. Within striking distance of an ISIS prisoner camp in a country at war, with no US embassy in sight, where they had no legal right to be, in any case. At high noon. With no water.

They were dead. If Coop let their attackers have their truck, they were dead.

Coop looked down at his keys. He looked at the boy. And he made a move to put the keys back in his own pocket.

The boy charged him. Emma realized that, just when she'd thought the situation couldn't get any worse, it'd gotten worse. With no truck, Emma and Coop were dead. But without Coop, Emma was dead faster. If he were killed on the spot right now, they might as well shoot Emma, too. It would be more merciful than dying of excruciating thirst wandering the desert.

Except they didn't shoot first. Like the child Emma pegged him to be, when Coop defensively shoved him mid-charge, the boy instinctively shoved back, forgetting he was holding a gun. Which gave the more prepared Coop the chance to kick him in the groin.

The one with the gun on Emma swiveled his head, undecided

between jumping in to help and sticking to his post. He likely feared that joining the fray would allow Emma to leap up and attack him from the back.

She had no intention of doing that. But if the concern prevented him from going after Coop, Emma was willing to keep doing whatever she was doing to maintain the illusion.

The kid who'd been booted in the balls hit the ground on his knees with a groan, but, remembering that he had one, redirected his gun in Coop's direction. His collapse, however, had given Coop enough time to reach into his shirt pocket and pull out a cigarette lighter.

That's odd, Emma thought, *I didn't notice him smoking*. Her second thought proved: *Is that really what I should be focusing on right now?*

Coop ignited the lighter and held it over the bag of medical supplies. He barked a threat Emma didn't understand. But the gesture he made with his free hand strongly suggested that one wrong move, and everything would go up in a fireball, including the pair with the guns.

The kid said something. Coop said something.

The kid took a step away. Coop kept glaring until he took another. And another.

Coop backed slowly towards the truck. He yelled for Emma to do the same.

She scrambled up from the ground, ignoring the gun still pointed in her direction. She believed her carjacker wouldn't hesitate to shoot her. But, for some reason, she believed that Coop would protect her, more.

"Get in," Coop ordered.

Emma did.

Coop opened his door and reached in backwards to turn on the engine with one hand while still keeping the lighter aflame and pointed at the medicine with the other.

Only when the truck had fully started, did Coop, in a single, fluid motion, slide into the driver's seat and floor the gas pedal so fiercely that the truck bounced and threw Emma against her seat, head smacking the roof.

It wasn't until they were out of firing range that Coop even closed his own door.

HE MUST HAVE TAKEN a short-cut back, because now they passed no settlements, saw no people. Emma didn't mind. She'd had her fill.

What had seemed deadly boring before was peaceful and safe now. Every living being they failed to pass was one less potential death threat.

They'd driven for what, thanks to her churning adrenalin, felt like minutes, but also, thanks to her lingering shock, like hours before Coop thought to ask Emma, "You OK?"

Was she? Her mouth still tasted of dirt. Her shoulders and back still ached. She had to keep blinking to clear her vision. On the bright side, she could breathe again. And not even in the kind of gasps that came after a crying jag. She could inhale, and she could exhale without worrying that either sound might prompt a hair-trigger assassination. That was an improvement.

"Were those the guys you were supposed to meet?"

"Don't know."

"So, they might have been intending to double-cross you, or they might have double-crossed the guys you were supposed to meet and taken their places."

"Doesn't matter."

"How can you say that? Don't you care where your medicine ends up?

"It's medicine. It'll end up with people who need it."

"Or they'll sell it at ten times the market value and use the profit to buy more guns to threaten the next people who drop by trying to play good Samaritan."

"The medicine will end up with people who need it."

She wanted to scream in frustration. Instead, Emma sincerely told Coop, "I wish I could be like you."

There went that half-smile again, the one he'd briefly flashed the other night. Except this time, it was directed at Emma. She was surprised by how much she liked it.

"I wish I could drink the Kool-Aid. I wish I could believe that feminism will end war, and co-ops will eradicate the wage gap, and all people are truly good at heart. But I know that plenty of women have started and fought in wars, and that *from each according to his ability, to each according to his needs* only works until the first traitor takes more than their share, and when no one's in charge the absolutely worst person inevitably is, and the girl who wrote cheery thoughts in her diary ended up murdered in a Nazi death camp. I wish I didn't know. I wish I was a true believer. Like you."

Coop's half smile slowly turned into a full one. A rarity, indeed.

"If I believed in anything," Coop said, "I could do nothing."

She wanted to ask him what he meant by that. But they'd barely pulled back into the compound they'd left the day before and Emma stepped out of the truck, desperately wishing to know where the shower facilities were so she could scrub layers of filth off her skin, before a coterie of volunteers recognized Emma and came rushing up to her. They chattered in a variety of languages, none of which Emma understood.

Coop translated, "Your daughter needs you."

EMMA FLEW UP THE STEPS to the room Libby once escorted her to. She found her daughter huddled in a corner, back against a cracking concrete wall, knees drawn to her chest, arms crossed, head lowered, sobbing hysterically. Rose was sitting next to her, stroking the side of Libby's head, smoothing back her hair, patting her on the shoulder and whispering in Russian and English, none of which seemed to be doing Libby any good.

"What happened?" Emma also hit the ground, ignoring the pain inflaming her existing injuries. "Libby, baby, sweetheart, what's wrong?"

Her daughter lifted her head. Libby's face was streaked with tears and patches of dirt, but otherwise unaffected as far as Emma could tell. She'd been expecting blood, injury, or worse. Whatever that was.

"Mommy," Libby, who'd barely ever called Emma that after the age of three, turned the cry into a plea. But rather than explaining how Emma could help, the sight of her mother sent Libby into a fresh bout of hysteria. She could barely inhale without gagging. Her body shook as if in the throes of malaria. Her fingers were ice cold while her cheeks blazed fire.

"Luba went on her first patrol today," Rose explained, speaking in a soothing voice which—she didn't know about Libby—but it drove Emma to the edge.

"And?" Emma demanded, looking from one to the other.

"And there were some—some unexpected complications," Rose cooed. "They were met with sniper fire. People got hurt. A girl standing right next to Luba, a very nice girl, we met her the other morning, Ameena was her name. She… she's gone."

"My God." Emma comprehended that Rose was trying to stay calm in an attempt to talk Libby down. But Emma lacked the self-control to do the same. She grabbed Libby's shoulders, feeling her bones the way she might have if her daughter had fallen out of a tree. If there had been serious injuries, obviously they'd have shown themselves by now, but Emma still needed to double-check. She squeezed Libby's arms, her legs, her ankles. Everything seemed solid. "Are you OK? Libby, are you OK?"

"It was awful." Each word came out preceded by a wheeze, followed by a gasp. "They shot her in the stomach. She didn't die right away. Not like if they'd gotten her in the head or the heart. She was awake and she was screaming, and all the blood. So much blood. I could see them. Her insides. She was thrashing around, begging us to help her. She grabbed my hand, and she kept saying, *please, Libby, please, Libby, please, Libby, do something.*"

"You're OK." Emma could think of nothing to say beyond that, so she merely seized her little girl and hugged her and rocked her and kept repeating over and over, "You're OK, you're OK, you're OK." Was she doing this for Libby's sake or her own?

Emma looked to Rose. "The three of us are getting on the next plane out of here. I don't care when it's scheduled. Coop says he needs money for fuel. I'll pay him whatever he needs. We're not staying here one second longer. Do you hear me? Not one second longer. I'm getting you out of here, Libby."

"No!" The hug turned into a wrestling match as Libby wriggled out of her mother's arms, all but pushing Emma away. "No. I can't. I can't leave here. I have to stay. I have to." At which point she began crying again, harder than ever.

"SHE'S NOT MAKING SENSE," Emma told Rose as they walked around the perimeter of the half-destroyed building where Libby had finally fallen asleep, collapsing where she'd sat. Emma wanted to move her onto at least a blanket, but Rose advised to let Libby be. They didn't want to risk waking her now that she'd calmed down somewhat, only crying out periodically in her dreams. Emma had tried to remain by her daughter's side, but Rose insisted it would do them both good to get out and cool off themselves. They couldn't be of help to Libby if they were reflecting her anxiety back at her. "How could Libby possibly want to stay?"

"She made a commitment," Rose reminded.

"Fuck that," Emma said. It was the first time she'd sworn like this in front of her mother. Neither of them fainted. "Dennis made a commitment. We saw where that got him."

"She needs to know that she can do this."

"She can't," Emma pointed behind her. "Could it be any more obvious? I don't care what Libby says. I don't care if I have to bind, gag, and drug her. I'm getting her out of here before her psyche is damaged so badly it'll take the rest of Libby's life to put it back together."

"Why can't you let her be? Why can't you let Luba make her own decisions?"

"Because you saw what happened just now! She had a complete mental breakdown. That's where making her own decisions led her!"

"I let you make your own decisions. Do you think I approved of your marrying Dennis? Do you think I liked him?"

"Everybody liked Dennis."

"Do you think I liked him for you?"

"You never hid how you felt, Mom."

"But I still let you make your own choices. I didn't stop you. Even when you came to America. Even when you turned your back on everything Jonas and I tried to teach you."

"I'm not like you, Mom." Emma didn't think she was revealing any shocking truths. "I can't… I can't not see what's in front of me. I can't pretend that things are good when they're not. And I can't let Libby march into what I know will be a disaster."

"It's her life."

"It's my life, too!" Emma exploded, realizing it was the first time she'd put the feeling that had always been there into words. "I read something Jackie Kennedy said once—no, Mom, I don't want to hear what a fascist her husband was. Jackie Kennedy said a mother is only as happy as her saddest child. I only have one child. When Libby is happy, I'm happy. When Libby is sad, I'm sad. And I can't bear it, I tell you. I cannot bear it." She glimpsed Rose's face in the moonlight. Her cryptic expression told Emma everything she needed to know. "You never felt that way, did you, Mom? Not about me."

Rose sighed. All the strength she'd marshaled to get herself this far drained from her ninety-one-year-old body. For the first time that Emma could recall, Rose Janowitz Cain looked her age.

"No," she admitted. "I didn't."

Emma hadn't meant to make her mother feel bad. She'd simply been trying to explain her position; why Rose could never share it. "It's OK, you didn't need to. You weren't one of those women where your kid is the only thing you have going on in your life. You had your work. You loved that. You had your politics. God knows, you loved that. And you had Dad…. You and Dad, you never needed anything but each other. That's kind of amazing. Inspirational, even."

"What do I have now?" Rose asked. "My work? Gone. My politics," she snorted. "Gone. And Jonas… my Jonas is gone."

"You have me," Emma said. "You have Libby."

Although she'd known all her life that they'd never been enough. And that they never would be.

Chapter Twenty-Nine

Libby proved no more rational following her restless version of a nap than she had prior to collapsing. Despite waking up shaking so badly Emma feared Libby would chip those perfect teeth Dennis had insisted on buying braces for, despite Libby scooping up handfuls of granite from the ground and scrubbing both palms against her forearms to scour away blood no longer there until her skin turned raw and red and began to crack, Emma's daughter refused to so much as hear, much less discuss, the possibility of cutting her misguided escapade short.

Emma tried to do as Rose commanded and view the situation through Libby's eyes. But what Emma saw then was that friendly girl from the previous morning, bleeding out, screaming, and, in Emma's mind, calling for a mother who wasn't there. A mother who could've prevented this, if she'd shown up in time to drag her idealistic daughter home. If Ameena's mother had forced her to come home, they might never have spoken again for the rest of their lives. But Ameena would have had a life to lead. And her mythical mother wouldn't be spending the remnants of her days second-guessing and whipping herself for her choices.

This, Emma understood, wasn't seeing matters through Libby's eyes. But Libby's eyes were wrong. Emma's eyes were the only ones truly seeing reality.

Rose certainly was no help. She listened to everything Libby babbled and nodded her head, as if it made perfect sense. Could Rose not spot the shaking, the teeth rattling, the fresh blood on Libby's arms, not from some doomed other girl, but from Libby herself?

Libby wasn't listening. Rose wasn't listening. Emma's options were to keep repeating herself at higher and higher volume or removing herself from the situation to calm down and regroup. Emma chose the latter. Not because she was the bigger person. Because she needed to recharge her energy, and come up with better, fresher arguments.

Emma left Rose and Libby to their echo chamber and stepped outside. She had no destination in mind. Not that there were many places to go. The shooting range was out, so were the community buildings. That just left the fields. Emma didn't know enough about agriculture to distinguish between crops. She saw some flora the size of small trees, others more like bushes, still others barely peeking out from the earth. Would they yield a harvest adequate to feed themselves? Share with other cooperatives? Emma had heard a lot of big dreams. She hadn't really seen much proof of their fulfillment.

She also saw Coop. He'd driven his truck to the edge of the field and was, once again, filling the back up with bags to take on his next day's deliveries. Emma couldn't let him do that. She picked up her pace, rushing to lay a hand on his shoulder, then quickly jerking it away when, for the second time in two days, she remembered that sneaking up on a trained soldier was less than ideal in a war zone.

Coop must have heard her coming because he didn't flinch. He only turned his head in Emma's direction to acknowledge her presence, then kept on with his task. Emma shadowed him on the back and forth walk from the fields to the truck, impressed by how quickly a man with a canvas bag full of produce swung over each shoulder could move. She needed to scramble to keep up. But this was important enough to ignore the burgeoning stitch in Emma's side.

"I need to hire you. For tomorrow. Fly my mother, Libby, and me out of here. Just get us to any functioning airport in the Middle

East, we'll figure out the rest from there." Emma had no idea how she would do that, but wishful thinking was the name of the game for now, as long as their most pressing, practical problem was fixed immediately.

Coop tossed his wares into the truck, then paused to study Emma with an expression she'd describe as amusement. "Booked tomorrow. And the day after that. And the day after that. Was planning to fly out next Tuesday. Three of you are welcome to hitch a ride."

"It needs to be now." Emma quickly filled Coop in on the crisis with Libby. "If we stay any longer, I'm afraid she'll crack and never recover."

"I don't shanghai rebellious teenagers."

"This isn't a kid staying out past curfew or sneaking beers and smoking pot. My daughter watched her friend get killed. She almost got killed herself."

There was nothing Coop could have said in response which would have infuriated Emma more than his silence. Chat break over, he turned his back on her.

Without thinking, Emma grabbed his shoulder again, this time spinning Coop around and forcing him to face her. "Do you have kids?"

"No."

"Then you have no idea what I'm talking about."

"OK."

Emma had no idea how to respond. She wanted a fight. But that would require dissent. "I was wrong. You're not a true believer. You don't believe in anything." Coop opened his mouth to respond, to maybe even offer the dissent Emma had been on the hunt for, but it was too late. "I know, I know. You told me that. You told me you didn't believe in anything. I didn't realize that meant you didn't care about anything. You don't care about this place. You don't care about these people. You don't care about the kids you ferry in to die for yet another hopeless cause, like kids always do."

He didn't agree with her. He didn't disagree with her.

Which, naturally, made Emma angrier. Had she come outside to cool off? It wasn't working. "What's in this for you? Are you just some kind of danger junkie? I read about that. Guys in the military, they become hooked on adrenaline or something. They have to keep risking their lives to feel anything at all." Had Emma really read that somewhere? Or was she thinking of the Russian Roulette scene in *The Deer Hunter*?

No matter. She couldn't yell at Libby. She couldn't yell at Rose. She couldn't yell at Dad or at Dennis or at herself. That only left Coop. Besides, he didn't seem to mind. Which, naturally, made Emma angrier.

"Cooperation," he said.

Now Emma was confused, in addition to angry. "What the— Who's cooperating? You are?" It sure didn't feel like it.

"My name. Coop. It's short for Cooperation. Cooperation Gump if you can believe it."

There were non-sequiturs. And there were silly names. This was Emma's first silly name non-sequitur. She had no idea what it had to do with anything.

"The rich San Francisco family," he prompted. "They own the department store. Gump's."

"So?"

"My mother was living in a commune when I was born."

"OK." Two could play the indifference game. Emma just wished she felt indifferent. No matter how much she hated to admit it, he had her attention.

"She ran away from her parents, denounced their consumerist lifestyle. Opted for free love, good vibes, peace, no possessions."

"How John Lennon of her."

"Believed nobody owns anybody else. Everyone belongs to themselves. And to the collective."

"Did they sing patriotic songs about it while gleefully stomping through fields, chopping wheat? Do you know how many times I acted out that scenario in my school plays?"

"They tried to grow food. They failed. Upper middle-class kids from the suburbs. Their liberal arts degrees rarely covered applicable skills. So, they stole."

"From the capitalist pigs' store?"

"From the store, from their parents, from visitors passing through, from each other."

Emma thought about giggly Awira of the women's commune. "How could you steal from yourselves?"

"They managed. Then there were the arguments over cars, over clothes, over drugs, over fuck buddies. My mother came looking for peace and love, and what she got was more of the same old, same old."

We tried to do what was better, Mikhail Gorbachev said after the dust had settled, *but we ended up with the usual.*

"She kept picking up and moving somewhere else. Sometimes before the cops got there with arrest warrants, sometimes after. Meandered all over California, Oregon, Washington, only to end up back in San Francisco. And the People's Temple."

Emma's horrified expression told Coop she knew where and what that was. He wouldn't need to explain.

"It's funny. Religion was another thing she was running away from. She thought how her family practiced was performative, zero spirituality. She wanted a deeper connection, true equality. Men, women, Black, white…. What she wanted from Jim Jones, it's the same thing your parents wanted from the USSR."

"How did you know about my parents?"

"Your mom's a talker."

So was Coop, apparently. When you got him on the right subject.

"Were you there, too? In Jonestown?"

A nod. The man of few words had no words for this.

"How did you… survive?"

"Do I look like the type to drink the Kool-Aid?"

She'd accused him of that. She'd used those exact words when… oh, God. Emma sucked in her breath, as if that could call back what she'd said the other day.

Coop clearly remembered. Coop, just as clearly, took no offense. Perhaps because he'd already lived through something a great deal more offensive. "Morning in November, I watched a handful of folks sneaking off into the jungle. One of the women, Leslie, she'd strapped her kid to her back. He was no baby. He was two, maybe three. Leslie was married to the compound's security chief. I figured if she was willing to take off into the wild, with the snakes and the jaguars and the tapirs, carrying a kid that heavy, she knew something major was about to go down."

"What about your mother?"

"She'd never wanted to leave any other place when I begged her. Why would she now? I was finally old enough to risk it on my own."

Later that November day, the man who'd brought them all to Guyana ordered 900 of his followers to ingest cyanide. Men, women, elderly, children, teenagers, babies. Jim Jones knew his South American reign was doomed. Kill a US congressman who'd come to investigate your operation, as well as the three reporters accompanying him, and even a megalomaniac grasped he could no longer hide and claim immunity from international law. Authorities would be coming for him. But just like with the Jewish zealots scraping to hold out on the mountaintop of Masada from the Romans, Jones made it so his pursuers came upon a massacre, no one left alive to arrest, except for an old woman who'd hidden under the bed, and a deaf man who'd slept through the suicide order. The press reported that less than a dozen people had escaped before sunrise.

"I got flown back to the US, dumped on my mom's family. They thought the illiterate little hippie they'd been saddled with could use some discipline. So, they sent me to military school."

"Quite the change."

"Surprisingly similar. Do what you're told, don't ask questions, dress like everyone else, and if you don't like it, keep it to yourself or get the shit beaten out of you. I adjusted quick."

"That's how you ended up in the Army."

"Path of least resistance. I learned to fly. Dropped some bombs. Rescued some people. Delivered some guns. Delivered some food. That's when I figured it out. Fascist, communist, dystopia, utopia, totalitarian, collective, individualist, one man-one vote, or one candidate-all votes. Just words. Words are meaningless. People matter. I help people. I ignore the words."

"So, I was close," Emma said. "You don't care about anyone. You care about everyone."

"Because your being right is what we've been discussing," Coop confirmed.

For a moment she thought he was serious; she'd put her foot in her mouth yet again. But then Coop smiled, giving Emma permission to do the same.

"Do you think they can make this?" Emma swept her arm behind her, towards the fields and the shooting range and the bombed-out buildings. "Do you think they can make this work?"

"I know I can bring food, medicine, and supplies to people who need them."

It went against every tribalistic, us versus them lesson Emma had marinated in growing up. And with Dennis. And by the USSR. And by America. But she understood.

"Libby hasn't reached your stage of enlightenment yet," Emma sighed, then admitted. "Neither have I."

"You don't have to stay here."

"But Libby thinks she does!"

Coop said, "I'm not flying anyone out of Rojava against their will."

"Are you refusing to sell me a service which you make available to others? There are laws against that, you know."

"Hysterical Mother is not a protected class."

"I'm Black," Emma reminded.

"This isn't an Alabama lunch counter in the 1960s."

"I'm Jewish."

"Or Germany in the 1930s."

"I'm a woman."

"Or a bank refusing to grant you a loan. You'll have an onerous time proving I denied you service based on any of those identities. Soon as you find someone to report me to."

Now he wasn't just smiling at her. He was laughing.

Which Emma thoroughly deserved.

She was being ridiculous. She was being, as he'd so accurately pegged a moment ago, hysterical. What she wasn't being, was dissuaded.

COOP WALKED BACK towards Libby's building with Emma. She wasn't sure if he'd been heading in that direction anyway, or if he'd decided to escort her. If the latter, she wasn't sure if it was because he wanted to continue talking to her, or because he feared she'd tie up Libby's hands and feet and stow her away on his next flight out of Rojava. Which she'd considered.

Emma's mother and daughter met them halfway. Libby, to Emma, still looked as shaky and pale as she had when she first collapsed recalling Ameena's death. Rose, however, looked triumphant. The combination made Emma even more nervous.

"It's decided," Rose pronounced.

Now Emma was downright scared.

"Luba will remain here in Rojava."

"No," Emma attempted to cut her off, momentarily forgetting that was an impossibility.

"And I will remain here with her."

Emma's initial objection died without making it out past her throat. A novel, greater one roared up to take its place. "Are you out of your mind, Mom?"

"I will look after our Lubochka."

"And who will look after you?"

"The same person who's always looked after me. Me."

"No." Though no question had been posed, Emma still answered it. "Absolutely not."

"If Luba, at nineteen does not require your permission, I certainly, at ninety-one, do not."

Emma turned to Coop. "There'll be two bound and gagged passengers on our flight."

Coop's response was a shake of the head and a palm raised.

Fine. So, he was no help.

"What's the matter with both of you? Why are you determined to get yourselves killed?"

"Because I have to," Libby insisted. "I made a promise. I made a commitment. What kind of person would I be if, at the first sign of trouble, at the first sign of personal discomfort, I gave up my principles and my values?"

 Alina Adams

"The kind of person who turns tail and runs after a few measly bear attacks?"

Libby didn't say anything. She didn't look at Emma either. Which told Emma everything she needed to know. Libby didn't want to be like her.

"Getting shot at, Libby, is not a personal discomfort. It's a sure way to never feel anything again."

"The people of Rojava don't have the option of picking up and leaving. Why should I?"

Because you're not from here, Emma wanted to say. *Because you don't belong here. Because, in our own misguided ways, your grandparents and your parents made decisions and took risks specifically so that you, our precious baby girl, would never find yourself trapped in a situation you couldn't pick up and leave from at a moment's notice.*

None of that mattered to Libby. For all her genuine empathy, for all her big heart and her politically raised consciousness and her conviction that if her generation didn't fix the world no one would, it was up to them, it was now or never; the only thing that truly mattered to Libby was the childish, the self-absorbed, "I can't let them down. They're counting on me."

You don't matter, Emma wanted to say. *You're a bigger liability to the trained soldiers than you are a help, and the women who've been surviving here for generations laugh at you behind your back and shake their heads at the fool who'd give up her charmed life in America to play radical.* The way Emma had overheard so many Soviets mocking her parents, in Russian, when they presumed Jonas and Rose wouldn't understand.

But if Rose still didn't understand as much, how could Libby?

She's doing this because of you, Emma had accused Rose upon reading Libby's email what felt like a lifetime ago. *So, you're the one who has to bring her back home.*

Arguing with Libby was a lost cause. The only chance Emma still had was bringing Rose to her senses. Maybe if Libby witnessed her heroic grandmother backing down and admitting she'd been wrong, Libby might be inspired to do the same.

"Mom." Emma squeezed her fists and inhaled through her nose to keep from shrieking at both of them. "You take medication for your heart, for your blood pressure, for your cholesterol. Where do you think you'll get your prescriptions filled here?"

"The other women don't need it. America is too much in the pocket of the pharmaceutical companies. They have pathologized a perfectly natural aging process."

"The kind that leads to death."

"You're aware of an aging process that doesn't?"

Libby giggled at that. It was nice to see her smile again. Even at Emma's expense.

"Why are you doing this?" Emma demanded. "Libby, I get. She's a kid. She doesn't know better. But you, Mom. You do. How many times have you done this? Run off half-cocked, then dug your heels in, insisting everything was great when anyone with eyes and ears could tell it was awful? Your last little escapade killed Dad. Now you want to do the same to Libby?"

"Mom!" Libby gasped.

Rose, for her part, didn't flinch.

"What I want," Rose informed Emma, "is to save Luba from making a mistake she will regret for the rest of her life. Like I did."

Chapter Thirty

===

"That's ridiculous," Emma blurted out. "You've never regretted anything you've done."

"Stop it, Mom," Libby said. "Leave Grandma alone."

"You think I don't regret my Jonas dying?"

"That's not what I meant."

"You think I don't regret having failed at absolutely everything I have ever attempted?"

"Quit it. You were crazy successful. How many times have I heard about you and Irna Phillips single-handedly inventing soap operas? You've got scrapbooks of clippings about the shows you wrote and directed for Dad. You even somehow managed to start a third career at an age when most people are comparing retirement plans."

"My husband is dead. My daughter..." Rose gestured in Emma's direction.

What would she say next? What could Rose possibly say about failing with her daughter that would be on par with Jonas' murder? Emma was desperate to know.

Emma was terrified to know.

"My daughter," Rose finished, "thinks I'm inconsequential."

"Since when do you care what I think?"

"You aren't listening to me," Rose said. "I'm trying to explain to you why it's imperative that Luba and I stay here. But you aren't listening."

"Because you aren't making any sense. What does Libby have to do with your regrets?"

"When I was Luba's age, I had a point of view. A view of myself. I thought I knew who I was, and what I was capable of. Those of us who volunteered to fight in the Spanish Civil War, we thought we were going to save the world. First, we'd end Fascism. Then racism, then sexism. And, once we did that, then we'd naturally cure poverty. Which would lead to prosperity. Which would lead to an end to crime, to violence. We would usher in a golden age across the globe."

"That's just what we're planning to do here," Libby corroborated.

"Oh, I get it." Emma relaxed. It wasn't nearly as complicated as she'd feared. "You failed in your Quixotic quest seventy-something years ago, and you've regretted it ever since. So first you dragged Dad into your Utopian do-over attempt, and now you're using Libby."

"No," Rose said. She didn't sound angry. She didn't sound upset. She just sounded tired. "That's not what I regret."

"Then what the hell is going on?"

Rose turned to Libby. Emma didn't blame her for opting for a friendlier audience, even if Emma had been the one to ask the question.

Rose took her granddaughter's hand. She squeezed it between her palms, then pressed it to her chest. "I was so much like you. Though you're much prettier."

"Come on, Mom!"

"What? You disagree? She's much prettier than I was at her age."

"Is this relevant?"

"I was so much like you, Lubochka. I thought I was prepared to do whatever I had to, to help liberate Spain, then all of Europe, then the world. We'd drive out invaders, colonialists; we'd free oppressed peoples, achieve universal suffrage, return the means of production to the workers. Education for all, healthcare for all, respect for all."

"You did your best, Grandma. It's not your fault it didn't work. History wasn't ready yet."

"I wasn't ready," Rose said.

"What?" Emma and Libby asked in near-unison.

"It wasn't my fault the revolution failed. There's enough blame for that to go around. There, I was utterly inconsequential, I have no delusions about that. But it was my fault that I, personally, failed." In response to their confused expressions, Rose went on, "I was just like you, Lubochka. I came with dreams, ambitions, plans. And I fell apart. I hated it. The filth, the cold. I hated sleeping on the ground and having nowhere to wash. I hated trying to choke down disgusting, moldy food. I hated how carsick I got on every trip, bouncing around on pitted roads, my teeth scraping, ribs smacking against hipbones. I hated squatting to urinate in fields while listening to planes flying overhead, wondering if they were about to drop a bomb, and is this how my body would be found? Can you imagine? The fate of the free world was at stake, and I was worried not even about dying, but about looking humiliated while doing it. And the blood. So much blood everywhere. Soldiers with limbs blown off, bits of brains, guts sticking to your clothes. You'd scrub it off, but the outline would still be there. I got lice and I got diarrhea. Young men and women were going blind, losing their ability to walk, to speak. And I was ready to turn tail and run because I had an itchy scalp, some bruises, and a stomachache."

"But you didn't," Libby stammered. "You were scared and miserable, sure, but you didn't run away. You stuck it out."

"The war ended." Rose laughed. It came out more like a whimper. "I got shipped home. The only reason I didn't throw in the towel and run sobbing and screaming home so my mother could remind me, *I told you so*, was dumb luck. I would have barely made it another week, much less a month or a year. I cried every night. I cried every day. Some of the injured soldiers, they even felt they had to comfort *me*. Can you imagine how disgusted I felt? How ashamed?"

"So why then," Emma interrupted, "are you so adamant in making Libby stick this out?"

"She isn't making me—"

Rose cut Libby off. "I hated myself. I hated my weakness. Everything I did after, working for Irna, putting up with the crap Jonas and I received, in America and in the Soviet Union—yes, Emma, I heard, I saw; I also saw no point in dwelling on it—coming back to New York and starting my life over again from scratch. All of it, I did to prove to myself that I could be strong. That I wasn't worthless. Or," she said, looking at Emma, "inconsequential."

Emma didn't know what to say. Libby didn't know what to say. Maybe Coop did. But he wasn't known for saying much.

"I want to protect you from that." Rose stroked Libby's hand. "I don't want my beautiful granddaughter to hate herself the way I hated myself. I want you to always have confidence. I want you to believe that you're strong, that you can do anything."

"You worked for that veteran's organization." Emma couldn't believe she had to remind Rose. "You met the men who came back from Korea, from Vietnam, from the Gulf, from Iraq. You saw how messed up some of them were. They are never going to be OK again, no matter how much therapy they get, or how many drugs the pharmaceutical companies pump into them. And these were men and women who had training, who were professional soldiers. They were not nineteen-year-old dilettantes with delusions of grandeur."

"I will not let Lubochka suffer the way I suffered."

"She already is, Mom."

"No. I understand now. The difference. I can make the difference." In all her fifty-four years, Emma had never seen Rose Janowitz Cain at a loss for words. Until now. Now, Mom seemed to be struggling to make herself understood. She actually paused and thought before she spoke. She hesitated between words, searching for precisely the right one to make her point, understanding this would be her one chance. "My mistake was, I thought I could do it alone. I thought I was smart enough, tough enough, righteous enough. But I wasn't any of those things. I was just alone. The solitary reason I dared take any subsequent risks in my life; it was because I wouldn't be alone. I had Jonas. I could have never moved to the USSR without him. I could have never stood up to Irna without him. I could have never been with him, without him." Rose laughed at the oxymoron, yet it was absolutely true. "Jonas made me bold. Because he made me feel safe. In Spain, I had no one to turn to. In Russia, I had Jonas. Whenever I felt I wasn't good enough, that I couldn't do this, that this is what would finally break me; I was an imposter, a fraud, I'd bitten off more than I could chew, I would fail, I would be a laughingstock. He was there. I wasn't alone. As long as I had him, nothing else mattered. At least, not as much."

Now Emma was the one lost for words. But it was OK. Because Rose still had a couple more for all of them.

"Let me, Emma. Please. Let me be for Libby, what Jonas was for me."

EMMA WASN'T SURE if it was Mom using Libby's American name for the first time, or her confession of not always being the self-reliant, self-possessed, self-confident—alright, the self-important—woman Emma had grown up resenting, judging, and admiring, which drove Emma to take a step back, both mentally and physically. Emma had nothing to say in response to Rose's disclosure.

No, that wasn't true. She had so much to say, that not a single word proved forthcoming. Emma imagined they were crowded up behind her lips, like multiple shoppers all trying to exit a department store's rotating door at the same time.

She didn't say anything. She merely nodded. First in Mom's direction, to indicate that she'd heard. She may not have processed everything, but she'd heard. And then in Libby's. She'd heard her, too. She hated what she'd heard. But she'd heard.

Coop ended up leading Emma away. She didn't remember giving him permission. She didn't even remember following him. One minute she was in front of Rose and Libby, the next she and Coop were in a shadowed spot below a cement wall, the top of which had been blown away, a tattered yellow, red, and green flag of Rojava stubbornly continuing to flap overhead. To Emma, it seemed a goading target begging for a fresh round of bombardment. But, as had been determined mere minutes earlier, Emma's ability to understand the nuances of a complicated situation was not the sharpest.

"Breathe," Coop advised.

Couldn't go wrong there. Emma breathed. Several times. In, out. In, out.

Nothing changed.

At least, nothing changed for the better.

"You'll be fine," he assured.

"Who cares about me? What about them?" When Coop didn't answer as quickly as he had last time, she pressed, "Aren't you going to tell me they'll be fine, too?"

"I don't know." He spread his arms to the sides. Then added, "Neither do you."

"Has anyone ever punched you for being so Zen?"

"It's not in the top five of reasons."

"Top ten?"

He leaned back against the wall next to her. "Classified information."

"So, who's crazier?"

Coop pointed to Emma, then to himself, raising his eyebrows questioningly. Emma shook her head, indicating first herself, followed by the retreating backs of Rose and Libby.

Coop gave it a long moment's thought. Then gave up and shrugged.

Not helpful.

"Am I just stupid then, letting them stay here?"

"Didn't hear you offered a vote."

"I thought everyone in Rojava voted on everything."

Just one eyebrow inched up this time. She got the message.

"What am I supposed to do?" Emma tried her best not to whine, but she suspected this attempt was failing as spectacularly as her earlier attempt at humor. "Am I supposed to just abandon my daughter and mother in a war zone?"

Coop sighed. As if each word were being dragged from him by force, a ship painstakingly pulled to shore via chain-link cable, he mumbled, "I'll keep an eye on them."

"Why?" There Emma went again, not thinking, just blurting. When he didn't answer, she guessed, "To shut me up?"

"Sure."

"Thank you," she told him sincerely.

"You can keep an eye on them too."

"You mean stay here? No. Three stupids don't make a... not stupid." The metaphor had sounded better in her head. Spoken out loud, it was just... stupid.

"Visit."

"You'll fly me?"

"You'll sue me if I don't?"

"Thank you," she repeated. This time the sentiment covered more subjects than she could say. "Thank you for saving me from getting shot. Thank you for keeping me somewhat sane. Thank you for listening. Thank you for..." that last one was the trickiest. She wasn't sure words even existed to describe what she wanted to say. What she felt.

So, instead of talking, Emma leaned over and kissed him. Quickly. She didn't want to impose. And she didn't want to give him the chance to resist. Emma brushed her lips against Coop's, and, just as quickly, pulled back. It was a peck. It was a gesture.

It was an invitation.

Epilogue

Rose Janowitz Cain knew where she was. She knew why she was there. What annoyed her was being forced to wonder whether she'd be allowed to stay.

"What are they doing?" Having conceded that her eyes weren't what they used to be, Rose passed her binoculars on to Libby, so that her granddaughter could spy on Emma and Coop. The beauty of occupying dwellings missing windows, chunks of wall, and entire roofs, was that you could pretty much see anyone, anywhere, at any time. Emma and Coop were standing behind a concrete slab that had once been a courtyard, which Rose and Libby could easily see over from a third-floor window across the way. Rose understood they were engaged in childish behavior. But if Emma was determined to treat Rose like a child, then Rose felt no qualms about acting like one.

"Just talking." Libby appeared calmer for the moment. To ensure that she didn't revert to dwelling on what had happened, Rose resolved to keep her occupied and distracted.

Her Lubochka. Her beautiful, perfect granddaughter. Rose had made peace with guilt, acknowledging that the way she felt about Libby was the way she should have felt about Emma. Her daughter should have been the center of her universe, her priority, the thing Rose would have sacrificed anything for. Emma had been right when she didn't so much accuse as remind Rose that she'd never felt that way. She would make up for it now. She would make up for it here. If only Emma would give Rose the chance.

"Are they talking about us?" Rose wondered.

"Probably." Libby asked Rose without taking her eyes off their targets, "That's not very collectivist, is it? Assuming we're important enough to be talked about? It's pretty individualistic."

"Individualistic would be if they were talking about one of us. Since they're talking about both of us, it's alright."

Libby giggled. "Mom said you were good at making words mean whatever you wanted them to mean even—Whoa! Mom kissed Coop!"

Rose leaned forward as Libby shifted the binoculars sideways to offer her a half-peek. "How intriguing."

Rose had advised Emma to truly experience Rojava. This was one way to do it.

"Do you think that's a good sign or a bad sign? For us, I mean?" Libby peered up at Rose, convinced her grandmother still held all the answers, despite Rose's earlier confession of never having had any to begin with.

The best Rose could offer was, "You do realize, Lubochka, that Emma has no right to dictate our future."

"Then why do you look so anxious?"

"Because," Rose sighed, "I'm afraid Emma doesn't realize that."

"She's coming this way!" Libby guiltily lowered her binoculars, while Rose arranged her features to appear as defiant and nonchalant as she was claiming to be.

Coop had peeled off a few yards earlier. Emma was alone when she jogged up the crumbling steps and approached her daughter and mother. Rose wished Jonas were here. Not merely because Rose always wished Jonas were here, but because he would have been able to connect with Emma in a way Rose had never managed. He and Emma had been so close, closer than Emma and Rose. How many days and nights had she spent at her desk, pounding away on her typewriter while Emma and Jonas played Hot and Cold under and around her, a tiny Emma giggling hysterically at the way Jonas could whisper while shouting, or project his voice without raising it. If Emma wanted something, she came to Jonas, trusting him to phrase her request in the manner most palatable to Rose. Jonas couldn't say no to Emma, and Rose couldn't say no to Jonas, so it was a very effective family communication system. At least Rose had thought so. Until, without Jonas, she realized she had no way of communicating with her daughter at all.

"Good show?" Emma inquired of Rose and Libby, indicating the binoculars.

"I have a few notes," Rose sniffed.

Why did she always do this? Why did she always meet Emma's sarcasm with more sarcasm? Why couldn't either of them say what they really meant? Unless, of course, they were both so far gone that this was, in fact, all that they really meant.

Emma burst out laughing. "You'll never change, will you, Mom?"

"Would you want me to?"

"I have a few notes."

"Did Coop convince you?" Libby interjected, cutting off any potential honest talk between Rose and Emma. "Can we stay?"

"What makes you think Coop and I were talking about you? Maybe he was giving me a lesson in *jineology*. Or criticizing my white woman feminism."

"Oh, don't tease, Emma. Put the poor child out of her misery."

Emma sighed. She looked from Libby to Rose and back again. "I don't suppose I have much of a choice in the matter, do I?"

"Thank you, Mom!" Libby squealed once she'd worked out that Emma was saying what Libby had so wanted her to say. She rushed forward to hug Emma. "Thank you!"

Over her granddaughter's head, Rose inquired, "Am I also included in your papal dispensation?"

"You're not nineteen anymore, Mom. Or seventeen, for that matter." Emma hadn't chosen that age at random. Rose understood exactly what she was saying to her.

"You're right."

Emma, arm slung over Libby's shoulder, the sides of their heads touching in an intimacy Emma never shared with Rose, observed, "I think that's the first time you've ever said that to me."

"Second."

She waited for Emma to remember the first. When her daughter had spat about Jonas, "They got the wrong person. It should have been you." And Rose had agreed.

Rose still agreed.

The memory sobered them both, even if it did leave Libby to awkwardly disentangle herself out of Emma's embrace and look from one to the other, wondering what she'd missed.

Emma enjoined Libby, "Take care of your grandmother."

"Sure. Of course. Absolutely."

"And you," Emma turned to Rose. "You had damn well better take care of her."

"I will," Rose swore. The same way she'd once promised to love Jonas forever. That was one promise she'd never broken. But even it paled in comparison to what Rose said next. "I'll take care of our Libby. It's the most important thing I will ever do."

END

Fact From Fiction

In my November 2022 historical fiction, *My Mother's Secret: A Novel of the Jewish Autonomous Region*, I delved into a little known historical fact: Nearly twenty years before the establishment of the State of Israel, that great friend of the Jews, General Secretary of the Communist Party of the Soviet Union Josef Stalin, magnanimously announced that "for the first time in the history of the Jewish people, it's burning desire for a homeland, for the achievement of its own national statehood has been fulfilled," courtesy of the USSR granting the world's Jews an autonomous region on the border of Russia and China.

While the majority of Birobidzhan's new citizens were from Eastern and Western Europe, as well as some from South America, many of those in charge of running the place were from North America, the United States, in particular.

When I spoke to book clubs, synagogues, and other organizations about *My Mother's Secret: A Novel of the Jewish Autonomous Region*, readers expressed disbelief that anyone, especially a Jew, would leave the US for the USSR. (Even then-Mayor Bernie Sanders, who loved the Moscow subways and thought the Soviet Union was an amazing place with no anti-Semitism, wasn't that foolish. He, like most of his fellow traveler Americans, preferred to love the USSR from his private home in Vermont.)

The fact that there were, in fact, Americans, including some Jews, foolish enough to relocate, gave me the idea for my next novel: An American couple who did precisely that.

But why would they? What could make an American couple believe they'd get a fairer shake in the Soviet Union?

Well, how about an interracial couple? Before Loving v. Virginia, the Supreme Court ruling which made my own marriage and family possible.

And what if their issues weren't merely personal, but also professional?

There is no denying that African Americans had a tough time booking acting jobs in the 1950s. Sure, they could get by on the radio, but what about on the newly popularized medium of television? It was one thing to be heard by the greater American public, it was another thing altogether to be seen—and accepted.

And which genre made the most substantial transition from radio to television in terms of hours broadcast?

Why, soap operas, of course.

Did you know that soap-operas were almost single handedly invented by a Jewish woman? Even though I worked for *Guiding Light* and *As the World Turns*, I never met the legendary Irna Phillips. The force of nature who appears in these pages was assembled based on first-hand reports from *Guiding Light: A 50th Anniversary Celebration* by Christopher Schemering, *Guiding Light: The Complete Family Album* by Julie Poll, *Worlds Without End: The Art and History of the Soap Opera* by the Museum of Television and Radio, and *When Women Invented Television* by Jennifer Keishen Armstrong. Insights into Irna were also gleaned from her protegee's book, *My Life to Live: How I Became the Queen of Soaps When Men Ruled the Airwaves* by Agnes Nixon. (Even though I worked for *All My Children* and *One Life to Live*, I only caught glimpses of those shows' creator as she blew by me at ABC industry events and functions like the Daytime Emmys.)

Thinking about an interracial couple emigrating to the Soviet Union naturally made me think of the 1957 World Youth Festival in Moscow. Having been born in the USSR, I heard the stories from my relatives about that brief window of openness when the world was welcomed in—and how, after they departed, those guests left a legacy of "rainbow children." What could be more appealing to an interracial couple than that? Especially when they learned that the USSR was also inviting thousands of African visitors to attend their universities.

My family knew about the Youth Festival. But they didn't know about the Harvard student drawing crowds in Red Square, or the representatives sent to deny the realities of the recent Hungarian uprising. As Soviet citizens at the time, they had no access to such information. I had to unearth it in my research over sixty years after the fact. (Just like my characters would have no access to information about how those invited African students were treated. Or maybe they just didn't want to know.)

I also did a bit of personal research. I asked my teenage daughter, "Can you imagine that you're the child of a Soviet-Jewish soap-opera writer and an overeducated Black man raised in Harlem?"

She scrunched up her forehead, concentrated really hard and said, "Yes, I think I can do that."

"If you had lived your entire life in the USSR—you remember how white it was when we visited Moscow—and you came to New York City for the first time, what would strike you as the most amazing thing?"

She instantly replied, "All the different hair textures and styles."

So that became Emma's most amazing thing, as well.

When it came to Dennis, his background was a hodge-podge of the Jewish children left orphaned after Stalin's Doctor's Plot, and of Vladimir Pozner, who spent his childhood in the United States, spoke fluent English, and was the Soviet Union's chief apologist… until suddenly, in what felt like an overnight switch post-Gorbachev, he wasn't. It was Pozner who co-hosted the real-life "Citizens' Summit" with Phil Donahue, which inspired my fictionalized version.

When it came to the glamorous life of New York City's progressives, I took bits and pieces from the biography of director Sidney Lumet by Maura Spiegel (which is where I also learned of the world's only Yiddish language radio soap opera and knew I had to include it in a book, long before I had this story in mind), and Tom Wolfe's classic "New York Magazine" article, "Radical Chic: That Party at Lenny's."

On the other side of the spectrum, (wild)life in the Free State Project was heavily influenced by *A Libertarian Walks into a Bear: The Utopian Plot to Liberate an American Town (And Some Bears)* by Matthew Hongoltz-Hetling.

Finally… Rojava. Like Emma, I also have a college-aged child enamored with the social and political experiment taking place in Northeastern Syria. He gifted me a book, *Revolution in Rojava: Democratic Autonomy and Women's Liberation in Syrian Kurdistan* by Michael Knapp, Anja Flach, and Ercan Ayboga, so I could understand the background of the movement. I added to that initial knowledge via The Kurdish Project, openDemocracy, and other mainstream news coverage. *The New York Times* offered insight on the ISIS prisons of Rojava.

Despite taking place in New York City, Moscow, and the Middle East, all of *Go On Pretending* is haunted by the ghosts of the Spanish Civil War. For the critical role of women in that conflict, I referred to the research of Esther Gutierrez Escoda, who made it her mission to set the record straight about the female soldiers of The People's Army of the Spanish Republic. The Abraham Lincoln Brigade Archives covered the international women volunteers.

There was one more thing that happened when I did book talks for *My Mother's Secret: A Novel of the Jewish Autonomous Region*, as well as its predecessor, *The Nesting Dolls* (HarperCollins, 2020): I was regularly interrupted by Soviet-born readers who took umbrage with how I described a historical event.

"That's not how I remember it," they said.

I pointed them to historical sources—with footnotes—which testified to the veracity of my research.

Nope. They didn't care. That's not how they remembered it. Sometimes, two members of the same book club would have different memories of the same historical event. And neither one matched what I'd written. (Boy, did I get an earful when I claimed there was no historical evidence to confirm the rumor that, only a few weeks before his death, Stalin was planning to deport all Soviet Jews to Birobidzhan. My listeners were sure it was true. They were there! They heard! They saw! Those historians have no idea what they're talking about!)

In the end, we writers can do our research, we can check and cross-check multiple sources, we can interview people who were there and people who devoted their lives to confirming the accounts of those who were there. But we are all still slaves to human memory and, even more important, human interpretation of that memory. As Pontius Pilate (talk about a controversial historical figure!) sings in the musical *Jesus Christ Superstar*, "We all have truths, are mine the same as yours?"

Go on Pretending is the truth about a variety of real-life events and real-life characters as seen through the eyes of imaginary people. It is as honest of a story as possible to create... while pretending.

Alina Adams was born in Odessa, USSR and immigrated to the United States with her family in 1977. She has written Regency and contemporary romance novels, figure skating mysteries, and NYT best-selling tie-ins to the soap-operas *As the World Turns* (*Oakdale Confidential* and *The Man from Oakdale*), and *Guiding Light* (*Jonathan's Story*), as well as the officially sanctioned continuation of *Another World*. She has worked for *All My Children*, *One Life to Live*, the Daytime Emmys, ABC Daytime, *Pure Soap*, *SoapLine*, and SoapHub.com, and written the book, *Soap Opera 451: A Time Capsule of Daytime Drama's Greatest Moments*. Her first historical fiction, *The Nesting Dolls* (2020), focused on three generations of women in the Soviet Union of the 1930s and the 1970s, and present-day Brighton Beach, Brooklyn. Her second, *My Mother's Secret: A Novel of the Jewish Autonomous Region* (2022), was set in Birobidzhan, a German POW camp, and 1980s San Francisco, CA. Alina lives in New York City with her husband, and three children. Visit her website at: www.AlinaAdams.com.